A former teacher, Kate Long was born in 1964 and grew up in Blackrod, Lancashire. She left teaching to pursue her career as a best-selling novelist and has also had short stories published in *Woman's Own*, *Woman & Home*, the *Sunday Express* magazine and the Sunday Night Book Club anthology. She describes herself as being inspired by family stories and power shifts in relationships, as well as by how people form personal identities. Other favourite themes are class, disability, and the power of the maternal bond in all forms, healthy or otherwise. Kate currently lives with her husband and two young children in a small village in Shropshire.

BEFORE SHE WAS MINE

Freya's two mothers couldn't be more different: Liv, her adoptive mother, is earthy and no-nonsense, whereas Freya's birth mother Melody is still apt to find herself thrown out of Topshop for bad behaviour. Hard as it has been for Freya to try to reconcile her two families, it has been harder for her mothers. Proud of her mature and sensible adoptive daughter, Liv fears Melody's restless influence. Meanwhile, forced to give up her baby when she was just a teenager herself, Melody now craves Freya's love and acceptance — but only really knows how to have fun. When tragedy strikes, can they finally let go of the past and pull together in order to withstand the toughest challenge life could throw at them?

Books by Kate Long
Published by The House of Ulverscroft:

MOTHERS AND DAUGHTERS

KATE LONG

BEFORE SHE WAS MINE

Complete and Unabridged

CHARNWOOD
Leicester

First published in Great Britain in 2011 by
Simon & Schuster UK Ltd
A CBS Company
London

First Charnwood Edition
published 2013
by arrangement with
Simon & Schuster UK Ltd
A CBS Company
London

A catalogue record for this book is available
from the British Library.

ISBN 978–1–4448–1770–6

Published by
F. A. Thorpe (Publishing)
Anstey, Leicestershire

Set by Words & Graphics Ltd.
Anstey, Leicestershire
Printed and bound in Great Britain by
T. J. International Ltd., Padstow, Cornwall

This book is printed on acid-free paper

For baby Hope,
and for Julia

Acknowledgements

Many thanks to Alison Winward for allowing me to use her brilliant notes on life in Nablus; to Matt from Holly Farm Nursery, Whitchurch; to my dear friend Julia Black for talking so frankly to me about her experience with cancer; to Jill Arnold and the fantastic team from Shrewsbury Social Services, and Alison Millen from Adoption UK; to valleyforge, Fritillary, The Woodman, Malcolm Banks, Phoebe, nakedgardener and Charles Halliday at Wild About Britain; to Nicky Hunter, Sandra Kinsey, Simon Williams, Simon Long, John Harding and Helen Day.

As we come out of the Arndale, Melody breaks into a run and we end up sprinting across the precinct, shopping bags swinging as we dodge leafleteers and people with clipboards. I ask her why we're running and she shouts back that she doesn't know. Passers-by must assume we're shop-lifters, evading pursuit. I can see them checking the crowds behind us for security guards. It's a wonder no one tries to make a citizen's arrest.

We stumble into the entrance of H&M and thank God it's cool and calm in there, Mika playing cheerily over the loudspeaker. Melody takes a moment to adjust her little skirt where it's ridden up round her thighs, and I unzip my camouflage jacket. No one turns a hair.

First thing that draws me in is a stand loaded with plimsolls, because my last pair got ruined when I had to check the cattle after it had been raining all week and the nature reserve was like a swamp. There are some navy trainers I think are smart, and I'm turning them over to see the size stickers on the soles when it occurs to me I ought to be keeping at least half an eye on Melody. I look round and she's in the far corner, trying on dark glasses and a beret and draping ten scarves round her neck and shoving twenty bracelets up her arm. As I watch, she prances off round the store, still loaded with unpaid-for goods.

Well, so far, so good. She's not upset anyone and the accessories I can strip off her before we pass through the security portal. Mika finishes, Take That comes on. Suddenly I can tell by her body language she's spotted something. She quivers, like a pointer. Then she starts rifling through one of the clothing racks, shoving hangers left and right, eager at first and then with increasing irritation. She scans the store, does a double take, strides over to a two-foot podium where a half-mannequin's kitted out in a Union Jack blazer, and clambers up to examine the label. Next thing she's trying to wrench the jacket off, tugging at the buttons, cursing the pins at the back. Other customers are beginning to stare.

I have the choice of either going across and claiming her, or walking out of the shop and leaving her to it. With my head lowered I make my way quickly to the podium.

'The smallest on the rail's a ten,' she says in explanation. Pins tinkle to the floor. The mannequin rocks.

'Get down. Ask a member of staff,' I hiss. 'They've probably got a box full of eights in the back.'

'It'll be fine. God, don't they want people to buy stuff?'

The blazer slides off, bringing with it the mannequin's lower arm. Melody jumps down smartly. Assistants are closing in.

'See,' she says, pulling on the jacket. She twists to look in the mirror. The labels from the hat and glasses dangle over her nose.

2

Here comes the manager, a young guy in a suit that's too big for him. There's a terrible shaving rash all down his neck. The rest of the staff part respectfully to let him through.

'Could you and your sister leave the shop, please,' he says.

Melody starts to laugh: she's laughing at my expression, at the boy-manager with his scraped-raw skin, laughing at her own laughter, and at the assistants frowning. Behind her the loose forearm rolls off the podium and bounces onto the lino. I think she might die of laughing.

I reach out and take her collar because whatever happens, we are not buying that jacket in this store today. And I tell him, 'She's not my sister, she's my mother.'

★　★　★

Later, back at Liv's, and I'm feeling peckish. There being nothing in the fridge and the bread gone to mould, I venture into what Liv refers to as the 'downstairs cloakroom' to see what's in the freezer.

Before I can get to the freezer itself, I have to pick my way through boxes of pamphlets on Meres and Mosses, towers of mammal traps, a pile of wellingtons and waders and grabbers and poles, and shift a stuffed otter out of the way.

Next, having tugged the door open, I spend a minute or two chipping off a layer of ice because the last person to close up — Liv, or possibly the idiot Geraint — didn't do the job properly. When I do free the top drawer I find it's empty apart

3

from a lone sandwich bag containing nibbled iris leaves. I shove the drawer back in again lumpily.

Pointless pulling out the second one down as it's permanent home to Victor the vole who Liv uses for field study training sessions. Melody claims the freezer also houses Billy the Bacterium and Gerry the Germ, but to be fair Liv's always scrupulous about how she stores her props. Inside his box Victor's shrouded in cling film, kitchen foil and a zip-seal plastic pocket. God forbid any harm should come to the vole.

The bottom drawer's worth a try. Usually there's a packet of emergency fish cakes to be had, or sausages, or at the very least frozen Yorkshire puddings. Very versatile is your Yorkshire pudding. You can eat them on their own, or with tomato soup, jam, beans, anything really.

But today all I see as I pull out the wire basket is a white polythene bag with something grey showing through. I lift the bag out and have a feel. Encouragingly, there are the remains of a supermarket label still stuck to the side. The shape is long and solid, cosh-like.

I think what we have here is a trout.

I consider for a moment. Yep, it's OK, I can cook a trout. All you have to do is stick it under the grill. It needs defrosting, but if I take it out now I could conceivably have it for supper, especially if I give it a quick blast in the microwave to start the process off. You sprinkle lemon juice and salt on; I've seen Nigella do it.

Grasping the trout in one hand I try to wrestle the drawer shut with the other. It won't budge. I swap hands. I put the trout down and try shunting with my knee.

Then Liv's voice calls across the corridor from her office: 'Freya? If you're in the freezer, don't touch the trout. Geraint wants to use it for baiting mink traps.'

And this is my other mother.

From Liv's diary, 12/04

First meeting over, I think OK.

Dropped Frey off at station entrance & went for pointless walk round back streets of Crewe. Christmas lights up, gloomy afternoon, eerie atmosphere like before a storm. Must have checked watch every 2 mins. Promised F I'd wait in car park till they'd finished but needed loo so had to go past station café anyway. Freya & Melody sitting in window, couldn't believe how young M looks. She was waving her hands around in the middle of some story. F completely rapt. Wanted to stand & watch but knew I mustn't.

Was dreading having to go in & get her in case seemed needy, but she came out when she said she would. M small next to her, gypsyish, in huge long coat. Pointy cat's face, eyes like a cat. F's face.

M came up to me & speech I'd rehearsed went out of head. Left F in the car & had ¼ hour with M. She said, 'It's a dream come true, isn't it?' Didn't stop for me to answer. I managed to get in that I was grateful for her letters, & tell her how well F doing at school, predicted grades etc. M began to talk about her own time as schoolgirl, best/worst subjects etc. Had to cut her short because it began to sleet & F waiting. Said we'd all meet again, hugged briefly. Thought she might say thanks for bringing up her daughter, but she didn't. Perhaps meant to & overwhelmed.

F quiet on way home. I didn't press her. When got back made cheese on toast, couldn't eat mine & found F's in the bin later. Suggested we watch Meerkats United *DVD*. F said she was tired & wanted to go up to her room. Whole house felt odd.

Later got out some of her toddler clothes & the wooden blocks Col made for her. F came back down & we had chat about her early years. She said she hated not being able to remember Col, that it was sometimes hard to believe he'd been real. I said, 'Oh, your dad was real & he loved you to bits.' Felt weepy but fought it. She said, 'It'll work out all right, Mum, I promise you.' Hope she's right. I want to be hopeful.

A THURSDAY

November

When I tell people I work in a nursery, I like to watch their faces. 'Oh,' they say doubtfully, 'do you really?' The expressions of relief when I explain it's the plant kind, not kids, because I know full well they've been trying to imagine me with my orange hair and black eyeliner looming over some bawling infant. Luckily no seedling has ever been traumatised by my appearance.

So then it's, 'I see. You mean a garden centre.' Because they've got me installed in one of those vast Percy Thrower emporiums, the ones that sell floral china mugs and scented candles, fluffy toy owls and hamster mazes and Barbour jackets. Whereas our outfit's not much bigger than a school playground, and our only non-garden sideline is ice cream in the summer. Or, for the winter, Christmas decs. We shift a fair few of those around now, though Ray insists on a garden theme — spray-painted fir cones, silk poinsettias, resin berries. Fair enough. It's his shop. Bird food sells steadily, and pansies, violas, some of the bare-root hedging plants, but if it wasn't for December 25th, we'd have a lean time of it this quarter.

I was in Greenhouse One watering the indoor plants — an acceptable gift for every occasion, just ask and we'll stick a ribbon round the pot — when the shop alarm buzzed. From spring to autumn the counter's staffed, but during winter when it's quiet Ray has us on general maintenance. It makes sense. No point paying someone to gaze at a wall of seed packets all day. I put down my can, wiped my hands, and went to serve.

My heart gave a little skip of pleasure when I rounded the corner and saw the frog-green Mazda parked by the gate. Christian was standing just inside the shop entrance, waiting.

'Excellent,' he said. 'I was hoping it would be you.'

I felt myself begin to glow. There are some people you meet in life who light a place up simply by being there. They smile and the sun comes out, they drop a compliment and you're bathed in warmth for hours afterwards. Christian's not just young and fair and good-looking; he's genuinely charming, a nice bloke, a man you want to be around. You can't help yourself.

'Shouldn't you be at work?' I said.

'Day off. I'm not required this session.'

'I thought you were indispensable.'

He grinned, and it was like sparkles on water.

'What's your current project?' I asked.

'We have to film a woman in Bradford who says she can't diet because she eats in her sleep.'

'Honestly?'

'That's what the lady claims. Sleepwalks to the fridge, sleep-makes-a-sandwich, sleep-roots-through-the-freezer-after-chocolate-brownie-ice-cream. Our job's to hang around her kitchen in the small hours and catch her at it. Only she's had to be rushed into hospital with a septic finger, so some of us are kicking about for a day while the producer re-schedules.'

'I bet he's pleased.'

'He won't be sending a get well card. But all's not lost apparently. Tomorrow we can whizz over to Nottingham to film a narcoleptic.'

He stepped back while I slid myself behind the counter.

'Sleep disorders, is it?'

'Yup. All delivered in our usual sympathetic style. We're hoping to sell to *Tru-World*'s freak slot.'

Made me laugh, the way he said 'we'. In the tiny Manchester-based film company he works for, he's third assistant to an assistant's assistant, right down the bottom of the food chain. Meanwhile, back in Oxford, his parents write out cheques to keep him in petrol and M&S ready meals. As far as they're concerned, he's a star in waiting.

'So why are you kicking around here? Your flat doesn't even have a garden.'

'I have a window box.'

'Which you use as an ashtray.'

'Not me.'

'Your meedja friends, then.'

He stood there, smiling at me. 'OK,' he said. 'I'll come clean. Can I trust you with a secret, Freya?'

Fizz fizz, my insides went. He does that to you, to everyone: makes you feel as though you're the most fascinating person in the room. It's hard

10

not to be sucked in by it.

'Go on,' I said.

He brought his face closer and lowered his voice conspiratorially. Behind him a bunch of silvered beech twigs twinkled with fake frost.

'Tonight I've decided I'm going to go for it. I'm going to ask Nicky to marry me, and, well, I need your help.' Fake snow on fake berries, fake robin lurching. 'Will you help me, Frey?'

''Course I will. That's great. No question. Fab!'

I don't know why the news shook me so much. It's not as if I'm in love with him.

★ ★ ★

The nursery's only five minutes' drive from home, so I can go back and have my dinner with Liv if I want. I considered it all the rest of the morning, as I helped Christian pick out half a dozen standard bay trees and four hundred outdoor fairy lights and organised the trailer and booked the delivery.

'I have this idea of an illuminated avenue,' he explained. 'So when she comes home, her front path's all magical. I've just been round to Joan and Derek's, squared it with them. They're going to wait in the kitchen till I call them through. I'll be behind the front door, with the ring. Derek's sorting out some champagne.'

Of course he is, I thought. What dad wouldn't be delighted to have you as his son-in-law? I could see it all in my mind's eye: her astonishment as she came to the end of the street

11

and saw the trees, the slow walk of wonder to the front step, the door opening, Christian outlined in light like the Angel of the Annunciation.

'What do your parents think?'

'I haven't told them yet. It's going to be a surprise. Obviously I'll give them a bell as soon as I have Nicky's answer. Do you think she'll say yes?'

I just looked at him.

After he'd gone, I went back to Greenhouse One and carried on watering. Then I swept the front yard and the area round the pots, unpacked a load of bulbs, filed the invoices, had my tea break, answered a phone enquiry about hedera screens, did some dead-heading and sold a door wreath. By then it was coming up to midday and I knew for definite that the place I most wanted to be was in Liv's kitchen eating tomato soup to the sound of Radio 4.

★　★　★

I couldn't find her in the house, but when I glanced down the garden I could see the garage door was open so I guessed she was working in there.

I hunted through the cupboard next to the fridge and located a tin of soup. While my dinner was heating, I wandered into the dining room and checked the morning's post. It was all for Liv: a flyer from Natural England, a form from North Shropshire Council's planning department, a receipt from the Game and Wildlife Conservation Trust. Nothing for me, as usual. To get letters, you have to write them, as Melody says. She doesn't get letters, though, just parcel after parcel of clothes off eBay.

The soup began to spit so I went back through, decanted it into a mug, stuck the pan in the sink and took myself up to the garage. I found Liv kneeling over a bucket of clay which she was mixing with her bare hands. She greeted me with her usual mild distraction.

'Ooh, is that a cup of tea?'

'It's soup.'

'Oh.'

'Sorry, I didn't think. I can make you one.'

She wiped her forehead with her wrist. 'No, it's OK, I've nearly finished.'

I watched her fingers knead and squelch. With her long red-grey hair spread across her brown cotton shirt she had a look of some ancient tribeswoman. She could have been grinding corn or casting runes.

'Was it busy at the nursery?'

'No.' I was thinking that now would be the time to tell her about Nicky.

'Pass me that trowel, will you?'

I did as I was told, and Liv began to scoop out the clay and drop it onto a small plastic tray packed with wet oasis, spreading the surface smooth with the action of a plasterer, or maybe an enthusiastic cake decorator. It was calming to watch.

'You after some animal tracks?'

She nodded. 'We've had a sighting of something small and dark-coloured by the main drain at Fenn's dyke. It's most likely a polecat.

13

But just in case it's a mink, I thought I'd stick a tracking cartridge down.'

Mink are Liv's nemesis. They sneak into her nature reserve and eat up her water voles and her wading birds. So she's eternally vigilant, though it's a fine line between watchfulness and obsession.

At last she got to her feet and stood, pushing her hair back behind her ears. 'Can you see the cling film anywhere, Frey?'

'Leaning against your display boards.'

She grabbed hold of the box, laid it on the workbench, and rolled out a length of film. Then she put the tracking cartridge in the middle and proceeded to wrap up the damp clay so it was airtight.

'Where's Geraint?' I made myself ask.

'At a Wetlands Trust conference down in Shrewsbury.'

I pictured him: the big belly and the fluffy grey beard, the round glasses, the eternal stripy sweater, the irritating sing-song of his Rhyl accent. And always a pair of binoculars hanging round his neck like an outsize talisman. Melody calls him Bin-man. I have other names for him.

'He says he's stopping the night there,' Liv went on. 'That way he can have a beer or two in the evening while he networks.'

'He likes his beer.'

'He does.'

She straightened up and dusted her palms together. 'Could you — ?'

In time-honoured fashion, I ducked out of the garage and turned on the outside tap for her to rinse her hands. The trouble with clay is it gets everywhere. It dries light on dark clothing, and dark on light. If Liv ever thinks to take in washing off the line, you can end up with a basket of clothes that need to go straight back in the machine.

'So it'll be just you and me tonight?' Cloudy water spattered down onto the soil between us.

'Uh-huh.'

Excellent. 'Shall I do a stew for tea? It's not too late to stick something in the crock-pot if I put it on high.'

'Oh, would you?' Liv was wiping her wet hands on her shirt.

'We could have it round the fire, in bowls.'

'I must clean out the grate, actually . . . '

'Come in now and help me chop some veg.'

I walked ahead of her down the path, kicking aside crusts of bread, gearing myself up to tell her about Nicky.

'We've definitely got onions. Well, I think we have . . . ' said Liv as we reached the back door.

Only because they last for bloody ever, I thought. But it was OK, I knew we'd had a meat delivery two days before, and there were sliced carrots in the freezer. She switched the radio on, *You and Yours*, and I dropped some tea bags into a couple of mugs to sit while I dug out a tin of tomatoes. Liv wiped down the chopping board. I said, 'I had a bit of news today.'

She squatted by the base unit next to the sink, opened the door and peered in.

'Christian's asking Nicky to marry him.'

Liv made a small noise of surprise at the back

15

of her throat, but carried on rooting in the cupboard. *Pensions,* said the man on the radio. *Successive governments, tax credit.*

'He's asking her tonight,' I said.

I'd have thought she hadn't heard, except she turned her head and raised her eyebrows at me. Then she pulled herself up, onion in hand. She placed the onion on the chopping board and regarded it.

'A nice bit of news, them getting married,' I said.

'Mmm. If it's what she wants.' Liv picked at the onion skin. Fragments of crackly brown came away and fluttered to the floor.

I could have hugged her for that flat remark. I so needed her not to be impressed or excited, and she wasn't. Where ordinary mothers would have clucked and fussed, for Liv an engagement like this barely registered in her consciousness. She wasn't stirred to ask about place settings or dress designs or reception venues; they didn't interest her. Fripperies, they were, examples of needless consumption. Now if I'd told her Nicky would be releasing helium balloons at the reception, that would have grabbed her (*'Do you know how many turtles are choked each year by balloons landing in our coastal waters?'*).

The blade sliced wetly into onion flesh, and at the far corner of the kitchen, the kettle clicked off. I poured the tomatoes into the pot. At the back of the fridge was a bag of cubed stewing steak. I drew it out, wrinkling my nose at the blood smell, and tore open the thin plastic with my nails. In days gone by, I thought, Liv would

16

probably have cooed over weddings: when she was with my dad and they were young and in love. And look at how fate paid her for it. In that sense, and that sense only, I could see the attraction of settling for an old gimmer like Geraint. He was never going to break anyone's heart.

Once the stew was stirred, I brewed the tea and sloshed in some milk. I wondered what Nicky was doing at this moment, in these last hours of being unengaged.

'It is nice, she's a nice girl,' said Liv. 'Tell her congratulations from me. Oh, and do you think she'd consider guests throwing bird seed instead of confetti?'

'She might but I bet her mum won't.'

'No, I bet she won't. Ask anyway. It does no harm to ask.'

★ ★ ★

It was dark when I finished at the nursery and drove back home. The red curtains in the lounge were still open — Liv was busy on the computer in the front room — so I dragged them closed across their ancient metal rails. I remembered her getting those curtains through *Loot*, driving down to collect them off a woman in Stoke, and the struggle we had afterwards to hang them. I was too young to be much help and they weighed a ton, being floor-length lined velvet. So sometimes, when I'm at this big window, I get this mental flash of Liv collapsed on the sofa, her head in her hands and a mound of red cloth at her feet.

The fire wasn't laid either so I started on that, pushing the cold cinders through the grate, removing the tray and sweeping up the escaped ash. And as I carried the tray outside, that reminded me of another of Liv's domestic crises, a pan loaded like this accidentally dropped in the middle of the dining-room carpet. Everything around it grey, like a bomb had gone off. It's awful when you're little and your mother cries and there's nothing you can do about it.

I came back in and shut the door against the cold. The night was clear and sharp: Christian had probably ordered it specially.

In the lounge I knelt by the hearth and laid eco-firelighters and sustainable kindling, scrunched up copies of the *Shropshire Star*. As I worked I imagined Christian's progress. He'd be jostling the trees into order — no, he'd be further on than that — draping the lights? Unravelling Derek's extension cord? More likely he'd already be in their kitchen, relaxing with a drink while Joan fussed round him. He'd have changed into a suit. The ring would be a slight bulge in his breast pocket.

What time would Nicky call me?

I checked the coal scuttle and calculated timings. Nicky got back from Chester about six. The proposal itself would be swift and immediate, but then you had to factor in family celebration and private rapture. So at about seven I thought I'd hear from her. I wanted to have talked it through with Liv by then. I wanted to be completely ready to shoulder the full weight of my best friend's happiness.

The stew was simmering nicely. I set the table, with my slab pot in the centre and some silver twigs from the nursery. Then I poured two glasses of elderflower cordial, switched on the radio for the news, and called Liv.

She emerged from the front room rubbing her neck and yawning. As she walked towards me, her silhouette against the hall light looked almost fat. She isn't, even though she's nearly fifty; she just has really wide hips. 'A child-bearing pelvis', she likes to say, ironically. Still, part of me can't help being pleased it's Melody's narrower frame I've inherited. Whatever other dodgy genes might have been included in the package.

'Had a productive day?' I asked.

She nodded. Emailing some university zoology department, she'd have been, or harassing a council planning officer, or researching the relationship between numbers of water-vole latrines and breeding females. To be fair, she doesn't generally inflict the details on me.

'This smells nice,' she said as I spooned out the stew.

'I don't know why you don't use the slow cooker more. It's dead easy.'

'I know. I will.'

Or Geraint could cook something for a change, I thought.

For a minute or two we ate in silence because the man on the radio was talking about a new ruling on farmers and set-aside land, and the possible impact on birds and invertebrates. Liv listened, frowning. I thought she looked tired.

19

The report finished and she came back to herself, I could see her re-focusing on me like a camera adjusting its depth of field.

'Bloody government,' she said. Then the words I'd been waiting to hear. 'So, have you spoken to Nicky yet?'

I took a gulp of cordial, put my glass down and drew a deep breath.

Which was when we heard the latch go on the front door. Geraint was back.

★ ★ ★

Nicky rang at two minutes past seven.

'Frey? Frey? Oh, Frey. I've got — yes, *I'm on to her now, yes, yes, I will* — Mum and Dad say hi — Listen, did you know? Did Christian tell you?'

'Tell me what?' I asked generously. I wanted her to have the pleasure of saying it out loud.

'Oh, Frey, he's proposed!'

Liv had taken herself to the kitchen to wash up, but Geraint was still at the table, watching me mole-ishly through his glasses. I took the phone into the hall and sat on the stairs.

'Congratulations,' I said.

'You knew, didn't you? The trees.'

'I had an idea.'

'Oh my God, there were all these lights, he'd strung them all along and it was just — I thought my dad had maybe put them there, although — *no, I know you don't, Dad* — and then I was putting my key in the lock and the door opened. I suppose Chris must have been waiting, he must

20

have been — *what? I knew you were* — he says he was watching for me through the window.'

'Or on his knees peering through the letterbox.'

She let out a shriek of laughter. I heard Joan say, 'What is it?' Then Nicky's muffled repeating of my nothing-joke. More mirth.

'You all sound high,' I said when she came back on.

'I am. I can't believe — Actually, it's Mum who's gone mental. She's been on her mobile for about an hour, ringing everyone she knows. Next she's going to start randomly dialling strangers. She's had a stack to drink. She's gone bright red. Yes you have, Mum. Look in the mirror. Like a tomato. Even your ears.'

'Have you set a date?'

'No — There's another bottle in the fridge, Chris. Oh, I don't know, Mum had it last. On the sideboard.'

'Look,' I said. 'Let's meet up tomorrow night. Then you can tell me all the gory details uninterrupted.'

'I'll come round to yours.'

'No, don't. I'm not sure where I'll be. I might be staying at Melody's for a day or two.'

'Oh, well, you come here, then. Yeah?'

'Yeah. Tell Christian congratulations from me, won't you?'

'You can speak to him yourself — hang on, no, he's on the phone, they're all bloody on the phone except my dad. Oh, God, Mum's started crying. It really is — God, I'm so bloody happy, Frey, I think I'll explode.'

21

In the background I could hear her mother exclaiming, the tinkle of glass being broken, her dad calling cheerfully for a cloth. I imagined the back-slapping and the hugging that had gone before, the way they'd be up tonight for hours talking, reliving events, as a family and then, later, as two couples. The months of planning and discussion ahead, the joy of detail. It's possible Joan Steuer would die of ecstasy. And I thought, I'm glad for you, Nicky, I really am. The truth is, whatever my own fears and failures, you need this more than I do.

★ ★ ★

Melody's house is a twenty-minute drive away in Nantwich, a tiny terraced cottage on a road called Love Lane. Her mum left it to her when she moved to Ireland. Since then Melody's redecorated completely and filled the place with colourful junk. Chaotic but chic, you might say. Like Melody, in fact. She gets most of her stuff from car boot sales and the market and her current obsession is birds, so she's on the lookout for bird pottery, bird fabric, fancy bird cages. She has a string of red and blue felt birds hanging by the bathroom mirror; a cushion covered in bird brooches rests on the floor against the bookcase. She's tracked down some swallow-shaped mobiles which she's strung up in the kitchen.

When she papered the walls (in pre-bird days), she used ends of rolls only, so each side of the front room is a different floral pattern, and the upstairs landing changes colour halfway along. The sofa's ancient and shot, but Melody's covered the torn fabric with a gold and red tapestry throw. Scratches on junk-shop furniture are hidden under embroidered mats and jewelled coasters and lava lamps and scrimshaw. None of it's seen a duster in years, but you're so busy taking in the quirky detail you don't notice the shabbiness. Well, I don't. It took Liv to point it out to me.

Amazing to think how physically close Melody was to us for all those years. That fantasy so many adopted children have, of bumping into your birth parents and not realising who they are, could actually have come true in my case. *Did* it ever happen, just momentarily? Say, in a shop doorway, or at adjoining checkouts? Sometimes I wrack my brains for hidden memories but I never come up with anything. Speculation's pointless now. When I did meet her properly for the first time it was at a coffee bar on Crewe station.

There's no parking on Love Lane itself so I left the Mini by Morrisons and walked. I rang the bell and, when I got no answer, tried the key. The deadbolt wasn't on, which meant she was around. I rang again and went in.

Evidence Melody wasn't far away: the sash window to the yard left up; a magazine open on the sofa; a steaming cup of tea on the carpet next to her pointy *Arabian Nights*-style slippers. Looking at the slippers put me in mind of a scene last Christmas. Melody coming to drop off presents, bouncing up Liv's front path in an ankle-length black coat, a Russian hat and fingerless gloves. Round her neck she'd wrapped half a dozen lengths of different material, lurex-threaded, fringed, bobbled, tasselled, spangled. 'She couldn't just wear a scarf, could she?' Liv had muttered.

I dumped my overnight bag under the table and shouted up the stairs. The only response was a dull thudding beat which, after a moment, I identified as Eddy Grant's *Electric Avenue*. So I flopped down on the sofa, took a quick sip of tea, then picked up the magazine that was lying across the cushion next to me. *How Do Men See You?* was the title of the article Melody had been reading. The pages were slightly yellow at the edges, and the model studying herself in the mirror sported a bubble cut and massive false eyelashes. I flicked to the cover: *Twenty-Twenty*, the magazine was called. This was the July 1976 edition. When I went back to the article I could see it was actually a questionnaire Melody had been filling in. *Take a Look through HIS Eyes*, urged the subheading. *You might be surprised at the view!*

This was what she'd put so far:

When you enter a crowded room at a party, do you:
a) *search about for a face you know?*
b) *shrink against the wall in terror?*
c) *head for the buffet table?*
d) *stride in like a warrior queen and scan for good-looking guys?*

24

She'd circled *d*. That made me grin, because I imagined it was true.

You're introduced to a man you find physically handsome, but he only wants to talk about car engines. Do you:
a) *try to steer the conversation onto something more interesting (like yourself)?*
b) *let him drone on — you're too polite to interrupt?*
c) *fake enthusiasm and join in as best you can? After all, men like women who are keen!*
d) *tell him he's got as much charisma as a wheel nut, and walk away?*

Melody had circled *a*, then crossed it out in favour of *d* again.

Your most attractive feature is:
a) *your smile.*
b) *your ability to listen sympathetically.*
c) *the way you dress. You're one foxy lady!*
d) *your sparkling wit.*

That one had rated a *c*.

The sexiest item in your wardrobe is:
a) *your denim shorts. If you've got great legs, why not show them off?*
b) *your romantic frilly blouse. It makes the guys come over all protective!*
c) *your strappy wedges.*
d) *your fave jeans.*

25

Melody hadn't marked any of these answers, and suddenly I knew what she was up to. She'd halted the quiz so she could go up to her bedroom, check through her outfits and rate each one for allure.

I put the mag to one side, hauled myself up and went again to the foot of the stairs. This time, when I called her name, the music quietened. I tried again. A door clunked open and I heard her voice.

'Freya?'

'Yep,' I shouted.

'I'll be down in a minute.'

The magazine drew me back; I took it with me into the kitchen while I made myself a drink. Tacky it might be, but the questionnaire held a kind of hideous fascination.

The pattern of your dating history is:
a) *there hasn't been anyone special, but you've had lots of fun.*
b) *one or two serious relationships from which you've learned a lot.*
c) *confused. Some unfortunate overlaps, a few bad boys — your love life isn't always as tidy as it could be.*
d) *one heartbreak after another.*
e) *seven long years of intermittently mucking about with a bloke who drives you up the wall but you've known him since you were twelve and it's easier than starting with someone new.*

It didn't really say e, but if it had, that's what I'd

have ticked. Melody was an *a* through and through.

★ ★ ★

At last she came downstairs wearing nothing but a Hello Kitty vest and knickers set, and a long open shirt in orange silk. I watched her weave, barefoot, between coffee tables and potted palms like a species of urban dryad.

'That's the sexiest item in your wardrobe, then? Seems a touch, I don't know, forward.'

She whipped the magazine away. 'Naff off.'

'And it's lovely to see you too, Mother-dearest.' I flicked on the kettle. 'Is it all right if I stay over tonight?'

Melody ran her fingers through her dark hair. 'Yeah, of course, hun. You know it is. Always. *Mi casa es tu casa.* You'll have to make up the bed yourself, though.'

No change there, then. If I wanted a hot meal I'd also be cooking again, since Melody prefers to follow the Picnic Diet — fruit, biscuits, yoghurts, cold meat, bread, cake, crisps and chocolate. Anything that can be unwrapped and eaten on the spot. Liv says it'll catch up with her when she's forty-five. In the meantime Melody grazes on junk and looks bloody good on it.

Her slender arm reached up towards the cereal boxes. Sugary ones she likes best, ones with cartoon monkeys on the front and pixies and mice in hats. I have this theory that, essentially, she froze at fifteen, which is the age she was when she had me. I think I arrested her development.

'So why are you doing crappy magazine quizzes?' I asked her.

'For fun. Keep myself out of mischief.' She took a bowl off the drainer and tipped in a handful of Coco Pops. 'Are you OK, hun? You look gutted. Something's up, isn't it?'

'No. I wasn't prepared for this disgusting level of cheerfulness, that's all.'

She pinched a cluster of cereal with her fingers. Why bother with a spoon when it only meant extra washing-up?

'Have you even got dressed today?'

'Yes! I've been helping Michael at the garage, actually.'

'*Helping at the garage?*' I tried to picture her lacquered nails clamped round an oily spanner.

'Only answering the phone, booking appointments, that sort of thing. He was stuck. I was free.'

'And it went OK?'

'Yep.'

'Is it going to be a regular set-up?'

'God, no.' A fragment of cereal burst from her lips. 'I told you, he was stuck. It was a favour. There's no way I could cope with my brother as a boss full-time. I'd brain him within a week.'

'Bet the feeling's mutual.'

'Could be. Hey, sorry, have you eaten?'

'Ish. I made a stew, but then when it came to it, I didn't have much of an appetite. I'm hungry now, though. Have you got anything in? Apart from cereal, I mean.'

The cupboard above me was still open and she nodded at it. 'Jam, honey, marmalade. There's a hunk of cheese in the fridge, anything you like.'

'I'm not having just toast. I've been shifting bags of Osmocote all afternoon. What's in the freezer?'

Melody looked vague. 'There might be some battered cod.'

'That'll do.'

'Don't know how old it is, though.'

'I'll take my chances.'

She wandered off, bowl in hand, back up the stairs. I lit the oven and carried on with the quiz.

★　★　★

The fish was pretty much ready to serve and I'd plated up some bread and butter to go with it. But when Melody came back down, she was all glammed up. Her skirt was a black sequinned tube down to her knees, and for a top she had on an emerald camisole which may or may not have been meant for outside wear. She'd twisted up her shoulder-length hair into a messy chignon.

I said, 'You look as if you're going out.'

'I am. Didn't I mention it?'

'No.'

'Sorry. You can still stay, though. We can catch up later. Do you want to open a bottle of wine?'

My spirits dipped. What I'd been hoping for, what I'd been sure Melody would provide, was a good long session of hard-core cynicism. I'd thought, I can tell her about Nicky's engagement, about the fancy preparation and fairy lights, and Melody will do what she always does on these occasions, which is to pour scorn. Flicking Vs in the face of happy-ever-after is one of her favourite entertainments. 'The only reason people marry,' she says, 'is for legal security. To nail down stuff like who turns off your life support machine, or who gets custody of the hi-fi system. The rest is bollocks. And weddings are the worst: poncy dress, boring speeches, half the congregation taking bets on how long till the divorce. It's a humiliation *I'll* never put myself through.'

She certainly seemed to be sticking to her word. In the five years I'd known her, I'd met maybe a dozen of her boyfriends, and every one she'd delighted in slagging off behind his back. The guy with the weakness for jewellery she'd initially called 'Jingle Bells'; after they split up, he became 'Pimp'. Another she tagged 'The Gobbler' because he ate with his mouth open. There was 'Lurch' and 'Mr Potato Head', and another she referred to as 'Whopper' (glad I didn't meet him; I wouldn't have known where to look).

'Why do you date them if you don't like them?' I remember asking her.

'I do like them,' she'd said. 'I'm just not stupid about it.' Another time she told me, 'It's a hobby.' I don't know whether she meant the men or the casual cruelty.

Sometimes it was funny, other times it got a bit wearing. But there's no doubt Melody's was a great place to be on Valentine's night. Two years in a row we spent the evening of the 14th getting drunk and watching *Dawn/Day/Land of the Dead*, then mocking the soppier of the love messages from the local paper. Happy hours, where I'd felt as though Melody was just about the only person I knew who was on my wavelength.

I'd thought we might do something similar tonight. She could bitch about Nicky and Christian and the Engaged in general, and I could scold her, and we'd both enjoy ourselves.

Except she was going out and leaving me to eat unwanted fish.

★   ★   ★

I did try before she went. While she was fiddling with the cap on the wine bottle, I related the story of Christian's proposal and Nicky's reaction.

'Jesus!' was Melody's first response, but then I realised she'd cut herself on the metal edge of the screw top. So while she sucked her finger, I gave her the news again, in summary.

'Oh yeah, Mr Posh-Pants,' she said.

'Don't call him that.'

'Why not?'

'Because I might come out with it myself.'

She dabbed her hand on her skirt and grimaced. 'When's the date?'

'Not sure yet. Mad, aren't they, though? She's only twenty-three. Don't you think that's too young?'

'Totally.'

She glanced round the room, frowning.

'What feels weird — ' I began.

'Shit, you haven't seen my phone, have you? It was on the window sill, I'm sure it was on the window sill. I definitely put it there.'

So we stopped to hunt. All the cushions off the sofa, her bag tipped upside down on the carpet, every pocket in every coat turned out. She found a tenner she didn't know she had, and a mysterious number on a scrap of paper. No mobile, though. Next she got dust in her eye, and I had to follow her to the big mirror on the landing while she poked under her lashes and swore. I was still trying to talk about Nicky, but she wasn't listening.

'Who is it you're meeting?' I asked as she repaired her eyeliner.

'Joe.'

'Joe who?'

'Sounds like a knock-knock joke.'

'I meant, what's his particular strangeness? Have you a nickname for him yet?'

Melody bared her teeth at her reflection, then started down the stairs. 'Nah. I only met him a couple of months ago.'

Two months? Plenty of opportunity to have dismantled his character, I thought as I followed her.

'Will I meet him?'

'Soon, hun. Promise.'

She looked back over her shoulder at me and she was doing this twinkling thing, this cutesy half-smile at me. I swear, if she'd had a fan she'd have fluttered it.

'What's he do?'

'He's a shop manager at Comet. Pass me my coat, will you?'

Hanging by the front door was the Union Jack blazer; she'd had to order it online in the end. It looked tiny, like a child's garment. I'm only a size twelve, but I feel like a cart horse beside her sometimes.

'Do I look OK?' she said, hooking the blazer off its peg and slipping it on over the camisole.

'You want to stop shrinking into the background. Stand out from the crowd for once.'

She smiled sweetly. 'Says the girl with the fluorescent hair.'

A car horn bibbed. Melody grabbed her bag.

'Where's he taking you? If you haven't got a phone and anything happens — you've not known him that long. Stranger danger.'

'Don't be a div.' I caught a whiff of her perfume as she opened the front door. 'Finish the wine, watch a DVD. Eat anything you can find. Don't wait up.'

And then I was on my own. Again.

★ ★ ★

I binned what was left of the fish, then sat and zapped through the TV channels, eventually settling on a stupid romcom where we were supposed to believe the gorgeous glossy lead was actually a moose. 'If only I could get him to notice me,' she simpered, flicking her hair about like she was in a shampoo ad. These films do your self-esteem no good at all.

Then the bell rang. I assumed it was Melody,

33

back after a row, or to retrieve some vital piece of kit. But it wasn't. It was Michael, returning the missing phone.

'She swore she hadn't taken it to work,' I told him as he stepped in, shaking the rain out of his curls.

'She'd left it in the toilet. God knows what she was doing with it in there.'

'Texting Joe, I bet.'

'Ah, Joe.'

'You've met him?'

'Only the once. He's younger than she is.'

'By how much?'

Michael shrugged. 'Visibly.'

'What's he like?'

'All right, I suppose.'

'Go on.'

'Nothing else to say. We didn't talk for long, they were going to see a film.' He laid the phone on the coffee table and perched himself on the sofa arm. 'What's up with you, anyway? You look like you've spent the afternoon sucking crab apples.'

'Get lost,' I said.

'Come on, Mrs Glum, give us the news. Let me see if I can't sort you out.'

He always adopts this teasing tone with me. He doesn't do it to other women; I've heard him in the pub, in the garage, and I know he can hold a perfectly normal conversation if he wants to. I suppose he likes to think of himself as a kind of uncle, except he isn't blood relation to any of us. His dad moved in with Melody's mum when Michael was five and Melody was thirteen, then

34

moved out a decade later, leaving Michael behind at his own request. 'I was doing my exams, I was settled,' he'd told me. 'Staying seemed the easiest thing.'

All of which makes him a paper-brother only. But he's still loose family and, having already been married and divorced, he does have a fair bit of life experience under his belt. He's not a bad listener either.

So I told him.

'Your best friend's engaged.'

'Yeah.'

'And, naturally, you're thrilled for them both.'

'I am.'

'You bloody great liar, Frey.'

'I *am*. Of course I'm happy for Nicky. She's my *friend*.'

Michael stared at me till I looked away. Then he said, 'She's all right is Nicky. I've never forgotten that time you had glandular fever and she came round every few days with books and fruit, pictures she'd taken on her phone, all that girly shit.'

'I'd have done the same for her.'

'Yeah, yeah.'

'I helped *you* when you fell down the inspection pit and broke your ankle.'

'That's true. You made me at least one cup of tea.'

'I should have poured it over your head.'

'Thank you, Florence Nightingale.'

'You pretended you couldn't get to the toilet and needed to pee in a milk carton. Is it any wonder I left you to your own devices?'

'Poor, gullible Freya.' He grinned and raised his eyebrows. 'Hey, I think I know what's bugging you. It's that you might have to wear a frilly bridesmaid's dress. In pink, I shouldn't wonder. You couldn't bear the humiliation.'

'If she does stick me in a daft frock, I'll make sure I have my DMs on underneath.'

'And your combats.'

'I wonder if they do camouflage taffeta?' I flopped down on the sofa next to him. 'Seriously, though, I must be a bit crap if I can't just be happy for her. She'd be ecstatic if it was me getting married. She would. Because she's everything I'm not. She's straightened out, and uncomplicated and grown up.'

Michael snorted. 'What are you, then? Still a teenager?'

'You know what I mean.'

'I don't.'

'Nicky — she's got everything, she's done everything in the right order.'

'What's the 'right order'?'

'She stuck the course out at uni, for one. Then she got her legal qualification. Then her training contract. It's all mapped out.'

'You chose to do something different.'

'I flunked it.'

He pushed affectionately at my shoulder with his knuckles. 'Not that again. Look, what's done is done. There's a lot to be said for admitting you're wrong and doing something about it. Unfairly maligned is the U-turn. I wish I'd walked away before I got married, it would have saved everyone a lot of grief. But you get so far

36

down the line and it's difficult to untangle yourself.'

'There's more to it than the degree. Nicky's going to leave her mum and dad's, get her own place. Choose curtains. Hold dinner parties.'

'I can run you to Homebase if you're desperate.'

'It's the moving-on thing. She's being *normal*.'

That made him laugh.

''Cause we all want to be that, Frey, don't we?'

'It's not as if I want her life. I don't want to get married. It's just — it's change. Yeah, that's it.'

'And you're not good with change, are you?'

'I know it shouldn't matter in the face of my best mate's happiness. But the thought of the wedding feels, urgh. Crap.'

He drew in a long breath. 'OK, listen, I'm going to put it to you straight, and I'm only asking because I think you need me to: are you sure this isn't a plain case of jealousy?'

'No. I told you, *I* don't want to get hitched.'

'You've got a crush on Christian.'

It sounded shocking, hearing it out loud. 'No!'

'You've got a crush on Nicky?'

'For God's sake,' I began.

At which point the landline began to ring. We both jumped.

'Go on,' he said. 'It'll be Melody, in some sort of bother. Forgotten her eyelash glue, broken a heel.'

So I picked up the receiver. There was a pause, then Geraint's voice came down the line, cautious, rusty, Welsh. 'Freya?'

37

'Yeah.' What the hell was he ringing me here for? Wasn't there anywhere I could go to escape his wheezy old-man presence?

'Can you come back?'

'What, now? I'm stopping here tonight. I told Liv. She was fine with it.'

'She's — '

'What? What's the matter?' I caught the fear in his voice, and that made me frightened too. 'Is there a problem?'

'It's Liv.'

'Is she ill?'

He made a sick strangled noise. 'Yes, I think she is.'

'What, Geraint? Tell me.'

'She's, she's found a lump. In her. In her. A lump in her chest. She's gone a bit — upset. Can you come home now? I don't know what to do.'

No, you never bloody do, I thought.

I replaced the handset with extreme care, Michael said, 'Frey?'

'I'm all right but I have to go,' I said shakily.

Funny how just one short phone call can be all it takes for your world to begin unravelling.

Case Notes on: *Melody Jacqueline Brewster*

Meeting Location: *42, Love Lane, Nantwich*

Present: *Miss Melody Brewster, Mrs Abby Brewster, Mrs Diane Kozyra*

Date: *11 a.m., 11/11/86*

Spoke with Melody and Mrs Brewster for approximately 45 minutes, both women chatty and forthcoming. Melody feels she is recovering well physically from the birth but is still very tired (appointment with health visitor two days previously, no concerns). She has been seeing friends at home and would like to resume school as soon as possible. She says she thinks going back to her normal routine will help her in forming her decision about the best course for her baby.

Mrs Brewster agrees that Melody would benefit from returning to her classes. However she would prefer her daughter to have made a firm decision before that date. Mrs Brewster is keen to see an adoption go ahead, and asked what they had to do to begin the process once the six weeks was up. Melody is as yet unsure how she wants to proceed. Spoke to them both about the timescale involved.

Melody asked how her baby was settling in with the foster carers and I was able to reassure her all was well there. She particularly wanted to know whether they were musical and if they were playing the baby music. Mrs Brewster stressed again that she favoured adoption as the way forward.

Melody asked if I could provide her with some sleeping pills and I advised her to contact her GP.

Next visit: 18/11/86   Signed: Diane Kozyra

A SATURDAY

December

There's no getting away from it: under all the tinsel and razz, Christmas is a majorly crap time. As the festive week approaches, there's always loads on TV and in the papers about vulnerable groups we need to keep in mind: the poor, the lonely, the bereaved. And obviously that's right. We should look out for these people.

But there's another group of people for whom Christmas is a particular trial, a group neglected by the media, invisible to charity campaigners, whose suffering falls beneath everyone's radar. I'm talking about those of us in the 13-23 age bracket, that no man's land when you've basically disconnected from your family but you haven't yet established a territory of your own. We are the dispossessed, the sulky. No one rattles tins on our behalf. We have no proper place, whatever the table settings say.

Everyone else has a clearly defined role to play. Under-twelves have a ball, of course, because *Christmas is all about children, isn't it?* Mums and dads are busy creating the framework of the day, while the elderly just sit back and consume. But what's our status? Apparently to make everyone else wistful for the days when we were little and cute. 'Do you remember,' Liv says

41

every damn year, 'when you sat on Santa's lap and wiped your nose on his beard?' Ho ho ho.

For the last five Christmases I've had the extra joy of balancing both mothers, a situation ripe with stress even when the rest of my life's been going pretty steadily. This year I was still feeling the shockwaves of Liv's lump-scare, still not quite daring to trust the future. That initial trip up to the hospital for the mammogram and biopsy, the nights before and afterwards I'd sat watching mindless TV till the small hours, the compulsive internet checking, had all drawn me right back close to Liv's side again. Though her tests had come back clear, there was this strangeness hanging about the house, the lurking sense of a terrible near-miss that stole over me every so often like a cold draught. In those shivery moments, Melody seemed a long way away, just a friendly eccentric I'd got tangled with one time and couldn't shake off. Not her fault. Not mine. Simply a natural ebb, like a tide in a basin; now pulled towards this shore, now towards that. Since I've found her, I've grown used to this constant motion back and forth between my mothers.

People who hear the story of how I found my birth mum — via Friends Reunited, and directly against the advice of social services who wanted me to have counselling and follow proper procedures — often react as if I'd told them a wonderful fairy tale. Genetic order restored. How marvellous that it didn't end in a Jeremy Kyle-type punch-up. And yes, when you think of all the tensions involved, it has gone incredibly well.

I suppose the first stroke of luck was that Melody turned out to be so wrapped up in herself, my re-appearance hardly shook her at all. I'd expected tears and hand-wringing; what I got was a ninety-minute monologue on her life so far. I don't think she stopped for breath. But it was OK. Melody is what she is: sparky, generous, sunny, and almost completely self-obsessed. Once you appreciate that, the relationship becomes a lot easier.

Obviously I asked pretty early on about my biological dad, but it turned out the night I was conceived Melody had been at a stranger's party and got herself drunk. Couldn't remember a thing about the incident, bar the fact they had very loud wallpaper in the bathroom, and gatecrashers had broken the fridge door off its hinges.

So there being no father for me to fret about, this left, family-wise, just Melody's mother, Abby, and Michael. Abby sent a vague welcome from Ireland but made it clear she didn't want to be involved in any reunion. Michael, who's hardly related to me at all, turned out to be brilliant. He was twenty-five then, and about to get engaged to a bunny-boiler, but he still took the time to listen to my history and ask me what I wanted out of my new family. I told him I wanted more of a sense of who I was, and he nodded as though he understood.

So I was bloody fortunate the way it worked out, because all I'd really pictured when I

43

thought about meeting my birth mum was a pair of figures embracing. Her and me, end of story. It honestly didn't register there might be wider effects. 'Which is why,' said the social worker afterwards, 'we advise talking the process through at every stage. It can be an overwhelming amount to take on board, especially for someone at your stage of life.' The trouble with being eighteen is you're in such a hurry about everything.

The other big miscalculation I made was that, when they met, Liv and Melody would either love or hate each other straightforwardly. I could imagine them being jealous, competing for my affection. Or alternatively (went my fantasy), it was possible their bond through me might make them extra-special friends, and we'd make a new tight unit of three with me in prime position at the centre, like jewels set in a ring. This was the scenario I liked the best.

Back in 2004 I'd exited Crewe Station with my brand-new mum Melody, crossed the road to the car park, and seen Liv standing by her Volvo estate, waiting to give me a lift home. Melody came over with me and they shook hands awkwardly, and I climbed into the passenger seat expecting to go. I was exhausted. I had lots to think about. But Liv took Melody's arm and led her a way off, and they talked for about fifteen minutes. I'd have given worlds to know what was being said. It looked friendly, from a distance, but that wasn't enough. I wanted to be involved. I mean, it was my day, I was the connection. Just as I was about to open the door and join them,

Melody leaned forward and hugged Liv round her neck very quickly. Then she stepped back. I saw Liv nod, laugh, shake her head, turn to me and smile. I remember thinking, 'It's going to be OK.'

Neat scenes like that are never the end, though, are they?

The next occasion they came together, Liv had invited Melody round for a meal. By then I'd seen the house in Love Lane — the extensive wardrobe, pristine kitchen — and I began to view our place as if through Melody's eyes. While Liv moved around clearing spaces between equipment, I registered her clogs, her cargo pants, dip-dyed T-shirt, wild hair. Our hallway was full of bat box kits, the dining table covered with a wall chart showing the processes in the formation of a peat bog.

Worst, though, was when Melody first breezed through to our kitchen with her bunch of freesias to find four plates of half-mashed barn-owl pellets and two dishes of tiny bones laid out along the worktop. It must have looked as if she'd interrupted a really nasty party game. *Are those the forks we'll be using to eat?* said the expression on her face. Liv was unabashed. 'We're monitoring small mammal distribution along the Prees Branch Canal,' she explained. 'These are wood-mouse skulls, and these are shrew, see the red-tipped teeth.' She tapped the dishes one after the other. I think I said something warning like, 'Not everyone shares your passion for rodents, Mum,' and she stared at me, amazed. I thought perhaps I'd got

45

through, but she went, 'Shrews aren't rodents, Frey. You know that!' I suppose Melody was wondering who the hell she'd given her baby to. Then, whilst Liv was assembling ingredients for the meal, Geraint turned up and washed one of the jawbones down the plughole before she'd had a chance to identify which species of shrew it belonged to. Michael told me afterwards that Melody thought Liv was mad.

When the time came for a return visit, it was the level of consumption Liv found impossible to deal with. 'So much *stuff*!' she said as soon as we got in the car. 'You could barely move. And I bet she's a stranger to FairTrade.' As soon as we got home she pulled up this website where you can calculate how much more of the planet's resources you're using than you should. According to the stats, Melody was taking 2.7 earths just to fund her clothes habit.

So there was a spot of rockiness at the start. I tried to reassure each of them. I said to Liv, 'I didn't go looking for my birth mum because you aren't good enough.' To Melody I said, 'Finding you makes me feel kind of complete.' To anyone who'd listen I said, 'It's not a competition, I'm not trying to find the best mum or anything.'

I soon realised, though, that any tension was straightforward dislike based on the fact they are two very different people, and the whole shared daughter thing didn't have much to do with it. The idea I'd had at the back of my mind, that having two mothers would feel like snuggling down under a double layer of duvet, turned out to be wrong. Trying to stitch together two ill-matched squares of blanket would have been nearer the mark.

And yet we *were* a family. Melody had become part of our Christmas, alongside other traditions like painting fir cones, hanging up a star for Colin and making a giant fat-and-seed cake for the birds. She got into the habit of dropping by early afternoon, before the big meal. 'What's your Christmas Day routine?' I remember asking her that first, critical year.

She'd laughed. 'Routine? Me?'

'Don't you have any little rituals?'

'I make sure I'm pickled by five,' she said. But she hadn't got drunk in the hour she stayed with us, and she'd left not only a present for me but some perfume for Liv as well, which caused panic as Liv had nothing to give her in return. 'Putting herself on the moral high ground,' said Liv, holding up the bottle of *Poison* critically. 'When would I wear scent, anyway? It attracts wasps and it interferes with the tracking pads.'

Thus started another tradition: the unsuitable gift exchange. So far Melody's received, among other things, a ladybird overwintering house, an energy-saving plug and a mug showing which areas of the earth will be devastated by global warming. To Liv she's given a massive pair of spangly dangly earrings, a voucher for a manicure and a DVD called *Make Mine Mink*. These may have all been chosen with a pure and innocent heart, but I doubt it.

This troubled year my birth mother turned up slightly later than usual, in a long, belted

Victorian nightie, burgundy knee boots and a green suede coat.

'I declare, it's Wee Willie Winkie,' muttered Liv as we watched Melody tug her sack of presents off the back seat of the car. But as usual, it was air-kissing and smiley-smiley as soon as she was in the hall.

'Have you re-decorated? The place looks bigger.'

'We shifted a couple of moth traps,' said Liv. 'Come through.'

Geraint was watching TV but he looked up when Melody came in. It's difficult to read what he's thinking. His small eyes squinted, taking in her whole length. Sensibly, she ignored him.

'The house looks nice,' she said, nodding at the home-made paper chains and modest tree. The tree's one of Liv's few festive concessions — real, but locally sourced off the edge of the Moss, and always recycled via the council chipper afterwards. We decorate it with strings of popcorn that can be hung out for the birds, and with teasels and physalis and dried orange slices. The colours may be subdued but it does smell nice.

'This is your present,' said Liv. She settled herself next to Melody on the couch, and handed over a small, slim envelope. I was surprised. Surely Liv wasn't giving cash?

Melody's perfect nails slit open the flap and drew out the card. 'Oh,' she said after a beat, 'chickens! You bought me chickens.' She began to laugh. 'Welcome to my smallholding.'

'Where's she going to keep chickens?' I asked.

'Melody doesn't get them, they go to a family in Haiti,' said Liv. 'Oxfam have this scheme. I could have bought you half a goat, or an eighth of a cow.'

'Chickens!' said Melody.

'I got you jewellery,' I said hastily, in case she thought I was in on the poultry deal. She wiped her eyes, put the envelope down and started on my present.

'Oh, that's beautiful, hun.' She lifted up the peacock brooch to admire. Then she fastened it straight onto her nightdress and blew me a kiss.

'More birds for you,' I said.

Beside her, Liv was picking at her own parcel, her fingers short-nailed, freckled, calloused, saggy about the knuckle. What she finally unwrapped was a box of Booja Booja ethical truffles, packaged in renewable cedar wood, dairy-, wheat-, gluten- and GMO-free. Her face was a picture and I almost hooted out loud. Ha! Wrong-footed this time, Liv. Cunning Melody, switching the rules.

'Well, now. They're lovely,' said Liv.

'Organic,' said Melody.

'So I see,' said Liv.

'Yum yum.'

Was that a wink or just a bit of eyelash-fluttering? Now Melody handed me two presents: a smart gold affair the size of a shoebox and a smaller one which looked as though it had been wrapped in wallpaper lining by someone wearing a blindfold. I attacked the scruffy one first. 'That's from Michael,' she told me.

I glanced up, surprised. 'We don't do presents.

49

I haven't got him anything.'

'I know. He said it doesn't matter.'

The paper tore away and I was holding a book: *The Rough Guide to Israel & the Palestinian Territories*. 'Oh. Wow. This is — unexpected.'

'Is it a gardening manual?' asked Liv.

I studied the palm trees on the cover. Whatever had induced him to get me this? The guide was clearly well used, the cover curled at one corner and the spine creased. Michael did like to mooch around second-hand bookshops; I could imagine him sliding it off a shelf, on a whim. But why pass it on to me?

'Hmm. Tell him I don't know how I've survived without it.'

I supposed he must have meant the guide as a dig because I never went anywhere. I've a terrible fear of flying, for a start — I suffer from a recurring dream where the plane I'm on climbs vertically and then drops like a stone. Abroad frightened me. I didn't even hold a current passport. In fact, the only time I've been out of the UK was for a school trip when I was thirteen and we took a ferry to Belgium for two days. I hated every minute. Holidays with Liv were taken in this country, always based around some ecologically interesting area — wetlands one year, shingle coast another. I didn't really mind because it was just what we did, and some of it was cool, e.g. map-reading and watching seals. If Colin hadn't come off his motorbike maybe we'd have done more usual stuff: sandy beaches, shopping, video arcades. Liv has a photo of

Colin and me, aged two, filling a bucket with seaweed. But there's no point dwelling on what might have been.

I used to go away with Liv till I was about sixteen, and then I rebelled so she left me to camp at Nicky's for the week. Basically, I stopped having holidays then. Even British ones seemed like more bother and expense than they were worth. And the idea of navigating InterRail timetables or foreign currency or health insurance froze my mind. How on earth do you arrange these things? Liv didn't know, wasn't interested, didn't approve of travelling around much anyway on account of the carbon emissions.

Nicky went with her parents annually to her mum's friend's villa in Portugal, but these trips were always organised by Derek; Nicky's only responsibilities were to pack and climb into the car. Melody's holidays were irregular, spontaneous and boyfriend-led. No room for an awkward daughter in the hold.

Get off your backside and see the world, Michael was saying to me.

By landing in a war zone, though?

'Don't forget my present,' said Melody.

The book slid to one side. I picked up the golden box.

When I lifted the lid, it was to find a silky nightdress covered in a rose pattern, a riot of pinks and purples. I lifted the chemise out by its straps, and two slender mauve ribbons unfurled and fell gracefully from the centre of the bust. 'My God,' I said. It was the kind of outfit that

51

would have looked fantastic on Melody. I knew it would make me look like a half-hearted transvestite. 'Add a touch of glamour to your life', read the label. A sudden memory of standing in Melody's bedroom early on, peering through the drapery of scarves and necklaces into her dressing-table mirror while she rubbed foundation into my jaw line. *Your skin's so like mine. I've waited years to do this, Frey.*

'Gosh, thanks very much,' I said.

'Every woman needs a bit of silk in her wardrobe, doesn't she?'

'Just wish I had someone to wear it for.'

'What about Oggy?'

'We're not seeing each other any more.'

Melody shrugged. 'Oh, you'll get back together, you always do. In the meantime, wear it for yourself. Be gorgeous for gorgeous' sake.' Across the room, Geraint lowered his face and hunched deeper into his chair. 'What did Liv get you?'

'A coat,' said Liv.

Which I had to pick myself, I thought ungraciously. The next moment I was ashamed. As if Liv hadn't had enough to worry about these last weeks. If it had been me with a scary lump, I'd have been a weeping mess, never mind arranging present lists.

'It's really nice,' I said. 'It's like a bomber jacket.'

'You going to show me, then?' asked Melody.

'It's hanging up in the hall. Come and see.'

'I need to check the turkey,' said Liv, getting to her feet as well. Geraint stayed where he was, only his eyes flicking to the side as we trooped past him.

Melody and I hadn't even reached the newel post when she stopped unexpectedly, making me bump into her. When she turned around, her face was alight.

'*Merry* Christmas, Frey.'

'Merry Christmas,' I said cautiously. Perhaps she had been drinking, after all.

'You did like your nightie, didn't you?'

'It was great. Very rosy.'

She clasped her hands in satisfaction. 'Oh, my God, everything's so perfect!'

I thought that was overdoing it a bit, so I stepped past her and reached for the sleeve of my new coat. I knew Melody would hate it. She'd call the colour sludgy, wrinkle her nose at the ribbed cuffs. 'Why do you dress like you're about to walk onto a battlefield?' she asked me once. 'All those nice funky clothes I bought you when we first met.' I remember thinking that if she'd chosen to keep me rather than give me up for adoption, she'd have kitted me out in pink and lace and artificial flower hair slides, and I'd probably have grown up clacking around in unsuitable shoes instead of scrambling up and down ditches in my wellies. And as we stood there in the hallway, I was transfixed by a sudden pang of longing to be a little girl again, holding Liv's clipboard for her and marking off water-vole burrows.

Melody lifted the other sleeve of the coat. 'Yeah, very grungy, Frey. Suits you.'

'Sure.'

'It does. It's your style, I'm not going to criticise. No need to look so down.'

'I'm not down.'

'You are.'

'I'm nostalgic. That's not the same.'

'Nostalgic for what?

'Oh, I don't know. Nothing. It doesn't matter.'

'Tell me, hun.'

I exhaled slowly. 'I suppose, a time when I fitted in. Christmas when you're a kid, you know where you are. It's safe. Now I'm not sure I belong.'

'Don't be silly.'

'I'm not explaining it very well. What I mean is, I can't rewind. I can't go back and find the place I felt right . . . ' *So I need to have got to the next stage. I need to have my own base, be starting some new venture of my own. A new job, a man, a family, even. Any step forward. Something other than this axolotl existence.* 'It's like they say, Christmas is for children — it is, though, isn't it? Those are the happiest Christmases. However the rest of us flounder about — and basically once you're past that stage it gets sad because you can't — '

I didn't get to complete the sentence because Melody put her finger to my lips and arched her brows dramatically. 'For children, you say?'

I nodded.

'As it happens, I might be able to help out there,' she said.

It took a few seconds for her meaning to sink in.

'You don't mean you're pregnant?' I hissed.

'I do.'

You're too old, I almost said. 'Does Joe know?'

'Of course he does.'

'Is he all right with it?'

'He's thrilled.'

'How far on are you?'

'Only just begun really. I used one of those super-early predictor tests.'

'You're sure you read it right?'

'Of course I'm sure. I'm going to see the midwife in the New Year.'

It was true, then. The next second I remembered my manners. 'Congratulations!'

'Shhh.' Melody glanced behind me towards the lounge door and the kitchen.

'Have I to keep it a secret?'

'Just for a few weeks. I want to try and get a scan photo, then I can show people the baby's picture.' She grinned and gave a little shiver of excitement.

You'll be keeping this one, will you? I couldn't stop the sentence popping, fully formed, into my head. For a terrible moment I imagined what would happen if I spoke it aloud, how her face would crumple, what devastation it would wreak after the years we'd been so careful with each other.

I took a deep breath. 'Yes, just think,' I said.

★ ★ ★

After Melody had gone, I put on my new coat and went and sat in our garage for a while, trying

55

to work out how I felt. The truth was, I couldn't take it in. Melody wasn't a mother-type. I just couldn't picture her with a baby at all. Hadn't she said herself she wasn't cut out for child-rearing, and it was the best bit of luck I ever had in my life that I didn't get brought up by her? Wasn't her running joke that she couldn't even be trusted to look after a goldfish?

And yet for all that, I know she didn't give me up straight away. Attitudes were different in the 1980s, and when she gave birth she was only fifteen, a minor. Jesus, at fifteen my idea of a crisis was a morning where my hair wouldn't go flat.

I know she only had me for forty-eight hours before I was taken away to foster carers. That she then had weeks of counselling, and she found it really hard to make up her mind despite Grandma Abby going on at her about what a fool she was to even think about keeping me. I know she dithered for three months, till her social worker said that really it was the best time for me to move, before I formed attachments.

I know she was asked to come up with a wish list for the type of adoptive family she wanted and she put that she wanted a big house with a garden and a piano. 'But they did say they couldn't guarantee anything,' she told me later. 'I just thought a piano would have been nice.'

I know that when she came to sign the final consent form, she got an attack of nervous giggles and they all thought she was going mad.

I obviously know that her social worker

encouraged her to write me a letter because I have it; Liv and I used to read it together from when I was about eight. It's half a side of loopy, childish script, with circles instead of dots over each i, which I've since read graphologists consider a sign of dishonesty, though I don't believe Melody is dishonest, no more than most people. The letter says pretty much what you'd expect. That she loves me but she wants me to have a better life, that she hopes I'll be good for my new mum and dad and grow up to be happy. That her name for me was Fay Johanna.

She wrote to Liv every year asking how I was doing, and Liv always replied, though no photos were ever exchanged and neither party knew where the other was based because the letters went via social services. Liv used to ask me what I wanted to go in our letters — teachers' comments from my report, lost milk teeth, school trips, any little achievement or adventure — but she was the one who actually wrote them. I didn't object because I thought it had to be that way. Maybe it did.

So I've grown up aware that Melody thought about me and wished me well, and in turn I knew stuff like when she bought a new car or changed her boss or tripped over doing salsa and broke her arm. I've always had a sense of her. Even as a shadowy pen pal she was part of my life. Remote, but there.

I tried again to imagine her with a new baby. The picture wouldn't gel. But a baby there would be, it wasn't going to go away.

I'd have to get my head round it somehow.

* * *

When I went back, Liv was still in the kitchen, battling with the turkey.

'Tell me about when I was little,' I said.

She looked up from basting, her face shiny with the heat. She'd tied her hair back with a duster, which must have been the first fabric to hand.

'I'll do the carrots for you.'

'Thanks.' She hefted the turkey over, basted it, and with an effort, slid the tray back into the oven. Then she put her palms flat on the worktop and hung her head.

'Do you feel faint or something?'

'It's warm in here. Open the back door, will you?'

I put the peeler down and did as she asked.

'OK,' she said, recovering herself and shifting to the sink where a plate of parsnips waited. 'Let's see. When you were little.'

'Was I a good baby?'

'Oh, the best. I think the people who'd had you before us had got you into a routine. You slept through, you were pretty keen on your food. You weren't talking or walking but you were bright as a button, we could see that straight away.

'What was my first word?'

' 'Ta'. You used it to mean please as well as thank you. And even when you couldn't say much, you'd wave your arms and legs around when we spoke to you. It was very sweet.'

I looked across at her as she scrubbed the

parsnips. Her eyes were gazing out over the garden, but unfocused, as though she was watching scenes invisible to me.

'How happy were you that you had me?'

'Happier than a king.'

I've asked her before; that's her stock answer. I never tire of hearing it.

'And you used to love watching water come out of the outside tap,' she went on. 'And the first time we took you to the beach, you didn't like the feel of the sand on your feet and you had a screaming tantrum. And later in the week you saw some shrimps swimming in a rock pool and you couldn't stop giggling at them. You won't remember, though.'

Melody popped unbidden into my head, Melody and her expanding embryo. I longed to confide the news in Liv. 'Do you like babies?'

'I liked *you*. Oh, and another thing you used to do: you really developed a taste for Calpol, and sometimes you pretended your teeth were hurting so we'd give you some. And of course it's poisonous if you take too much, and I never knew whether or not you were faking. Colin would be saying, 'Oh, give it to her,' and I'd be saying, 'No, let's wait.' You were a devil for it.'

'A druggie before I was two.'

She stopped cleaning the parsnips and her shoulders drooped again. I wondered whether she was remembering Colin. That's the trouble with reminiscing. You don't know what else you'll drag up.

'Do you want to sit down for a minute?'

Liv just shook her head. I left my carrots and

went to see what was wrong.

'Oh, God, Mum.'

'It's fine,' she said, in a choked voice.

'Yeah, 'cause you always cry for no reason.'

'I'm not crying.'

'My mistake.' I put my hand on her shoulder, and as I did so, a tear dripped into the sink. 'Look, I shouldn't have got you to talk about the past, especially not on Christmas Day. How stupid am I?'

'No, it's not that.' She unknotted the duster and wiped her eyes with it. 'It's absolutely nothing. Forget it.'

'*Mum.*'

'No, really.'

'For God's sake!' I felt like snatching up the peeler and waving it in her face. Why did we always have to play this daft game, Guess What's Wrong? Melody spilled out everything the instant it formed in her brain, but Liv needed it coaxing out every time. It made me feel deficient, somehow, as though I should have noticed without the prompt.

She patted her chest. 'All right. It's only this stupid lump.'

The lump. Three weeks ago I'd come hurtling back from Melody's to find Liv locked in the bathroom and Geraint dithering at the foot of the stairs, clasping his hands like a mad bell-ringer.

'She dropped a bottle of blackcurrant, it's all over the floor,' he'd whimpered.

'Go clean it up then,' I'd yelled. Bloody useless article. It had taken twenty minutes to get her to open the bathroom door.

In the days that followed I'd made a GP's appointment, walked with her to the surgery, driven her to hospital where some doctor had taken cells out of her boob, got them checked and pronounced them sound. End of story, I'd thought.

But something wasn't right. Now I looked at her properly, she still had shadows under her eyes and a hard set to her mouth, as if she was right near the edge.

'You got the all-clear, didn't you? Didn't you?'

'Mmm. You were terrific, Frey.'

'It had to be done.'

'Geraint's not good with hospitals.'

Whereas I find them a laugh a minute. 'Look, I know the whole business must have been a shock, and you're going to take a while to put it behind — '

'I was being ridiculous, wasn't I? All I could think that night was, I needed some space. And then once I got inside the bathroom I didn't want to open the door again. It was pure panic, and Geraint didn't know what to do to help, bless him.'

Yeah, bless him. 'It doesn't matter.'

'No. Only, only I think it's grown, Frey.'

'What?'

'The lump. It's got bigger. And it's changed. It's got sort of grainier.'

I blinked at her. 'Are you sure?'

'Geraint says it might be the effect of the biopsy needle poking about. He's probably right. I'm being silly again. I told you it wasn't anything.'

Despite the grey smudges under her eyes, something in her face looked relieved to have confessed. But she had me frightened now.

'You have to go back, then,' I said.

'I've another check-up in April.'

'Sooner than that!'

'I don't want to waste anyone's time.'

'Are you absolutely positive it's got bigger?'

For answer she tightened her lips.

'Then you've to go back in the New Year and demand another biopsy. Which is better? Feeling a bit embarrassed in front of a few nurses, or keeping quiet and . . . '

I hadn't thought the end of the sentence through. Liv grasped my hand, a gesture I wasn't expecting, and we knocked the peeler onto the floor where it clattered and spun. 'I'm sure it's nothing, but promise me anyway,' I said.

Then the doorbell rang, and she let go of my fingers. After a moment, I heard Nicky's voice in the hall.

'Fuck,' I said under my breath.

Liv wiped her eyes again and went back to the potatoes. 'I'll be through in a minute,' she said. 'Give me a minute on my own, eh?'

Sometimes you wish you could just pop on an invisibility cloak while you get your act together.

★   ★   ★

When I walked into the lounge, Nicky was perched on the edge of the sofa, talking at a baffled Geraint.

'Hiya,' I said, as brightly as I could manage.

Nicky jumped up at once and gave me a hug. She was wearing a berry-red jumper and neat black trousers, and I thought she looked older than twenty-three. Getting engaged seemed to have changed her already. She was more confident, somehow, more adult.

'Hi yourself. Having a good time? The house looks great. Love the paper chains! Wow, are these your pressies?'

I showed her my modest pile: the coat I was still wearing from having sat out in the garage, Melody's inappropriate nightie, money from Grandma Abby, hand cream from Mrs Noble who used to collect me from school and give me my tea when I was little, a bottle of wine from Ray at the nursery. Geraint and I buy nothing for each other, an arrangement Liv wisely leaves alone.

'Cool!' went Nicky, to everything I showed her. This is kind of her because she gets ten times what I do. Joan and Derek have a string of siblings each, plus a wide circle of generous friends. Santa nearly has a hernia getting down their chimney. *But then think of all the boring thank you letters I have to write afterwards,* I remember her saying in an attempt to cheer me up. *And so much of it's tat. Banana-shaped purses and musical toothbrushes. Would you want it?* For a few moments I held that image of teen Nicky holding her banana purse like a microphone, singing *Dancing in the Moonlight* down the stalk end. 'Well, here you go,' she said, handing me a shiny blue paper bag with a flower on the side. 'Add this into the mix.'

Inside the bag were three *Hammer House of Horror* DVDs and a pamphlet on calligraphy.

'Calligraphy?' I said.

'Yeah, I thought you might like to give it a whirl. Could be fun.'

How empty did she think my life was, that I wanted to spend hours practising handwriting? 'Excellent,' I said. 'The DVDs are top. I'll have to make you sit down and watch *The Two Faces of Evil* sometime. For your hen night, maybe.'

'No hen night, I told you.'

'Girls' night in, then.'

Liv appeared at this point, dry-eyed and calm, and carrying a plate of kettle chips. I gave Nicky her present, which was a subscription for *Brides* magazine. When she undid the envelope, she actually shrieked with happiness.

'Is it all right? You've not subscribed already?'

'Oh, yes, no, it's fantastic. Oh, *thanks*, Frey. Thanks *so* much.'

You'd have thought I'd pledged to buy her wedding dress for her the way she carried on. I was pleased, because buying such a sensible present nearly killed me. On one side of the High Street was WHSmith and its stand of magazines, while on the other was a shop I'd spotted selling glow-in-the-dark croquet sets. Pre-engagement, I'd have plumped without hesitation for the croquet set, knowing in the months afterwards we'd all have played under the stars, drunk and hilarious. But as I dithered on the pavement, it dawned on me we'd now passed that stage and I needed to buy my best friend something suitable and grown up, even if that knowledge felt like a girder laid across my heart.

'How are the wedding plans?' asked Liv, wrestling the poker out of its slotted stand and prodding the fire.

Nicky's face took on an almost holy radiance.

'Terrific! I've got this special book, a diary-memorandum thing I've been filling in. Mum bought it for me. We've got a wall chart, too.'

'And when's the actual date?'

'Next October. The twelfth.'

That's ages off, I was about to say, when Liv went, 'Not long, then.'

'I know,' said Nicky. 'Scary. We got in on the back of a cancellation, which was lucky. Although not lucky for the people cancelling. That's really sad, isn't it? I can't think of anything worse, can you?'

'When Colin and I got married, the wedding before us never happened because the bride pulled out. Right at the last minute, with everybody waiting.'

'You never told me that,' I said.

Liv pursed her lips. 'Didn't I?'

It felt odd to hear them talking together so enthusiastically about weddings. Liv wasn't interested in that kind of fluff. And yet there they were, sitting opposite each other, leaning forward eagerly, while Geraint and I looked on from outside the charmed circle.

'Will you be having a hot meal or a buffet?' Liv asked.

Geraint caught my eye, and shifted in his chair.

Fuck off and die, old man, I told him silently.

Why don't YOU bugger off and leave home, he signalled back. *It's about time, and then some. At your age I was driving an eighteen-tonne truck between London and Swansea every week. Shape yourself, girl.*

' . . . after a rustic effect,' Nicky was explaining to Liv.

'And what does Christian think?'

'He's not bothered. I mean, he says I can have whatever I want, it's for me to choose. It's my day.'

'No battles yet with your mum or your mum-in-law?'

Even though I was on the other side of the room, I thought I saw hesitation flicker over Nicky's face. 'Oh, no. Mum's just, you know, really excited, same as me, and Corinne's, Corinne's great. She has lots of ideas, lots of energy. She's been so helpful already. They're a lovely family. I'm incredibly lucky.'

'They're the lucky ones,' I said.

Nicky turned to me and beamed, and I thought, *I truly meant that. Christian's parents should be on their knees thanking God he's picked someone as sound as you. I hope they appreciate you.*

'I've been having a think about your dress, too, Frey,' she said, and the warmth I'd been feeling towards her evaporated immediately.

'Go on.'

'Well, I've seen something in a shop I want you to come and try on. It's green, so it'll go with your hair. Not dull green, not green like your coat, a bit brighter than you usually wear.

Emerald. Nice. And it's ankle length with a low front, sleeveless, very glam. I thought the two little bridesmaids could wear green and cream. Maybe you could have long cream gloves. You'll look brilliant together. It's going to be brilliant.'

A day of bliss evidently awaited me, trussed up like a burlesque stripper, shepherding Nicky's nieces about for hours in the freezing cold. 'Sounds fun,' I said.

'Do you think so? God, Freya, I don't think there's anyone happier than me in the world right now. It feels almost wicked.'

'You couldn't be wicked if you tried,' I said.

'I can't wait for next October, can you?'

'Absolutely not.'

'It's nice to have something positive coming up,' said Liv.

Then I understood why she'd shown such an uncharacteristic interest in the wedding plans. 'Yeah, something to focus on. A bright spot on the horizon. It will be good, won't it?'

I wondered whether Geraint was getting this, but his attention was fixed on the TV screen. After a few moments, his hand came up to scratch his scalp, and a flake of something detached itself and floated down to land on the chair back.

'Have I shown you my idea for how the invitations are going to be folded?' said Nicky.

★ ★ ★

The last visitor on Christmas Day was an unexpected one: Michael.

67

'I thought you might need rescuing from the festive joy,' he said, standing on the doorstep with his hands in his pockets.

'I do. Where are we going?'

'Anywhere you like.'

I ran to get my coat.

'So Melody's having a baby,' I said as soon as I'd climbed into the van.

He laughed. 'Remind me never to trust you with one of my secrets.'

'I assumed you knew.'

'I did. But that's your good luck.' He swung the van away from the pavement and we started off into the night.

'Sorry. I've been holding it in all day. It was a hell of a shock.'

'You're telling me.'

'What do you think?'

He took a hand off the wheel and rubbed the back of his neck. 'Makes no odds what I think, does it? Although, between you and me, I'll believe there's a baby when I see one.'

'You don't mean she's making it up?'

'No. I think she could be mistaken, though.'

'She's done a test.'

'OK. It's early days. That's all I'm saying. These things don't always go according to plan.'

I spent a moment or two digesting this, watching the white lines loom out of the darkness then disappear under the bonnet. What did he mean, exactly? That she might get rid of it? It seemed an uncharacteristically cruel thing for him to say. Melody was so high on that baby, anything other than a happy outcome would be a

68

disaster. Even to consider it felt like the worst disloyalty.

I was still frowning when he glanced across at me, his face guilt-stricken. 'Sorry, Frey, I don't know what made me come out with that. Obviously I hope it's fine for her.'

'Yes,' I said. 'So do I.'

We turned off the bypass and headed out towards Whixall. Hedgerows loomed past, bleached and skeletal in the headlights. The tarmac sparkled with frost.

Without warning he swung the van off the main road, onto a farm track. The cab bounced hard on the rutted ground and I slammed against the door and hurt my arm on the handle. 'Ow,' I said, but Michael seemed not to hear me.

'You should know,' he said, 'three months after I got married, Kim had a miscarriage. Fucking nightmare, it was. It was one of the problems that helped spilt us up.'

'Oh, God, I'm sorry. I had no idea.'

'You wouldn't have. We didn't tell anyone; well, I told Melody on the QT. Kim didn't want it spread about. Madness, to be honest, because it meant there was only really us in on it.'

'That must have been hard.'

'It bloody was. We'd sit there of an evening and there'd be this great black space between us. She was so cut up, I didn't know what to do to make it better. The whole business was shit. What I'm trying to say is, these experiences, they stick in your mind forever afterwards and spoil a piece of good news. That's the only reason I said what I did. I hate myself for even mentioning it.

Melody's charmed. I'm sure everything'll be fine.'

He slowed the van and we passed between the last hedges and out into open space. The engine died and he switched off the headlights. Ahead of us lay the fishing lake, a glimmering stretch of flat black water.

It was a struggle to find the right words. 'What Melody didn't hear won't hurt her.'

'Yeah, that's the last thing I want to do. Just, any day now she'll be decorating the nursery like it's the Sistine Chapel, and sticking some four-hundred-quid pram on her credit card. If I could just somehow be the voice of caution. God, I don't know. Shut up, Michael. Forget I ever said it. What's your take, anyway?'

'On Melody being pregnant? Urgh. Too weird.'

'More scary change on the way for you.'

'Bog off.' I lowered the back of my seat and closed my eyes. Gradually the tension between us lifted.

Michael said, 'You'll have a sibling, of sorts, a proper one. Have you thought about that?'

A little sister or brother. Some squirming infant dropped into my arms while I stood petrified I was going to drop it or choke it or let it cry itself into a fit.

'Like I said, it's just too bizarre, I can't picture it at all. And Melody, she's been *my* mum for twenty-three years. I thought that was it. I thought she'd finished with babies. Can you imagine her dealing with a nappy, honestly? Her scarves and pendants dangling down in the poo, her velvet clothes with sick on them? And all those bits and pieces in the house that a baby'll pull down or swallow or fall over. She'll have to change. She can't carry on being Melody.'

'Does that matter?'

Yes, I wanted to say, *I need her to stay as she is.* But even through the whirling mess of thoughts and possibilities I realised how selfish it would sound. Melody was never really my mum; why shouldn't she move on and mother someone else?

'You know what? Makes no odds if it's happening anyway. I mean, change is part of life. You have to go with it.'

'That's the spirit, kiddo.'

Something brushed across my scalp and I opened my eyes. Michael, I realised, was attempting to ruffle my hair.

'Patronising git,' I said, batting his hand away. 'I shan't bother telling you anything in future. Oh, and do you mind telling me what your present was in aid of? 'Hey, Freya, why not bugger off to a war zone for a spell?''

'It was only an idea. The guide kind of leaped out at me.'

'Because . . . ?'

'I don't know what it was, except in junior school we used to have this ancient book called *Flight Six: The Holy Land.* I remember sitting in the library looking at the pictures, and it dawning on me for the first time ever that places you heard about, like in assembly, Bethlehem and that, actually existed and you could go visit them. So when you grew up you could go anywhere in the world if you wanted to. Maybe it's that.'

'Couldn't you choose somewhere more peaceful, though?'

'It's not all fighting round there. There's people living ordinary lives, a different culture and stuff. Some of it's very historical.'

'I'll give you 'historical'. Next year, foist your junk-shop finds on someone else.'

He laid his arms across the steering wheel and rested his chin there, staring out at the far-off orange glow from the bypass. 'I wonder what it would be like to go out somewhere so different and far away. I might have it back, your book, and make use of it myself.'

'You wouldn't.'

'I might.'

'We're talking the other side of the world.'

'Exactly.'

'You don't know the language. There are terrorists.'

'I think I can work out how to use a phrasebook. There are terrorists everywhere these days.'

'For God's sake.'

'What?'

'You love the garage.'

Michael sighed in exasperation. 'I don't 'love' it. It's OK. But there's other stuff I want to do. It might be nice to travel the world, properly travel, meet different people who've grown up thousands of miles from you and had completely different experiences. All right, maybe not the West Bank, that probably is a bit radical, but *somewhere*. Are you telling me you want to spend your whole life here, in this two-horse town?'

'What about the people here?' What about me, I suppose I meant. 'Aren't we enough for you?'

I guess I'd not appreciated how much I relied on Michael. He was someone I could always moan at, confide in, laugh with. He'd given me lifts home when I was stranded, bailed me out of a small financial crisis, helped me find my first proper job. Plus, quite aside from any emotional support, he represented free car maintenance, something which must have saved me a small fortune over the years. If all of a sudden he wasn't around, it was going to leave such a hole.

Not that our relationship had always been so positive. When we very first met, I'd developed a small and secret crush on him. This crush evaporated overnight when I came limping back from uni and he took it upon himself to give me a right telling-off. He actually took me out for a meal to do it: massive great bollocking in the beer garden of the Dusty Miller. 'For God's sake, Freya,' he'd ranted, 'I wish I had half your brains. You don't appreciate what you're chucking away.' Oh, he's changed his tune since then, but at the time he was furious with me.

For half a year after that we avoided each other. Then I went to his awful, sad wedding and I just felt sorry for him. It's difficult to stay angry when you discover the bridegroom round the back of the registry office with his head in his hands.

'Wouldn't you miss your friends and family?' I asked him now. 'Your workmates, and the pub,

Oulton Park? What about all those autojumbles you go to?'

The edges of the fishing lake before us were busy with little silver streaks of movement — coots, moorhens, mallards, or perhaps only the ordinary disturbance of water against reeds. To me it looked beautiful. And the clouds pearly against the half-moon, and bare tree branches outlined by distant sodium lamps, and every few minutes the twinkle of headlights passing.

Michael spoke without turning his head. Each sentence misted the windscreen faintly. 'I don't know, Freya. I don't know whether it's enough. I keep thinking lately, there's got to be more than this.'

'At least we're safe here.'

'Are we, though?'

I thought of Liv, tried to sound careless. 'There's no place like home, Toto.'

'How would you know unless you ever left it?' he said.

From Liv's diary, 1/05

Bad start to the day as Alan H rang to say mink reported on reserve. F in mood at breakfast saying she didn't know what to wear, everything I suggested wrong. Stress between us dreadful even though I try not to show reaction.

Arrived M's house around 10. When she opened door I thought we'd got her out of bed, but nightie/slip turned out to be a dress. Can't understand how she wasn't frozen.

Hard to see where to sit. Whole space crammed, clutter on every surface, lacy mats & cushions & nick-nacks like an old lady's house. F thinks it's trendy. Wonder if M has a condition.

Met the 'brother-who-isn't', as he calls himself. Seemed sensible & polite, slightly hunted look about him. Very tolerant of M's teasing. He told me in kitchen when on our own, 'Freya is obviously a well-brought-up girl'. Wanted to ask him whether he thought F seeing too much of M, whether healthy, but worried about how I'd sound so didn't. F ridiculously giddy throughout visit. Not the daughter I know!

Back home made us scrambled egg & bacon, asked if F wanted to come check mink rafts with me. Said she would, but then Michael rang & she got chatting to him. Not heard her laugh so much in years.

The trouble is, they are all so young.

A WEDNESDAY

January

Under different circumstances it could have been quite a fun half hour.

'*Woken Nightly by my Haunted Stairlift!*' read Liv, holding the tatty magazine aloft and showing me the headline for proof.

'*Jealous Neighbour Fed Me Poisoned Trifle,*' I countered, flourishing my own mag. '*Dr Doom Sold My Kidney.*'

'*I Used My Giant Boobs to Squash a Burglar.*'

'*Mum Cooked My Guinea Pig.*'

Other patients in the waiting room frowned and looked away. 'Sorry,' said Liv, to no one in particular. The double doors opened and a hospital porter wheeled an empty trolley past reception. Liv followed it with her eyes till it was out of sight.

'Can they be true?' I said, to bring her back to me.

'The stories? I've no idea.'

'Someone's been through my magazine and clipped half of them out. Now that's disturbing.'

We shifted on the hard plastic seats, checked our watches, sighed. Behind the safety of her desk, the receptionist busied herself on the computer. 'Do you think it'll be much longer?' asked Liv.

'No. There's only that couple in the corner who were here before us.'

Her left hand crept up to clasp her right bicep, a habit she'd started over Christmas. I suspected it was a way of covertly feeling the lump, by pressing her wrist above her nipple. 'The Breast Care Nurse did say to call if I had any more worries,' she'd confided on Boxing Day. 'Then do it,' I'd urged. 'Ask for another appointment. Get a scan.'

'*Locked in the Loo by Evil Burglars!*' I read out hastily.

'As though there might be any other kind of burglar,' said Liv. 'Do you ever feel as though you've led the dullest life?'

When they did finally call her, she wouldn't let me go in even though I pleaded.

'Let me do this my own way,' she said, which left me no room to manoeuvre. Instead I sat among the magazines and read about a teenager who'd given birth in a jammed lift, a Girl Guide who'd used her uniform to rob pensioners, and a man who kidnapped his old maths teacher. My maths teacher in secondary school had been about a hundred; he'd never have stood to be bundled into the back of a van and driven around with a pillowcase over his head. Oggy's daft comments alone nearly gave him a heart attack. Once someone planted a Little Snapper mouse trap in his desk drawer and he had to have the week off for the shock. And then I remembered Melody standing in our hallway, sliding her hand into Liv's shoulder bag to retrieve a set of keys, and her shriek as her fingers touched cold slime. Liv hurrying in, reassuring: *It's only rotted apple. I keep it to attract the voles.* Melody's eyes wide and disbelieving as she took the proffered towel.

The scanning-room door opened and Liv emerged. Her face was so grim I couldn't help but assume the worst. 'Well?' I said as she sat down next to me.

'I'm not sure they think there's a problem,' she said tightly.

'Oh.' That I hadn't been expecting. 'Did they see it had grown?'

'Only by half a millimetre, and that's not significant. They allow a margin of error anyway.'

She hung her head.

'Let them do this second biopsy,' I said.

'I don't know. We could just go home. Aside from the lump I feel perfectly healthy.'

'You're here, though, it's all set up.'

'I don't want to be a bother.'

I stood up. Several patients turned their heads in my direction. '*Bother?* What the *hell* are you talking about?'

'Freya.'

'Well, for God's sake, Mum. What are you trying to do to me?'

'Sit down,' she hissed. 'All right, I'll go. Just don't make a fuss. It's bad enough as it is.'

Which made me feel like a kid being told off for having a tantrum. It's funny, even decent mothers have a way of making you feel like crap sometimes.

★ ★ ★

78

Straight after the biopsy they gave Liv a special pager. We were supposed to go for a wander round the hospital, then, when we got the bleep, come back in for the results.

'Where do you want to go?' I asked.

'I'm not sure there's anywhere *to* go. Walk round the grounds, maybe.'

'It's raining. Does that matter?'

'I think I'd like to be outside, Frey.'

We strolled across two giant car parks, shiny with the wet, and I thought about the opening sequence of *28 Days Later* where nearly everyone in Britain has died of the Rage virus and the hospital's been left smashed and deserted. This place felt uncaring in its bustling efficiency, its normal busy-ness.

Round the back of the maternity unit, where it was quieter, Liv found an interesting hedge containing an old blackbird nest, and we watched some finches and siskins fly back and forth between two maples.

'This biopsy's only double-checking,' I said, pushing back my hood so I could see her better. 'Everything's been clear so far. Just get this last hurdle out of the way and you can put it all behind you.'

Liv's hand came up again to her bicep, even though I knew she wouldn't be able to feel anything through her coat.

'It hurts,' she said. 'A surprising amount. It hurts a bit when they scan you because they squash you so hard, but it bloody hurts when they put the needle in.' She studied the white sky. 'I suppose that's nothing.'

She meant compared with cancer treatment.

I said, 'Hey, guess what, Melody's pregnant.'

Her mouth fell open. 'Melody?'

'Yup. It's a secret, though. Don't say anything.'

'I can't believe it. Melody? How many weeks?'

'Not many. About eight.'

'Good grief. Was it planned?'

'I don't know.' I hadn't thought to ask. 'Not much in Melody's life is, so I doubt it.'

'Well!'

'She's really pleased. I mean, even if it was an accident, she's happy, she's going to keep it.'

'And her boyfriend? There is someone around, is there?'

'Some guy called Joe. He's hot news, apparently. I'm meeting him tonight.'

'It's all go, isn't it?' said Liv. She walked ahead of me for a few paces, then stopped and looked back at me through the rain. 'You know, I honestly can't get my head round this. How on earth does she think she'll cope with a new baby at her age?'

'She's not that old. In some ways she's pretty young.'

'Quite.'

'She'll have to change her lifestyle — '

'Won't she just?'

'Get some more practical clothes, at least.'

Liv snorted. 'I'll send her some muslin cloths to drape over her shoulder. Elegant they're not, but they do the job. You know, she's going to be in for an almighty shock. She's never had to care for a newborn before.'

Nor have you, I thought, but I kept that to

myself. 'Anyway,' I said, 'you mustn't let on that you know. Don't tell a soul. She's not announcing it till the scan.'

'When's that?'

'They do an early one at twelve weeks. And they want to do an amnio test because of her age, except she's not entertaining that because she says it's too big a risk and even if there's something wrong with the baby she wants to keep it, so there's no point. But this is all in confidence. Don't breathe a word to anyone, yeah?'

She pushed a strand of wet hair away from her cheek. 'Don't worry. My lips are sealed. It is an extraordinary move, though, isn't it?'

'Keeping it secret?'

'Getting pregnant.'

I hadn't registered it as a 'move'. 'I don't know. I think it just happened.'

Liv shot me a cynical look. 'I suspect there's a bit more to it than that, Frey.'

I guessed what she was thinking. *Once a feckless mother, always a feckless mother. Even in these days of condoms, pills, implants, caps and coils, the woman's incapable of controlling her own fertility. Ridiculous. Twenty-three years on and she's the same silly girl.*

'It's still a happy event. I mean, babies are meant to be fun. Having a little kid around, a new member of the family. We can take it for walks along the riverbank, show it where the otter poos.'

'I'm sure Melody will love that.'

'Show it the damselflies, then. It'll be cool.' I

tried to sound enthusiastic.

'If you say so.'

Then the pager bleeped, and all thoughts of Melody and her baby schemes fell away.

★ ★ ★

This time she let me go in with her. As soon as we saw the nurse sitting at the back of the room, I guessed what was coming.

'It needs to come out,' said the consultant. He was middle-aged, quietly spoken, and his manner was very matter-of-fact.

'The first biopsy was clear,' I said.

He nodded. 'Yes, I appreciate that. But what matters now is that we remove the lump and possibly some of the lymph nodes too, and then we thoroughly examine the tissue we've taken out.'

'What if that doesn't cure it?'

'There are a number of routes. We'll know more when we've operated.'

Every sentence he addressed to Liv, but she wasn't responding. Her eyes kept flicking from one face to another, to the poster urging self-examination, to the Seurat print of a boat on a lake.

'How soon?' I asked.

'Within a fortnight. A lumpectomy's a relatively quick, straightforward operation. You go in as a day case.'

'Will she need chemo?'

'We can't say at this stage. Again it depends on what we find.' Still Liv hadn't uttered a word.

The consultant turned and indicated the nurse behind him who stepped forward, smiling.

'If you have any questions,' she said, 'or there's anything you'd like to talk through you can come next door, have a chat.'

I looked at Liv, but she only shook her head.

'Or you can call me, and talk over the phone. It's a lot to take in, isn't it?'

That last note of kindness seemed to undo Liv. She stared at the wad of pamphlets the nurse was holding out to her. 'It's silly, but I can't think. I just want to go home.'

'Come on, then,' I said.

I took the papers and opened the door for her. As I did so, I remembered Geraint, busy in the dining room with his urgent cataloguing of wetland leaflets, and sent a vibe of hate his way.

Then we walked out into the waiting room, and a different future.

⋆   ⋆   ⋆

I dropped Liv off then went straight on to the nursery because I'd told Ray that unless the appointment was massively delayed, I'd be fine for the afternoon. He was filling a bucket under the main tap and saw me walk across the yard, but when I didn't come over he left me alone. I knew he wouldn't say anything to the others, either. He's a good boss, is Ray.

Everyone else seemed to be planting up liners in Greenhouse Four. I went into the office to collect my overalls and check the jobs list. 'Slow-release fertiliser', someone had written on a Post-it and stuck it at the top of the planner. So I pulled on my gloves, took a barrow down to the store room, collected compost, spade, measuring scoop and a bucket of Osmocote, and wheeled the lot round to the concrete mixer. I set the mixer going and hauled the compost bag onto the ground by its squashy middle. Once it was laid out flat I used my Stanley knife to slit the polythene open.

Crumbly peat spilled over the edges of the cut. I tugged the knife further down the length of the bag, so that the opening was wide enough for my spade. A scent of leaf mould and growing filtered up through the cold air. I grasped the spade handle and began to shovel compost into the mixer. It's a rhythm you get into quickly: bend, push, lever, lift, turn, tilt.

And as I dug away, it seemed to me I ran through every thought it was possible to have about breast cancer. How could they have got it wrong? How *could* they have got it wrong? Who'd cocked up: was it the nurse, the labs, the admin? Or was it just that the cells had changed on their own? I wanted to talk about this on the way home, but Liv said it didn't make any difference. I thought it did, a lot. I wanted someone to be angry with. I imagined Liv with no hair, Liv on a drip, on a hospital mattress, dead.

I remembered a play on the radio I'd heard where a burial was taking place and a squirrel dropped an acorn on the coffin, and I thought how pleased Liv's ghost would be if that happened to her, even if the rest of us were bawling our eyes out by the graveside. I wondered what we'd say to each other if she found she was dying; what might get said at the funeral service; whether she'd stipulate an eco-burial or not bother. How, if Liv was dead, I could finally say what I liked to Geraint, throw him out of the house, burn his mouldy old possessions. Then I'd be left wandering between silent rooms on my own.

That image quickly became unbearable, so instead I imagined Liv being given the definitive all-clear and holding some type of celebration — a party, a hot air balloon ride. Liv with a scar, with no breast at all, with burns and tattoos from radiotherapy, rolling up her T-shirt and looking at herself in the bedroom mirror. I thought of support groups and special padded bras and of a magazine ad I'd seen for Macmillan Cancer Support showing a green coffee mug. There'd been a girl at school whose mum had died of breast cancer when we were only in Year 7. I still recalled our tongue-tied horror, how we avoided her at break. What bitches we were. And I thought of a sponsored run Nicky's solicitor colleague had taken part in last year, and how I'd only put down two quid. Two pounds! At the time I'd been short of cash and reasoned it was good of me to give a stranger anything. Perhaps Liv was somehow paying for my heartlessness.

The mixer now being full with compost, I turned my attention to the tub of Osmocote. The lid was on tight and the sharp plastic ridge round the edge hurt my fingers as I struggled to prise it off. My mouth was parched too — I'd wanted a drink in the hospital an hour ago but it had seemed more important to get Liv home. On and on the mixer churned and rumbled as I fed in scoops of fertiliser, counting under my breath, and the steady rhythm of the mixing drum and my thirst and my aching arms and the smell of the wet earth were somehow a weird comfort against all the chaos in my brain. I would carry on making compost till I dropped.

I wasn't even aware of Christian till he was upon me.

'Didn't you hear us shouting?' Then he nodded at the mixer, and laughed. 'Stupid question.'

I reached for the off switch.

He was wearing a plain light-blue shirt and jeans, simple but somehow just right. I thought I could smell his aftershave or hair lotion, something woody, spicy.

'Is Nicky with you?'

'She's just stopped off in the shop to get a drink. You look as though you're burning up, Frey.'

I knew what state I was in, red and sweaty and smeared with dirt.

'I'm OK. It beats going to the gym.'

'Let me feel those biceps.' He put his fingers against the top of my arm. 'Ooh, yes, very impressive. Seriously solid.'

'Seriously wrecked. I take it you've got the day off again?'

'They're editing today, so I'm not involved. Thought I'd swoop across to Chester to see whether I could persuade Nicky to come and have lunch, and she managed to wriggle out of a whole afternoon's work. Can you believe it? I think the boss fancies her, actually.'

'And you're here because — '

'She wants inspiration for her floral displays.'

I pulled my gloves off and wiped my forehead. 'How are the wedding plans?'

'Insane. I've got weddings coming out of my ears. The whole project's tuning into a juggernaut, with me running about a mile behind. Not that you'd better repeat that comment to Nicky. She'd spit-roast me, or her mother would. Now they're all locked into some dispute over bridesmaids. Little ones, not you. You're safe.'

'There's a relief. What's the issue?'

Christian snorted. 'Mum has this distant cousin with a likely infant, but Nicky maintains she doesn't know her from Adam and anyway she's already too far along with the preparations to add another dress into the mix. She's of the opinion an extra child would make the church look untidy. So the kiddy's out in the cold. It's causing a spot of tension.'

'Oh dear. Never mind, isn't it traditional to have loads of rows during the lead-up?'

'It's only the women who are getting in a state. You girls. Flutter flutter.'

'*I'm* not like that.' I gave him a light punch on the shoulder to make the point.

He caught my wrist. 'No, you're not. That's why we love you.'

The moment froze in sunshine and birdsong.

'Hiya!' It was Nicky, water bottle in hand,

picking her way across the rough ground. Customers aren't technically allowed in this part in case they come a cropper and decide to sue.

'All right?' I said, pulling my hand free from her fiancé's grasp.

She nodded, all aglow. 'I wanted to come and look at your flowers, Frey. The florist keeps emailing these ideas at me and I don't know what she means. Pelargoniums, hedera, what the hell are they? I want to see for myself. Because it's not just the bouquets, it's the buttonholes, hair corsages, the decorations for the lychgate and church entrance and lectern and pew ends and altar, and then all the dining tables at the reception and the guest-book table and the flowers to say thank you afterwards. It's a lot, you know?'

Christian was chuckling. 'Where is the woman I proposed to? She's been swapped for this bridezilla.'

'Get lost. Flowers are about the only thing your mum's left me to organise.'

He put his arm across her shoulders.

'Come on, then. Let's get the job done. If I have to adjudicate over some plant or other, let's not hang about. Are you coming to give us your professional advice, Frey?'

I put on a sorrowful face. 'Sorry, some of us have work to do. Can't leave this or the boss'll go nuts. I'm a slave to the machine.' And I switched the mixer back on to drown out any argument.

They wandered away together, walking close, brushing against each other for the pleasure of it. As they drew level with the spring bedding,

Nicky pulled on Christian's sleeve and he stopped walking. I saw them consult together, then he lowered his face to hers and drew her into a fierce kiss. His arms were wrapped round her back, and their bodies pressed together, and her head tipped back in a kind of surrender. How wonderful to lose yourself in a kiss like that. My own muscles reacted in sympathetic longing, and then a spike of pure jealousy passed over me, making me flush. How long was it since anyone kissed me that way? How long since anyone kissed me, full stop? Not since the summer, and Oggy's birthday bash in the Red Lion, when I was too drunk to argue.

I sensed someone come up behind me, and when I turned it was Ray.

'I could throw a bucket of cold water over them, if you want,' he said.

'If you would. Actually, chuck one over me while you're at it.'

'Don't let the happy bastards get you down, Freya, hey? They all come to grief eventually.'

He strode away and I looked back at Christian and Nicky. They were still kissing.

* * *

There's nowhere like your own bedroom when you're under fire. Mine's a pretty unremarkable space, and yet it's amazing how much I missed it when I went to uni. The rooms in my hall of residence had cold lino on the floor for ease of cleaning, and only a little rug instead of carpet. There weren't enough surfaces for my clutter.

Also I was unlucky with my view, which was the canteen yard and bins. What really freaked me out, though, was the noises at night, the footsteps and coughing and drunken shrieks and snatches of music. Sometimes there'd be sobbing. Sometimes it was me.

But when you've lived in a place all your life it fits you like a skin. It's your history. Literally, because the suite itself used to be Liv's mum's, and is Fifties G-Plan, and ugly chic. Some of my clothes hangers came from her house, and the glass lampshade's hers as well. The shawl draped over the back of the chair was one of the first presents I ever had from Melody; the ammonite I use as a door stop was found by Colin at Seatown near Lyme Regis. There are posters in this room I've had up since primary school — a chart of garden birds' eggs, a zombified Britney Spears — and dozens of photographs of Nicky and me going back ages. On the dressing table, behind the tray of make-up, is my model toadstool collection, some of which I made myself during art lessons at school. My hair products I've arranged along the window sill, which means every time I open the curtains there's a good chance I'll knock a tub or tin or tube onto the floor, but that's just the way it is, the sill's their home. My boots and trainers live in a neat row with their toes tucked under the wardrobe. Above my headboard hangs a cross-stitch fox Nicky sewed for me, and a print of a harvest mouse I won in a nature-writing competition when I was eleven, and, from the same era, a pair of pipe-cleaner bee antennae Liv made me wear on a Go Wild for Nature fun day.

On my bedside table sits my bottle of water, my iPod, a Ryvita tin containing plasters and tea tree oil and Germolene. There's also a wedding picture of Liv and Colin in an oval stand-alone frame. The hiking socks I wear round the house instead of slippers lie across the pillow, together with my tartan pyjamas.

I love this room. I love the massive house spider who lives in the gap where the skirting boards come together, and the bedding box which is full of old toys I can't bring myself to throw out, and the dusty lever arch files of A level and uni notes, and the lopsided sisal bin, and the bleached patch on the curtains from where teenage Nicky got careless with the Sun-In. There's a dent above the door lintel where I hurled a pot of Supa-Wax after failing to pick a fight with Liv. These events and their records may be small, but they're mine.

I've sat on this leaf-print duvet and struggled over homework, surfed the net, messaged schoolfriends, gossiped, dreamed, devoured unhelpful women's magazines. It was on this bed I first heard Christian's name: a breathless call on my mobile one evening, Nicky shouting over the noise from some student bar. I had my first kiss lying here and a whole lot more besides, though none of it amounting to very much in the end. Simon Ogden, Oggy, here today and gone tomorrow, a man who liked to think he got his lovin' on the run but in reality was just a twit. I've lain here and cried over Oggy more than once.

And it was in this room I first tracked down Melody's Friends Reunited page with its excited profile notes and crazy photo. 'Those men who've left messages, are they all ex-boyfriends?' I'd asked her, that initial visit.

She'd grinned, her eyes little slits of mischief. 'Some of them wanted to be. 'S just a game, just fun. It doesn't do to let anyone get too close. And I never *ever* fall in love. Take note, Freya. Love's like rust, it eats your insides away even if you can't see the damage on the surface.'

Liv said Melody reminded her of Miss Havisham, out to break as many hearts as possible while keeping well out of range herself. But Miss Havisham never walked abroad in a sequin pencil skirt, flashing her eyes and goosing random men on her way to the bar. 'Never let yourself get attached to *anyone*,' Melody advised me. 'My philosophy is, if there's any heartbreak going around, it ain't gonna land on me.'

She spoke casually about the guitar teacher who'd stood and wept on her front lawn, where all the neighbourhood could see him; of the Greek guy she met on holiday who really was going to sell up and leave his community to be with her; of Letter-man who wrote every week for five months after she'd given him the boot. 'Their choice,' she said. 'No one can hurt you unless you let them.' And to be fair, she's always clear from the start, she never deceives. The smart ones just enjoy themselves and jump off the roller coaster when their time's up.

'Joe's different, though,' Michael had told me over the phone. 'She's started using words like 'stability' and 'long-term'.'

'Bizarre. What's he really like?'

'You're meeting him tonight.'

'Do *you* like him?

'He is what he is.'

'What's that, then?'

'You'll see, won't you?' he said, frustratingly.

★ ★ ★

Melody had chosen a town-centre pub for our meeting. I spotted her straight away, partly because she was wearing an electric-blue smock, and partly because her Union Jack blazer was hanging on the chair opposite her. To her left sat Michael, and to her right, the famous Joe.

'Here comes my gorgeous daughter,' said Melody as I drew near the table.

My first impression was that Joe was much younger than she was, at least ten years, at a guess. He was handsome in an obvious kind of way, with close-clipped hair, tanned skin and a strong jaw line, something cocky about the tilt of his head. When he moved, his scalp glistened with gel or wax. His white shirt was dazzling.

'Wow, you're smart,' I heard myself say.

Joe glanced at me, then away.

'He wears a suit to work,' said Melody.

'Great, wow, that's great. Well done you. Can I get anyone a drink?'

'Nah,' said Joe.

'Orange juice for me, hun,' said Melody coyly.

While I waited at the bar I watched them together. She was making some fuss about her

93

stomach, patting it and standing sideways, even though there was no bump at all. Michael was nodding. Joe sat back, one hand round his glass.

'And I've gone right off tea and coffee,' she said when I got back. 'They taste like cack. Strange, 'cause I used to drink bloody pints of Typhoo. Tuna, I can't stand now. But I could murder some runny cheese. It's such a pain: the things I can have, I don't fancy, but I'm craving the stuff I'm not allowed.'

'Isn't that always the way,' said Michael.

'Have you had morning sickness?' I asked her.

'No. It's brilliant, I feel brilliant. Just a bit woozy in the mornings, but that soon passes. I am dog-tired, though. I'm knackered by the evening, falling asleep by nine. I'm no company, am I, Joe?'

'No,' he said.

'I pop my feet up on the sofa and then wham! I'm out like a light.' She giggled.

'Whereabouts do you work, Joe?' I asked, because I was keen to hear him say something.

'Comet,' he said.

'What's that like?'

'OK.'

'Do you get a staff discount?'

'A small one.'

'I bet you meet some funny customers. We do at the nursery. Last week we had a woman try to smuggle out crocus corms down the side of her boots. We nabbed her as she was hobbling across the car park.'

'What kind of saddo steals bulbs?' said Melody. 'Can you imagine, Joe? TVs, yes,

94

laptops, whatever, but not crocus bulbs. Hardly ambitious, is it?'

Joe shrugged. I could tell he was completely aware of his looks. Perhaps there was no need to struggle for sparkling conversation when your cheekbones were that finely chiselled.

'Hey, what about the old bloke you were telling me about, the one who wanders into the store and talks back to the televisions?'

'He's harmless.'

'You said he's funny, the stuff he comes out with.'

'I suppose.'

We waited for elaboration, but none came. *Oh, for goodness' sake, make an effort, man,* I thought. I felt weary and anxious and not remotely in the mood for small talk; I kept recalling Liv's stiff face, and that bloody painting of yachts in the consultant's room.

'So what's been the reaction to the new iPod, Joe?' asked Michael. 'Has there been much demand?'

'You could say.'

There followed another longish pause. I gave up and slid my phone out of my pocket so I could text Nicky.

'Frey was interested in getting satnav for her car,' Michael persisted.

'Right.'

'It was only an idea,' I said, squinting at my mobile. 'I'm not that fussed.'

Joe looked away towards the fruit machine. Michael frowned at me, vibing me to ask more, but I carried on with my text.

In pub hell. Wish u wr here. Hows chris?

'It's crazy, the baby's only the size of a grape but I've had to buy a bigger bra already,' said Melody, looking down at her own chest. 'The woman in the shop said I could go up as much as four sizes. Four sizes! I'll be like, enormous. I'll need scaffolding.'

I sent the text and shut my phone. 'Oh, are you telling everyone you're pregnant now? Because I thought you wanted to keep it quiet till you had the scan.'

'I know, that was the intention. But pregnancy's too good to keep to yourself. I tend to blurt it out. And everyone's so nice when they hear. You're like a hero or something.'

Joe's expression was vacant, he could almost have been wearing earphones. I had to look twice to check he wasn't.

'But it's so cool,' she went on. 'I lie there wondering when I'll get the first kick, and how I want the birth to be, whether it's going to be a boy or girl. What I'm going to call it. If it's a girl, I'm going for 'Sasha'. If it's a boy, 'Donny' or 'Alain'. That's '*Alain*', like Alain Prost. This time my baby gets to keep its name.'

A dig at Liv.

'And I've seen this fantastic night light in Argos, the shape of a hot-air balloon. I'm definitely having that. Do you think they'll tell me at the hospital whether I'm having a boy or a girl? They don't in some counties. Does anyone know? I have the strongest feeling it's a boy. What do you think, Freya?'

'No idea.' It struck me as a silly question.

'Your little brother. Or sister. It'll be good, won't it?'

'Fantastic.'

I decided to give it one last shot with Joe.

Turning to face him, I said, 'What does your family think about the news, your mum and dad? Are they excited?'

He looked down and straightened his watch strap. 'I haven't said anything.'

'Oh.'

'She told me not to.'

Melody flapped her hands at him. 'That was before. I've changed my mind, everyone can know, everyone.' She stood up and pushed back her chair. 'Hey, guess what?' she said loudly.

No one paid any attention.

'Give us a break, Mel,' said Michael.

'Am I an embarrassment?'

'Yes.'

She grinned and sat down again.

'You need some energy to keep up with her,' I said to Joe. He shifted in his seat and his eyes met mine, and there was just nothing there. Nothing. Not humour, not awkwardness, not a spark of interest, not even hostility. Certainly not excitement, or love.

'My round,' announced Michael, standing up.

As he passed my chair, he pulled at my collar. 'Come and help me carry the drinks back, lazybones.'

The second we were out of earshot I said, 'God, it's like pulling teeth. Is it us?

'Don't think so.'

'What the hell's going on, then?'

97

'You tell me.'

'Joe's just not *there*, is he?'

'No shit, Sherlock.'

We leaned against the bar, elbow to elbow. 'Have they had a row?'

Michael shook his head. 'I'm guessing not. Because if they had, she'd be sulking, massively. There'd be barbed comments flying all over the place. She doesn't hold back if she's got a grievance, our Mel.'

That was true enough.

'OK,' I said, 'what about this: they've had a row but she thinks they've made up and he thinks there's still unfinished business.'

'He's not exactly angry, though, is he?'

'Is it like 'suppressed anger'? Shutting down, passive-aggressive, sort of thing. Or is he always that way? You've met him before.'

We both sneaked a look across the bar to Joe and Melody's table. She was grinning and stretching over to stroke his lapel, while he remained upright, disconnected. Snapshot of a relationship.

'First time I met him he was quiet but normal, you could have a reasonable conversation with him. He was never a babbler but there were none of these dead-end silences like tonight. Melody was chatty as ever, of course. Then the next time, he was that bit quieter and she was that bit louder.'

'Why didn't you warn me?'

'It's never been so bad as it is tonight. This is a man who's winding down.'

'He's going to finish with her?'

98

'Oh, the writing's on the wall.' Michael ran his hand around his stubbly chin. 'Unless I'm being over-pessimistic.'

'But if Joe's that unhappy, he'd say, wouldn't he? He'd already have made a move to get out. He wouldn't sit there and suffer.'

'It's not always that easy, Frey.' I guessed he was thinking of his ex-wife. 'There's this baby, for one thing.'

'Yes. It's a bit of a mess.'

I couldn't stand the thought of Melody in distress on top of everything else.

'Let's hope you're wrong, then. Let's put it down to a crap day at work. Stroppy customers, a smart-arse boss.'

'Maybe. Although even if it is, it's not like he's got the monopoly on crap days. I've had a nightmare.'

'Lost a wheel nut down the grid again?'

'Ex-wife bother. Kim left a dead rose on my doorstep this morning, then, ten minutes after I got home, some guy turned up with a Chinese takeaway I hadn't ordered — hoi sin duck, so I know it's her. Stupid, piddly stuff but it wears you down. You can do without it.'

'I expect you can.'

I had a sudden rushing need to tell him what was happening in my world, trump all these petty troubles and complaints. Then he'd understand what a crap day really was.

Oh, sweet Jesus. Liv's got cancer? Oh, Frey. You must be really freaked. But listen, treatment rates are better than ever, and they've caught it early, haven't they? Don't panic till you know all the facts. *Thousands and thousands of people recover from cancer every year. Statistically there's every chance she'll be among them. Hold onto the science for now. Keep calm, and find out what you can.* That was the kind of thing Michael would say. That was the kind of thing I'd like to hear.

I knew I couldn't tell him, though. We weren't talking some silly half-secret like Melody's, where breaking a trust didn't matter beyond a bit of good-natured tutting and eye-rolling. It was imperative I keep my mouth shut at least until we knew the prognosis.

'There's damn-all you and I can do about it anyway,' Michael was saying. My breath caught in my throat, and then I realised he was still talking about Joe.

'Michael, would it be rude if I went home after this drink? Are you staying much longer?'

'Yeah, I'll stick it out till closing. You get off if you're not feeling so good. You do look a bit washed out. Is something up?'

'Women's trouble,' I mouthed.

'Oh, that. Long as you're not properly ill.'

'Sod off.'

'I will.' He picked up his drink and Melody's. 'By the way, I think there's someone over there trying to attract your attention.'

As he walked away, I squinted across the bar towards the saloon doorway where a tall figure waved. Oggy. He held a pool cue in one hand and he seemed, from a distance, sober and buoyant. His hair was shorter than I'd last seen it, but still spiky at the front. He was wearing a

100

Weebles T-shirt I'd bought him two years ago, during a period we'd dated for eight months solid and he'd begun to feel like a real boyfriend. Rogue, mate, bastard, good laugh. That was Oggy.

He smiled at me, and my heart lifted just a fraction.

I thought, I could deliver Joe's pint, then come back and play a quick game of pool, catch up on news, enjoy an hour of easy, mindless banter. God knows, I could stand a dose of that.

So I waved back, and picked up both drinks. At the exact same instant a girl I'd never seen before came up behind him and put her arm round his neck possessively. He jumped in surprise, recovered himself, smirked at us both in turn. *Hey, what can a guy do?* said his expression.

Oh you prize tosser, I vibed back, like someone who couldn't care less. Still, the moment was his. He disentangled himself from the girl and turned away from me, but before he did he raised his cue at me in a Zulu-style salute. I'd have given him the finger if I'd had a hand free.

I took the drinks and trudged back to Melody. When a day's as tough as this, there's really nothing to do but get on with it.

Case Notes on: *Melody Jacqueline Brewster*

Meeting Location: *42, Love Lane, Nantwich*

Present: *Miss Melody Brewster, Mrs Abby Brewster, Mrs Diane Kozyra*

Date: *11.30 a.m., 09/12/86*

Melody has been experiencing faintness and dizziness in the last week, both at home and at school. A recent blood pressure check by her GP was normal, so I asked whether she might be anaemic, or had any other explanation for the faintness. She said the fits came on when she felt under pressure, e.g. for a biology test or when she thought about making a decision over her baby. She asked me whether I thought people would believe she was 'shabby' if she chose adoption. Mrs Brewster said that people would think a lot worse of her if she kept the baby and it 'wasn't fair to put the family in the firing line.'

Shortly afterwards Melody said she had a headache and asked to go upstairs for a lie-down. While she was out of the room, Mrs Brewster suggested the faintness might be a ploy for attention. I asked whether Melody had ever suffered fainting fits before and she said no. I advised Mrs Brewster to keep a record of when

Melody felt faint and to note any possible triggers so as to try and avoid them. I stressed the importance of fully supporting Melody in making what was a very difficult decision. Mrs Brewster said she would try, but it was hard because she herself had never felt like a very confident mother and also Melody was sometimes 'her own worst enemy'. Gave her the BAAF number again.

Next visit: 16/12/86   Signed: Diane Kozyra

A TUESDAY

February

When we were younger, Nicky and I loved to make plans for the future. What pets we'd have, what jobs we'd do, where we'd live and in what kind of houses, who we'd marry. How we'd lose our virginity, and who to. We'd make actual written lists. Sometimes I'll be tidying my room, or re-visiting a favourite book, and find one. If I'm in a mellow mood they make me smile. I was going to keep chickens, train Palomino horses, breed chinchillas, run a wildlife sanctuary. I would be a vet, an artist, a web designer, a TV cameraman, a TV naturalist, a crofter, a postie. I'd live in a cottage on the Stiperstones, in a gamekeeper's lodge, a windmill, a camper van. I was marrying the man who drove the veg-box van, Simon Willis in Year 6, Tom Settle in Year 8, Liv's student research assistant, the presenter of *Countryfile*, Oggy. And I would lose my virginity either in a moonlit attic or a mossy New Forest glade against an autumn sunset while a robin sang in the background. 'Watch out for midges!!!', I remember Nicky writing underneath this last entry.

I've often wondered whether she kept her own lists. To my shame, I can't remember much about them, barring the fact she was in love with the music teacher we had in Year 10, and she quite fancied city living or moving to a Greek island and keeping her own boat. The wanting to be a solicitor didn't figure till she was in the sixth form. I think she may have offered to help run my chinchilla farm at one point.

I was pondering all this now, our shared history of dreams, as I waited in the bridal-wear foyer for Nicky to come out in her seventh dress. The area was spacious and plush with springy carpet and you could tell someone had been round with an air freshener before opening. We were drowning in vanilla. Three walls were taken up with racks of snowy gowns and I sat in the middle of the room on a chesterfield sofa while an assistant eyed my Doc Martens and fingerless gloves.

They always put me on the defensive, bridal shops, as if I should be accounting for where I am in life and somehow apologising for it. I wanted to take the assistant by her matronly shoulders, give her a good shake and say, *I'm not jealous of this, you know. I wouldn't be seen dead in a big frock and a tiara. Don't look at me with that pitying gleam.*

On the wall by the changing-room entrance a shadow moved. The assistant looked up brightly and here came Nicky, stepping out in a bandeau-top ivory gown with tiered skirt. She stood in front of me, her face taut and unhappy.

'What do you think of this one?' she said.

I thought it was vile. It compressed her already small chest, whilst at the same time puffing out her hips to the extent that her bottom half looked almost fat. Essentially she was the same shape as a toilet brush.

'Nah. Not unless you want everyone to think you're up the duff,' I said.

At once I saw I'd made a mistake in being so blunt. She flushed and nodded, and turned quickly away.

'I love this detailing here,' said the assistant, darting forward and plucking at the ruffles round the waist. 'Such a curvy shape, makes your waist look tiny. And if you want more balance on top, you could always wear a stole. We do them in fur, chiffon, taffeta, silk. They're ever so popular. Shall I get you one to try?'

'No, you're fine,' said Nicky. 'I wasn't that struck. It's too tight under my arms.' She looked absolutely miserable.

Freya, you big-mouthed idiot, I was thinking. Liv had warned me about women and their wedding dresses, how you have to pretend every outfit's wonderful because it's not your decision to make, and also if the bride-to-be gets excessively emotional then the whole expedition's scuppered. Nicky glanced over her shoulder, frowning, and tried to press down the back of the bodice.

I said, 'If it's not comfortable, you won't be able to enjoy the day.'

'Do you want to try the next one?' said the assistant, who knew when she was beaten.

She led Nicky back into the changing rooms and I was left to my thoughts again. I found myself remembering, out of nowhere, the summer we broke into old Mrs Finch's garden to carve rude messages on her marrows as revenge for her complaining about the noise we'd made playing hosepipe wars. I'd assumed, as we'd crawled about behind the bean-plant frames, that Nicky was doing what I was, which was to be as filthy as my nine-year-old brain could manage. But I discovered later she was adjusting my graffiti, turning the words BUM into BUMP! and FUCK into PUCKER UP XXX. The cartoon boobs I cut into one huge yellow squash she adapted into googly eyes, and my attempt at a hand giving a two-fingered salute she changed into a rabbit's head, complete with whiskers. At first I'd been annoyed and called her wet, but she'd explained she couldn't bear for me to get into real trouble (and it would have been me, because Mrs Finch was my next-door neighbour). As it was, the vegetable decoration, when it was discovered, was more or less dismissed by Liv as an inventive joke, which it certainly wouldn't have been if my messages had been left unedited.

That's the thing about Nicky: she's always been able to face the future better than me. I've a kind of shutter that comes down and blanks out consequences. When we first started drinking as teens, it only took one time for her to get sick-drunk and then she knew her limits and stopped when she was getting near them. I, on the other hand, regularly ended an evening by puking into a hedge. At school she always completed her homework before the deadline, whereas I'd be scribbling to finish during morning registration. For the whole of Year 9 I

107

used her lab coat because mine had gone missing and I couldn't be bothered to sort out a new one; not once did she huff about this irritating state of affairs or tell me to bloody well get my own.

There are two other incidents I particularly remember, little moments where her loyalty saved my skin. The first happened when, only a month into high school, I was kept in after lessons for forgetting my trainers twice in a row. Detentions were a big disgrace, and supervised by the deputy head, Mr Prentiss, who was an utter git. I was petrified all day and spent lunchtime in tears. But when the three-thirty bell rang and I was led away, Nicky not only waited an hour for me, mooching about in a drizzly playground and missing the bus, but she kept my spirits up by sneaking round the side of the building and holding funny messages against the window. If Mr Prentiss had caught her, she'd have been in serious bother.

The second happened while we were on a school trip to Formby, and I had a period disaster. Nicky bundled me into the toilets and offered there and then to lend me her jeans. 'What the hell will you wear?' I'd hissed, near-hysterical. 'I can pretend my tunic's a mini dress,' she said. 'It'll be fine. See, it's not far off my knees.' Only the fact her jeans would never have fitted me prevented her from peeling them off and handing them over. In the end she gave me her cardi to tie round my waist and hide the bloodstain. Gestures like that seal a friendship forever.

And she's always just *been* there. Even when she was away at uni, she called me every week. She's listened to me slag off Oggy for hours, yet not got snippy when I've ended up back with him. She's never, to my knowledge, betrayed a secret I've confided, nor has she made me feel inadequate for jacking in my degree even though she completed hers with flying colours (no surprises there). The nearest we've ever come to falling out was in Year 9 when she wanted me to go on the French exchange and I wouldn't, and she called me a coward and we didn't speak for five days. It nearly killed us both.

So although I'd rather have been pretty much anywhere than marking the minutes away in this shop of frills, I was more than willing to do it for my pal. I just wished she'd hurry up and make a decision.

There was a rustling, a cry of alarm as something evidently caught and had to be freed, and then out shuffled Nicky once more.

'Woah,' I said, determined to be more upbeat. 'That's a bit special.'

Her body was encased in a sheath of close-fitting silk, widening out only at the last minute to pool round her ankles. The neckline was high but the dress was sleeveless, so there was still plenty of Nicky's pale flesh on show. It made her look as though she'd been chiselled out of icing sugar.

'Do you like it?' she said.

'It's incredibly glamorous. You remind me of that woman who opens Columbia films.'

She laughed nervously. 'I'm not happy with

this cowl-effect here. Plus I can't walk in it.'

'That is a bit of a downer.'

'But I love the skirt shape.'

'Could you not wear roller boots underneath? I could shove you up the aisle. And on the way back down from the altar there's a slope, it'd be a cinch.'

I thought this image would amuse her, but instead she only frowned and put her hand to her brow. 'Trying to work out what's best . . . I want this one, but with number five's bodice and the sleeves from that first. Or number three without the embroidery and that stupid bow.'

'We do have an alterations service,' said the assistant.

Nicky whipped her head up crossly. 'I'm not talking little nips and tucks, I'm talking about a whole re-design. I just want a dress that suits me. Why is that so hard?'

The assistant nodded and made soothing noises, and my eyes swept over the racks and racks of gowns.

'Why do they all have to be so . . . '

'What?' I asked.

'*Wrong*,' she said, and turned and hobbled back into the changing room.

Behind the thin wall of the changing room there followed a heated consultation. I could hear Nicky's indignant tones as she argued about the fit of the dresses and their general fussiness, and then the assistant's lower, slower voice attempting to instil some calm. At one point Nicky cried, 'I wish my mum was here.'

'Pretend I'm your mum,' said the assistant.

There was an ominous silence, then she came rushing out and snatched four or five dresses off the rails. It was hard to see the detail of any of them because the action was so quick, but I got the impression of a great fishtail train, iridescent sequins and ruched, puffed sleeves. *Oh good grief, you've so not understood*, I thought. The next moment she'd whisked back behind the wall and the arguing started up again. In desperation I opened *Wedding* magazine and attempted to read an article about how sugared almonds were making a comeback.

Eventually I heard Nicky snap, 'We're not all built like Page Three girls, you know!' There was a sound like someone wrestling cellophane. I put the magazine down and waited.

'Come on, Frey,' she said, sweeping round the corner, jeans and shirt back on and her hair all mussed up. 'I've had enough for today.' She grabbed her coat and jerked open the door. I felt a blast of lovely cold air.

Outside I said, 'Do you want to go for a drink?'

'I don't know. Do I?'

'Come on.'

I took her arm and led her across the shopping precinct to a tiny newsagent's. From there I bought a couple of cans of Coke and a bag of Haribo because we both needed a sugar boost, then I guided her down a side street to the amphitheatre ruins and found us a bench where we could get our breath.

I knew what a contrast we must make, her in her long, smart, tailored grey coat, and me in my khaki jacket clutching two tins in my mittens. Passers-by probably thought she was my care worker.

'I had this dream last night,' she said. 'This nightmare, that Christian was marrying Corinne and not me. It was hideous. I kept telling her it was against the law but she just waved me away.'

'I once dreamt I was teaching Michael Portillo to ice skate. Dreams mean nothing.'

Nicky reached up and tried to smooth her fringe. 'What do I look like?'

'Your eyes are a bit pink.'

'It's only because I've no make-up on. They won't let you try on any dresses if you've a face full of slap.'

'In case you smear the goods.'

'Uh huh. God, what's the matter with me, Frey? It should have been a really happy hour, trying on dresses.'

'It wasn't your fault. She was a madam, that assistant. Anyway, you can go back later and see some more, once you've got a shot of caffeine in you.'

'No, no, I can't. It's not that sort of a shop. You have to make an appointment.'

'Oh,' I said, feeling the weight of my own ignorance.

A bulky woman walked past us trailing a little girl. The girl was walking with her head tipped right back, staring at the sky, allowing herself to be blindly led.

Nicky said, 'Do you ever wish you were about six again, and all you had to do was play with your Barbies and colour in worksheets?'

'I never had Barbies.'

'You did. You had one, for definite.'

'I wonder who bought me that, then? It wouldn't have been Liv. She thinks Barbies sum up all that's evil about western consumerism.'

'Well your Barbie paid the price. Don't you remember? You stuffed her in a tree up near Yockings Gate. I bet she's still there.'

'Unless she's been drilled apart by death-watch beetles.'

'Undone by earwigs.'

'Death by invertebrate.' I swigged my Coke thoughtfully. 'I used to wish I could run my life backwards. But recently I've been wishing I was about forty, and my life was behind me, you know?'

'Forty? Eugh. You don't.'

'It looks a doddle, being forty. Everything's in place, you don't have to struggle any more. There's no uncertainty. Your major decisions have been taken. It's all a nice slow slide from there.' I could see myself, grown middle-aged, standing at a sink in a farmhouse kitchen somewhere, a shadowy male in the background, shadowy chickens in the shadowy garden. I'd be wearing an apron. There'd be a cake in the oven.

'When you turn forty you have to start wearing enormous pants. I can't say I fancy it much.'

'I don't think the enormous pants thing is law. Did you solve your bogus bridesmaid problem, by the way?'

She nodded. 'The kid'll be on holiday in

America, it turns out, so I don't have to have her. Honour satisfied. Only there's a new fuss, over caps. You don't want to wear a cap, do you?'

Bloody right I didn't. 'What kind of a cap? Like a jockey?'

'Some type of bonnet, I think Corinne had in mind. I don't know where she's got the idea from. She thinks bridesmaids should have something on their heads.'

'I'm not wearing a cap or a bonnet, Nicky. Much as I love you and Chris.'

'No. The trouble is, because she's paying, it's hard not to sound ungrateful when you reject her ideas.'

'Tell her *I've* said no.'

Nicky pulled her coat collar more tightly round her neck. 'It's funny, she liked me before I wanted to marry her son. Christian says it's the pressure of the wedding that's making her go all picky, but I'm not so sure. I'm beginning to see she's quite a complicated woman. For instance, did you know she still buys all Christian's shirts for him?'

'You're kidding.'

'She orders them from some up-market catalogue. Always has done, apparently. But this is the freaky bit: she chooses without ever asking him. Just orders what she likes. Because she says she knows his tastes.'

'And does she?'

'She seems to, yes.' A cloud of steam escaped Nicky's lips in a long sigh. 'Sometimes she makes me feel like an outsider. I think that's her intention, too.'

114

I held out the Haribo bag. 'What's the dad like?'

'Julian? He's charming; charming, with a sliver of ice down the middle. Although he's like that with everyone except the dogs, so it's nothing personal against me.'

'That doesn't sound too terrible. Have a gummy bear.'

We sat for a while, chewing sweets and watching tourists straggle across the grassy floor of the amphitheatre.

'Look at it this way,' I said. 'All mothers are protective of their little boys, however old they are. It's Oedipal. It's not that she's taken against you. She'll get over it, and then she'll just be really pleased she has you for a daughter-in-law and not some cheap strumpet. And the bottom line is, whatever stress you go through planning this bash, Christian's worth it. Isn't he?'

She turned her face to me. 'Oh, he is, Frey, he is.'

'Well, then.'

I imagined them as they'd be on their wedding day, arm in arm, enveloped in their own private bubble of bliss while the rest of us looked on.

'Right,' I said, 'this is what you do. Whenever darling Mother-in-Law's getting on your nerves, I want you to go to the loo, tear off a sheet of toilet paper, find a biro, and draw her face — '

'She's not that bad, really — '

'Then, when you next pay a call, you can use her to wipe your bum. In fact, I'll do you a roll for your wedding present. Let me have a photo and I'll get straight on the case. Anyone else's pic you want adding while we're here? Madam from the dress shop? That bloke in the office who claimed you'd lost his file? I'm happy to take orders. Revenge bog roll, it could really take off.'

Nicky was laughing in spite of herself. 'Oh, Frey. I knew there was a reason I appointed you chief bridesmaid. Pass us another bear, will you?'

And I did.

* * *

Liv was laid out on the sofa watching some mad therapy show when I got back.

'This is the weirdest programme,' she said. 'They've just had a woman on claiming owls are ruining her life.'

'Owls? For God's sake.'

'I know.'

'Does she run a mouse farm or something?'

'She has a phobia.'

'She'd best not go see any of the Harry Potter films, then. How are you feeling?'

'Sore. All right apart from that.' She touched the neckline of her dressing gown, about where the bandage was sited.

'Look, I'm going to hoover upstairs and change the bedding now. Is there anything I can get you before I start?

'Stay here for five minutes and be company. I'm so bored. I want to be up and busy.'

'Give it a couple of days, the consultant said. You've had a general anaesthetic, remember.'

'I could sit at a computer screen. There's a stack of GPS data to input, all the mammal sightings from last autumn.'

On the TV screen, a painfully thin old woman was screaming at a teenage girl in a sweat top. I muted the sound.

'Geraint can do that job,' I said. 'Where is he anyway?'

'He had a call about someone trying to start a bonfire on the Moss. I told him to get straight down there and see. We don't want to have to call the fire brigade again.'

Hadn't even left her a tray before he buggered off; hadn't bothered to move the phone so it was within her reach. I bet myself fifty quid there'd be a bowlful of washing-up waiting for me in the kitchen.

She must have read my thoughts. 'I'm fine. I'm not an invalid. I've had a small lump taken out of me, that's all. This time next week I intend to be back at work.'

'Don't be ridiculous.'

'Yes, Frey. I don't mean anything heavy, I'm not going to be donning waders and going out dredging or pulling reeds. But I can plonk myself in front of a desk and go through my correspondence. Honestly, love, if I sit at home and brood, I'll go mad. I need to be occupied. Do you understand?'

I nodded.

She swung her legs down and patted the sofa for me to join her. 'Tell me, how was the fitting? Did Nicky find the dress of her dreams?'

'Not exactly,' I said, settling in next to her. 'Actually, she had a bit of a strop. For Nicky, I mean.'

'What happened?'

'She flounced out of the shop. There was this completely annoying assistant who was like a wasp round a jam pot, wouldn't give Nicky space to breathe and kept shoving these horrible creations at her. I've never seen so much sparkly netting.'

'Did she panic?'

'I don't know. I think mainly she got bored.'

Liv's expression softened. 'I panicked when I had my second fitting. The dressmaker had to stand there while I gibbered into my underslip — silly, because there was never any doubt it was Colin I wanted. But there's a specific point during your wedding plans when you realise the enormity of what you're set to do. It comes like a jolt because you think you already know, but you don't. And so you have a wobble. That was probably Nicky's.'

I couldn't imagine Nicky having any kind of wobble over Christian. 'I think it was to do with her mother-in-law, really.'

'But Nicky likes Corinne, doesn't she?'

'She didn't like her much this morning.'

'Oh dear.'

Liv sank back so I could see her bandage clearly underneath the collar of her dressing gown. It made me wonder how much the wound hurt and how frightening it must be to be wheeled down to an operating theatre, a needle taped to the back of your hand. In my own safe life I'd never had so much as a tooth out. I wanted to reach over and cover the bandage up, out of sight.

The TV screen was now showing an advertisement for a savings account, golden coins spinning down from a hole in the sky.

'Corinne's been dictating terms,' I went on, 'and waving her purse about when Nicky objects. Basically going, 'I'm paying, so we're having things the way I want.''

'Ouch.'

'Wants to stick me and the other bridesmaids in some stupid hat. I said, no way. Tell her from me she can bog off. Just because she's loaded.'

'Haven't they got two houses?'

'Three. They've one in France and a flat in London. And the main one's a bloody mansion, well, it's about four times the size of ours. Nicky's shown me photos. And what about this: Corinne's got jewellery that's worth so much she has to keep it in Barclay's bank for safety.'

I knew that last would make Liv smile. Her own jewellery collection lives in a chocolate box covered in shells, and consists of African beads, polished wooden bangles, metal-cast leaf brooches, a tumble of semi-precious stones. The only pieces she owns of any conventional value are a gold and opal pendant and two gold rings bought for her by Colin. I know that if a fire broke out, it's those she'd probably run to save. But she never wears them. They belong to another life.

'It sounds to me as though there's a culture clash going on,' she said.

'They're snobs.'

'Oh, I don't know. It can be tricky when people from different social classes come together. There's bound to be tension on both sides.'

I pondered this. 'What social class are we?'

'Hippies like us fall outside the curve.'

'Nicky's lot?'

'Oh, they're firmly inside. Middle class, the middle of the middle class.'

Obviously. Derek Steuer with his BMW, his Rotary Club crested shirts; Joan with her cruise-ship wardrobe, her shelves of Caithness glass. 'Not posh enough for Corinne and Julian, though.'

'It's possible Corinne might be staging some kind of protest, subconsciously or otherwise.'

I was appalled to think of Nicky under siege from some stuckup bat.

'Well, if she thinks she's going to split them up — ' I began, and then the phone rang, making us jump.

'That'll be Geraint,' said Liv, sitting up.

'You stay there. I'll speak to him.'

But when I picked up the receiver it wasn't Geraint.

'Bastard,' went Melody's voice. 'Bastard bastard bastard.'

* * *

I called Michael before I set off because I didn't want to have to deal with the crisis on my own.

It had begun to lash down, so when I reached Love Lane I let myself in rather than wait around to soak on the doorstep. The house was dark and quiet.

'Melody? Melody!'

I blundered across the living room, knocking

into jardinières and footstools and coffee tables, till I glimpsed her through the window. She was standing in the yard without even a coat on. The rain fell in stair rods.

Melody's back door sticks so I had to really wrench it open. The noise made her look round.

'What in God's name are you doing?' I shouted. 'Get inside. You'll catch your death.'

'Like I give a fuck,' she yelled back.

'The baby does.'

That made her shift. As she slouched towards me, I noticed that the dark paving slabs around her were scattered with nuggets of coke, the bunker lid was open, and when I glanced at her hand, her fingers were black with grime. 'Why have you been chucking coal around the place?'

She halted in the doorway, dripping, and just looked at me.

'This is going to take ages to clear up,' I said, handing her a tea towel. 'Oh, God, you've no shoes on either.'

'Genius.'

I didn't have to come over, I felt like saying. She slid past me into the lounge, leaving a trail of small footprints across the kitchen floor.

'Do you want to go and put some dry clothes on?'

'No.'

'Give your hair a rub? I could get your slippers at least.'

That she didn't argue with, so I nipped upstairs and into her room. It's chintz on chintz in there, and small items can easily get lost amongst the busy colours. I remember helping

121

her hunt for an earring once, and we were nearly half an hour before we discovered it sitting in plain sight on the bedspread. Luckily the slippers were laid sole up across her red velvet dressing chair.

'I suppose you're going to say you saw it coming,' she said when I re-appeared.

'Tell me what happened, exactly.'

'What do you *think*?'

'I don't know. That's why I'm asking.'

She snatched the slippers from my grasp and whacked them down on the sofa next to her. Then she reached for her wet socks, tearing at them so fiercely that she left scratch marks on her ankles. Each sock she pulled away, squeezed into a ball and hurled into the empty grate.

'I'm so fucking angry. Apparently he does *care* for me, but he's not 'ready for anything long-term'. Can't cope with it, it does his head in. I told him, a bit fucking late in the day to be making statements like that. And he said he'd never signed up for the family package, he never would have, he's too young for all that. The baby was a unilateral decision.'

Well, it was, I thought.

'So that leaves me and this kid. I mean, fucking hell.' She put her hands over her eyes, and when she took them away there were coal smudges on both cheeks. It made her look like a refugee.

'It might be temporary,' I said. 'A wobble.'

'It isn't. He's fucked off, gone. Bastard. 'S like I've told you before, don't ever get properly involved with anyone. Don't do it, Frey. Always keep them at a distance, then you can never be hurt. Because if you don't, *this* happens. Why I ignored my own advice — '

'Put your slippers on,' I said.

Back in the kitchen I dried the floor with a paper towel — the last thing we needed was a skidding incident to add to the mix — and filled the kettle. The rain had eased right off till it was barely spitting, so I thought I might try clearing up the worst of the coke while Melody dried herself. There was a brush in the cupboard under the sink, but I needed a dust pan to scrape the nuggets into. Squatting, I peered inside and located the brush straight away on top of a jumble of silk roses, DVDs, a battery-operated nail polishing kit and seven or eight poster tubes. I moved the tubes aside, uncovering a bottle of Parazone and a single sprouted potato, but nothing shovel-shaped.

'What do you use to bring the coal in?' I asked her.

She wouldn't answer.

I stepped outside and had a quick shufti around the bunker; turned up a child's enamel pail with a painted duck motif and a Victorian crumb tray. I looked down at the brush dangling from my hand by its string and reasoned that I could at least sweep the coal into one corner, then she wouldn't be treading it into the house or turning her ankle on a stray nugget.

So I got to work. It was satisfying to flick at the little pieces and send them skidding across the stone flags. Some of them I kicked, viciously, when they lodged between the cracks. Skippity-skip thock, they went. Ker-pang. Smash. Never underestimate the therapeutic effect of violence against the powerless.

By the time I'd finished — she hadn't half done a thorough job — Michael had arrived. I glanced through the window and she had her arms round him, her head against his chest. It's moments like this I remember they're not blood-related, for all she calls him 'brother'.

I went in and closed the back door behind me. Then I stood at the sink and washed the dust off my arms and hands, brushed my trousers, gave my shoes a wipe with a tea towel. There was grittiness between my teeth when I clenched them.

'All right, Frey?' said Michael as I came into the lounge. Melody relaxed her grip on him and he stepped away. I did a double take when I saw his face; under his eyes were great weals, as though he'd been branded.

'Have you hurt yourself?' I said.

'How do you mean?'

'Round your eye sockets, you've got red marks.'

'That's from my goggles. I was in the middle of welding when you rang. Just dropped everything and jumped in the van.'

'Were they OK at the garage about you going?'

'We're slow this week, it's been really quiet.' He indicated Melody, now slumped on the sofa. 'What's the deal, then, Melly?'

'I've been dating a bastard.'

'So I heard. You want me to take out a contract on him?'

'It's not funny!'

'Shall I make us a cup of tea?' I asked.

'Fucking tea,' I heard Melody grumble.

'Oy oy,' said Michael warningly. 'Don't get shirty with us. We're the rescue squad.'

He pulled up a footstool and sat down opposite her.

'You *knew* what was coming,' she said. 'I *saw* you and Freya whispering together. You could have warned me!'

'No, Mel, I'm not having that. You must have known as well, or you'd never have picked up on what me and Frey thought.'

I took myself back into the kitchen and began assembling mugs and spoons. I heard Melody say, 'I really, really *wanted* him to be right.'

Michael's voice: 'I know you did.'

'He wasn't like anyone else. You could see that, couldn't you?'

'I could see you were keen.'

'Him, though. He was different.'

'Was he? Was he really?'

Nothing, and then Michael spoke again. 'I'll tell you what I think, shall I?'

I flicked the kettle on. Above the flex was a calendar on which Melody had been marking off the weeks of her pregnancy with little biro hearts. 'Joe', she'd written in every other night. Joe, Joe, Joe.

'The real difference,' Michael went on, 'the only real difference was that he got you pregnant. Just that. And you wanted the father on the scene, you wanted to make everything fit together. Obviously. You convinced yourself it was a serious thing you had going. But you were wrong. Your heart's not broken, it's your pride that's hurt. You're angry. Be angry. There's a lot of energy to be had off the back of anger, and you need all the energy you can get.'

The spoons rattled as I poured boiling water into the cups.

'It *was* more than the baby,' said Melody.

'I don't think so.'

'Before — '

'Ssh.'

' — when I was a kid and I got caught with Frey — '

He spoke again, but too softly for me to make out the words. I opened the fridge, took out the milk, unscrewed the lid, watched the tea blanch. I wondered whether I ought to take the drinks through, or simply stay in this kitchen forever.

Michael solved the problem for me by appearing in the doorway. The imprints from his goggles were still there, giving him a comic surprised look. 'Is there any beer in that fridge?'

'There's a bottle of wine.'

'Let's have it out, then. Yeah, bring the tea as well. Biscuits, anything. We'll get some sugar and alcohol down her.'

'We can't have her drunk. The baby.'

'Shit, yeah. Well, PG Tips'll have to do. Load it up.'

We used a chopping board in lieu of a tray and he carried it through.

Melody had at last peeled off her wet sweater and was sitting in her shirt, leggings and slippers. She sat with her hand across her belly protectively, her head drooping, the picture of an abandoned maiden. 'What am I going to do?' she said.

'At any rate, he's liable,' said Michael, doling out the food and drink. 'However much of a slippery beggar he is, he has to support you financially. We can take him to court if he won't cough up. You know where he lives.'

'I told him that. I told him he'd have to pay towards it.'

'What was his response?'

She lowered her head.

I drew a deep breath and said, 'What actually happened, Melody?'

'I was being practical, that was all! I've never talked about the future with a boyfriend before. I've not been bothered, there's never been any need. But this time — how can you not, with a baby on the way? I showed him the scan photo and then I said I was thinking of selling this place and moving to Wrexham. To his. You can't be ferrying a baby back and forth between two houses, can you? It makes no sense. I wanted everything tidy. Not like before.'

A glance in my direction.

'You were going to move in with him?' I asked cautiously.

'I was going to . . .'

'What?'

'All I said was, if we got married, yeah, it would be a lot simpler with benefits and stuff. I only meant legally, to tie off any loose ends. It was half a joke anyway.'

'Married! Oh my God. But you always — '

'That would have made sense,' Michael broke in over my protests. 'Once you have kids on the scene, a marriage certificate straightens out everyone's legal position. It's daft not to at least look into it. Plus, coping with a baby's a hell of a lot easier if there's two of you on hand. I imagine. So it was a sensible suggestion. Yes, it was, Mel. Come on, now. You've no call to think you did the wrong thing. If he felt he couldn't cope, that's not your fault.'

'If I hadn't rushed him, though,' she said. 'I don't know why I said it.'

'The clock began ticking the minute you got pregnant.'

'*What* am I going to do?'

Michael shifted closer and took her hand. He nodded at me to take the other and we posed for a moment in a kind of defensive circle. 'You'll be fine. You've got us, you've got a roof over your head. Your mum'll see you don't starve. Hasn't she sent you some money already?'

Melody nodded.

'OK, then. Why don't you ask her over for a visit to help out? Abby would come, I know she would. And you'll manage. Trust me. It's a baby you're having, not a nuclear bomb.'

'It's better to be on your own than with someone unreliable,' I added. God knows, I'd been told that enough times myself.

She'd drawn her knees up under her chin and was rocking herself gently among her bird cushions. Her eyes were fixed beyond us, into the distance somewhere. I thought, *It's unbelievable she's going to produce a child before the end of the summer. Whatever kind of set-up is the poor kid going to find when it emerges?*

'My head needs to catch up,' she said.

'Yeah,' said Michael. ''Course. We've all the time in the world.'

Out in the yard it began to rain again.

★   ★   ★

Melody went to bed at nine-thirty, saying she was tired out.

'I'll stay for an hour or so,' I told Michael when I came back downstairs, 'check she's settled. Have you got to rush off?'

'I'm OK,' he said.

'You sort out another brew, then, and I'll stick a DVD on.'

'Here we go. Two hours' extreme screen violence,' he said, but took himself off to the kitchen anyway.

The film I chose was *Grave Break* because it was a while since I'd seen it and I was in a nostalgic mood. The case was still shrink-wrapped; I admit I'd probably been thinking more of myself when I gave it to Melody as a birthday present. I drew off the cellophane and stuck the disc straight in because I knew there were at least four minutes of trailers and piracy warnings to wade through.

'Ah, zombies,' said Michael. He put the cups down and came to sit next to me.

'It's a zombie kind of evening, don't you think?'

'Not really. Since you're asking.'

The film began with a grainy aerial shot of a lorry driving across a moorland landscape during a storm. The camera moved in every now and again with snapshots of windscreen wipers labouring against the downpour, wheels slooshing over waterlogged tarmac, the MOD logo on the cab door, the anxious face of the driver. Cut to wind turbines on the horizon, then swoop ahead to a waterfall crashing down some jagged slate. Sheep's skull, crows' bodies left to hang on barbed wire. Back to truck interior, driver's finger against map. Then the camera pulling right out to show us a stone bridge coming up and a river in spate. A dead cow lying bloated in the middle of the road. The lorry swerving, a sequence shot first from above and then from tarmac-level, played out so the crash took twice as long as it would have done in real life. We saw the wheel arch smash into the bridge, the driver's face smack against the side window, then the vehicle careering to the opposite side of the road, bursting through the low wall and pitching forwards. The instant where the lorry entered the river was done in slow motion against quavering violin music. Then, at the last second, everything speeded up again and we heard the roar of the water, saw the tailgate buckling and the cargo of deadly-looking canisters cracking together, rolling out and sinking into the murky depths.

After that the titles started. More aerial views in one continuous edit of the river in daylight, following the course downstream as it wound between villages and towns to settle at the finish in a huge reservoir.

I said, 'Do you think we're always going to come running every time Melody has a disaster?'

Michael shrugged. 'That's what families are for.'

'Don't you mind?'

'Nope. Mel was very good to me when I was growing up. She was just about the only person who ever took an interest. I owe her.'

He looked at me searchingly, and the silence said, *Don't you?*

Not like you, I thought. Not the way I owe Liv. But I remembered Nicky admiring my new Melody-inspired clothes and hairstyle, telling me, *Your birth mum's really changed you, you know. She's kind of relaxed you. Finished you off.*

On the TV screen, black clouds rolled.

'Is it too late to ask for something more upbeat than people having their limbs gnawed to shreds?' said Michael.

'Horror films *are* upbeat.'

'Right.'

'No, they are.'

'How do you work that one out?'

DANGER DEEP WATER read the sign on the reservoir gate. Two teenage boys leaned their bikes up against it, laughing at a shared joke. They had swimming gear under their arms.

'Do you remember,' I said, 'when we visited Hack Green and saw a simulation of the effect of a four-hundred-kiloton thermonuclear weapon dropped on Birmingham? Afterwards we came out into the sunshine and you were like, 'My God, the world's so beautiful.' You were sniffing handfuls of grass and stopping to ogle clouds.'

'It had been a disturbing couple of hours. Touring a decommissioned nuclear bunker isn't everyone's idea of a grand day out, Frey.'

'The point is, by the end of this zombie film, we'll be so glad our drinking water isn't actually turning everyone into the living dead, and society isn't collapsing into hideous violent chaos, our own problems'll have dwindled to nothing. We'll go home after this just relieved and happy that the world's still normal.'

'Normal? My ex-wife squirts perfume through my letterbox and superglues my locks. I wouldn't describe my world as normal.'

'She's not ripping your head off and drinking your blood, though, is she?'

'Give it time.'

Inside the water purification plant, a broken filter hung uselessly from a pipe end.

'Anyway,' he continued, 'what have *you* got to worry about? Whether your fertiliser's mixed right, or your seedlings are going to be eaten by pigeons? What precise shade to dye your hair next?'

As he spoke, an image of Liv broke through as I'd found her the night before, sitting at the computer screen in the near-dark, ostensibly reading a report on buzzard poisoning but with a shrunk-down tab at the bottom of the screen labelled 'Survival rates breast'. I know we were both thinking, *Imagine if the lumpectomy turned out not to be enough, if they hadn't got it all, if she was sitting there waiting for her next appointment with the cancer ticking away inside.*

If I allowed myself to contemplate the worst, the terror was dizzying.

I blinked it away. 'Yeah,' I said to Michael. 'Pigeons and hair dye, you're right, that is the sum total of my daily grief.'

On screen someone turned a kitchen tap and a glass filled slowly.

From Liv's diary, 9/05

Trying to get F to focus on uni, reading lists, packing etc. She says she will sort things but then doesn't. Mind elsewhere. Nicky came round, she's completely organised & ready to go, as ever.

Obvious now M using F to create a mini-me. F wandering round in ludicrous braided jacket, not her style at all, plus dreadful purple nails. Then this morning F asked why I never insisted she wear a 'decent night cream'. I said I'd always made sure she wore midge repellent when we were by the water. She said it wasn't the same & anyway I should be using night cream myself. Told her we were both beautiful enough. She stropped about, wanting to pick argument. Later, out of the blue, said 'Why can we never just buy stuff? Why does it always have to be ethical? Why not, for once, go mad & shop the way every other normal person shops?' Luckily doorbell rang (Alan R with bag of Longworth traps — must email Gwyn & let him know need ones with shrew holes. Also order more blow-fly pupae).

F wants an iDog for birthday, tacky plastic dog that sits on desk & moves to music. Claims she is 'making up for not having had cool toys in the past'. Asked her if she remembered caterpillar races we used to have, & the wood-mouse obstacle course, but she was texting & didn't reply. Seems right now as though past doesn't count.

G says she's just 'flexing her wings' & I've not to take it personally. If she's happy, I should let her go. Well of course I know that, but is M making her happy??

A FRIDAY

March

I had to bully Geraint into coming to the hospital with us. On the morning of Liv's appointment he stood there in the kitchen in his stripy blanket-jumper, mumbling about having hired a digger for the day so they could clear some ditches. 'We need to get on. The machine's to go back to the plant hire yard tomorrow.'

I said, 'Call Alan H. He knows how to drive a digger, he won't mind taking over.'

'But then he'll be out of the office. We can't leave the office unmanned.'

I'll bloody un-man you in a minute, I thought, twirling Liv's egg whisk between my hands. 'No, because you've got that Field Studies Council trainee with you this week. He can answer the phones and take messages.'

Geraint's mobile lay on the worktop between us. Our eyes locked onto it at the same time, but he was too slow. I snatched it up, found the number I needed, pressed call and spoke to Alan H. In less than two minutes, while Geraint shuffled and hemmed in the corner, I had it sorted.

'There's really no need,' Liv had insisted the evening before when I'd talked about getting him to come along.

See, his expression had said. *She doesn't want me.*

'Of course he wants to be there for you, Liv. Why wouldn't he?' Geraint had looked about ready to murder me. 'And afterwards we can pop into that big garden centre on the roundabout and check they're stocking sustainable peat.'

That had cheered her up.

Now Geraint gave it one last shot. 'I was going to start putting together the programme of summer schools events this morning.'

'You can do it this afternoon instead,' I told him briskly.

I more or less heaved him down the hall and out the front door. Liv didn't seem to notice, but then she had a lot on her mind.

This appointment was make or break. If the doctors thought they'd got all the cancer out we were OK, maybe it was over, finished. If not, then God knows what lay in store. I'd lain on my own bed the night before, squeezing my own breasts for lumps, wondering what on earth it was like to have them cut open, or off. Unimaginable. I remembered when I was too young to have breasts, the secret worry that they might never grow. How in Year 6 I'd become obsessed, continually sneaking anxious glances at other girls' chests and comparing them to my own flat front. I remembered buying my first bra and how excited I'd been, even though it was hideously embarrassing to go behind the shop curtain and be measured by an old woman who smelt of nicotine and mints. I thought about Nicky trying out a gel-filled booster bra, how

137

we'd prodded it about and even weighed it on her mother's kitchen scales. I remembered Oggy peering down my cleavage and sighing; even Christian staring once, admiringly, when I was bending to shift a planter from outside the nursery shop. His faint blush when I lifted my head and caught him, the secret prickle of acknowledgement that passed between us.

I just couldn't fathom what it must be like to lose your breasts, or to live in fear of them because they might be quietly killing you.

Even if I'd been allowed to speak any of this outside my own head, confide it to the world, I don't know whether I'd have dared.

★ ★ ★

The clinic was pretty full. Even though it was one big room, in my mind it felt like two waiting areas in one: the women who were destined to go in to see the consultant and get the all-clear mixed in with those about to be told they needed more treatment. This second group would be made to wait again to visit the Breast Care Room and discuss 'options'. I glanced fearfully at that door. *Engaged*, said the sign outside.

Every so often a patient would emerge from the consultant's, dazed and shaky, a loved one hugging them tightly. For a while I watched those exits, tried to guess each time whether it was good or bad news. But soon that felt intrusive, so I fixed my gaze on the wall-mounted television instead. The volume was too low to hear but I couldn't have taken much in anyway.

After forty-five minutes Liv was called. I got up to go with her. Geraint stayed where he was, so, against all my physical instincts, I bent and took him by the arm and dragged him off his seat. His face reminded me of the Cowardly Lion from *The Wizard of Oz*. Liv's expression was poker-straight. 'Let's get it over with,' she said.

I knew, I think, as soon as the consultant stood up to greet us. From then on the morning became a bit of a blur.

Liv wasn't in the clear. She would need a mastectomy and possibly a course of Tamoxifen afterwards. 'This cancer's oestrogen-positive,' he said, as if we knew what that meant. There was to be no chemotherapy.

'How long before the operation?' Liv managed to ask.

'Two weeks or so.'

He gave some statistics, some prognoses I couldn't take in. There was this, which might result in that, though no one could be sure; another drug that worked, or didn't work, depending on your genes or menopausal status or just plain luck. I know I lost track so I'm sure Liv was in a total whirl. It seemed as though every opinion had to be qualified, when all we wanted to hear was firm fact.

Then we were outside the door, and other patients were watching me hugging my mother, Geraint laying his palm against her shoulder blade.

★ ★ ★

Inside the Breast Care Room the nurse talked options.

'There *are* no options. I need a mastectomy, Mr Harlow's just told me,' said Liv.

'Yes, but there are different types,' said the nurse, producing a kind of catalogue and laying it on the desk between us. She flipped it open and showed us a series of photographs, women's chests post-surgery. 'This is what we're here to chat about. You can have the full breast taken away completely, leaving a flat surface, like this one. Everything's removed, see?'

We saw.

'Or you can have reconstruction. We might pump the breast back up with expanders, like balloons, till it's stretched enough. That's a several-stage process, you'd have to keep coming back in for that. Or we can look at using muscle and fat from elsewhere on your body, implants — '

'What are you asking *me* for?' said Liv. '*I* don't know what's best. You're the one with the medical training. You tell *me!*'

The nurse laid down the folder and waited.

Liv waved her hands in frustration. 'Why is it so complicated? Just *tell* me what I need.' She turned to me. 'What should I do?'

Geraint sat mute and useless.

'I'm just showing you what's available,' said the nurse.

Out of God knows where I heard myself say, 'Look, whatever my mum chooses, there's been enough messing around. This is serious now. We want a second opinion.'

'On what?'

140

'On the tissue samples. How do we know she definitely doesn't need chemo, for instance? Because the labs didn't pick anything up first time. Did you know that? Have you read the notes?'

It wasn't her fault, of course, it's just that we needed to be angry with someone. She closed her folder quietly. 'OK.'

'If we have to pay, we'll pay.'

'You'll need to speak to the consultant about it. I'll give you his secretary's number.'

I hadn't the slightest idea whether Liv could afford to go even temporarily private, or if she'd countenance it on political grounds.

'Meanwhile, take this literature,' said the nurse. 'Read it at home. You see us again next week and we can talk more then, or there's a contact number here, call me any day.'

It was me who moved towards the desk and gathered up the pamphlets. Liv's earlier outburst seemed to have drained her. She rose from her chair like an automaton, her arms hanging limply by her sides. Already she looked like a sick woman.

A *glimpse of what's to come*, I thought miserably as I guided her towards the exit, Geraint trailing behind.

★ ★ ★

I dropped them at home, but remained in the car as I was supposed to be going on to Melody's.

Just days after Joe dumped her she'd been struck with an idea for a kind of party where, in return for help decorating the nursery, she'd supply a running buffet and drinks into the evening. 'That way people can duck in and out all day. Why should I have to struggle on my own?' she'd said. 'There's more than one way to curry a goose.' Michael and I had been amazed by the way she'd rallied. We'd signed up to help at once.

Right now, though, Melody's was the last place I wanted to be.

I thought I might take a short diversion to get my head together — drive out on the heath road, maybe, park on the cinder path and go for a half-hour walk across the common. I needed to think about how I was going to tell the world my mother had cancer.

The main street out of town's one-way, narrow, and easily blocked by delivery lorries. Although I wasn't exactly in a hurry, my temper still flared when I found myself stuck behind a van unloading stationery. I sat behind the wheel cursing and hating everyone. A parked car beside me indicated to pull out, but I only edged closer to the van to close up his escape route, pointlessly mean. A middle-aged pedestrian squeezed in front of my bonnet on her way to the opposite pavement, and I glared at her, thinking the next person who did that would get a faceful of windscreen wash. No swerving for rabbits out on the bypass today, either. If they were stupid enough to sit in the road, they deserved flattening. Why should I care when the universe so patently didn't care for me?

At last the van doors closed and the driver

hauled himself into his cab. Even then he didn't set off immediately but sat there with his engine idling and a great line of cars stretching out behind. I bibbed my horn and saw an irritated movement in his wing mirror. Finally we rolled forward, me over-revving in a way that would have made Michael wince.

The van crawled up the High Street, pausing for incompetent parkers, elderly shoppers, dithering stray dogs, till we got to the mini roundabout at the top. 'For fuck's sake!' I shouted at the dashboard, because I could see the way was perfectly clear and there'd been no need for him to pull up. With grinding slowness he allowed himself to cross the Give Way line, till he was far enough forward for me to barge past him. Thank God he was turning left (though with no indication or anything helpful like that). I swung the car round and to the right and plunged down a rat run I knew would take me straight onto the bypass. I'd be on the heath road within two minutes.

Except I'd reckoned without them digging up the road behind the civic centre. Too late I registered the yellow digger, the temporary traffic lights and warning triangle, and at the same moment I was distracted by the figure of Oggy emerging from the walkway by the library with a cat basket — cat basket? — in his arms. I knew enough to slam on my brakes, but not hard enough. It would have been OK if there hadn't been a flatbed truck in front of me.

I didn't set my airbag off, that was something. In the seconds that followed, I stayed where I was, still clutching the steering wheel, and waited for trouble to come to me.

And here it was now: a pot-bellied, crop-haired thirty-something climbing out of his driver's seat to inspect the mess I'd made. He walked slowly round, pulling all manner of discouraging faces, then brought out his camera phone to record the detail. I rolled the car back a foot or two and shut off my engine.

Crop-head knocked on my window. 'Dear, dear,' he said when I wound the glass down. 'In a hurry to get to the beauty parlour, were we?' Beyond him, two workmen grinned and exchanged winks. I suppose it was big entertainment for them.

'Is there much damage?'

'Much damage? Oooh, I'll say.' He sucked in his breath pityingly. 'You insured? You'd better be, girl.'

The next thing I knew, Oggy was crouched by my side. 'Stick your hazards on or you'll have someone up the back of you.' When I didn't react, he leaned in and pushed the button himself. I wondered what he'd done with his cat basket.

'Daft mare,' said Crop-head. 'Daft fucking female drivers. Too busy looking at herself in her mirror. Putting on her lipstick. Yacking on the phone.'

'Watch your mouth,' said Oggy.

'Watch my mouth! I like it. Hey, lads, I've to watch my mouth.'

The driver of the digger was laughing.

'Look, there's no damage to your lorry,' said

144

Oggy. 'She's scraped her own bonnet. You're fine.'

Crop-head raised his eyebrows. 'Yeah? What would you know about it? Work in a garage, do you? Got X-ray vision? How do you know she hasn't cracked the exhaust mount or buckled the tail-gate hasp?'

'Because she was nowhere near the exhaust and I can see myself the tailgate's untouched. She went in under it, and only just clipped you.'

I thought perhaps I should get out and see for myself, but when I reached for the door handle, Oggy signed for me to stay put.

'You know what it's like to be self-employed, mate?' said Crop-head. He'd stepped forward and was now well into Oggy's personal space. 'Anything goes wrong with this vehicle, it comes out of my pocket. My pocket. I want her details so I can claim.'

'No you don't.'

'I'm sorry,' I called.

'I bet you are, love,' said Crop-head.

'For fuck's sake,' Oggy exploded. 'Do you think she did it deliberately? Do you think she decided to bash in her own bonnet, for the hell of it? Fucking *look*. There's not a mark on your lorry.'

'That you can see.'

'You really are asking for it.' Oggy raised his fist. The workmen whooped and cheered. One of them was videoing us, I noticed. We'd be on YouTube by the end of the day: Feeble Female v Porky Git.

Crop-head re-arranged his features so as to

convey mock-revelation.

'Oh, I get what you're up to, I see it now. You reckon this is gonna get you into her knickers, yeah? Fucking hell. Rather you than me, mate, s'all I can say. Vinegar-faced tart. You deserve each other.'

Oggy took a swing, but the lorry driver saw it coming and ducked neatly out of the way. That's it, I thought, a full-scale street brawl and somehow it's my fault. I rummaged around for my mobile so I could summon help.

But the conflict was over before it started. While Oggy was recovering his balance, Crop-head turned and strode towards his cab, pausing only to gob on the pavement. He hauled himself back inside, slammed the door and fired up the ignition. 'I've got your number,' he shouted through the open window. 'You'll be hearing from my insurance.'

'Aw, piss off, fatso,' called Oggy. 'Shift before I deck you.'

'I don't fight kids. You're not worth the bother, son.'

'Time to go home and change your pants.'

Luckily the light turned green and Crop-head was able to pull away, to the ironic applause of the men in fluorescent jackets. Soon there was nothing left of him except a pall of diesel fumes.

'That saw him off, didn't it? Wanker.' Oggy looked pleased with himself. 'Park up properly and I'll take you for a drink.'

'I can't. I'm on my way to Melody's.'

'You're not fit to drive. You need to calm down.'

'I'm absolutely fine.'

He just raised his eyebrows at me, secure in the knowledge he was right and I was wrong.

Bastard, I thought, ungratefully.

*　★　★　★*

I took the car round the corner to the bowling club car park, then walked back to where Oggy was waiting with his cat carrier.

'Trust you to be there at the exact time I'm making a fool of myself,' I said.

'I know. It's like ESP. Our special connection.'

We passed under the covered walkway and onto the high street.

'Whose cat's that, anyway?'

'It's not a cat,' he said, holding the cage up for me to see through the front grille. 'Least, if it is, it's got problems.'

A dark mass the rough size of a turnip was lodged in one corner among some wisps of grass. As I squinted in, the animal flexed its body, shifted round and a black snout appeared. A hedgehog. I could hear its snuffly breathing and the scratch of its spines against the plastic walls.

'Why are you carting a hedgehog about town, Oggy? They're a BAP species, protected. You shouldn't interfere with them.'

'I'm not going to hurt it. I'm looking for somewhere to release it.'

'Where did you find it?'

'Caz's garden. Caz, you know. In the pub.'

'Your girlfriend.'

'In a manner of speaking.'

'A 'manner of speaking'? I'm sure she'd love that.'

'All right then, she is.'

The hedgehog scuffled to keep its balance.

'Why couldn't it stay in her garden?'

'She saw it go under the shed last night and freaked out. She said they have fleas and they'd come in the house. I had to promise to fetch it out and take it over the other side of town, out of the way.'

'So you're an amateur pest controller these days as well as a cattle-feed rep? Honestly. This animal needs to go back to its home territory. It'll only just have come out of hibernation and it needs to feed up somewhere it knows. Tell your girlfriend to get a damn grip. She's more likely to catch fleas off you than off a hedgehog.'

'Cheers, Frey.'

'No problem. Let's go round there now and we can find a garden nearby and release it. Whereabouts does she live?'

'Cottle Court. I thought you wanted a drink though?'

'We can hardly take a hedgehog into a pub. Anyway, we've a job to do.'

We made our way down Piper Street in the general direction of the new estate and the park.

'Are you really OK?' Oggy asked me as we crossed the road. 'You look dead pale.'

'I'm shaken, that's all. Pissed off. With myself as much as anyone. What was I doing to miss the lights like that?'

'Oh, it's easily done. I mashed up my front wing on a bollard month before last. A scraped panel's not the end of the world. I once drove for a week with no side window, if you remember. Can't the famous Michael mend it?'

I shrugged. He would, but he'd give me an earful in return.

Oggy said, 'Don't waste energy worrying about that tosser in the truck either. All mouth and trousers, I know the type. You won't hear from him again.' He nudged me with his elbow in a friendly way, and I heard again the scrabble of claws from the darkness of the carrier. 'Not having a good day, are you?'

I had to look away as tears unexpectedly filled my eyes. 'You don't know the half of it.'

★　★　★

We decided to release the hedgehog near the end house, six doors down from Caz, because the garden went round three sides and was pretty overgrown. Oggy put the carrier down and opened the front so it faced into the stems of a large laurel bush. Nothing happened, so he bent down and reached inside. Next thing he'd whipped out his arm again, shaking his fingers as though they'd been burned. 'Fuck!'

'Oh, for God's sake. However did you get him in there in the first place?'

'I just sort of nudged him with my foot. He was very cooperative actually.'

'Well, look, drag your coat sleeve over your fingers and hook him out that way.' I squatted on the pavement to show him.

The hog, when I drew it out, was tightly

curled, so I scooped it up between my wrists and placed it under the bush.

Though we waited a minute without speaking, it didn't move.

'I'm sorry about Liv,' muttered Oggy eventually. 'I dunno what to say.'

I don't know what I want to hear, I thought.

I said, 'What's bothering me most right now is the idea of telling everyone, having to announce it over and over again. And then people being shocked and sorry for us, or embarrassed. I'm not sure I can stand it. Mad, really, because for weeks I've been desperate to tell someone, I've hated the secrecy. But now I feel the exact opposite and I want to keep it all completely private. How stupid is that?'

'Life's shit.'

'Yeah, it is.' Oggy would know; he'd been with his gran when she actually died, walking back from the shops with her and the next minute she was collapsed on the ground and having a heart attack. I remembered how shaken he'd been by that, and how he'd stopped playing football with the lads and had sat with me on the rec wall every lunchtime, talking. We'd have been in Year 10. Our form tutor was Mrs Dewsbury and she was a right unsympathetic cow.

A rustle under the laurel told us the hedgehog was beginning to move. It was the black snout I saw first, coming forward jerkily, then the beady black eyes and the leathery feet.

'One hog can have up to seven thousand spines, you know.'

The snout twitched in our direction.

150

'Hey up, mate,' said Oggy.

'How could anyone be scared of that?'

'She's a bit of a div, is Caz.'

'Don't feel you have to do her down on my account.'

'No, but she is.'

The hog came up to the edge of the path, sniffed about, then turned and shuffled away into the depths of the garden. It's always a funny sensation in your heart when a wild animal leaves you: half pride, half panic. Part of you wants to run after, re-rescue it. 'You will keep an eye out, won't you? Make sure she doesn't whack it with a pan or anything?'

Oggy nodded and picked up the cat basket again. His face was hopeful.

'Look, I know I wasn't a great boyfriend, Frey, but I can be a good mate. It sounds as though you need one right now.'

'I don't know what I need, to be honest, Oggy.'

'Fair enough.'

I looked at my watch. Melody would be waiting. 'I need to get going,' I said.

★ ★ ★

Her front door was open and the hall and stairs carpet sheeted over. Music floated down from the bedroom, something with a ska beat. The coat pegs were loaded with strange garments.

I could have gone straight up, but instead I took myself to the kitchen to gather my courage.

There wasn't much evidence of a buffet going

151

on, though there was an impressive collection of bottles out on the worktop. No one was going home thirsty. I checked in the fridge and found only half a tray of scotch eggs, a tub of Philadelphia and a multipack of Frubes. But the freezer, when I opened it, was crammed with Iceland boxes. I pulled one out: ready-to-bake mini quiches. 'Cooks in 20 mins!' read the tag line. Without even stopping to think about it I stuck the oven on and began to hunt for plates.

I do know where it comes from, this need to make myself domestically useful. Where my classmates let their parents wait on them hand and foot, would moan if asked so much as to ferry a dirty plate to the sink, I've always enjoyed helping run the house. It comes from the years after Colin died, when Liv was all over the place emotionally, and I learned even as an infant I could do us both good by hiding away my toys under the bed, making my own cups of Ribena, packing my school bag myself etc. If she came out of her study to find the waste-paper baskets emptied, it lifted her mood slightly, which meant I was a winner too. Now setting things in order is automatic for me and a kind of therapy. I can still remember Liv's face the first time I stripped the beds myself, or when I laid a proper fire.

I was trying to locate Melody's egg timer when Christian appeared clutching a bunch of mugs in each hand. Even like this, in his paint-spattered T-shirt and grimy chinos, he looked like something off a boy-band album cover.

'Hey, you wonderful girl!' he said when he saw

what I was doing. 'Trust you to be busy.'

'How's progress on the upper storey?'

'Good, good. Melody had already moved all the furniture out and taken up the carpet, so we were able to get straight on.'

'I hope she didn't lift anything too heavy.'

He frowned. 'I never thought about that. She's been taking regular breaks, though. She's sitting on the stairs now, having a breather.'

'Who else is up there?'

'Tanya who used to work at the farm shop, Lindy from next door, Tom from across the road, some bloke called Angus, don't know where he's from, plus Nicky's joining us after work. And Michael, of course. There might be more coming later.'

'It's a wonder you can all fit in.'

'There is a certain amount of jostling involved. We've already had a spillage.'

I said, 'Liv's got cancer.' I had to get it out quickly, before the words stuck in my throat.

Christian's smile fell away. 'What?'

'We were up at the hospital this morning. Liv has breast cancer.'

'Oh good God. Oh, God, Freya, I'm so sorry.'

I felt a huge weight settle on my shoulders, chest and heart. As I'd feared, now the news was coming out, that made it truer than ever.

'What do the doctors say?'

'She needs a mastectomy, drugs after that.'

'What drugs? Chemo?'

'They say not.'

His body language relaxed slightly. 'Well, then. That's — chemo's really nasty. She doesn't have to go through that, at least. Oh, Frey. Come here.'

He held out his arms for me and I let myself lean against him. It was so sweet to be held by a pair of strong arms.

'You OK?'

'Not really.'

He hugged me tighter. 'You know, if there's anything I can do, you've only to ask.'

You can let me stay like this indefinitely, I nearly said. But this wasn't my place. I had no right to be seeking comfort from my friend's fiancé.

'I'll be fine,' I said, pulling away. 'I'll have to be.'

'And Melody, does she know?'

'No. No one. You're the first person I've told outside the family.' Already I was editing Oggy out of the day.

'Do you want me to speak to her?'

'I'll do it.' Both of these women were my responsibility. If anyone was the bridge between them, it was me.

★　★　★

Christian made a new round of teas, and took himself back upstairs. I waited till the quiches were done, persuaded them onto a sheet of foil to cool, then tipped some frozen sausage rolls onto the baking tray. Fifteen minutes they needed. By the end of fifteen minutes I'd have told Melody.

I heard her before I saw her. She was singing

154

along to 'Mirror in the Bathroom' but imperfectly, just the odd lines she knew. I rounded the top of the stairs and found her holding Christian's hands and bobbing about as though she was in a club. She was kitted out in a baggy lumberjack shirt and black leggings and her hair was bound up with an orange chiffon scarf. All around her stood displaced furniture and junk.

'Bloody hell, Melody.'

'What?'

You should be in there helping the others, you're nearly four months pregnant, that's someone else's boyfriend you were dancing with.

'Nothing,' I said. 'How's it going?'

'Brilliant, totally brilliant. Take a look.'

I poked my head round the spare-room door: the room that once, briefly, I might have claimed as mine. There was a plump girl on her knees gloss-painting the skirting boards, an ancient but fit-looking man up a stepladder, a sixty-something woman with very short hair fixing masking tape round the window sill, and a thin young guy with dreadlocks filling in the centre of the back wall with a roller. The girl I'd met before, and the white-haired man, but not the others.

Melody was rattling on. 'Do you like it? I chose blue because I just love that shade, doesn't matter if the baby turns out to be a girl, newborns can't even see colour. And I'm going to stick some decals of clouds under the picture rail, and seagulls, maybe do a mural of a tree or something in the corner. I've found these gorgeous curtains with stars on, plus I'm fitting a blackout blind because of the street light, and I managed to get that lampshade shaped like a balloon. Not thought about a cot yet, but Tanya's cadged me a cane chair her dad was chucking out because the cushion needed re-covering. I can drape a throw over it, and it'll be fine. That can be my feeding chair. And you know, Frey, you can still stay over, any time. I've got that zed bed.'

I took in the scene, trying to summon up the appropriate level of enthusiasm.

'For God's sake, cheer up. Go in there and sniff some paint or something. We're all high on the fumes. Aren't we, Chris?' She grinned and rolled her eyes at him.

'Well,' said Chris.

'Such a shame Liv couldn't make it.'

'Liv's ill,' I said.

'She's not got this flu, has she?'

'Worse than that. I've got something to tell you. Something serious.'

That sobered her slightly. She glanced from me to Chris, and back again, and a little crease appeared between her brows. 'Oh, OK. Do you want to go in my bedroom, hun?'

She led me in and we shut the door. A string of tiny brass bells rattled as the latch clicked home.

'Frey?'

'It's cancer.'

There was a beat, then Melody mouthed the word after me. 'Oh fuck.'

'Yeah.'

156

'Where?'

'Her breast. She's having a mastectomy.'

Melody's eyes widened with horror. I knew in her world there wasn't a lot worse than disfigurement. 'Jesus. Will she lose her hair too?'

'I don't think so.'

'That's something.'

Like it's a big deal here, I thought.

'Will she . . . is it — '

'We don't know how it'll all turn out. I suppose they won't know till they've done the op.'

'Cancer, though. She must be fucking terrified. I would be. I can't believe it.'

Melody began to pace about the room.

'The stats are pretty encouraging,' I said. 'I know what counts in the end is the individual case but, overall, treatment's getting better and better. I think we have to hang onto that. That's what Liv says.'

'Cutting off her boob, though.'

'They can reconstruct it,' I said defensively.

'I'd be, like, mental, if it was me.'

Yes, but this isn't about you, I thought. She was on the verge of annoying me.

'How long has she known?'

'She found a lump before Christmas.'

'And kept it to herself?'

I sighed. 'No, she did tell me and Geraint, only she wanted it kept quiet till she'd had the results.'

'I count as family here too, Frey.'

Only just. Whose cancer is it anyway? It was bizarre. Of all the reactions I'd been expecting, a

157

battle over ownership was something I hadn't predicted. 'So I'm telling you now.'

Melody sat down on the bed and pulled her scarf away, ruffled her hair free with her fingers. I could have been wrong, but I thought she took a split second to check herself in the mirror. 'What can I send her?'

'You mean, like a card?'

'That and what else? I want to send her a present, let her know I'm rooting for her. Not flowers, though. I know she's funny about where they're grown. Does she use moisturising face masks ever?'

'I wouldn't say it's high on her list of priorities.'

'How do you know? It might be just the pep she needs. Everyone loves a nice facial.'

I wanted not to be irritated. I knew she was trying. 'It's up to you, Melody.'

'And you, you're so calm, so grown up about it. I don't know where you get it from. Not me.'

'I've had time to get used to the idea.'

'Yeah, I suppose. God, it's awful isn't it?'

'Yes,' I said.

★ ★ ★

Later, when the second crowd had arrived and the house was full and hot, I wandered from room to room feeling disconnected and miserable. I wanted to be back home, but the home it was before Liv got ill, when a rough day meant Ray snapping at me for misplacing a delivery invoice, or Geraint hogging the bathroom for

158

beard maintenance when I was gagging for a shower. You don't appreciate ordinariness when you have it.

Nicky caught up with me in the backyard where I was standing alone, watching the sun set over the roofs of Nantwich.

'You OK, sweetheart?' She put her arm through mine. 'Chris told me. I'm so sorry. You must all be reeling.'

'Yeah. Well, Liv's not too bad at the moment. She says she wants it over and done with and then she can get on with her life. Geraint's acting as though nothing's happened, but that's par for the course.'

'I'm sure it'll be all right, you know. She's going to be fine. Trust me.'

Nicky's face was shining with sympathy, and suddenly I felt furious with her. *How dare you make that claim on Liv's behalf? This is actually happening, it's not some schmaltzy TV drama. None of us knows what the future holds and I for one won't be tempting fate by assuming the best.*

I wriggled out of her grip, turned and found myself watching Christian through the window. He was handing round pretzels, charming smiles off everyone he spoke to, the way he does. When he caught my eye he gave a little wave.

Nicky reached out for me again. 'You should know, we're both here for you.'

Oh, go play with your Virtual Wedding Bouquet. How can you possibly understand my situation, the way your life is right now?

'Thanks,' I said. I think I sounded sincere.

159

We went back inside the kitchen and I found myself standing next to Melody, who was flirting energetically with the dreadlock man.

'When's Michael getting here?' I asked.

'He isn't. He rang me to say he'd had to deal with some problem for Kim and couldn't make it.'

My last hope crashed. Aside from anything else, Michael was common sense; he always knew the right words to say. I realised how much I'd been depending on seeing him this evening.

'Hey, I'm sure it'll work out OK in the end, hun,' said Melody, grasping my sleeve.

I just about managed a nod.

Then, before anyone else could be kind to me, I moved away quickly and through to the lounge. Without bothering to explain or say goodbye I pushed past the bodies and out to the front door, into a smarting red sunset.

Case Notes on: *Melody Jacqueline Brewster*

Meeting Location: *42, Love Lane, Nantwich*

Present: *Miss Melody Brewster, Mrs Abby Brewster, Mrs Diane Kozyra*

Date: *2.30 p.m., 22/1/87*

Initially Melody wouldn't speak to me. Mrs Brewster told me her daughter had been tearful all week and also had become convinced her hair was coming out. I asked if she thought Melody wasn't perhaps coping as well as we'd hoped. Mrs Brewster said it was hard for everyone and Melody needed to 'pull herself together'. I suggested that now Melody had made the decision to relinquish her baby she might be going through a grieving process, and that this was perfectly normal.

Shortly after this exchange, Melody began to examine her hair in the mirror. I said I thought her hair was looking just as full as on my previous visit, and she replied that I should see the state of her brush or the plughole after she'd used shampoo. She said she felt 'everything was falling away'. I advised a chat with her GP. Again assured her I really could detect no obvious hair loss. She seemed slightly calmer by the time *I* left.

Query: beginnings of depression? Note on follow-up session.

Next visit: 30/1/87   Signed: Diane Kozyra

A WEDNESDAY

April

I've always liked April. It feels like the proper start of spring, when the cold weather lets up slightly and you get the first patches of blossom coming in the hedgerows. Blue tits fly in and out of the nest box, our pipistrelle bat re-appears, the evenings are light again. You can't help but feel cheered.

More significantly, Liv's at her best in April, after the long drag of winter. The water-vole reports start coming in and she can begin to map that year's colonies. Now's the season for habitat surveys, before the vegetation gets too mad: groups of earnest adults paddling about by the water's edge, parting reeds and hunting for burrows and latrines. My job on survey days is usually to mark the map — a square for feeding signs ('Think of a square meal,' Liv says); a circle for a burrow; a star for their little starry footprints etc. We never glimpse any actual water voles, but sometimes there's a plop as one dives into the water upstream of where we're working. I've seen kingfishers and any number of dragonflies and damselflies, woodpeckers and grey squirrels and shrews and frogs and toads. Once I spotted a pike, and it was massive.

Or in this month we go checking dormice, still

asleep in their boxes. I'm in charge of the clipboard there as well, because you're not supposed to handle a dormouse unless you're registered, but sometimes Liv's let me stroke one when it's needed microchipping and it's still under anaesthetic.

I also remember April as the month I got to know my birth mother. Our initial meeting on Crewe station had been back in the December, but those first weeks had been cautious and restrained. I think both of us were on our best behaviour, pretending to be people we weren't. Then one early spring day she'd driven over and I'd taken her for a walk down by the canal. I wanted to show her some of the places I used to hang about as a kid.

The first thing I'd spotted was some otter spraint on the kerb under the bridge. I was so excited I forgot to be cool. Took a photo on my phone, got down on my knees and actually sniffed it, while Melody shrieked with horror. 'Professor of poo, are you?' she'd said. And I'd told her Liv had taught me to identify ten different types of wild mammal scat, and if she thought that was gross, then tough.

'God, you're so serious, aren't you?' she'd said. 'Chill out. I can do nature, you know. That's a heron.' She'd pointed across the canal to where one flapped lazily across the field. 'Well done,' I'd said. Maybe flushed with success, she'd taken a run at a beech tree and hauled herself up onto the lowest branch, marking her bleached jeans with mould and wiping cobwebs across her long chenille coat. As I stood there on the towpath she'd scrambled up two, three, four more branches till she hung right over me, her face triumphant. She rocked back and forth, showering me with spiders and grubs to try and freak me out. But she must have rocked too hard because the next second there was a rushing noise and a thud and she was on the hard ground in a heap of black chenille. Even before I had a chance to panic she was sitting up and laughing. 'Call me Kate Humble,' she'd said when she got her breath back.

I never told Liv about the episode because I suspected she wouldn't approve and I was quite protective of Melody in those days; she seemed hardly older than me.

Those were the Aprils of the past, though. This one had seen Liv recovering from having her breast taken away, drains and an implant inserted.

Geraint and I had struggled. The house with only the two of us in it was dire. She was only away five days at the end of March, but our systems began to unravel even in that short space. It wasn't as if I couldn't cope domestically — I'm keener on routine and order than Liv — it's that I resented looking after Geraint. Where I wouldn't think twice about tumbling a basketful of clothes into the washing machine, I couldn't bring myself to wash just his stuff. I objected to picking up even a single mug or bowl he'd used, and rather than cook for him, I bought in a load of processed meals-for-one and ate them in my room, leaving him to forage for himself. I watched him cut his toenails one night

165

and thought, *There's no way I'm hoovering that up*. The upstairs sink was rimed with unswilled beard trimmings, the towels were left on the floor by the side of the bath, the peelings pot sat on the kitchen worktop crammed and sweltering. As for cleaning the toilets, forget it.

We needed Liv between us.

The result was that the day before she was discharged, both of us had to go round the house in a mad panic to return it to a fit state. To be fair to Geraint, he did as he was told. Because neither of us had bothered to put the wheelie bin out for collection, we now had surplus bags of rubbish sitting by the back door and it was Geraint who drove them down to the tip. When he came back he swabbed the kitchen floor (once I'd shown him where the bucket lived, what cleaning agent to put in and to use hot, not cold, water). In between all my jobs, I stood over him while he changed the sheets on Liv's bed, and followed him about to make sure he draped wet clothes tidily over the radiators, rather than stuffing multiple socks and underpants in a sodden wodge down the back.

It had been worth the effort. Liv's face, as she came through the door and saw the vacuumed carpet and flowers on the hall table, was such a picture I'd have high-fived Geraint, if either of us could have borne the physical contact.

Now she'd been home two weeks and I was sitting in the dining room surfing eBay on my laptop, while in the lounge next door Liv attempted to talk to Geraint about what it was like having cancer.

'My chest still feels huge,' she was saying. 'Though they say the swelling will go down. I hope it does. I hope I'm not lop-sided. Do you think I will be?'

I assumed he was shaking his head.

'In the end,' she went on, 'I was laughing. You know, when the consultant said about using the smallest size implants. Because it was that or cry. There's no dignity about any of it. I used to be so shy about my body, but after all this . . . It's still really tender and bruised, but otherwise not too bad. Not like when they took the drains out. That hurt.'

Another pause.

'It looks as though the nipple's going to be OK, too.'

A grunt.

'Do you want to see?'

I focused on my laptop screen, scrolled down columns and columns of unwanted Doc Martens, Fly boots, Camper sandals. Searching, searching. Restless shoes crossing the length and breadth of the land. I heard Geraint clear his throat painfully.

'So I'm going to try and get hold of some flaxseed oil,' said Liv. 'The woman in the next bed mentioned it. Not sure what it's supposed to do exactly. I might research it later.'

I can help, I thought. I brought up Google and typed in 'flaxseed oil cancer', and within a minute was reading about the controversial Budwig Diet and how some people thought phytoestrogens might prevent new tumours from developing and shrink existing ones, but others said there wasn't enough evidence. There were testimonies and blogs and scientific papers and forum posts, and every site claimed something different, every author seemed convinced they were right. I trawled through eight or nine different reports, and at the end was no wiser.

In all that time, I was aware that Geraint had said nothing at all: made no reassurances, no soothing noises, no meaningful response of any kind. Then, just as I was closing down Windows I heard him go, 'Oh, Alan H rang this morning. Apparently the new conservation leaflets have a photograph of hazelnuts nibbled by wood mice instead of dormice, so they'll have to be recalled.'

I snapped the laptop shut so hard I nearly broke the catch.

There are times when the only course of action is to run away.

* * *

I had somewhere to be anyway. That afternoon Melody had her twenty-week scan appointment.

'You're coming with me?' she'd asked, her tone bright-bright-bright with a hint of desperation.

'I'm at work that day. I can't keep taking days off.'

Her brow had come down like a sulky child's. 'You went with Liv. You've been to hospital with her loads of times.'

Bloody hell, it's not the same, I wanted to say. 'It's a hellish busy period for the nursery. Ray

168

needs all hands on deck.'

'So I have to struggle on my own.'

'Can't Michael go with you?'

' . . . have to sit in the waiting room with all the happy couples, big sign over my head saying 'Single Mother'. It was bad enough the first time, but at least then I had my mum with me. I don't think I can bear to sit there completely alone. I'd rather not go at all.'

'Don't be daft.'

'I mean it, Frey. I need you, hun. *You*. My flesh and blood. No one else will do.'

So in the end I'd caved in, gone crawling to Ray to beg yet another advance day off. It meant I'd be working twenty-six days solid, without any break at all (and weekends are frantic; there's a queue even to get in the car park).

On the way to pick her up I decided to call in at Michael's garage. I was running early, due to stropping out of the house, and also I just wanted to see him. He has this knack of straightening out my head just when I need it.

Peacock's is one of those old-fashioned outfits where their mainstay is still basic mechanical repairs rather than computer diagnostics. Most of their custom is Classic Vehicles, what I'd call old heaps. These Michael loves, the more distressed the better. Often we'll be out round town and he'll start raving about some tatty old Renault Fuego or Alfa Spider or Reliant Scimitar, and what he could do to it if he had a free hand. The rise of eBay's been a particular boon, tempting customers to make all kinds of nostalgia-led impulse buys they haven't a hope of

169

restoring themselves. Then it's Peacock's they come to for help. A lot of modern garages won't touch upholstery, for instance, but that type of project's meat and drink to Michael and his workmates. I've seen him restore cars that have no floor under the pedals, whose bonnets are lacy with rust, cars you'd think were only fit for the crusher.

And if the customer waiting area's a manky old portacabin with nothing more than three ancient *Autotraders* to read and a busted kettle on a tray, that's all part of the ethos. The cars are what matter.

Because I'd dropped in on spec, I knew there was a good chance he'd be up to his elbows in engine, and he was: right in the middle of disembowelling a white, tyreless Ford Capri. I called across the bay to him and he looked up and shook his head. Then he checked his watch, frowned, glanced at a Triumph Dolomite parked by the door, and flashed his spread palms at me twice — twenty minutes. Larry came out of the office and waved a mug at me. I gave him the thumbs up and went to wait in the portacabin. After ten minutes I got a hot drink, and after twenty-two, Michael joined me.

'Am I a nuisance?' I said.

'You are. But everyone's entitled to a tea break. How's tricks?'

'OK, I suppose. Apart from I want to strangle Geraint with his own binoculars.'

'Tell me something new. How's Liv doing?'

'Tired. But now the op's over, and she seems all right with the Tamoxifen, I think she feels

170

she's got through the worst. We'll know more when she goes back for her review.'

'You want this second opinion on the cells they took.'

'Yeah.'

Michael put his mug down on the table. 'Well done for pushing.'

'You think?'

'Of course. Why?'

'Because — ' I dragged my hands across my face. 'I wonder if I should've interfered. It's not like it's *my* cancer, is it? And now it's hanging over her, another question mark, extra stress. Which she doesn't need. Geraint hates me for it.'

'Geraint can go shag a badger. What matters is they get the diagnosis right.'

'I suppose. Yeah. It is, isn't it?'

'Liv needs someone to look out for her. Don't feel guilty for that, Frey. If these other tests show up nothing, then that's all fine, you can forget it. If there is still something that needs dealing with, then — '

'Don't,' I said. 'I can't think about that. Hey, you know Melody sent her a whole folder of stuff on cancer?'

He looked mildly alarmed. 'No, I didn't. What kind of stuff are we talking about?'

'Articles, clippings from about a thousand women's magazines.'

'She does like her fashion mags.'

'It must have taken her ages to go through them. Some of the pages are in those see-through plastic pockets, but I think she must have run out a quarter of the way in.'

171

'What was Liv's reaction?'

'Not sure.' I remembered her expression as she leafed through the articles one by one. *Cancer, My Battle; The Cancer Diaries; Eat Yourself Strong* — *the role of nutrition in cancer recovery.* Best was *Leeches Saved my Boobs*; she'd enjoyed that one for the wildlife content. 'It's a bit overwhelming,' she'd said as she packed the articles away. 'But thoughtful. Very thoughtful of her. Tell her thank you.'

The windows of the portacabin spotted with rain. Onto the forecourt rolled a smart blue Hillman Avenger, driven by a bald man wearing mesh-backed driving gloves.

'You're really busy, aren't you?'

'The devil makes work for idle mechanics.'

'So I shouldn't keep you.'

I made to rise, but he reached out and pressed my arm to keep me in my chair. 'Before you go, tell me.'

'What?'

'What else is bothering you. I've never seen you look so wrecked, Frey.'

'Silver-tongued charmer.'

'Seriously, spit it out. You'll feel better afterwards.'

I wondered whether he ever got the urge to nab one of the cars he was working on and just set off in it, to hell with everyone.

I said, 'OK, you asked. You know how, when I'm working at the nursery, one of the things I do to stave off the boredom sometimes is run through what action I'd take in the event of an apocalypse?'

'I didn't know that, no. But now you say, it doesn't surprise me.'

'So, like, what I'd do if I had a few weeks' or even months' warning: I'd stock up on veg seeds, get a coil fitted, and take crossbow lessons.'

'Crossbow lessons?'

'Less to go wrong on a crossbow than a gun. Plus they're silent, and you can retrieve your ammunition more easily. Now, if I only had a matter of days before the apocalypse, then I'd get myself to Millets and stock up on camping gear. I'd raid Lidl for as many tin openers as I could carry, plus bottled water, food and first-aid equipment.'

'Right.'

'Obviously I'd be filling my petrol tank and spare containers to the brim, packing my solar chargers and driving over to Hack Green bunker —'

'You realise you're sounding mad?'

'But if we only had a few minutes before the bomb went up or whatever, I'd dash over to Nicky's because she has that fresh-water spring in her cellar, plus she lives next door to the pub.'

'What, and you could nip in for a swift half as the sirens sound?'

'Alcohol's very useful in an emergency situation, actually.'

He was laughing. 'What can I say? You'll survive the end of the world and I won't.'

'No, you will, 'cause I'll come and rescue you.'

'I'm touched.'

'Just being practical. We'll need mechanics.'

'So, to rewind, the reason you've been fretting

173

is you think an atomic bomb's about to drop on Whixall Moss?'

'No. I'm using it as an *example*.'

'Of what?'

'Of a situation that would be overwhelmingly hideous but where I'd still feel like I was in some control.'

'Sorry, you've completely lost me, Freya.'

'The point I'm trying to make is that ordinary, day-to-day life's worse. Because now I'm faced with a nightmare situation that's really happening, and I don't have any answers. I keep waking in the night and thinking about dying. I think about Liv dying, what if they haven't caught it, what if it comes back. I think about me dying, all of us. I lie there in bed and it's like I can feel the cells in my body ticking away, dividing and moving round my body to do their different jobs, and the idea gets into my head that maybe some of them are turning rogue and making tumours and I wouldn't know because they're silent and secret. I'm so scared, Michael. My boobs are black and blue from checking myself.'

Another man might have sniggered at that, but he only smiled gently.

'And then I start thinking about growing older, and Liv, even if she survives the cancer, being an old woman and infirm and needing help, going doolally maybe, and it's not that I'd mind caring for her, it's that I'd be the one who was in charge, like a role swap, and I can't imagine that. I'd be all exposed and freaking out. Like the mice.'

'The mice?'

'When I was about seven, right, we had these wood mice that someone brought in, a little nest of babies from inside a timber pile. They'd been handled so the mother wouldn't have come back to them. Liv put them in one of my kiddy-size shoe boxes, nest and all, cut a little doorway so they could come and go, and stuck the box inside a plastic tank. And they did OK, they were furred and Liv fed them every few hours and they didn't even seem too stressed out considering they were in our front room. Only, a couple of weeks in, I went to check how they were doing and they were all huddled up inside the box and wouldn't come out. I lifted the lid to get a better view, and they went completely mental. You've never seen anything like it. Treading on each other, pushing in all directions. They were panicking because they had no cover.'

I could see those little brown bodies squirm in utter mindless panic. I remember I'd dropped the lid back on and scarpered, never mentioned it to Liv.

'And you feel as though someone's lifted the lid off your box?' asked Michael.

'I know. It's pathetic. I don't know how you coped when your mum walked out.'

'I don't remember it, do I? Like you don't remember Colin. Far as I was concerned, it was always just me and my dad. The family you grow up with is what's normal. Then Dad moved in with Abby, and she was like a mum, but so was Mel in a way.' He grinned. 'She used to check my dinner money, stick the tops back on my felt tips. Sometimes she picked me up from school.

175

And Saturdays she'd take me into town and buy me a Slush Puppy.'

I was trying to listen but all I could see was Liv flicking through her cancer articles, turning them over from time to time to read about the new handbag shape, the ankle-strap shoe revival, the summer-fresh foundation.

'You'll be all right, Frey,' Michael said. 'Whatever happens. Think of it this way: get through this, and you'll be a much stronger mouse.'

'You don't think I'm being pathetic, then?'

'Nope. You're just reacting to a tough situation. If you get the 3 a.m. terrors again, stick the TV on, or put some comedy on your iPod, then at least you're not lying in the dark worrying.'

'I will, yeah.'

'What you're frightened of will happen one day, but not for ages and then you'll deal with it. You'll be ready.'

'Huh.'

'At least you're managing to put a brave face on for her. You wouldn't have been able to do that when I first met you.' He nudged my foot with his. 'And we all have to hop out of the box eventually. In the case of your mouse, that would be so it can run across the carpet while I'm watching CSI and nearly give me a fucking heart attack.'

My phone bleeped.

'Sorry,' I said, and pulled it out of my pocket. 'Oh, for God's sake.'

'What is it?'

I dropped the phone back. 'Hogden.'

'Who the hell's Hogden?'

'A hedgehog. It's Oggy, pretending he's a hedgehog and texting me. He does it all the time. He ate a bowl of cat food last night, apparently. The hedgehog, I mean, not Oggy.'

Michael turned away and picked up an *Autotrader* to study.

'I know, he's a fuckwit. I don't encourage him,' I said.

'Don't you?'

'No.'

Perhaps I should have argued but sometimes the more you protest, the falser it sounds. Outside, under a spitting sky, Larry was assessing the Hillman Avenger, walking round it with the owner and making notes on a clipboard.

'I wish you were coming with us this afternoon.'

He chucked the magazine back on the table. 'Yeah, well. If we weren't up to our eyes here . . . But give that baby a wave from me, won't you?'

'I will.'

'And remind Mel to buy a scan photo.'

'Like she'd forget.'

He laughed. 'You're cool now?'

'I am.'

'Go have fun, then.'

He walked me across to the Mini, holding an *Autotrader* over my head to keep off the rain.

It was only as I drove away that it dawned on me, with a pang of terrible guilt, what memories a pregnancy scan room would have held for him.

177

Melody was in high-energy mode when I picked her up. She talked at me all the way to hospital, so that by the time we got there, my head was ringing.

'I already need a pee,' she said as we signed in. 'I'm bursting. How am I going to last till two-forty?'

'The toilets are by the vending machine,' I said, pointing.

'But I can't, I'm not allowed. My bladder has to be full.'

'You'll have to cross your legs, then.'

She took herself to the nearest chair, and I watched her as she walked. The bump, though there, was neat and not too pronounced. Glancing round the room I could see that some other women looked vast by comparison. 'It's to do with whether it's a boy or a girl,' Melody had explained when she was about fourteen weeks. 'You carry them differently.' 'Rubbish: old wives' tales,' Liv had said when I'd passed it on. I suspected it had more to do with how taut your stomach muscles were, and your general build.

'There are some women who don't even know they're pregnant till they give birth,' said Melody, picking up a copy of *Heat*.

'How far on were you with me when you realised?'

She made an Oh God face at me. 'It took a while before I'd accept it. I kind of knew when my first period was late, but I kept thinking, I'll be all right. And then my school skirt got tight and Abby spotted me struggling with the zip, and she cottoned on straight away.'

'But she was fine about it, wasn't she?'

'In the end. At first she was bloody furious.'

'You always told me she was cool.'

Melody squinted at a photograph of Cheryl Cole. 'Yeah, I did, didn't I? But to be truthful, she was mightily pissed off, for ages. Basically she couldn't be bothered with a baby, the expense, the lack of sleep. Plus she was annoyed there was no father to pursue, and also she hated the idea that the house would be full of people in suits marching in and telling us what to do, judging us.'

'Did they? Tell you what to do?'

'Not really. My social worker was great, actually, because she was neutral where every bugger else around me seemed to have an opinion. I felt like a parcel of meat sometimes, sitting there while they talked over me.'

'What was Michael's take on it?'

'He was only seven or eight, he had no idea what was going on. His dad just wanted to hunt down the boy who got me pregnant and lamp him. Mum was OK in the end, once I'd agreed to sign the forms. Mainly I remember her going, 'It's too much, we can't cope.' But I don't blame her. She was pretty much right. The one thing I did know through all the confusion was that I'd make a crap mum.'

With someone else that might have been a cue for me to go, 'No, no, you'd have been brilliant,' but it would have sounded hollow; we both knew it. Even a well-organised fifteen-year-old would

179

have struggled, never mind one as chaotically minded as Melody. Instead I said, 'That was ages ago.'

'Yup. And this time, it's going to be different. You'll see. I'm grown up, I'm independent. I'm going to do a bloody good job. A whole new start for both of us.' She patted her belly, pleased with herself.

'You'll have to streamline the house. All those ornaments and tassels and beads, a toddler'll have a field day. You'll be forever at A & E.'

'I've thought of that. I'll just shift everything swallowable up to a higher level, get Michael to help me stick some shelves up. I'm not going all wipe-clean and sterile. God, no. This baby's going to grow up surrounded by colour. And music. I'll rock it to sleep with reggae and I'll wake it up with ska. And we'll dance.' She went misty-eyed for a moment. 'I danced with you, you know, hun, in those few days we had in hospital before they took you off. You won't remember, but I did. I used to hold you and bop about the room. 'I Wanna Wake Up with You', I used to sing. You liked it. It stopped you crying.'

I'd heard that story before. In fact she'd given me the single (Boris Gardiner, Creole Records) on our second ever meeting.

My phone bleeped again and I jumped guiltily.

'You're not supposed to have them on in here.'

'I know, I'll shut it off. It's only a text from Nicky to say she's found the perfect pair of white satin shoes.'

Melody sniffed dismissively.

'I've had it with men,' she went on. 'Had it. They're way more trouble than they're worth.'

'Joe was an idiot — '

She waved her hand to stop me. 'You don't have to keep telling me. I'm over him. Michael understood; I got myself in a state but there wasn't any real feeling behind it. It was like, when I was little and I fell over, I'd sometimes carry on crying after I'd stopped hurting because Mum made a fuss and it was nice. So with Joe, I knew I ought to be upset, and it felt good to go through the motions, but there wasn't any depth there. It was more the shock of it.'

Briefly my mind jumped to Liv, frowning as she held up a page from Melody's folder and reading it out loud. ''Hippy to Hip — Killer Dressing for Pear Shapes.' Is that supposed to be me? 'Hide your behind with a flattering smock-top?'' 'It's only the back of something else,' I'd replied. But it wasn't. The other side was just more of the same.

I said, 'Was it deliberate, the baby?'

'To keep him, you mean?'

'No. Well — '

'It's OK, I don't mind you asking. I know what people have been thinking. The pregnancy wasn't a strategy. It was more like, a last chance. I thought I'd stop the Pill and just see. See if I could have a baby of my own. And then if it happened, it happened, everything would come together. Dad included.'

'Couldn't you have picked somebody nicer?'

'Oh, he could be incredibly charming, could Joe.'

'You're kidding.'

'You didn't see how he was at the beginning. He could charm anyone when he smiled. But nice smiles are poor currency, when it comes down to it. You should know that, Freya. I should know it. God, I'd sell my soul for a pee. How many patients do you reckon there are in front of me?'

I glanced round the room. 'Two, three. It depends how many scan rooms they've got on the go.'

'Only, if I don't get in soon, my bladder's going to explode.'

'Does it hurt, giving birth?'

'It nips a bit, yeah. And you, you got bloody stuck, you did. Turned the wrong way, so you were facing the front, and then my pelvis was too small and they had to use forceps.'

'Sorry.'

'So you should be. I couldn't sit down for a week afterwards.'

I'd seen photos of Melody when she was a teenager. She'd been one of those girls who looked their age; certainly no older. Her hair had been permed in a long poodle style, held back at the left side with a comb. She'd favoured long, oversized jumpers and leggings, and when she did wear make-up, it was amateurish and brash. How many double takes must she have attracted as she walked down the street, the woman's swollen belly and the round young face. Yet she didn't hide away. 'I wasn't ashamed of you, hun,' she told me at that first meeting.

182

Another woman was called. Melody sighed and shuddered.

'What's up?' I said. 'You've not wet yourself?'

'Not yet. Listen, I know it's a bit late in the day to be asking, but you are OK with this, aren't you?'

'With the baby?'

'Yeah.'

And if I said no, what then?

'Because it was a different time, when I was pregnant with you. I did what I could, what was right for then, and what was right was that I handed you over to someone who could look after you properly. It wasn't that, you know, you mattered less. Do you understand?'

'Yeah, 'course.'

Melody thought I was jealous. But how could I be when Liv had wanted me so badly? No child could have been more joyfully received into a household than I'd been. Growing up I'd lacked for nothing except a dad, and that was no one's fault.

But when I thought about Melody holding a newborn, conjured the image and focused on it, something did prick at me. Not jealousy — envy. The idea of this brand new person coming into the world with a blank sheet, everything to look forward to, no failures and cop-outs and disappointments trailing in its wake. Only years of being looked after and supported and having decisions made for it. How blissful would that be?

'I'm fine, it'll be great.'

'Oh, well, that's good,' she said with obvious relief.

183

'Anyway, I don't really think of you as my mum.'

Her eyes widened slightly, and just for that fraction of a second I knew I'd hurt her. It wasn't even true; I don't know why I said it.

'What I mean is, you're like a friend. A very special friend.'

The thing about Melody is, she recovers quickly.

'Of course I'm your friend. You've no other friend like me, that's for sure. God, I honestly am going to pee my pants if we have to wait much longer.'

Then the door of the scan room opened and a couple came out, and at the same moment a receptionist called Melody's name.

I levered her up off the chair, and we went to meet the baby.

* * *

The scan room was small and hot with a leather-covered table in the centre. The sonographer was a starchy-looking woman with tight grey curls.

'Bladder nice and full?' she said.

Fuck off, said the thought bubble over Melody's head.

With a little difficulty she slid herself onto the table. I noticed a suspiciously phallic attachment hooked up by the foot end, and was struck by a sudden fear that they'd strip her and I'd have to see her privates. I wasn't clear about what a scan involved.

Melody seemed to know, though. She pulled up her top so it was round her bra line, and wiggled her leggings down to the level of her pubic bone. I thought she'd be chatty and hyper about the whole business, but instead she lay quietly, waiting for the scan to start. There was that atmosphere about the room, almost like a chapel or a confessional. I sat myself in a corner next to a trolley full of latex gloves and sterile wipes, to wait.

The sonographer squirted a dollop of something slimy on Melody's bare skin that made her gasp. Then the overhead bulbs dimmed and the scanner screen lit up, and the sonographer came forward holding what looked like an oversized computer mouse and started it push it against Melody's bump. Up and down and around she stroked it, sweeping the area, squashing hard into the flesh. I couldn't see the screen that well from where I was, so I tried to edge round the trolley for a better view. By craning forward I could make out fluid white shapes appearing on the screen, ovals of bright and dark blooming and retreating, specks and blobs. A tiny head, a spine, I glimpsed, picked out in light. I felt a surge of excitement that made me gasp.

'What is it?' asked Melody.

I assumed the sonographer would swing the screen round to show her, but she just carried on moving the sensor back and forth. Then I happened to glance at her face. Her expression was utterly, heart-stoppingly grim.

Oh, God, no, I thought. *Let this woman's*

misery be for something else. Let her simply be ready for a coffee break, or still stewing over a row she had with her husband this morning. Let her break into a smile and say, 'Here's your baby, and everything's grand.'

But the silence carried on, the grinding of Melody's uterus, the unreadable glowing shapes. With every passing second, bad news became more of a solid presence in the room with us. At last the machine froze and whirred, froze and whirred.

'Please, what is it?' said Melody again.

'I need to speak to a colleague,' said the sonographer, pressing a pager.

'Is there something wrong?' Melody tried to sit up so she could study the screen. 'My twelve-week scan was fine. If the baby's disabled, I don't care. I'll love it anyway. If it's got Down's. I don't mind, anything, I can give up my job to look after it. Or if it needs an operation, that spine thing, it doesn't matter. I want it. Please.'

The sonographer met her gaze briefly, then looked back at the screen. I think we all knew it was hopeless.

'I'm sorry,' she said. 'I'm afraid this pregnancy's not going very well.'

From Liv's diary, 11/05

So furious not sure what to do with myself. Can't believe F would drop out of degree course so soon, without even giving it a proper chance & to tell me over phone, so cool! 'You need to come pick me up, Mum.' What she expecting me to say? Knew if I let myself start I'd never be able to stop so I managed 'If that's what you want.' Wouldn't mind so much if F leaving to pursue some specific goal but far as I can see she's just stepping out into void! Thank God it was telephone & she couldn't see my face.

Must be to do with M, major unsettling influence, critical time. How can it not be her fault? Feel like calling her up & shouting. That would make me the villain, though. Determined to stay the 'understanding one'. Only card I have left to play.

G says to step back, let F get on with it, but easy for him because he has no children. Can't believe, after all these years of motherhood, I've failed at the final fence.

A SATURDAY

May

'If you want to talk,' said Liv, 'it might make you feel better.'

We were sitting on a soil bank at Wenlock Edge, looking out over the rest of the world. The plum blossom was out and frothy, the new beech leaves above our heads bright green, the sky gloriously blue and white. Nearby a robin pecked about hopefully.

Liv was looking better than she had for weeks. The walk had brought colour to her cheeks and with her hair blowing back from her face she looked defiant and almost pretty, for her age. On the way up we'd spotted wild violets and strawberry flowers, primroses, bluebells and an early purple orchid. She'd turned over a stone and found a pill woodlouse; I'd rescued a tired bee off the path. It was like stealing another day from my childhood. I didn't want to be called back to the present.

'I'm trying not to think about it,' I told her. But it was impossible. Every time I let my brain relax, I saw the doctor's expression as he explained that the baby had stopped developing weeks ago; the way Melody had stumbled as we'd walked through the doors of the maternity unit; the awful drive home. Over and over the film re-played.

'That poor girl,' said Liv.

I put my fingertips to my temples, as if there might be some kind of volume control there. 'It's so horrible. All of it, just horrible.'

The heart, they'd said, had stopped at sixteen weeks. They didn't know why, though Melody could ask for a post-mortem if she wanted one. After we'd waited for a while in a side room, a nurse had come in and said she was going to give her some tablets. I went out to the foyer then to call Michael and let him know the news. When I came back, Melody was crying hysterically. 'They won't give me an operation!' she was saying. 'I have to give birth!' Apparently she was too far on for them just to knock her out and remove the baby that way.

Worse was to come: she needed to go home and wait for the drugs to work. 'How long for?' I'd asked, appalled. 'Forty-eight hours,' the doctor said. 'But I want it out!' screamed Melody. She'd been beside herself, and to be honest I'd panicked. Once again I'd run outside and phoned Michael, gabbling at him a load of rubbish that it took him ages to unravel. I wanted him there at the hospital, but it didn't make sense to have the two cars so in the end we agreed it was best if he went to Love Lane and made the house ready for her. 'Whatever else you do, take that kitchen calendar down,' I said. 'She's got all the stages of the pregnancy marked on it.'

For that couple of days we never left her alone. We watched TV a lot, sat up into the small hours, snacked on rubbish. Then it was time to

189

deliver the baby. Michael drove us to the hospital. I was petrified. I didn't want to go. Before we left I argued secretly with him. I said, 'I was there at the scan, it's your turn. I shan't know what to do. I'll make things worse. She's your sister.' It was horrible of me, but I was desperate. He let me rage and whine, then handed me my coat without comment.

She had a private room, which was something. I didn't stay with her right through because doctors kept coming in and doing things to her, so then Michael and I would wait in the corridor. Over and over I cursed him for forcing me to come.

Once she was settled they gave her morphine, which chilled her right out, and we were all three able to chat for a while. We talked about politics, and some TV shows Michael and Melody remembered from their childhood that I'd never heard of. But then she started getting pains and shifting around the bed, and I slipped out to the corridor again. A midwife bustled past me and into the room. She never even glanced in my direction.

I cried a bit, then listened for sounds from Melody, but I couldn't hear any. After about half an hour the midwife came back out with something wrapped in a blanket and walked briskly away.

Then Michael called me in, and told me to clean Melody's face and hands with some wet wipes. She was just lying still, bleak and pale and somewhere else. I kept making soothing noises, and dabbing with this wipe, while Michael fished about in the hospital bag she'd brought. None of us spoke.

Then the door squeaked and we all jumped. It was the midwife and she was carrying the blanket. I think I might have flinched. I know Michael shot me a warning glance. 'Help her sit up,' said the midwife, so we pulled Melody into a sitting position, and the bundle was laid on the bed, across her lap. I thought she'd shy away, but it seemed as though she'd asked for the baby to be brought back. She picked it up, pulled back the material covering its face.

'Oh,' she said wonderingly.

Please don't make me look, I was praying, but she reached out and drew me in by the lapel of my shirt. I took a breath and lowered my eyes. And it was a baby's face I saw, peeping out. Tiny, really tiny and very red, but definitely the face of a baby. I think I let out a yelp, a kind of hiccuping sob.

'It's a girl,' whispered Melody. 'I want to call her Elizabeth.'

Michael moved round in his seat and I saw he had a camera with him. 'Mel,' he said gently. She angled the baby so he could get a proper view, and he fired off four, five, six photographs.

'The hospital told us to take pictures,' she said. 'Because, because — ' And there she'd broken down completely.

That hospital smell, the clanking of trolleys in the corridor, Melody's eyes full of bewildered pain. I would be in that room forever.

'Freya,' said Liv, into my ear. 'Frey. Freya.'

I was back on Wenlock Edge with the breeze

stirring my hair. A buzzard circled. Bluebells shimmered through the trees. Over the fields we'd crossed the grass was whorled into penny-sized tunnels where small rodents had forged their undercover runs. Nature thrummed with life, while Melody's baby was dead.

I scrambled to my feet, shouting into the wind.

'Why did she have to go and get pregnant anyway? There was no *need*. Everything was fine as it was.'

Behind me, silence.

'Tell me that was awful of me. Tell me that was an awful thing to say.'

I turned and saw Liv rock herself forward onto her hands and knees, then stand up stiffly.

'I hate babies,' I said. 'I hate people being pregnant and getting married and making . . . upheavals. I hate the way you can be in a shop and everyone's cooing over a pram, going 'ahh' at some snotty toddler. It's not some great achievement. But you'd think it was, you'd think it was like climbing Mount bloody Everest. And then when things go wrong — I hate being dragged into the drama. And there always is a drama. It's like you're waiting for a bomb to go off. It's like shrapnel flying.'

Liv's eyes, grey and steady.

'I'm *never* having children. Or getting married. I don't want to be a part of any of that. I might go live on an island somewhere. In a Scottish croft, on my own.'

'You'd be missed.'

If I could have clicked my fingers and been

192

five hundred miles away, I'd have done it. 'I don't care.'

'I do.'

Way below us the fields were smooth and velvety, even the newly ploughed ones. Cloud shadows crossed the landscape, chasing over yellow rape and reddish soil and mossy-dark hedgerows. We stood for a long time, watching.

Liv said, 'It's funny being so high up. It gives me a sense of power.'

'Does it? Makes me feel the opposite. That we're dots in a massive landscape, worth nothing. Worth as much as a beetle.'

'You're worth a lot more than that to me, Frey.'

'Perhaps we're all just beetles, scurrying about, and we don't realise it.'

'Perhaps we are.'

★ ★ ★

On our way back down to the car park Liv was delighted to find a badger sett. Round the base of a big oak the banks had been dug up and scraped, the sandy soil smoothed and trampled, paths worn through the grass.

'How do you know it's not just a gang of chunky rabbits?'

'The entrances to the sett: see how wide they are? Badger holes are badger-shaped. Oh, and look, Frey, this is a latrine.'

'You don't say.'

She bent to examine the massive pile of sloppy poo. 'It's a significant one. Can you see the older droppings underneath?'

'Only if you wave the flies away.'

'This badger's been eating fruit. You can make out the pips. And insect cases. Are those little bones?' She edged round, squinting to get a better view. Her face was alight, she couldn't help herself.

'What are badgers, exactly?'

'They're mammals.'

'Yeah, but what group do they belong to? They're not rodents, they're not canids.'

'They're mustelids. Like stoats and weasels, mink, otters, ferrets. Pine martens. Polecats.'

'Why are they so fat, then?'

'I don't know. Because their legs are too short to do aerobics.' She straightened again and I noticed her hand go up to her breast automatically and pat the place where the lump had been. Something about the movement disturbed me, reminded me of how anxious she was before the op. I thought we'd passed that stage.

'Liv?'

'Hmm?' Now she was peering at some animal hairs caught in the barbed-wire fence.

'When are you due to get the lab results?'

'I've had them.' She carried on fingering the little tuft of fur. 'They called me in when you were staying at Melody's.'

'And?'

'We'll talk about it later. It can wait for another day. It's not important.'

'Mum!'

'No, I'm not laying anything else on you just

at the moment. You've had enough with Melody. Melody must come first.'

For God's sake, I wanted to shout. *It's not a bloody competition.* 'But now I'm really panicking. You have to tell me.'

She sighed. 'It was only the results of the re-grading. Turns out I will need chemo.'

'What? Why didn't you ring me?'

'You were in Nantwich. I didn't want to drag you away. Geraint went up to the hospital with me, so I wasn't alone.'

Bet he was some bloody use, I thought. 'And?'

Finally she left the wire and turned to face me. 'Well, they've had a good old look and re-graded the tumour. Which, in a way, is a relief. For once it's just, 'This is what we're going to do; lie back and let us get on with it.''

'When do you start?'

'Next week.'

'Jesus.' So ignorant, I wasn't even sure what chemo was. Some kind of beam or ray? A tablet? Did they inject you? 'I'll go with you, keep you company while you have it.'

'That would be nice.'

The wind stirred the grass, the leaves. She linked her arm through mine and started to walk me back down the hill. Part of me wanted to wrench free and yell at her for making me feel so guilty. I was angry, too, that the cancer stuff wasn't gone and Liv wasn't free just to be my mother, safe and normal. There seemed to be no refuge anywhere.

'Listen,' she went on, holding the kissing gate for me. 'I've had a space to mull things over, and this is where I am: the operation's done and healed, the tumour's out, my lymph nodes were clear. So that's the biggest part over. The chemo's only mopping up. Twelve sessions over eight months, and that'll be it. I can draw a line under it all.'

'If it wasn't for me, you'd already have drawn your line.'

'Frey. Don't be ridiculous! I should be *thanking* you. That day they told me it was cancer, my brain just scrambled. I was useless. But you, you took charge, you made the doctors check again. And you were right. I look back, and you were terrific. Eight months,' she said, 'eight months to get through. The fight with the cancer's over, now I'm battling chemo. And the sooner we start, the sooner we finish.'

'Your hair?'

'It's only hair, for goodness' sake. Dead cells.' She teased out a few strands, wound them round her finger. 'When it grows back, I might go for a new style. Something shorter. Then it wouldn't get in the way when I'm doing my surveys.'

The thought of her hair going made me feel more wobbly than anything to do with the cancer so far. Liv *was* her hair. That spread of sandy grey across her shoulders and down her back, wavy hanks of it sliding forward each time she bent over her keyboard or stooped to examine some ditch. It was her most striking feature. It set her apart from other mums her age. Witchy, I'd heard Melody call her; Wild Woman; Dances-with-Voles.

Voices from the time before.

I remembered, out of nowhere, Liv taking me out of primary school to go get a tooth drilled, and how she'd coaxed me with promises of treats afterwards — a Beanie mouse, an extra bedtime chapter of *Kittens in the Kitchen*, a go with the new Longworth trap. I longed to conjure up something to make things better for her, the way she used to for me. What a comfort it must be to hold that sort of power. Perhaps that was why people had children, for that brief opportunity of fixing someone's world.

An ache in my jaw made me aware of how I was holding myself, my teeth gritted, my shoulders tense. Against me, though, Liv felt relaxed. We made our way through fields of cowslips and dandelions, down lanes edged with wood anemones.

On the last stretch down to the car park she said, 'Anyway, Alan R is going to run the Meres and Mosses events this summer for me, and Veronica's logging the invertebrate sightings.'

'That's good,' I said. The world might be ending, but if the bog insects were being catered for, all was well.

'It is, isn't it? Small, good things.'

And we carried on walking, two human specks in the middle of the great uncaring hillside, trying to brace ourselves against what was to come.

★　★　★

I'd been planning a risotto for tea, so I took myself straight to the kitchen. Lying inside the tray of the weighing scales was the corpse of a stoat in a clear plastic bag. So far, so Geraint. Yet I could also tell by the sizzling sound and smell of meat that there was proper food in the oven. Apparently he'd got himself together enough to stick in three potatoes and a chicken.

'You star,' said Liv. Amazing how little you have to do to win praise if your default setting's Idle Bugger.

I had no appetite, so I took my plate upstairs where I could dispose of the contents discreetly.

Then, instead of eating, I lay on my bed with my earphones in, listening to Keane. I stared at the ID chart of harlequin ladybirds and let the memory come of a biology GCSE paper Nicky and I both sat, and how upset she'd been as we walked out of the exam room. 'I missed out a whole question at the end,' she moaned. 'Mum's going to kill me.'

'Your coursework's good, though. Even if you totally cocked up, you'd still scrape a pass,' I'd told her.

She'd shaken her head. 'Mum doesn't work like that. It's top marks or big trouble.' And she'd slouched away, looking miserable. Sometimes I've blamed Liv for not pushing me harder, but would I really want someone like Joan Steuer standing behind me, prodding me in the back every time I dared take a breather?

That made me think of the phone call I'd made from my hall of residence, sitting on the narrow bed in that sweltering box of a room, to tell Liv university wasn't for me and I was jacking in the course. Expecting her to blow up, or complain; dreading it, but being obscurely disappointed when she went, 'So do you want me to come and pick you up?' It's true she did say a few times afterwards it was a shame, but never with much conviction. Nicky was too loyal to comment beyond a regretful shrug. Melody was just pleased to have me back. Only Michael voiced any real criticism. 'Who the hell are you to stick your oar in?' I'd asked him, outraged. 'Your friend, I hope,' he'd said.

I thought of a summer fête at the high school, how Nicky and I had been manning refreshments when we spotted some Year 10 bitch sniggering at Liv's hippy dress. I'd filled a jug of squash and ice, and Nicky had shimmied through the crowds with it till she was near enough to tip it down the girl's back. Even now I could recall the screaming and swearing, Nicky holding perfectly her expression of innocent surprise.

I thought of a common newt I'd squashed with a planter in our garden, and how Liv had taken the floppy body between her fingers, like a shred of slimy meat, and somehow revived it so it swam off into the depths of our pond, with only a shudder.

The memory flicked to Oggy's hedgehog, then to the Red Lion where Oggy sat at a table in the saloon bar boasting he could take the metal cap off a beer bottle with his teeth. It was me who'd run him to casualty afterwards, at near-midnight in freezing fog.

I thought of planting crocuses round the base of Colin's Special Tree. And I remembered, the day after I turned eleven, Liv taking delivery of a tank of harvest mice and installing them in the front room. This was the nearest I ever got to owning a pet ('I'd have bought you a pet,' Melody used to say. 'If you'd been mine.') The mice were part of a captive breeding programme, but after a certain number of litters they were laid off. Their cute factor was huge: eyes like black map pins, curling tails like monkeys', tiny tiny claws which they wrapped around the grass stalks. Everything perfectly miniature, a miracle of nature.

Like Melody's baby's face.

That image I pushed away quickly. I wanted to remember comforting things, like Liv bringing me Horlicks with brandy when I'd broken up with Oggy. But the memory slid out of reach and became Liv straight after her operation, weak and groggy and talking garbage while Geraint sat by the hospital bed and picked at his thumbnail. I struggled for another, something nice from when I was very small. A Christmas, a birthday, maybe. Recollections half formed — a clump of fly agaric under our birch; Liv telling me to sit on the riverbank and make a noise like an apple. Once, when we went to get her wellies from the greenhouse, there'd been a mouse inside one of them and I'd actually wet myself laughing. But these times seemed far away, like scenes from a programme I'd watched on television once.

Why don't we notice when we're happy? Liv says that as part of the bedtime routine when she was little, her grandma used to make her tick off all the good parts of the day and thank God for them. I reckon there ought to be a secular version of this, public information films reminding us to count our blessings. They could stick them on the end of the National Lottery Draw. *You may not have won a fortune, but, hey, at least you've got food and shelter, which is more than millions in the world have.* That way, more of us would start each day grateful to have escaped disaster —

Suddenly, out of the corner of my eye, I saw the screen of my mobile light up. I wrenched off my earphones and made a dive for the phone.

Nd 2 C U. Rd Ln 8? N, said the text.

On my wy, I messaged back.

Nicky would save me from myself, for tonight.

★ ★ ★

We used to come to the Red Lion all the time when we were in the sixth form. Friday and Saturday nights for definite, and some lunchtimes too. It was our unofficial common room.

In the corner sat the fruit machine where John Jones, previously unluckiest boy in the school, had stuck in a random quid and won fifty back, golden coins sliding out in a fantastic cascade. The win made him a bit of a hero and the kudos stuck, enabling him to get a girlfriend and invitations to parties and an amnesty on planting weird objects in his locker. Amazing how a single incident can reverse your entire cred.

The bar top was the same one Neil Froggat ricocheted off, after boasting Lily Peterson had given him a blow job in the car park and earning a fist in the face off her brother. The dartboard Oggy used nearly every night back then was still on the wall, despite a recent spruce-up by the brewery. And opposite was the hearth where Sasha Morris once attempted a strip after persons unknown, but likely to be Oggy's friend Tyler Dawes, spiked her drink with about a litre of vodka. The tacky carpet in the girls' loos had gone, but the cracked mirror was still up, as was the condom machine with the smiley-faced dick felt-tipped on the side. I must have spent thousands of hours in those toilets, gulping water out of the tap and bitching and mopping tears and tormenting my hair.

'Let's get one thing clear from the off: I don't want to talk about my family,' I said to Nicky as we pushed through the swing door into the public bar. 'I just want to hear about weddings and films and clothes and reality TV and any kind of general crap you want to throw at me.'

She nodded. 'Let me get the first round in, then. I won't feel so guilty about bending your ear after.'

I went and bagged our usual place, near the back entrance. A couple of tables away sat a crowd including Denny Fletcher, who I'd dated briefly in between interludes with Oggy. I sat up in my seat and tried to catch his eye but he didn't take me on. Already he was getting paunchy, even though he'd been skinny at school. In those days, though, he was on the athletics team and training every weekend. Now he worked behind a desk at the builders' merchants off the ring road. As I watched he put his arm round a girl with long dark hair and rosy cheeks. I vaguely recognised her but couldn't dredge up a name.

'Marie Evans,' said Nicky, when she returned with our drinks. 'Don't you remember? Got so drunk at Kipper Harrison's eighteenth, she went home in someone else's shoes. And knickers, if you believe the rumours.'

Marie saw me looking, and smiled. Then she spoke to Denny, who turned and nodded. My eyes strayed to her stomach.

'Shit, she's pregnant,' I said to Nicky.

'She's married. They got married last year.'

'You never told me.'

'I did. I think I did. I only know because I saw it in the *Herald*. Are you bothered?'

'Of course not. God, he was as exciting as a flatfish. She's welcome to him. And all his little fry.'

I was smiling, but the swollen belly had been a shock. I didn't want anyone to be pregnant right now.

'And John Jones is married,' she went on. 'He lives in America now, has a job in Washington. Tyler Dawes got hitched but he's in prison.'

'What for?'

'Not sure. Affray, maybe.'

'How do you hear all this stuff?'

She shrugged. 'Local papers. Dad. Dad's on so many committees all the gossip passes his way eventually.'

I thought, that'll be me, I'll be a story doing the rounds. *Did you hear about Freya Hopwood? Running between two mothers, both* of them a mess. *She's the girl who had to leave the Fox Howl camping trip early because she was homesick. What's her job these days? Didn't she go to university?*

I said, 'How's Christian?'

Nicky frowned. 'Busy this week. They're filming psychic phenomena in the Norfolk area. He's not due back for days.'

'Bad luck.'

'Oh, I don't know. I don't know if it is.' She pushed her glass away from her and leaned back in her chair. 'We've been getting on each other's nerves. Sniping about the wedding plans. About his bloody mother. About mine. You know how it is when you're organising a wedding.'

'Yeah,' I said, even though I didn't.

'Everyone has an opinion and no one's prepared to compromise.'

'I can't imagine Christian sniping.'

'Believe me, Frey, he can.'

'Well, I expect he's under a lot of pressure.'

'Aren't we all,' she burst out. 'I've had a gutful, for a start!'

It wasn't like Nicky to raise her voice, especially not in public.

'Is it — have you had a row?'

'Not a row. Not outright.' She swept her hair back off her face in a gesture that was both cross and weary. 'You know, it's not even really him. It's his stupid family and his mental mother. All of a sudden Corinne wants her local church, now, not mine, because apparently there's a tradition going back a hundred and fifty years of Bliaises marrying there. I told her, it's a bit late

204

in the day for that, isn't it? You never thought to mention it right at the start? Not that it would have made a difference if she had. I mean, it's always the bride's home church you use, isn't it? And anyway, Mum's been a member of St Alkmund's for years, she'd have had a fit if we'd even talked about holding the service anywhere else. Plus, how are we supposed to ferry everyone all the way to Pinewoods for the reception? It's a stupid idea from start to finish. The trouble is, historically Christian's lot have married locals, so it's only ever been a hop between parishes and no one's minded. This time they're having to travel all the way up to the grim north — '

'Grim Midlands.'

'Everything above Banbury's north as far as they're concerned.'

I said, 'She can't be serious. She can't expect you to shift everything at this late stage.'

'She isn't. It's just a power trip, a last-ditch attempt to assert the Bliaise authority. If they'd only ignore her! But she twitches her little finger, and the rest of them jump.'

'Your mum's met Corinne, hasn't she?'

'Once, in Tewkesbury, for a Sunday lunch. I thought it had gone OKish. And they talk on the phone, in fact I know who it is straight away because Mum puts on this ludicrous lah-di-dah voice as though she's in conference with the Queen. Corinne must laugh her socks off.'

'Your dad and Julian?'

'Mostly they've ignored each other. During the meal Julian read a newspaper, which I could tell Mum thought was incredibly rude but she didn't dare say anything. Oh, and he used the F-word about his scallops, twice. That nearly sent her into a blue fit. There she'd been beforehand, tying herself in knots in case she used the wrong cutlery, and then Julian turns out to have a mouth on him like a docker.' She grinned weakly. 'It was very upper-class swearing, though. Sort of, 'fahhk', 'fahhking'. None of your nasty working-class vowels.'

Across the bar, Marie was pushing her chair back while Denny was poised, solicitous, to help her out of her seat. I thought how nice it must be for someone to be that aware of what you needed.

I made a sympathetic face. 'And you don't feel Christian's giving you enough support?'

'I don't, no! I *asked* him to come up this weekend so we could talk it through, get him to see he has to be on my side, and he said he couldn't because of the filming. But I don't think the filming's got anything to do with it. I think that's an excuse. He's frightened of her. And what kind of marriage is it going to be if his mother's always on our case?'

'Have you spoken to your mum about it?'

'You must be joking. She's the last person I could confide in.'

I thought of Joan, her blue-toned dresses and her sturdy bosom, her flower vases and matching tableware and frilly valances. Yet she and Nicky had seemed close when we were younger.

'Don't you understand?' said Nicky. 'They're coming at me from all sides. This wedding's like my mother's happiest day ever. She won't allow anything to jeopardise it. All that crawling to the secretary of the Ladies' Society, all the lunches she hosts for the English Heritage Book Club, those fine-cuisine courses she goes on: this is her pay-back. Her only daughter's about to marry a toff. There's a danger she'll expire with excitement.'

'That's a good thing, though? I mean that you're bringing her so much joy.'

'No. Because after this it'll be something else. She'll never let up. Once I've bagged Christian, and had the most perfect wedding ever recorded, then she'll be on at me to produce a perfect child. Then a perfect sibling. Then places at the best kindergarten, prep school, high school, university. It'll never stop. I know. I've had years of it already.'

Her shoulders drooped.

'Aw, Nicky. I don't know what to advise. I wish I did. But what do I know about fiancés and weddings and in-laws? You might as well be asking me about calculus. I wouldn't know where to start.'

She glanced up. 'Don't worry, I'm not looking for solutions. I wanted to off-load, that's all.'

Denny and Marie came back from wherever it was they'd been, hand in hand. He guided her into her seat and sat down opposite, all the while never taking his eyes off her.

'At least you've done something with your life,' I said. 'Unlike me. Miss Dead-end.'

'Don't be daft.'

'Miss Job-with-no-prospects, Miss Still-living-at-home-with-her-mum. Miss Single.'

'The nursery suits you. Better than some stodgy office. You like being outdoors and making things grow, rolling along with the seasons.'

'All those science A levels I'm not using.'

'OK, think about this, Frey. How would your mums have managed this year if you'd been at the other end of the country, holding down some research post in a lab or something?'

Nicky took a long drink. Then she said, 'Michael's got the measure of you.'

'Oh, Michael. Yeah, he always knows everything.'

'He knows *you*. He once told me you were one of these people who works on a slow burn. One day you'd go whoosh and take off, like a damp firework everyone had given up on.'

'So now I'm a soggy Roman candle?'

She grinned. 'I really like Michael. He's straightforward, blunt.'

'He is that, yes.'

'I mean, you're lucky to have found him. I bet you can tell him anything, can't you? He's got that levelness about him. I could do with a male friend like that.'

The baby's face flashed before my eyes again. 'He's all wrapped up with Melody right now.'

Across the bar, Marie was laughing, her cheeks shiny and plump with health. I didn't dare let my focus rest on her rounded shape.

'Anyway,' I said, 'I'm quite taken with that image of a rogue rocket. I'll be holding onto it.'

'You do that.'

We finished our drinks, ordered more. I stood

at the bar, calm amid all the chatter and movement and light, all the planning and debate and flirting and fret.

You lot, you want to watch out, I thought. *I could go off in your faces at any moment.*

★ ★ ★

After Nicky and I had parted ways, I took myself home via the narrow streets round the back of the post office so I could walk past Oggy's. For old times' sake, I told myself. Because this route was only a minute longer than going via the high street; because I was bored and a bit drunk and it felt nice to walk alone in the clear air of the night.

Once I got to the railings by the house next door I halted. There was a light on in Oggy's top-floor flat. For some reason, that cheered me up. It was a little beacon of normality in a dark, confused world. I remembered my first visit here, how proud and strangely shy he'd been, showing off the odds and ends his mum had donated and the items he'd picked up off the market or scrounged. I'd been impressed, though looking back a lot of his 'refurbishment' was stuff like draping a duvet cover over the knackered sofa, or sticking down a carpet sample over the hole in the lino by the kitchen door. Decorating for him meant Blu-tacking posters over the stains on the wall. Really, his flat was just his teenage bedroom translated.

Later, when he got his rep job, he did make a stab at proper decorating. We weren't together then, but I know he had a carpet fitted and he re-painted the woodwork himself. The last time I was there the place had been fairly tidy and, though there was still a definite junk-shop feel to the furniture, and I doubt if he could have laid his hands on more than two matching plates, it wasn't a bad effort for a single guy without a clue.

God, we'd spent some evenings up there, creating disgusting cocktails, telling rude jokes, providing alternative commentaries to crap TV shows. One time I cooked an enormous lasagne and Nicky and some weedy guy came round to share it and we ended up playing Shag, Marry, Shoot. And there was a birthday party where a bloke with one of those very thin beards had a good go at chatting me up, and Oggy threw a glass at the wall out of temper.

I remembered nights kissing on his sofa by the light of his electric fire, and others listening to him try to pick out *Badge* and *Sunshine of your Love* on an old acoustic he'd blagged off a mate. I remembered him saying no one cooked chilli as good as me, and the afternoon I was hunting for some paracetamol and I came across a drawer full of my cards and notes which he'd kept. Oggy was my formative years; my formative years were Oggy.

I wondered what his flat looked like these days. Would there be a strange toothbrush in the bathroom, Tampax in the cupboard, flimsies drying on the radiator? I'd had toothbrush rights, once.

All of a sudden I was seized with such a

210

longing to be up there, behind his stripy curtains, sharing a beer and a laugh and a cuddle. Our last dating session, I'd helped him begin a stop-frame animation called *Kitchen Wars: the Mightiest Battle of All*, fruit versus veg, with tomatoes changing sides halfway through. There were weapons — asparagus spears, carrot batons, sprouts played the part of cannonballs — and individual bouts e.g. melon versus cauli for the heavyweights, apples versus beetroot in the medium class. I carved crocodile jaws out of a parsnip, and he'd been particularly impressed. Had he ever finished the film? Had anyone else shaped his root veg for him?

There was the muffled clunk of a door round the back of the building, then the sound of footsteps down the flat's side access path. I panicked in case it was someone come to tell me off for behaving like a stalker — or worse, Oggy's girlfriend. How incredibly sad would I have looked? But it wasn't her, and it wasn't a stroppy neighbour come to say they'd rung the police. It was Oggy. He was in his slippers, and holding some kind of parcel at arm's length.

His head dipped uncertainly as he squinted against the glare of the street light. 'Freya?'

'I was passing,' I said feebly.

'Yeah? And I was binning some stinky fish. It must be fate.' He flipped open the lid of the wheelie bin and dropped the parcel in. 'How you doing?'

'Ah, you know.'

'Uh huh.' I watched him brush his palms together, then sniff them. 'Phew. I'm going to have to fumigate the place. Or buy one of those poncey perfumed candles. Mackerel and lavender, mmm.'

'Sardine and vanilla.'

He moved towards me. 'Are you pissed? You look a bit out of it.'

I shook my head. 'How's Hogden? I haven't heard from him this week.'

'He's had a lot on. Fleas, mostly.'

'Do you really see him every night?'

'Nah. He hasn't shown up for about a month or so. I reckon he might have moved on to a better area. Higher quality slugs, less dog shit.'

'But your texts.'

'I hate to break it to you, Frey, but they weren't really from Hodgen.' He made a mock-contrite face. 'I'm sure he's fine, though. He's probably romancing some lady hog as we speak. Hey, how *do* hedgehogs screw?'

'The female flattens her spines so the male can climb on without getting impaled.'

'Just as well. Ouch, otherwise. Might end up with a nasty little prick.'

'Nature always finds a way.'

Oggy stepped closer. I caught a faint whiff of fish. 'We could go look for hedgehogs now, if you wanted.'

'Where?'

He cast his eyes upwards, towards his lighted window.

'In your flat?'

'You never know. There might be a little one hiding in a crevice somewhere.'

'What about your girlfriend?'

Oggy smiled and laid his finger on his lips.
'What about her, though?' I persisted.
'She isn't here.'
Then he stepped away and beckoned for me to
walk up the path.
And, like an idiot, I did.

Case Notes on: Melody Jacqueline Brewster

Meeting Location: 42, Love Lane, Nantwich

Present: Miss Melody Brewster, Mrs Abby Brewster, Mrs Diane Kozyra

Date: 2.30 p.m., 11/2/87

Began the session by explaining to Melody that the report on baby Fay has been accepted at panel. She seemed pleased and asked me what would happen next. I advised that she needed to be thinking of what kind of adoptive family she'd like, and what she wanted for her baby's future. She said she was frightened to picture anything too specific in case it didn't come off.

I reminded Melody that she'd wanted musical foster parents, so perhaps that was something she valued for Fay. After some thought she asked if we could get a house with a piano because she'd always wanted one but her mum said there wasn't room in their house. So we began a list which I've left with Melody in the hope she can add some ideas to talk about next time.

Before I left I spoke to Mrs Brewster without Melody present. I asked whether she thought her daughter was in better spirits. Mrs Brewster said that they were having a lot of rows over trivial incidents, and that Melody 'seemed able to be pleasant with everyone but her'. I advised her it would take time for Melody's emotional state to return to normal.

Next visit: 20/2/87   Signed: Diane Kozyra

A FRIDAY

June

'How's she doing?' I asked Michael as we drove out of the forecourt, on our way to Melody's.

'Bad,' he said. Then, 'Slightly better than she has been.'

'That's something.'

I knew how much he'd done for her since she'd lost the baby. At least two nights a week he'd been staying round at hers, to make sure she was eating and sleeping at proper times. As well as replacing the kitchen calendar, he'd contacted Joe both to fill him in and tell him to keep away; dropped notes through the neighbours' doors; spirited away her pregnancy books and magazines. Even gone online to unsubscribe her from all the New Mother forums and mailings she'd signed up for. 'I'd never have thought of that,' I said when he told me.

'We had to do it with Kim. Or rather, she had to do it.'

A memory of Melody from last summer, standing by the war memorial in town and applauding some scruffy busker. She was wearing a patchwork maxi skirt with a frill round the bottom, very gypsyish. I'd said to her, 'Please don't dance, not here.' And she'd done a little twirl just to wind me up.

'It's good she's back at work,' Michael was saying.

'Is she fit enough?'

'The doctors seem pretty pleased with her, physically. Just her mental state, that's what we need to watch. I warned her not to accept any pills if she was offered but they never suggested any. I think they've got stricter guidelines these days.'

We crossed the roundabout onto the A road. The hedges were lush, quivering with birds. The sky was an uninterrupted blue.

I said, 'I expect she's too busy to think much when she's in the shop.'

'That's right. And they're a nice bunch in there. Sympathetic, without being over the top. She can have hospital counselling if she wants. There's a group that meets up every month.'

'Can't imagine that'll be a barrel of laughs.'

'It's hardly meant to be. The question is, would it help?'

His tone was so snappy I blushed, turned my head and looked out of the window. *Why bother asking my opinion? You're so close to her, you tell me.*

Michael cleared his throat. I reached forward and turned the radio on.

'Sorry,' he said, after an interval of two songs. 'It's been, you know. Not much fun. Dealing with it. And I've had Kim round asking for money.'

'Did you give her any?'

'Some. Don't look at me like that, she had

nowhere else to go.'

'Wonder why. I hope she said thank you.'

'She posted a load of chopped-up photos through my letterbox. Anyway, enough of my social life. How are you?'

'Me?'

He shot me a glance. 'Yes, Frey. I'm asking how you're doing. What have you been up to?'

Everything sounded like a reproach. *What's been so urgent in your hectic lifestyle that you haven't had one hour in three weeks to pop round and see your birth mother?* 'I've been busy,' I said.

'Yeah?'

Don't mention Oggy; for God's sake don't say you've been seeing him again, even though this other girl's definitely still around, sometimes leaves messages on the answerphone when I'm there in his flat and it's the crappest way to behave, like I've no respect for her or for myself but oh, the relief of having somewhere to go to get away from all the shit that's going on, of having a bolt-hole, of having a laugh, of having a sex life again.

I said, 'I've been busy with the wedding, fittings and such. Nicky's on the phone every day, nearly. And I've been helping Liv. I went with her to choose a wig.'

Michael nodded, and I felt safe again. 'That must have been difficult for her.'

'The wig woman was a bit snotty. Liv had to show her proof that she was really entitled, when the chemo would start, what type of drugs she was having. Like anyone would fake cancer just

218

to scam an NHS wig. But she got an OK one, an ashy-blonde bob. It makes her look so different. Well, weird, because her face is the same. It's hard to describe.'

'She's started the chemo?'

'One session down, eleven to go.'

'How was that?'

'Boring, mainly. She had to sit in a room with big armchairs all round, and drips. What was freaky, though, was when the nurse first came with the bottle and she's handling it with rubber gloves because it's so toxic, and Liv leans over and says, 'That's going inside me!' But it doesn't hurt, apparently. You feel it creeping up your arm like cold water, and later on she said her throat felt tight, and she had a nasty taste in her mouth. Afterwards we went to the café and she had a peppermint tea. When she got home she went straight to bed.'

'I bet she was glad you were with her.'

'Yeah, I think so. Next time we'll take magazines and wildlife reports and puzzle books. We'll be better prepared.'

'Geraint could go along to some of the appointments.'

'He'll have to. I can't take every session off work. But you should have seen his face when I told him that. He looked sicker than Liv.'

'Some people do find it hard,' said Michael, and I briefly wanted to punch him.

'You don't *always* have to be fair.'

'OK, then. If you say so. I'll be a model of intolerance.' But he was grinning. We were back on track.

By the time we arrived at Love Lane, I'd worked myself up into a state of nerves. I didn't know how I was going to face her. I knew I shouldn't have left it so long.

'You go in first,' I told Michael.

Perhaps I was expecting the place to have been blasted apart by grief, but thank God everything looked normal. Melody herself was dressed soberly, in a long navy cardigan and an ankle-length black skirt, and she'd pulled her hair back into a simple ponytail which didn't really suit her. But her figure seemed back to its usual shape. She looked OK, at first glance.

'Freya!' she said, and the quaver of gratitude in her voice was like a knife through my guts.

I went to give her a shy hug. She clung to me so hard I could feel her heart beating. *What next?* I thought. *What do I say?*

'I'll make us a drink,' she murmured, detaching herself at last.

It was so odd to see her without all her jewellery and scarves. She wore no make-up, either, the first time in all our acquaintance I'd seen her without. When she walked ahead of me to the kitchen, it struck me she was moving differently, too: more deliberately, the way someone might step along an icy footpath.

'You sit down, I can sort it.'

'There's no milk, though,' she said hopelessly.

Michael tutted. 'You noodle, Mel. Why didn't you give me a ring? I could have picked some up on the way.'

'Shall I go out for some?' I asked.

'Nah. I'll nip up the road. I'll only be gone five minutes. You girls put your feet up, have a gossip.'

He was gone before I could protest. Melody went over to the sofa and sat down, waiting for me to join her.

I settled myself awkwardly at the other end. 'You look different. I've not seen you like, with no make-up on.'

The insides of her eyes were habitually lined with black kohl, but now I could see the naked wet pinkness of the rims. Stripped of mascara, her natural lashes were a gentle brown. Her cheeks and nose were more freckly than I'd realised, and her lower lip dry and flaky. It made her look shockingly young — easy just now to imagine the fifteen-year-old Melody — except for the faint crow's feet, the two small vertical lines between her brows. And the hard expression to the eyes and mouth: that was recent.

Examining her like this reminded me of Liv, the way I'd so recently stood behind her in the wig room and gazed into the mirror at the familiar face beneath the unfamiliar hair. Liv's lines were deeper, deep creases running between the sides of her nostrils and the corners of her mouth, crêpeyness at her neck, frown marks carved into her forehead from years of squinting after wildlife. I had no lines on my face yet, only a blank elasticity.

'It's good to see you, Frey. I thought you might have come before.'

'I texted every day.'

She gave a grudging nod.

'Mainly I've been helping Liv.'

Melody sniffed. 'She has Geraint to do that.'

'You've got Michael.'

'No, I haven't.'

'Excuse me, but who was that just walked out the door on a mission to refill your fridge?' I tried to keep my tone light, but she was so near the edge.

'It's *not* the same, Freya! I haven't 'got' him. I haven't got anyone. Michael's not mine. He's just around.'

I didn't dare speak.

'God, I'm sorry, I'm so sorry. I don't know what I'm saying.' She put her hands over her face, and when she took them away she looked stricken. 'I'm sorry about Liv, too. I really am. How is she?'

'She's sent you a letter, here. Plus she wanted me to give you this.' I reached into my bag and pulled out a white angora shrug Liv had bought off one of her hippy friends. 'It's knitted out of rabbit combings. The woman who made it breeds them, she's got hundreds. They're well cute. Feel how soft it is.'

Melody put out a hand and stroked the shrug gently, as though it were alive. I had a sudden memory of her spotting the model wasp nest hung up by our back door and asking if it was Liv's best hat.

'That's nice of her.'

'She said it was the nearest she could get to giving you a hug at the moment. She sends her love.'

'Tell her . . . thanks.'

In a series of painful movements, Melody dragged off the cardigan and pulled the shrug up over her arms. It looked strange and frivolous over her other clothes, but it clearly felt good because she kept tilting her head to feel the wool against her cheek.

'How is Liv?'

I took a breath, to consider. 'Tired. Funny about her food. She's eating raw green beans by the bucketful. Some book she's read — no, an article you sent, actually — about raising your white blood-cell count. So she sits in the corner, chomping.'

'Her hair?'

'All right for now, but she's been told she'll lose it soon.'

'That's bad.'

'Yeah. I'm on standby to cut it off when it starts to fall out.'

'You can wear these caps with ice in, I saw it in a magazine.' Melody cast about vaguely, as if the article might somehow manifest itself and float into her hand.

'She knows about those. They're supposed to protect the follicles. But they're pretty horrid to wear, and I think Liv just wanted to get on with the treatment. She's chosen a wig, though — amazing, really, there were all these wig blocks, like decapitated heads. Rows and rows of them, different shades. The NHS wig woman was saying you could style some of them, you know, with tongs and stuff, but Liv never styled her own hair so she's not going to start now, is she? In the end she went for a bob. Fairish. It looks OK.'

Melody's eyes had glazed over.

I said, 'Oh, and my bridesmaid's dress is ready, we've had the final fitting. It's vile. You'll laugh like a drain when you see me in it.'

She was watching a space on the wall where nothing was.

I said, 'Oggy sends his regards.'

I said, 'Do you fancy a glass of wine while we wait for the milk?'

She came back to me, her eyes re-focusing. She looked so lost and bewildered.

'Melody?'

'Do you know what my mother came out with last time she phoned? She said, 'You can always try for another.' As if babies are inter-fucking-changeable! As if, oh, that one doesn't matter. As if I can just put it behind me and move straight on. Forget her. Like she didn't count.'

'I'm sure Abby didn't mean it like that.'

'No understanding that my baby was a person, and that person's gone. You can't replace her! It doesn't matter that she wasn't full term. She was real, and now she's not here and I had to leave her in that hospital and go home alone. Abandon her. Do you know how that feels? All the things I'll never get to tell her. Cuddle her. And she's still lying there — '

I knew we were waiting for test results on the body. 'Michael says the hospital holds memorial services. You can plan a lovely one.'

'But you don't associate birth with death, do you? It's all wrong. And what I don't get is that everyone seems to be carrying on as normal, and I think, How? *How* can you be doing that? Just getting on with your lives? I blamed the house, you know,' she said, her gaze flicking upwards. 'I made Michael change the spare room back. I thought it was my fault because I'd been getting ready, *presuming*. I'd even bought a few little pieces, a knitted jacket off a market stall, a blanket, scratch mittens. Idiot! That was asking for trouble, wasn't it?'

'No,' I said.

'I must have done something wrong. There must be a reason.'

'I don't think so.'

'Never let yourself love anyone, Frey. They always get taken away from you in the end.'

I wondered where Michael was, hoped to God he'd be back soon.

'And then I step outside — ' She shivered. 'There are pregnant women everywhere, and babies and prams and toddlers. Every bloody woman in Nantwich seems to have a kid in tow, or be expecting. They come and stand behind you in the newsagent's, or the queue for the cash machine. They smile at you. It's like a slap in the face. Why my baby and not theirs? I know that sounds evil, but it's what goes through my head, I can't help it. So fucking *unfair*.'

At last, here was something I could identify with. 'Yeah, I've felt that too,' I began.

'No, no. You can't understand unless it's happened to you. It's one of those events — no one else gets it, at all. There's this huge, huge loss, and it separates you off from everyone.

You're completely on your own. It's like, it's like bleeding to death in the middle of a great flat desert.'

'Michael says there's a support group that meets at the hospital.'

Her eyes were wide and full of pain. She'd clasped her hands on her lap in a kind of beseeching gesture. '*Nothing* will help! Don't you get it? *Nothing's* going to bring Elizabeth back. That's all I want, and nothing else will do. All us bereaved mums can sit round and share our stories but the one thing I really need — '

The front-door key rattled in the lock, startlingly loud. Oh thank Christ, I thought. It's Michael, come to save me.

He stepped into the room and lowered a plastic bag onto the coffee table in front of us. As he bent forward, his hair fell across his eyes and when he straightened up he had to flick it out of the way with his fingertips. Watching, I felt a spasm of fondness, because I knew that gesture so well; it was part of him. And I thought about what Melody had been saying, how Michael wasn't anyone's, just himself. I wondered who he went to when he was fed up, or angry, or wanted to off-load. There must be someone. Maybe I'd ask him, on another day. Bog off, Frey, he'd probably say. Mind your own business.

He nodded at the bag. 'From Lindy next door.'

'What is it?' said Melody.

'Some comedy DVDs. A box set. She said she thought you'd find them funny.'

'Yeah, right. Because I'm so in the mood for laughter.'

'Oh, give them a go, Mel. People just want to help.' He nodded at the shrug. 'Nice cardi, by the way.'

I got up and followed him through to the kitchen, where I closed the door behind us and switched the kettle on. Under the rumble of its boiling I said, 'She's still in a state, isn't she?'

Michael blew out his breath in a long, disappointed sigh. 'I thought she was getting better. Better than she's been, anyway.'

What the hell scenes had he witnessed to make him think that?

'How long do you reckon it'll take for her to get over it?'

'As long as it takes. Ages. And there'll be good days and bad days.'

He picked at the milk bottle's plastic lid.

'Oggy was upset for months after his grandma died. At least a term.'

'What's Oggy got to do with anything?'

'Just saying.'

The plastic ring tore free and Michael unscrewed the cap. As it came loose, he glanced across at me. 'Oh, Frey. You're not back with him, are you?'

'It's none of your business who I go out with. Why are you always so judgemental?'

The kettle clicked off.

Michael sloshed near-boiling water into the mugs, then fished the tea bags out with his asbestos fingers and flung them into the sink. Tannin splattered up the steel sides and pooled round the plughole.

'More fool me. It's called caring. Or would you rather I didn't bother?'

He slopped the milk into the tea angrily, so that half of it spilled across the worktop.

'You've never liked Oggy.'

'No. Because he's a tosser.'

I didn't feel I could argue with that, so I took a mug and followed him out.

To our surprise, Melody was on her knees in front of the television, sliding a DVD into the player. 'Might as well,' she said, hauling herself back up and dropping against the sofa, her cheeks framed by a fuzz of angora. We sat down with her and she zapped the remote at the screen.

After a moment, cheery pizzicato music started up, and a graphic of floating, interlocking squares. 'Oh,' I cried, '*Coupling*! This show's brilliant. Haven't you seen it? No? Oh, you'll love it. It'll really take your mind off things.'

Perhaps, perhaps, perhaps, went the opening song.

The first shot showed two perky young women walking down a city street, chatting about boyfriends. The camera then cut to two fittish blokes making their way down a different street, discussing their girlfriends. It looked as though they were all converging on the same wine bar. One of the girls was very petite, like Melody, her clothes smart and chic, and that gave me an idea. By the window, draped across a footstool, was Melody's beloved Union Jack blazer. I longed to see her slip it on again, on her way out to the pub.

'Hey,' I said, speaking across the script. 'I've thought of something that might cheer you up.'

Both of them turned to look at me. In the back of my mind was Liv and the way she'd been so consoled by getting someone to supervise her bog insects.

I said, 'Obviously you're feeling pretty low right now, Mel, but there is a bright side. You'll be able to get back into your favourite jacket a whole lot sooner than anticipated. I mean, that's got to be good, yeah?'

There followed a hideous silence. The characters on the TV screen kissed and snarled and waved their arms about; their lips moved but their words had no meaning. Melody's face was frozen.

'What, though?' I said. 'What? What?'

Michael put his head in his hands. 'Nice one, Freya,' he said.

★   ★   ★

There is a bus between Melody's and Liv's, but it's actually easier to go by rail as Melody lives right near the station. A short, slow train comes out of Crewe and plods its way through Shropshire down to the South Wales coast, stopping at all points in between. Seconds after Melody fled upstairs, shedding long white angora hairs in her wake, I'd grabbed my coat and walked straight out the door. *Of course I wasn't saying the baby didn't matter. You're taking it the wrong way. I was only trying to cheer her up, you must see that.*

I crossed over the roundabout at the bottom of the road, passed the Railway Arms, and slipped through the station entrance to climb the old iron footbridge onto the Shrewsbury platform. At the top I halted. If I flung myself off, I might stand a chance of silencing the howls of indignation roaring round my brain. *I only want her to be her old self. Why is that so wrong? It might actually help her if she thought about getting back to normal.* The tracks below me gleamed, briars reached out pleadingly from the embankment. It had become a sweltering-hot day, prickly and close, asking for a thunder-storm. Let it pour down. Let it sweep me away, drown me, wash me up like roadkill on the side of some deserted lane. *You try and do a good turn and all that happens is you get beaten up for it.*

The other side of the station was dotted with commuters: a man and his guide dog, a woman and two fighting kids, a Goth girl, a backpacker, a couple snogging. *You wouldn't judge me, would you?* I asked them silently. I was never going to speak again; I'd go home and superglue my lips together. *I just want to get away from this extended bloody family. You're more trouble than you're worth. As if I needed any more drama in my life! I wish I'd never contacted you, never got involved with any of it. We were OK, me and Liv. That social worker was right, it was too much to take on so young. I should have left well alone. Why should I be held to account? Who are you to judge me?*

Rapid footsteps coming up the bridge,

Michael's face appearing over the top step. 'Freya! Wait. Don't go like this.'

I turned away from him.

'Please, Frey, wait. Mel's not herself. What she's been through, the slightest comment cuts her to the bone.'

'And that's my fault?'

'No, of course it isn't.'

'See, this is why I kept away. I'm no good with these situations where you can't do anything practical to make it better. I haven't the skill to deal with them. I only make them worse.'

Four hundred metres away the front face of an engine rounded the bend. The people on the platform below began to shuffle and pick up their bags. Michael grasped my upper arm to stop me walking away.

'That's not true. Look, just come and have a coffee, straighten things out. I can't bear for us to part this way.'

'You need to get back to Melody,' I snapped. 'I suppose you'll go round telling everyone now the stupid thing Freya said.'

'Why would I? Why would you think that?'

'Oh, I don't know. Maybe the murderous look you gave me before she ran off in tears. Look, I'm sorry, all right? Obviously it was the most idiotic thing anyone's ever said in the history of the world, and I wish I could cut my own tongue off. But I can't, so I'll stay out of your way instead. Less painful for everyone.'

'No, Frey.'

'Yes. Now excuse me, I have a train to catch. I

promised my *mother* I'd be back by five.' I wrenched myself free and set off towards the far stairs.

'Please!'

The syllable came out like a yelp. I hesitated. Michael was not one to lose control, especially in a public place.

'*What?*'

'You know, I said something to Kim once.'

'How do you mean?'

'After she miscarried. I was trying to cheer her up.'

'Go on.'

'I've never admitted this to anyone. I told her that at least if there was no baby on the way, we'd be able to afford to go on a decent holiday. I wasn't thinking. I genuinely thought it would make her feel better.'

He stood there in the middle of the bridge, his eyes screwed against the sunlight. For the first time I could see grey flecks in the hair at his temples.

'Was she upset?' I asked, like a fool.

'She went for me with a barbecue fork. Yes, she was upset. I do understand, Freya. In these kind of situations you want to help and you can't find the right words, so you end up saying the wrong ones.'

'Melody doesn't understand.'

'She will. She's out of her mind right now. But she will.'

'She hates me.'

'No, she doesn't.'

'Can I go now?'

He hung his head. I took two paces, then ran for the train.

* * *

The weather broke as the train passed through Wrenbury. Suddenly we were driving into lashing rain, the windows assaulted by solid sheets of running water so that you could no longer see out. The countryside was a green blur and the carriage a gloomy, rattling box beneath the angry sky. Just my luck if we were hit by lightning, or derailed by a burst canal. Some of the other passengers looked agitated, but right then I didn't care whether I lived or died. My brain was in overdrive.

In the past I'd had this vague idea of family as a sort of web with me in the centre, surrounded, supported. Now I understood it was nothing so passive. Being part of a family was more like one of those platform video games Nicky and I used to play, a rolling program of dodging, leaping, reaching, reacting, climbing, shooting and point-scoring.

You can't understand unless it's happened to you, Melody had said, and she was right. When I thought of the baby I felt upset and freaked, but I didn't get that overwhelming sense of loss she obviously did. Those memories of hospital I wanted to block out, not dwell on them; couldn't understand why she insisted on reliving the experience over and over. Perhaps there was something wrong with me. Was a late miscarriage as bad as nearly losing your mother? That was all

I had room for, grief- and fear-wise. Not my fault. Yes, my fault. What had I said? The words went round once more, meaning less and less.

I gave up brooding and rang Liv because I needed to hear a friendly voice. Instead I got Geraint.

'Your mate's here,' he said.

'Who?'

'Nicola.' He sounded as if further speech would choke him.

'Oh,' I said. 'I'll be home in twenty minutes.'

The train pulled up at our tiny unmanned station and I stepped out into a monsoon haze. I nipped through the gate, scooted down the side of the car park, crossed the road and made my way along the top edge of the council estate to the public footpath that leads through fields to the end of our street.

Melody always laughs at my summer gear, but there are occasions when the kind of clothes I wear really come into their own. The swampy grass and puddles I was forced to splash through now were no match for my Doc Martens; my sweat-top hood was pulled up round my face, and my camouflage jacket zipped to the neck. I might have been a touch warm, but I was dry.

I walked fast, with my hands in my pockets and my head down, forging into the wall of rain. I was going at such a pace, in fact, that I almost ran into the thin little figure coming in the opposite direction. Just in time I skidded to a halt and lifted my hood, to see Nicky, coatless, doing a good impression of a drowned rat.

'What the hell are you doing out here?' I shouted.

She put her hand to her face and tried to wipe some of the water away, a pointless action. Her hair was plastered to her head, her T-shirt clung rudely to her boobs, and her pale capri pants were splashed to the knee with mud. Her canvas shoes looked to be disintegrating.

'I couldn't wait,' she gasped.

'What's the matter? Oh, fuck, is something wrong with Liv?'

'No,' she said, and the word was like a gulping sob. 'It's Christian.'

More tragedy: he'd been run over by a lorry; he'd revealed a terminal illness; he'd finally flipped and committed matricide.

'Dear God, what? Is he hurt?'

'No, but I wish he was!'

She stood there in the pouring rain, her face furious and excited.

'Tell me, Nicky.'

'The wedding's off. Off, just like that. Mum's in a complete state, doesn't know whether to phone all her friends or draw the curtains and go into purdah. Doesn't know whether to blame me or him or Corinne or herself. Dad's threatening all sorts. It's hell. I had to come to yours or I'd have thrown something through a window. Myself, possibly. Meanwhile we don't know for certain who needs phoning, because Corinne's got all the paperwork and Mum daren't call her. Even the spare room's full of wedding regalia. It's wherever I look, Frey, I can't escape.'

'I don't believe it.'

'Me neither. Oh, God.' Her teeth had begun to chatter, though I don't think it was with cold. I wondered whether she might be in shock.

'Let's get you inside, at least,' I said, taking her hand.

Together we half ran up the slope that formed the edge of the field, and then down the other side onto the cycle path and the street below. Water was coursing down the gutters; our feet squelched as they slapped the pavement. At last I was hauling her up the drive and fumbling for my front-door key.

We practically fell into the hall, shaking ourselves like dogs. Liv appeared, wearing the kaftan she uses as a dressing gown. 'I've put towels on the stairs ready for you. You know, I told her not to go, but she wouldn't wait.'

'Come upstairs,' I said, tugging Nicky's sleeve.

'Do you want me to pop your clothes over the radiator?' asked Liv.

''S no bother, I can do them. Come on, Nicks.'

We thumped up to my room, shutting the door noisily behind us. While she towelled herself down I hunted out spare socks and leggings for us both. It felt as though we'd gone back in time, somehow, and were teenagers once more. God knows we'd sat in here often enough over the years, discussing break-ups and boyfriends, and every one deadly serious. There was her crush on Lucas Moffat which burned right through the autumn term, only to end with him kissing Imogen Styles at the school Christmas disco. There was Davy

Morgan who she knew she needed to finish with because of his insane clinginess, but didn't dare in case he did himself a mischief and named her in his farewell note. There was Rhod Williams who seemed at first to be a completely brilliant, level kind of guy, but who turned out to be seeing a thirty-two-year-old divorcee behind Nicky's back. She'd spilt it all out to me, against a soundtrack of Oasis or the Sneaker Pimps or Mansun or Garbage or Space. Always the end of the world, except it wasn't. Me and Oggy, me and Denny, me and Oggy, angst to infinity. Don't you wish sometimes you could go back and give yourself a bloody good shake?

'How did it happen, Nicky?'

'I don't know. That's the stupid part.' She finished folding her wet clothes, placed them on the end of the bed next to her. 'One minute we were discussing table plans, well, arguing, because Corinne wanted about ninety per cent of the high table reserved for her family and I said that wasn't fair — and the next Chris was going, 'What are we doing?' So I said — you know, not really thinking — 'Perhaps we shouldn't be getting married right now,' and he said, 'No, I don't think we should.' And he walked out. I thought he'd come back inside after he'd had some fresh air, it was so bloody hot, only when I looked out of the front-room window, his car had gone. That's when I knew it was serious.'

'Fuck. And he hasn't been in touch since?'

'He sent me a text saying we should meet up

next week to 'sort things out'. I don't know what he means by that.'

'Can't you go down and tackle him?'

'He's filming in Dumfries till Tuesday.' Her face was still shiny and damp. I could tell she didn't know whether to risk being hopeful or not.

'So he said you shouldn't be getting married 'right now'. That's only postponing it, yeah?'

'Do you think? God, Freya, my head's all over the shop. And my mum's gone absolutely mental. She came in with a cup of tea for us and when he wasn't there it was, 'Why didn't he come and say goodbye?' and then, 'Is everything all right?' and then 'You said *what?*' And then it was like someone had died. Weeping and wailing, phoning my dad to tell him to leave work early. That's why I had to come here. I must have looked a fright because Geraint offered me brandy.'

'I'd have kept it quiet if I were you.'

'You think I don't know that? But Mum's — urrgghh. She winkles it out of you. I've never been able to keep any secrets from her. She just keeps on and on till she wears you down. I mean, would Liv ever have read your diary?'

'Even if I had one, she'd never have found it under all the junk,' I said. This was true. When I was a kid, the upstairs of our house in particular used to be filthy. Every window sill was a graveyard for bluebottles and micro moths; the cobwebs that hung from the light fittings were fat and furred as wool. But then cleaning was so dull in comparison with setting up a bat detector or installing a pond cam. 'To be fair, though, I could have left a diary wide open on the table and Liv wouldn't have read it. She's pretty good in that respect.'

Nicky gazed round the room distractedly. 'I still can't believe it's happened. No wedding. Gone, wiped out, like that.'

'How do you feel?'

She got up and went over to the window, staring out at the wall of ivy. 'Right now, numb. Nothing. They say when you've been in a terrible accident there's no pain. Like, your leg could be hanging off and you're fine about it. It's hours later that reality kicks in. By midnight I'll probably be a howling heap alongside my mother.' Her head tipped forward so her brow was resting against the glass. 'Oh God, God, what have I done? What's even the etiquette here? How *do* you dismantle a wedding? Although I wouldn't be surprised if my mother's got a book on how to do it properly. You know, she will never *ever* forgive me for this.'

'Well, she needs to get a grip,' I said. 'No one's died. You've changed a date on the calendar, that's all. Send out cards saying the date's been altered, details to follow, no explanation. Stick the dress and all your other bits and pieces in a plastic wrapper and put them in the loft.'

'The reception, the hotel?'

'Get Lady Corinne to sort that one out. It's her deposit she's chasing.'

Nicky raised her head and let out a little moan. 'The florist. Oh, the vicar. The photographer. The travel agent! Do you think we're still having a honeymoon? Or is that off as well?'

'Listen,' I said soothingly. 'Don't all couples have a big row during the run-up to the wedding? It's one of those ancient traditions: something old, something new, huge great row over a piddling little detail. Give Christian some space to cool off and then you'll be back on track, you'll see. You have to make it up with him, if only to wipe the smug smile off Corinne's face.'

'God, yes, the woman's probably popping the champagne as we speak.' She came back and sat on the bed next to me. 'Holding a celebratory dance in the village hall. Dishing out free cider to the serfs.'

'You really don't like her, do you?'

'It's not so much her, Frey, that's the thing. It's that Christian sides with her constantly. He *will* not stand up for himself. He says he doesn't want to ruffle anyone's feathers, but he doesn't mind ruffling mine. She's a 'dear', apparently, when you get to know her. 'Just a little bit set in her thinking.' He can't see the way she manipulates him. 'Funny old bird', he calls her, as if she was some lovable eccentric instead of a scheming witch. She doesn't think I'm good enough, that's basically the problem. Although what woman would be, I've no idea. And I'm thinking, *do* I actually want a marriage battling against that? Is that why I snapped at him? Was it my real feelings coming out?'

I pictured Christian's bright beautiful face, his clear blue eyes, and gave her a friendly shake. 'Of course you want to be married to Christian. He's gorgeous. You love him. You can't let someone like him get away, not over a little spat.'

And we sat there for a minute while I re-played his visit to the nursery the day he proposed; what it must feel like to have someone make that much of an effort for you. *I have this idea for an illuminated avenue, Frey. I want it to be magical.*

'This,' I said firmly, 'is a blip. You're going to meet up with him next week and he'll be as sorry as you are. There'll be no need for apology cards or cancellations. Then in twenty-five years, when you're planning your Silver Wedding party, you'll look back at this, this week, and you'll laugh.'

'You reckon?'

'I do. And here's another thing: you really can't let Corinne win, can you? You've got to go through with this marriage just to put her in her place. Mad old cow. Actually, how old is she?'

Nicky gave a wan smile. 'Hard to say. Younger than Julian. She's got such good bone structure it's impossible to guess.'

'OK, picture this: one day she'll end up in a home for retired bitches, and then you can really have some fun. You can go visit every Sunday, and spend an hour reading out the opinion pages from the *Guardian*. You can fill her iPod with death metal and smear Marmite on her false teeth and plant mealworms in her commode. You can take away all her novels and replace them with copies of *Socialist Worker*. Let's see how superior she manages to be then, yeah? What goes around comes around.'

241

I felt this was a good speech, one that would go some way to restoring a sense of balance and cheer. For once, I had said the right things. Nicky did look less upset than she had been, and in any case I truly wasn't just saying what I thought she wanted to hear, I genuinely believed myself. Couples did bicker while they were engaged; I'd read that in magazines. These small skirmishes didn't mean anything sinister. Corinne sounded a complete shrew, but all Nicky had to do was show her who was boss. Certainly nothing to throw in the towel for. I thought, *She'll remember this pep talk. In years to come she'll tell people how my words of calm common sense stopped her panicking and saved the day.* I felt almost high on it.

Don't get me wrong. I would never ever have gained enjoyment from witnessing my best friend in distress. I love Nicky, and I only want to see her happy. Nonetheless in the minutes after, there was something, a distinct and tingling thread of pleasure running down the centre of my chest. I think it was the being here together again in my room like the old times, like the Christmas she ruined Joan's best table mats with glitter glue, or when she let the family guinea pig get eaten by a cat. The relief of burying my own problems underneath her drama, a drama that really demanded nothing more of me than to sit back and listen and give sympathy. Not messing up by blurting something stupid.

'Honestly, though,' she said. She still wore that stunned, not-quite-there look, but the colour had

242

come back into her cheeks and her hair was drying.

'I know.'

'You think you're on track, you think it's all going along smoothly, and then, then, bang! Everything totally disintegrates.'

'Tell me about it,' I said.

★ ★ ★

After she'd gone I texted Oggy to check the coast was clear. I knew it was stupid and wrong, but right at that moment it was the only place I wanted to be.

From Liv's diary, 12/05

And now she hates G. Hates way his toothbrush leans against hers in bathroom glass, way he wipes round plate with piece of bread, that he puts empty packets & jars back in cupboard, that he doesn't flush toilet if he gets up during night. None of this F's said straight out but you'd have to be dense as a brick not to pick it up. This evening she said to me, 'I'm not sure it's working.' I feigned ignorance. 'What isn't?' I said. 'Three of us in the house,' she said. I said, 'It is difficult moving back in when you've been away.' She just scowled, didn't try to correct me. Think she's as frightened of direct confrontation as I am.

Instead she niggles, won't let him have TV remote, sighs when he comes into room, makes great fuss if he finishes something from the fridge or cupboard. E.g. was moaning on & on last night no peanut butter left, yet she hates the stuff & I've seen her texting while he's talking & I know she's sending messages about him. Tuesday night some comedian on BBC making jokes about beards, F snorting & casting meaningful glances in G's direction.

Last night v low, but G was great, showed me website about reintroduction of beavers to UK, & cheered me right up. This is what F doesn't see, he is a kind man, steady, & he loves me. For first time in years feel supported by another adult.

Want to say to her, 'You have M in your life &
I don't particularly like it, I have G. That's how
families work, compromise.' G thinks should put
that to her. Terrified I'll lose her, though. Not
even G could make up for that, & he knows it.

Notice she's stopped calling me 'Mum', but
haven't reacted.

Wonder what she calls M to her face?

A WEDNESDAY

July

We had a beautiful day for Liv's shearing.

I'd known it was imminent, but had pretended not to notice how her scalp was showing more and more, especially at the front. Then, early that morning, we were standing by the kitchen window watching a nuthatch on the feeder, and completely without thinking I reached across and plucked a loose hair off her shirt sleeve. She looked at me as though she'd been slapped. Before I could tie myself in knots apologising, though, she'd said, 'It's time, isn't it?'

So after we'd had our breakfast I took a chair into the garden and set it on the lawn by the pond. I went back for scissors, a brush, a towel, a plastic bag to hold the clippings, and the wig.

Liv came out and sat in the chair and I began to brush her hair through. Handfuls of it pulled away between the bristles. I shook out the towel then laid it across her shoulders, lifting her long tresses aside. Then I took a hank of hair between my fingers, brought the scissors close to her scalp, and cut.

'Stop!' she said.

I nearly dropped the scissors. 'Oh, God, what, did I hurt you?'

'It's — You don't have to cut my hair for me,

Freya, this is silly. I can do it myself. In the bathroom. I'll go and do that, shall I?' She started to peel off the towel.

'It's fine. Please, let me.'

'I don't know what to do.'

'You don't have to do anything, Mum. Sit back. It's fine. Close your eyes if it helps.'

After a moment she shook herself and smiled thinly. 'Go on, then.'

I replaced the towel and began again.

I tried to work symmetrically, so that what I took from the left I next took from the right. It seemed important to do that. Still it felt outrageous to be shearing her at all, exposing the pink skin with its freckles and marks she never knew she had. There were creases at the back of her neck, a silvery scar above one ear. Secret Liv.

As I chopped, she gave a running commentary on a pair of grey squirrels frolicking in next door's spruce. One was mean and the other was feeble. Feeble kept venturing out onto the garage roof, and then Mean would come after and chase him back up the branches.

'Is it territorial or are they getting ready for mating?' I asked.

'I'm not sure. Squirrels aren't my area of expertise.'

Geraint appeared at the kitchen window, then retreated again.

At last I paused to take stock of the job and a hot wave of fear washed over me. Almost all her hair was gone now, only a few short clumps remained. Liv would be appalled when she saw herself.

I peeled away the towel and ran it gently over her scalp to dislodge any last loose wisps. 'How does it feel?'

'Exposed.'

'Do you want to go in and look, or would you rather have the wig on first?'

She turned in her seat. 'I'll try it with the wig first. My lovely chic head-warmer.'

I imagined her in front of the mirror at bedtime, staring at herself, trying to take in her newly naked face. Geraint would be propped against the pillows, offering nothing or with his nose in some book about the history of peat bogs. Whatever, I knew she wouldn't get much support from that quarter.

While she pulled on the wig, I stooped to pick up the hanks of hair lying among the grass and started to poke them into the plastic bag.

'No,' said Liv, 'don't throw them away.'

'Are you keeping them?' I was surprised.

She took a length of hair from me and ran her fingers along it. 'No, drape it over the hedge. It'll make wonderful lining for mammal nests.' She laughed at my expression. 'You have to look on the bright side. My loss might be some wood mouse family's gain.'

So together we spent a minute or two distributing her hair around the garden at various mammal-friendly stations. Only Liv could have turned such a morning into a wildlife event. Then she went back in while I gathered up my tools and carried everything indoors. I slid the chair home under the dining table, and I was on my way to take the brush and scissors up to my bedroom when I passed Liv standing perfectly still in the downstairs cloakroom. I hesitated, wondering whether this was a private moment, but she called me in. Her fingertips fluttered uncertainly across the wig.

'It is still me, isn't it?'

''Course it is.'

'Bloody cancer,' she said.

Later, on the way upstairs, I met Geraint. As he passed me he cleared his throat. 'Thanks,' he said.

''S OK,' I said. Neither of us broke step.

*   *   *

Once I'd put everything back on my dressing table I went into the bathroom, locked the door and ran the shower till it was warm. Ironic to be dyeing my own hair minutes after Liv had lost all hers, and I wondered whether I was perhaps being a bit tactless. But I needed this shot of colour to give me courage. In less than two hours I was meant to be at the hospital chapel, saying goodbye to Melody's baby.

I plunged my head under the running water, squirted shampoo, lathered, then held myself under the needle jets, losing myself in the hiss and steam. To be honest I could have stayed there forever, till I dissolved away to nothing and disappeared down the plughole alongside the gobbets of froth. In a hour or so Geraint might batter the door down and find nothing but a slimy trail of Pantene.

I couldn't bear the thought of going to the

funeral and yet I also knew I couldn't stay away. When Michael had texted me at work with the date, my first reaction had been wild panic. It would just be too horrible. I knew I wouldn't be able to stand the intense focusing of all that sadness; I'd be like an ant under a magnifying glass, grief would fry my brain. And what if I somehow managed to say the wrong thing again? I'd have to leave the country, possibly the planet.

Frantically I'd tried to think of possible excuses: a crisis with Liv, a last-minute migraine, general mental breakdown. I even contemplated deliberately pranging my car on the way to the hospital.

But when I'd texted back to ask what time I should be there, Michael had replied: *Might jst be me + mel.* And that — the blunt unexpectedness of it — had gutted me. I'd actually felt sick when I read it. Because obviously what he meant was that I'd been such a crap daughter over all of this, Melody couldn't bear to have me around. That I couldn't be trusted to behave like an adult. I had to be shut out.

I switched off the shower and reached for a towel, scrubbing hard at my scalp, remembering how I'd spent the four hours after his text consumed with self-pity. Blundered about the nursery, glassy-eyed. Wouldn't speak, refused to serve in the shop, spilt a bin full of grass seed all over the car park. In the end Ray made me go sit in the office and eat an out-of-date flapjack to raise my blood-sugar level. *This baby was my sister*, I'd raged to myself. *I had a right to be there. I could have taken flowers. Read a poem.*

Just stood and held Melody's hand. Claiming me as part of the family and then shutting the door again — who the fuck did they think they were? Then, when I'd got home that evening, Liv told me Michael wanted me to ring him, so with a pounding heart I had done.

'It's at 11.30, if you can get the morning off,' he said.

'Does she want me there?'

'Of course she does.'

'I thought — '

'Oh, she was all over the place, Frey. She didn't even want me to go, at first. Then she only wanted her mum over from Ireland, and then, would you believe it, my dad, which obviously was crazy. And we had a huge row about the post-mortem results because I think it's good they haven't found anything but she feels let down. She does need us there. Trust me.'

'Isn't she cross with me?'

There'd been a sigh, a kind of warm noise, like an aural hug. 'I promise you, she's not cross any more. She needs you there. We both do.'

And in that instant I'd gone from dreading the idea of being at the funeral to wanting to be there, standing between them, a unit. I could do it.

'OK,' I'd said.

The noise of next door's dog barking brought me back to the present. I wiped the cabinet mirror free of steam and assessed the state of my hair. I combed it flat, frowned at the result, then mussed it up again, ready for the dye. Bold Red, I would be today. I pulled on the plastic gloves

251

and unscrewed the cap. A liquid similar to venous blood blobbed out onto my palm. Quickly I clapped my hand against my scalp, and began to work the dye through, so that within minutes I resembled the victim of a frenzied zombie attack. The residue as usual was splashed about the bathroom, across the tiles, smeared gorily around the taps. Bloody foam slipped down my fingers. There were even drops of it down the toilet bowl.

Like I was suddenly seventeen again and back at Oggy's mum's house the afternoon I lost my virginity, staring at the smear of blood on the toilet paper and wondering whether I'd done a very clever or a very stupid thing. 'What will your mum say about the sheets?' I'd asked him. 'Should we wash them before she gets home?' He'd howled with laughter at that, but I tell you, I never could look her in the eye afterwards.

And I thought of last Sunday, at the flat, Oggy draining his beer and telling me he'd reached a decision: that he'd finished with the other girl and he knew now I was the one for him, what had we been doing messing about all these years, hadn't it always been us. Kissing, kissing, stumbling to the bedroom, stripping off our clothes and falling into bed, with his malty breath on my neck. 'Freya, Freya,' he'd kept saying. Had there been tears in his eyes? I'd waited for him to stop and reach for a condom, but he never did; the moment was too fierce. 'Wait,' I'd tried to say, but he'd covered my lips with his and ground into me so that I was carried away too. I shivered now at the memory.

It was right, the sex was right and we were right and I'd been right to go back to him. Afterwards, as I was dressing, he'd pulled open a drawer and gone, 'This is for you.' I'd looked up to see him holding a chunky old-fashioned ring between his fingertips. 'Don't get the wrong idea, it's not an engagement ring. You wouldn't want one of those anyway, would you? But this, I found it on the canal path, and I thought you'd like it. It's got animals round the sides. You're into animals.'

Too shy to examine it properly, I'd dropped the embossed copper band in my pocket. It felt strange to have him serious after these years of flippancy.

'Wear it,' he said. 'Please.'

For a second, Michael's disapproving face had flashed up, and my heart had dipped with nerves. But then I'd thought, *Actually, you can sod off, Michael, it's my life*.

Oggy and I had kissed for a long time on the doorstep. The old loves are the best, always.

Now I turned to face the bathroom mirror again. The light in here was harsh and my face looked drained under the black-red slick of my hair. I knew, though, that I would get through these next few hours, and it would be all right. And then I'd escape to Oggy's.

I patted the ring where it hung on a chain under my shirt; nobody needed to know.

★ ★ ★

The service passed in an unreal blur. There was Michael, unfamiliar in suit and tie. Other people, couples, I didn't take much notice of. A cream-painted room with rows of black chairs, a simple altar block, two stands of flowers. Melody sitting between us, Liv's angora shrug on her lap. The hospital chaplain reading out names. A hymn only he had any voice to sing. Prayers. I squeezed my eyes tight shut, and tried to recall Colin's funeral, but the reality is I have no memory of it at all. The cold nugget of the copper ring burned against my breastbone.

Then it was all over, and we were filing back out into the foyer, wet-eyed and stunned. Some of the parents were queuing up to write in a book of remembrance.

'I need to go outside,' said Melody. 'Give me ten minutes on my own, yeah?'

We watched her make her way slowly through the double doors and out onto the grass verge.

'Can you stick around or do you have to get away?' Michael asked me.

'Well . . . ' I'd promised Ray I'd try and be back at the nursery for three.

'It's fine. That you came, that you were here for the service is what matters.' He took my arm and I was grateful for the contact. 'I'll walk you to your car.'

We passed a teenage boy on crutches, a pensioner in a wheelchair, a young man with his arm in a sling. Smokers huddled in doorways, some wearing dressing gowns. One guy was still attached to his drip.

'Do you think she'll be better now?' I asked.

Michael shrugged. 'It's another hurdle crossed. She's actually been brilliant, sorting out the right

254

forms and filling them in, phoning the right people. You know Melody and paperwork, and deadlines. But she got on and completed them. She's going over to Ireland for three weeks now, to be with her mum. It'll be a break for her. She's handed in her notice at the shop, though. I wish she hadn't.' He scratched the back of his neck, a gesture of bafflement. I thought he was looking very tired. 'How's Liv doing, by the way?'

I patted about for my phone, found it, brought up My Photos. 'Here. I cut her hair this morning. This is her with the wig on.' Already it wasn't quite such a shock to see. Before I left, I'd made myself gaze at the picture till it was imprinted on my brain.

Michael brought the screen close. 'It suits her. Tell her I said that: she suits her hair shorter.'

'It's just, it's different from what we're all used to.'

At the exit to the car park, a man was swearing at the barrier.

'Hey, I bumped into a friend of yours yesterday,' said Michael. 'Your mate Nicky. I was in town getting some dinner and she was in the queue behind me. We got chatting. She's not having a great time of it either, is she?'

'Did she tell you much about it?'

'I'll say. We ended up going to the Crown, and she poured it all out. She said she and her fiancé'd had a meeting but it had turned into another row. They've not spoken since. His mother put the phone down on her. Fucking mess, eh?'

'Well, the wedding might only be postponed.'

255

He raised his eyebrows.

'Christian's taking a breather,' I said. 'To get his head straight.'

'Right.'

'You reckon he's got other plans?'

'He's certainly pissing her about. And it's a damn shame to treat a girl like Nicky that way. She could have any bloke she wanted. I said as much.'

'That's what I told her, too,' I said quickly, trying to ignore the little flare of jealousy in my chest.

'So I dunno what he's playing at.'

I saw again Christian's wide blue eyes. 'He's only being honest. Better to say early on if you have doubts.'

'Better not to behave like a prick.'

'They'll work it out. It's nothing, in the scheme of things.' Funny to think how, twelve months ago, Nicky's wedding hitch would have seemed like the absolute worst disaster.

We reached his van and I leaned against it. 'OK?' he said. 'Not feeling giddy, are you?

'Exhausted, all of a sudden. Don't know why.'

'Release of tension. You did well, Frey. You really did. These things are never easy.' And he stepped forward and gave me a huge hug. It felt nice to rest against him and close my eyes for a minute.

'Hey,' he said at last, loosening his hold, 'you didn't happen to hear Wem FM on your way in?'

'No. I was listening to a CD. Why, what did I miss?'

'Kim. On a phone-in about love rats.'

'Shit, no. Did she actually give out your details?'

'She tried but they wouldn't let her, kept saying, 'No full names'. I think they warn callers before they go on air. Libel laws and stuff. The station doesn't want to end up in court.'

'And what did she claim you'd done?'

'Mostly what I did. That I ended the marriage because it wasn't working and because we were both unhappy. That makes me a bastard.'

'What did the presenter say?'

'Cut her off after a minute or two because she was starting to rant. A couple of other women phoned in later to agree I sounded like a git.'

'You could have done without that.'

'Yup. God, I'm glad you came today, Freya.'

He looked at me for a long moment.

'Anyway, you'd better get back to Melody,' I said, stepping away and tugging at the handle of the van door.

'I think you'll find that's my vehicle.'

I groaned. 'God, see what state I'm in.' But as I moved round the bonnet of the van, I noticed a paperback book lying on his dashboard. 'A History of VSO? What on earth are you doing with that, Michael?'

He looked away, thrust his hands in his pockets. 'You know.'

'Not really.'

'Just that it does me good to think I could take off, if I wanted. That there's the option. You could come too. Stuff some clothes in a rucksack, hop on a plane, easy. Whoosh.'

'Yeah, right, me on an aeroplane. I'd be

hysterical before we even took off.'

'You wouldn't. You could go to the doctors and get some pills. Anyway, think of the pay-back. Don't you need something like that in your life, at least to dream about?'

'You must be kidding,' I said. 'Neither of us could disappear right now. Too many people here need us.'

He muttered something I couldn't catch and turned away. 'What? What did you say?'

He looked back, wearily. 'I said, 'Don't I know it.''

Then, before I could reply, he was striding away across the car park.

★　★　★

Driving back from the hospital I wanted only to take myself home and crawl into bed. By the time I reached the nursery, though, I found my mind was racing, my brain and muscles completely wired. I had this sense of having walked across a lake of fire and come out the other side. The funeral was over and I'd got through it without disgracing myself. Surely I'd never again face any test as tough.

Ray clocked my state at once and sent me out to the raspberry field so I could be on my own. It's a cool, green, ordered space, well back from the greenhouses, adjacent to farmland. Several occasions I've been working here and a fox has trotted right past me; another day I saw a sparrowhawk eat a woodpigeon just the other side of the fence.

I unrolled my ball of twine and set to work. For the first half hour there was only room in my mind for painful images of the chapel, of the maternity ward, of Melody newly pregnant. The world was tipped upside down and would never be right again. But gradually, gradually, I began to feel a little bit calmer. The quiet of the field helped soothe me, and the repetitive threading and knotting as I moved along the nets.

I thought of a morning spent shopping with Melody early on in our relationship, telling her as we wandered through the rails of clothes about how Liv would only ever take me to play in the one playground that was near the brook so she could look for water voles. Complaining that Liv, with her untamed hair and men's shirts, stood out embarrassingly from the other mothers. Moaning about Geraint. Melody laughing at my descriptions. Another day, Melody stroking a blusher brush tenderly across my cheek. It had been so cool at the time to suddenly be hanging round with Melody's crowd, with the laid-back Michael and his weird, fragile fiancée. *You might have Geraint but I've got another mother*, I remember thinking as I watched Liv fill out her boring old Natural England reports. When I came back from uni and set up camp at Love Lane, it was supposed at least in part to be a punishment for Liv. *Let her struggle with the housework on her own. Or, if she wants me back, let her boot her boyfriend out, a straight choice.* Not that I ever put that to her. I did stop calling her 'mum', though. She never said anything, so I presume she didn't notice.

Then I thought of Nicky asking me straight out why I hated Geraint so much; it was an Easter Monday and we'd been holed up in her bedroom watching some utterly dire romantic comedy about a completely stupid, rubbish couple who deserved a good slap. And I'd gone, 'Because Geraint smells like a badger,' which wasn't even true but seemed like the most hilarious thing to come out with at that moment, and Nicky had choked on her creme egg. *Because he's there*, is what I really wanted to say. *Because he's not my dad. Because he's too old for Liv, and too beardy, and because he has this way of looking at me that makes me feel as though I don't belong there. He wants me to move out, move on. Even though it's my house. Even though it's none of his business what I do with my life.* But I didn't say that because I was embarrassed to be back home again after uni, after Love Lane. *Great hairy oaf.*

And then I found myself recalling, of all things, a conversation I'd once had with Nicky's mum Joan when I was about sixteen. We'd been in the garden because she was having a barbecue and she'd had a fair amount to drink, which wasn't like her. She'd sidled up to me and gone, in a voice full of tragic-sympathy, 'Nicky and I always think you're marvellous the way you've handled being adopted. So brave. Because it must be difficult, Liv not being your' — she'd lowered her voice — 'real mum.'

'Well, you know, it beats being put out on the street,' I said to her. Then I'd asked if she knew

260

how many kids in my class lived with someone who wasn't their biological parent. She'd looked sick and made a swift exit, so she never got to hear the answer, which was: *At least half of them*. Because the plain fact was that in every other household you'd have found a stepmum or stepdad, a granny or aunty or even in one case a neighbour standing in for absent kin. There were IVF and ICSI babies, born from donated sperm and eggs. And I knew other adoptees, too. In my maths group we had a Vietnamese boy called Hung whose dad was a ginger Scot and whose mum was half-Italian. Who says families have to match? Love's the glue that holds people together, not genetic fit. Hell, if genes alone did it, every biological family would be a shining unit like something out of *Hello!* magazine. Not Tyler Dawes taking a pop at his dad with an air rifle, or Sheree Lewis throwing hot coffee over her mum during an argument about skirt lengths.

We weren't just talking modern times, either. I'd done history GCSE and I knew that mix 'n' match parenting was perfectly acceptable pre-1950. For a start, people didn't live that long. Women died in childbirth and men in wars, so millions of households would have had to draft in a new mummy or daddy to keep the place ticking over. Children from poor homes would get sent away to live with rich relatives; wealthy parents employed nannies or boarding schools to do their child-rearing for them. That was the norm. You'd have been thought odd if you'd resisted. Also, till the Sixties there was rubbish access to contraception or abortion so if the wife played away, how many husbands would have been bringing up sons or daughters they knew weren't theirs? What about all those 'natural' offspring, all those 'wards' with their mystery benefactors? And how many young unmarried mums were forced to pose as big sister to their own baby? I'd had years to think about all this, marshal my arguments, and my conclusion was that the whole business of raising kids has been a make-do patchwork from year dot.

Of course, Nicky's mum had been beside herself when I first contacted Melody. 'What about Liv?' she wanted to know. 'Won't it feel like a dreadful rejection?'

I told her I'd asked Liv and she was fine about it. That's what she'd said: 'fine'. That she was happy if I was happy. Why would she lie? Everyone involved had been completely cool.

At that Mrs Steuer had tossed her head. 'I don't believe it's been as easy as you make out. I think you've been protected from an awful lot.'

Bloody Joan Steuer. What did she know about it? Another memory: me shouting down the stairs at Love Lane for bleach to clean the toilet, Melody telling me not to bother, she'd been squirting bubble bath down the pan for weeks and it did the job OK.

The sun filtered down between the green rows of plants as I moved along the top edge with my baling twine, looping, knotting and clipping. Magpies and crows rip holes in the net, and we wage a constant battle against hungry rodents and insects. Once we had a tribe of badgers run amok; the damage they did was unbelievable. The trouble is, everything loves raspberries. If they were growing in my garden I'd be happy to share them but as Ray says, this is a commercial enterprise, not a wildlife café. I went on mending nets in the still of the afternoon.

I had thought I was pretty hidden between the tall canes, so it made me jump when someone called out, 'Freya.' The knot I was working on pulled tight, and I raised my head to see Christian advancing down the row towards me. He wore a white shirt and pale chinos and I wondered what kind of a mess the soil was making of his Italian shoes.

'Hello, you,' he said, his voice softer and less jaunty than usual.

I let him come forward and kiss me on the cheek. 'You're not really supposed to be back here. If Ray catches you, I'll be in trouble.'

'It's fine. It's just, I needed to see you.'

'How's Nicky?'

Immediately he looked stricken. 'I don't know. I can't — I've been filming in Lincoln, and it's been — I did try once or twice, but ... Is she still upset?'

'What do you think?'

'Fuck.'

He ran his hand through his hair. Sunlight dappled his smooth pale complexion, and gave a green cast to his shirt.

I said, 'You need to sit down with her and explain what's going on. People ask her how the wedding plans are going and she has no idea

263

what to say, it's horrible for her.'

'Oh, God. I don't want to hurt her.'

'Then don't.'

'It's not that simple, Frey. I wish it were.'

He put his palms against the leaves in a despairing pose, and even in the midst of my panic I thought, *That would make a lovely painting.*

'What's the deal, Christian? Tell me.'

'Look,' he said, coming very near, so I could smell his aftershave and see the golden stubble on his chin. 'You know her the best. You'll understand when I tell you.'

'What?'

'I can't go through with it. I can't marry her.'

'Jesus.'

'Ever. I should never have asked.'

'Why did you, then? Don't you love her?'

'I do, I do.'

'Then there's no issue. She loves you. She's potty about you. She wants nothing more than to be Mrs Bliaise.'

This time he actually doubled up as though I'd punched him in the stomach. After a second or two's hesitation, I put my arm round his shoulders, the way you might do if someone's being sick.

'Christian?'

When he straightened, he did look ill. But perhaps that was just the effect of chlorophyll.

'I *hate* this,' he said. 'It's killing me. Whatever I do, I'm going to be hurting someone. If Nicky could understand, she'd see it was better to end it now.'

'Is there someone else?' Some young up-and-coming actress, I was imagining, some media type with clicking high heels and perfect nails. That was it. He'd fallen in love on the job.

'No! God, how could you even think that?'

'What's the problem, then? Because from where I'm standing, you've got the perfect match! The perfect life! Don't fuck it up for no reason!'

He took both my hands in his, gazed into my eyes. 'Oh, Freya, Freya, I love you, you're so *straightforward*.'

My cheeks flamed.

'It's *background*,' he went on. 'That's the issue.'

'How do you mean?'

'You see, I never gave it any thought, but my mother saw it at once. Nicky and I, we're just too different, it's too big a gulf. We'd make each other unhappy in the long run.'

I still wasn't totally with him. 'By background, you don't mean like the house she grew up in, and what her dad does for a living?'

'Some of those things. But they're not key. God, we're not snobs. It's to do with attitude, and expectation, and, and, it's hard to define. It's *difference*.'

'Difference can be good.'

'She wouldn't fit in. I wouldn't fit into her world either. She's not happy when she comes down to stay, you know. Within a few days we're bickering, she's sulking over some tiny slight she's imagined. There's always a terrible atmosphere.'

That's your bloody mother's fault, I thought. 'It doesn't happen when you stay with Joan and Derek.'

'No.' He seemed uncertain.

'I know for a fact they bend over backwards to make you comfortable. Joan cleans the house for days before you arrive, Derek gets special whisky in. They think the sun shines out of you.'

'It's not the same as 'fitting in'. I don't feel comfortable there. Not really.'

'Joan would be devastated if she could hear you.'

He loosed my hands despairingly. 'I can't lie. That's how I feel. It was naïve of me to think it didn't matter. Love's made up of so many different elements, it's not enough just to say 'I love you' and that's an end.'

'Isn't it?'

'No. Life's tough — '

'You don't have to tell me that, Christian.'

' — and to battle through it you need someone by your side who's, who's the same, who sees the world from the same perspective. It's crucial for an enduring match.'

That's so your mother speaking, I thought. 'Look, why did you come here? What did you hope I could do?'

'Speak to Nicky for me. Help her understand. You know the way to talk to her.'

I shook my head vehemently. 'Not my job. This has to come from you. And anyway, I don't think you will go to her and announce it's over. You're better than that. Saner. Christian, you'd be mad to throw everything away.'

There might have been tears in his eyes. 'I'm not mad, Frey, I'm just not sure this marriage is right.'

'Then all I can offer you is that I'll be around to pick up the pieces afterwards.'

He put his fingertips to the side of my face. 'Of course you will. I'll try to make it clear and quick.' Honest goodness radiated from him; or perhaps that was the light dazzling through the canes. 'And I hope I can count on your friendship, whatever happens.'

Whatever happens. The air was very still, a robin sang liquidly in the hedge behind.

'Yes,' I said, feeling my cheek tingle.

Case Notes on: *Melody Jacqueline Brewster*

Meeting Location: *42, Love Lane, Nantwich*

Present: *Miss Melody Brewster, Mrs Abby Brewster, Mst Michael Carden, Mrs Diane Kozyra*

Date: *10.45 a.m., 23/3/87*

Melody seemed upbeat during the whole visit, and full of energy. She wanted to talk about her own future and where she sees herself in ten years' time, she doesn't want to be dependent on her mother any longer than necessary and is keen to leave home. Currently she is hoping to pass her CSEs then go on to study design at sixth-form college. She showed me some of her sketch books and patterns.

I explained to her how smoothly the first meeting had gone between baby Fay and her adoptive parents at the foster home, and how they were enjoying their parenting classes. I stressed how closely their contact with Fay would be monitored throughout the whole process. Melody listened and said several times she was pleased, but then quickly changed the subject back to her college plans. I think this information needs revising at next visit, to make sure Melody has fully absorbed what stage we're at.

Towards the end of the session Melody's stepbrother Michael came into the room (he has been off school with an ear infection). She made him sit by her, brought him a drink and put a cushion behind his head so he was more comfortable. I observed to Mrs Brewster that Melody was an attentive stepsister. She said, 'She never leaves him alone.'

I congratulated them on how well Melody is doing, and on the general level of family support.

Next visit: 30/3/87   Signed: Diane Kozyra

A SATURDAY

August

Dreamed I was being chased by the zombies out of *Resident Evil*, then woke at two in the morning convinced I'd heard the phone ring. Everything was quiet, but I needed a pee so I got up anyway. On my way back from the bathroom I stopped to rescue a scalloped oak moth that had got in through the landing window and was leaving frenzied dusty streaks against the sill. I opened my hands and the moth dropped away into the outside dark; at the same moment I noticed a faint light coming from the bottom of the stairs.

I crept down half a dozen steps and listened. I thought I could hear Liv's voice, low and emotional. Carefully I made my way down to the hall where I stood for a minute or two, trying to work out what was going on. The dining-room door was ajar and still it was just Liv talking. Geraint must be doing his usual impression of a pudding, sitting uselessly while she poured out her heart. But then I heard her go, 'Yes, it's hard when you feel that way,' and I realised she was having a conversation with someone I couldn't hear. A Samaritan, I guessed. She used to phone them occasionally after Colin died. Or maybe she was taking to one of the cancer helplines.

I hesitated, not wanting to eavesdrop but in that instant gutted she would call a stranger in the night rather than speak to me about her worries. It really was as though I came last in this house.

' . . . when people suggest you can overcome cancer just by Being Positive,' she was saying. 'That gets me down sometimes. It's a physical disease, for heaven's sake. You wouldn't tell an amputee they could re-grow a limb by keeping chipper, would you?'

Silence while she listened, and then a little laugh.

'That's right. Yes, and when they say, 'It's going to be fine,' and they have no idea whether it is or not. I want to reply, 'Oh, I didn't realise you were a qualified oncologist.' That's awful of me, isn't it? I know they only want to help. So I put on my coping face and smile . . . But on the other hand, pretending everything's OK actually does help me feel stronger. Even though the cancer's constantly on my — Oh, wait.'

I ducked back under the stairs but it was too late, she'd seen movement.

'Frey? Is that you?'

If I could have turned and run, I would. But that would have been the action of a child. 'Checking you were OK,' I said, pushing open the door wide.

She was still holding the receiver, while her other hand pulled the kimono across her wounded chest. Her head was bare, which was a shock because she normally wore the wig at all times, even round the house.

271

'I'm sorry,' I said, appalled to have caught her in this state.

'No, no, it's fine.'

Liv pressed 'end call', and made a grab for a tea towel that was drying on the radiator. Then she wound it hurriedly round her scalp so no bare skin was on show. That felt hurtful as well. Didn't she think I could cope with her nakedness? I was the one who sheared her, for God's sake.

'Who was on the phone?'

'No one.'

I gaped at the blatant lie.

'Well, Melody.'

'What did she want?'

'Just to chat, really.' She gave a quick, meant-to-be-reassuring smile. 'Bullfinch' read the caption over her brow: the tea towel was a British Garden Birds design, bought when we last went round Hawkstone Park. We'd sat in a sandstone cave to shelter from the rain and she'd read out a leaflet about Shropshire myths and legends. Later we'd climbed the tower and dropped pigeon feathers from the parapet.

'To chat? At two o clock in the morning?

'Way past your bedtime, that's for sure,' she said, as though I was about nine. She pushed back her chair, rose, and switched off the light so we were left in near darkness.

How can you shut me out? I wanted to ask. I'm not a kid any more. I need you to let me support you, it's less frightening that way. I'm in limbo otherwise. Can't you see? The words were loud in my head. Melody lets me in.

Something fluttered against the window pane. The air was hot and thick. I only had to speak out.

'Night night, Freya,' Liv said.

* * *

I had meant to get an IUD fitted, I really had. I knew there was a five-day window after unprotected sex where a trip to the doctor's to get a coil fitted would see you right. I'd looked it up on the internet. Should have been easy.

But we'd been so unbelievably busy at the nursery, and there'd been Melody and Liv to deal with, the time had somehow just slipped away. I'd crossed my fingers very tight, hoped that would be enough. And here I was, my period two weeks late, with no idea what to do.

When the realisation first poked its way into my mind like a little poisonous seedling, my first reaction was denial. This was my life, and pregnancy couldn't happen to me. Upheaval on that scale only happened to others. I was too young. My body wasn't coordinated enough to have managed a proper grown-up conception. Mother Nature would never allow a child to land in the lap of someone so unprepared. I could not be having a baby.

But as the days ticked on, the idea became more real and I was forced to consider some of the things it might mean. I saw myself waddling up the high street, conspicuously huge, while people I knew from school sniggered and whispered behind my back. I imagined the disappointed face of old Mrs Noble, ex-babysitter from my childhood, who used to save me jam jars so I could make beetle traps. Nicky desperately, painfully encouraging while her mother tutted in the background. Geraint putting on his special Welsh glower on account of my bringing trouble to the house.

The actual birth was supposedly like pooing out a watermelon, and somewhere during the trauma your bits tore in half and then you had to have them sewn back up with a massive curved needle and they were never the same again. And that was only the beginning of your trials. I had an idea of what motherhood entailed because I'd heard women moaning about it on TV. There was a lot of shouting and tantrums and cheek, and sick and changing bed linen in the small hours. I'd seen women shut themselves in the kitchen and weep, while above their heads doors slammed and music boomed. Babies never slept, and were incontinent, and you couldn't go anywhere and just leave them on their own, not even down the road to the corner shop because that was against the law and your name would be splashed across the papers and people would scrawl stuff on your door. Newborns were ridiculously fragile, too, and had to be held a special way or their heads came off. There were a million things for a mother to get wrong.

Impossible to imagine what I'd do with a real live baby. Where would it go? Our spare bedroom was only the size of a cupboard, and currently stacked full of a display on the Wonder of Wetlands. Liv wouldn't want her pots of moss re-housing. Liv wouldn't want waking in the night, or hours of non-stop wailing or extra smells and clutter and mess. Geraint would say to me, 'How can you put your mother through this new stress?' and I'd have to kill him.

Then there was Melody. Dear God, Melody. My insides shrank with horror when I imagined breaking the news to her and Michael. For me to produce a child right now would seem like the ultimate insult. She might even think it was deliberate. I'd be out of that family for good.

But even as I fretted and raged, I couldn't stop my brain twisting off along other, less horrible scenarios. An image flicked up of Oggy and me lying on a hillside somewhere with a laughing child between us. Clouds would be scudding across the blue sky and Oggy would be tickling the child — a boy — with a blade of foxtail. He'd wave the grass head above the boy's fists, let him grab it. The sun would be warm and the breeze fresh. And I thought suddenly, *What if Oggy's actually pleased with the idea of being a father?* If his reaction's positive and supportive, being pregnant might be bearable. More than bearable. Perhaps this was all meant to be.

Because I'd have a direction in life at last. I'd *have* to pull myself together. I would move out finally, get a proper place. Get a place with him. Oggy as a dad — was it so bizarre? I knew he had a tender side because I'd seen it a fair bit lately. It was as though we'd found a recent level of understanding, an acknowledgement that, whatever had gone before, we were ultimately meant to be together. I'd taken to wearing his ring on my finger even though it did leave a green mark.

We were grown-ups, for God's sake. When Liv was my age, she'd been married two years; Grandma Abby had Melody at nineteen. So twenty-three was plenty old enough. Oggy and I would have a baby and muddle though, because people did. I knew how to run a home, I could do the things that mothers did. Another of these false memories flashed up, this time an older boy dressed in old-fashioned shorts and a red jumper; I must have got the picture from an Enid Blyton cover. We were down on the Moss fishing for stickleback with a seaside net. I saw us hunting for adders, whistling blades of grass, climbing gates, lifting bark to catch woodlice. It could be the making of me, being a mum. It didn't have to be a disaster. If that was what fate had handed me, maybe it was up to me to do the best with it.

Oggy and me: our coming of age.

*　*　*

I let myself in with the key he'd given me.

As soon as I walked across the threshold I smelled weed, and my heart sank. Oggy was lying on the sofa with his eyes closed, despite the combined noise of the TV, Napster's Hot Five, the kitchen radio and the washing machine on spin.

'What are you doing?' I shouted over the row.

'Not a lot.' He grinned as he watched me go round switching off appliances. The scent of skunk was faint but tangy. I opened a window and stood by it. 'I wish you wouldn't smoke that stuff.'

He pulled a face but made no comment.

I lifted the ashtray from the arm of the sofa and took it through to the kitchen, where I emptied it into the bin under the sink. On my return I found he'd zapped the television back on and we were now watching *Chucklevision*.

I said, 'I need to talk.'

'I need you,' he said. 'Come here.' He wriggled his hips until there was a margin of cushion for me to perch on. As soon as I sat down he buried his face in my shirt. 'Oh, Freya, Freya.'

'Get out of there.'

He peered up at me, his eyes small and slitty. 'Your hair's very red today.'

'Never mind that. Listen, are you in any state to have a serious discussion?'

Something in my tone must have penetrated because he frowned and half sat up. 'I'm OK, just chilled. If you want to talk, you go for it. Uncle Oggy's all ears. You tell Uncle Oggy what's bothering you. And if it's that twat Michael . . . '

A bluebottle circling the room distracted him and he lost the end of the sentence. He followed the insect with his eyes, till it settled on the window sill.

I took his face in my hands. 'Listen. Are you happy?'

'Fucking ecstatic.'

'With me. Us.'

'Like I said.'

'What about,' I said carefully, 'if there were three of us?'

A blank. Then an expression of slow puzzlement crossed his face, followed by an insane, beaming smile.

I couldn't believe it. My heart soared with relief, I felt dizzy. He did want to be a dad. It was going to be OK.

Then he said, 'You talking about a threesome?' He began to giggle. 'God, you're full of surprises, you. Fucking hell, fucking hell, who — '

'No, *not* a threesome. Not that. No. Jesus, this is hopeless.'

'It's not.'

'Yes it is, Oggy. I'm going to leave you and come back tomorrow.'

'Whatever's the matter, woman?'

'Nothing. It can keep.'

He snatched my wrist and held it tightly. 'Something's wrong, yeah? Tell me now. Come on. You look upset. I don't want you to be upset. Oggy says you mustn't be upset . . . '

The fly was on the move again.

'I'll give it one shot. Then I'm done.'

I waited till he re-focused.

'Go on.'

'How would you feel if I told you I was pregnant?'

'Dunno. Is it something you're likely to say?'

He sniggered again. I stared at him till he sobered up.

'Fuck,' he said. 'You're not, are you?'

'I might be. There's a good chance. I've never been this late before, and there was that time when you wouldn't — '

'I thought you were dealing with it.'

'I meant to.'

'Have you done a test?'

'No.'

He flung his head back, despairingly. I could see his mind was engaged now, but the wheels were moving slowly.

I said, 'I wanted to see what your reaction was. In case I am.'

'Should've done a test,' he mumbled. 'Anyway, listen, it's . . . You don't have to worry, yeah, because I'll go with you . . . '

'To the hospital?'

'Wherever they do it. I'll help with the fee, I don't know how much it costs. I'll put something towards it, anyway. There was that girl, Jo whatsit, used to knock about with Robbie Birch, she went to Wrexham for hers. You could ask around . . . '

It dawned on me what he was getting at.

'I wasn't thinking of an abortion.'

Oggy made an indeterminate noise in his throat.

'How far are you on?'

'I'm two weeks late.'

'Then it's a bunch of cells, that's all.'

'It's more than that, Oggy. It's you and me.'

'Aw, shit, don't get so . . . You were prepared to use the morning-after pill. It was just cells then.'

'That was before. It feels, it feels like a baby now.'

'Fuck.' He put his arm across his eyes to block me out. 'I can't get my head round this.'

'Imagine what it would be like, though, having a kid. A little person hanging on your every word. Who thinks you're brilliant, your number one fan, yeah?' I tried a smile. 'Because, I mean, what are you doing with your life as it stands? Nothing. You're like me, drifting about. And that's OK for a while, but you have to, you have to *settle* at some point, you have to achieve something. Make a difference. Otherwise, why were you born? What's the point of it all?' No response. I waited, then I leaned over till my lips were next to his ear. 'Oggy, be honest with yourself: *are* you happy?'

I really thought this speech might have hit home. Surely the doubts that plagued my confidence and kept me awake at three in the morning sometimes were the same ones that bothered him? The sense that I should have achieved more, was being left behind, had failed to make the grade. Would never make it. I didn't want to be stuck in no-man's-land any more, I wanted something to move me on. He and I could move together.

'I was happy,' he said. 'I am happy — '

'But are you really? Truly?'

'Yeah, Frey, I am. My life's fine. I don't need any add-ons. I *want* everything to stay the same. Same's good.' The next instant the fog seemed to clear and he looked at me sharply. 'I get it. This is about you, isn't it? What's bugging you. You've decided having a kid will be like, I dunno, a safe harbour where you can sit and be a mum and no one'll bother you, for years. Maybe the council'll sort you out a house. Then you can veg at home and watch CBeebies all day, all that shit.'

'No!'

'Oh, I think so, Frey. Well I'm not ready for my world to shrink, even if you are.'

I pointed angrily at the television screen where a man was riding a runaway lawnmower through a campsite of yelling Scouts.

'That's the kettle calling the fucking pot, that is. What are you watching, then? Sodding *Newsnight* with Jeremy Paxman? What do *you* do with your days except coast through your job, go down the pub, crash in front of the TV, get up and start over again?'

'Yeah but there's stuff I want to do in the future, sometime. Like, I've never been to America, you know? I want to have a go at snowboarding, go round a race track — '

'I thought you said you didn't want change.'

'That's, it's, I meant — ' Then: 'Fuck it. This is stupid. Do a test. Come back when you know what the fuck's going on.'

The lawnmower hit a tree and catapulted the driver head first into a convenient wheelie bin. The credits rolled as his legs waved.

'You know, plenty of girls are late. Two weeks is nothing. We're probably fine,' said Oggy, more quietly.

No, I thought. Whatever a test shows up, one thing we aren't is fine.

★ ★ ★

I didn't go straight home. Instead I followed the backstreets into the centre of town, then walked slowly up the main road in the direction of the

281

chemist's. No hurry. I wanted to hold onto this space-of-not-knowing, stretch it out, savour it. I didn't want to be pregnant, I didn't want not to be.

Once you're tuned in, evidence of fertility's everywhere. Right in front of me an elderly woman stopped to admire a baby in a pram, while the mother smiled down indulgently. Up ahead, a man holding a girl-toddler by the hand threaded his way through the crowds towards me. Two junior-age boys cycled past, calling to each other and laughing. All around me society was busy producing.

Nearly every shop window seemed to boast children's books or toys or baby gadgets, adverts for school uniforms, christening gifts. I passed Thorntons where five months ago I'd stopped by and bought two identical boxes of chocolates for Mother's Day; took a minute to imagine someone giving me a handmade card, crayon scrawl inside. Once I'd made Liv a daffodil card out of an egg carton, and another year our teacher had got us to cut out teapot shapes and sellotape a tea bag on the back. Liv had kept them all. Even Melody had one of my cartoons on display, a picture of the two of us I'd doodled on a flyer during one of our nervous early meetings. It lived on her kitchen wall, next to the calendar and takeaway leaflets. 'I like to see it every day,' she'd said. I hadn't appreciated what that meant till now.

I reached the chemist and hung around outside, delaying the moment. I had no reason to suppose I was pregnant bar the late period, and periods can just be late. Twice before I'd taken a chance, and got away with it. Why should I be caught this time? If I did the test and I wasn't pregnant, I was going to go out tonight and get smashed. If I did the test and I was —

Join Our Parenting Club! read the banner across the chemist's door. The bell jingled as I pushed it open. Surely everyone would stop what they were doing and turn to watch the harlot complete her walk of shame? I kept my eyes away from people's faces, concentrated on scanning the shelves till I located the rack of pregnancy testing kits. On the same aisle, not two stands away, there were packets of nappies and tins of milk powder and teethers and bibs, doll-size nail scissors, special baby-gentle bath lotion. My stomach lurched. I grabbed the nearest kit and took it to the counter.

Found myself standing hip to hip with a woman who looked about nine months gone. I cast her a sly look, and she nodded back.

'When's it due?' I heard myself say.

'Another six weeks.'

Another six weeks? Blood and sand. Her belly was already as enormous as it was possible to be without exploding. 'Oh,' I said, and let out a stupid high-pitched giggle.

She collected her prescription, gave me a quick anxious smile, and heaved herself away from the counter.

I kept the box hidden under my hand till she'd gone.

★   ★   ★

I'd turned off my phone while I was visiting Oggy. Coming out onto the high street again I switched it back on and found six missed calls and two text messages, all from Nicky. I rang her at once.

'Where are you?' she said.

'In town.'

'So am I. Can we meet in Walkers?'

'When?'

'Now. Please.'

I clutched at my little polythene bag. 'Is it urgent? What's happened, Nicks?'

But she'd rung off.

As soon as I saw her, sitting at the table near the window with an untouched cup of coffee, I knew something major was up. Her face was white and her lips pinched tight as though she was struggling to control herself. I slid in opposite and wondered what we must both look like, two women caught up in our own separate train wrecks.

'Is it Christian?' I asked. Though even as I spoke, I was thinking, *What more can he do?* He'd already delivered the final blow, surely, when he told her they were through. That had been bad enough. Michael and I had taken her out that night and sat like bookends while she puzzled and ranted and cursed and mourned. 'It's the *waste*,' she kept saying. 'Nearly two years wasted on him, thrown down the drain.' And Michael going, 'Hell of a bigger waste if you'd married him.' And me going, 'He's the loser here. You've got everything ahead of you.'

Later I'd helped her write her lists, some of

284

them practical ('Try again to get dress deposit back'), some of them more fantastical ('Go on internet and add Christian's details to spineless-gits.com'). I'd listened to her litany of ways in which the future was ruined — she'd been a total idiot, she'd never trust anyone again, people would always know her as the girl who got jilted, all weddings and everything to do with weddings was now spoilt forever, her mother was on the verge of a breakdown. I'd mopped her tears and told her a million times she was still attractive. I'd agreed that Christian would live to regret his decision, would probably never marry at all or if he did it would be to an evil witch type, and that Corinne would eventually die alone and unloved in grandiose squalor.

Meanwhile, across the table from me now, Nicky was swirling her coffee around danger-ously. 'Of course it's Christian. Bastard.' She clapped the cup down on the saucer. 'Him and his bloody bloody mother.'

'The thing is, Nicky, you don't have to have anything to do with her now. That's the silver lining in the cloud. No more snotty Corinne, ever, yeah?'

Nicky shook her head. 'It just goes on and on. I found out this morning that she never booked the reception. Never booked it, Frey.' She paused to let me digest the news. 'So that means not only was she a lying deceitful cow, but she *always knew the wedding wasn't going to take place.* That's why she offered to arrange it all, wouldn't let me or Mum do anything towards it, and why she talked about swapping the venue so late on.

285

Of course you can swap something that never even existed!'

'Oh my God.'

'I only discovered it because it was on my list: 'Make sure you're unsubscribed from potential mail shots'. Michael advised me to do that. He said it would be upsetting if I got wedding literature through for months afterwards.'

'But I remember you going round the hotel and looking at the banqueting room. You chatted with a woman at the desk. You showed me a sample menu.'

'That was before Corinne supposedly made the booking. Why would it ever cross my mind she hadn't done it? You know, I've been taking people up there to show them, I drove Aunty Paula and Uncle Vic round the grounds but we didn't stop at reception and check any paperwork. I didn't think there was any need. Corinne told me she was dealing with everything. All I had to do, she said, was tick the menu options and give her the names of guests who'd be needing rooms. I can't believe it, Frey.'

'And your mum never rang the hotel to check details?'

'Corinne told her not to in case it caused confusion. Everything was supposed to go through her, to 'avoid mixed messages'.'

'Didn't your mum and dad mind her organising everything?'

She pulled a sour expression. 'They assumed she knew best. You know what they're like. Anyone speaks with a posher accent than theirs and they just roll over. Corinne's such a forceful

286

woman anyway, it would have been like arguing with a bulldozer. Not to mention she was the one putting down the deposits. Except she wasn't.'

The waitress came and took my order. I touched Nicky's hand.

'I don't know what to say. It's just shit. Have you spoken to Christian about it?'

'I don't ever want to speak to him again. I hate him. I'm filled right to the brim with hating him.'

'When he hears, though. Presumably he'll be as shocked as you are.'

'Why 'presumably'?'

'Oh, he wouldn't be involved, Nicky. He wouldn't have had any idea what his mum was up to.'

'Wouldn't he?'

'No. Come on. It makes no sense.'

'What *does*?'

I thought of his smooth, blond cheeks, the tilt of his chin. 'He may be weak, Nicky, but he's not malicious.'

'You always stick up for Christian, don't you? I know you were sweet on him.' She looked tiredly back at me. 'Everyone was.'

'I was not.'

'If you say so. It doesn't matter.' My heart was pounding. Nicky lowered her gaze. 'None of it matters any more. It's just that I thought I'd got to the end of this mess, and then something else crops up, and something else, and something else. I realised last week there was a load of my stuff still at his parents'. So I've that to worry about now.'

'They're only things. You could always walk

away. Or get him to parcel the lot up and send it through the post, assuming Corinne hasn't already made a bonfire out of them.'

My Sprite arrived and I drank it gratefully.

'Can't abandon it. There's family albums — we were looking at past wedding dresses — and there's some clothes and jewellery. Too precious to leave, too heavy to post.'

'Fuck.'

'But it's OK because Michael said he'd drive me over next weekend. You can come too if you want, though I don't suppose it'll be a very jolly outing.'

'Michael?'

'I popped round the garage to give him back a book he'd lent me, and I ended up telling him about my gear, how I couldn't face going to retrieve it on my own. He said he had to pick up an engine in the area and could factor a stop-off at the Bliaises' into his journey, if I wanted. How lucky is that?'

'That is lucky,' I said.

'We'll have to go in his van. Which will give Corinne another reason to sneer at me.' She pushed her lips into a sulky trout pout which I assumed was meant to represent her mother-in-law. 'But Michael's so kind, isn't he? He's twice the man Christian is. A really decent guy. I never really took much notice of him before, but now I've got to know him . . . He's been great with me.'

'He has, yes.' And I remembered standing in the hospital car park after the memorial service and Michael telling me what a nice girl Nicky was; how she could have any bloke she wanted. An unhappy suspicion crept into my mind. 'What was the book he lent you?'

'Something about volunteering work overseas. It was brilliant, actually. You know, the difference people can make to struggling communities around the world. Teaching, building and engineering, advocacy — that's what I might do if I went — healthcare and social work. Lives turned around. Makes my job here look pretty irrelevant. Michael would be a mechanic, he reckons. Well, obviously.'

I swallowed. 'Did he ask you to go with him?'

'Not outright. He seemed to be dropping some pretty heavy hints, though. He was so — *lit up* — when we talked about it. His enthusiasm's infectious. I wanted to pack up there and then and go too. Leave all this mess behind.'

'You love being a solicitor.'

'My mother loves me being a solicitor.' She gazed mournfully into her coffee. 'I don't know, Frey, when something like this happens you end up questioning everything. Why shouldn't I just take off in a different direction? Leave them all standing gaping.'

'We could all go together,' I said recklessly.

Nicky looked startled. 'You?' There was no need for her to say any more. Me, who couldn't even manage to stay the course on a school camping trip twenty miles down the road. Useless, samey, stick-in-the-mud Freya.

All of a sudden I wanted to stand up and shout in her face that I was pregnant: that in fact I was starting out on my own adventure, about to take a huge and irrevocable step that would change my future forever in ways she couldn't imagine. For once I'd be the one leading the way, striking out into uncharted territory. A child of my own, I'd have. Top that.

'Are you all right?' she said. 'You look furious. I'm really sorry if I sounded like I was being — '

'It's fine. I was imagining punching Corinne in the gob for you.'

She laughed. 'I wish someone would.'

'Get Michael to do it for you while he's down there.'

I regretted my tone at once, but she didn't pick up on it.

'I just can't believe I had so much and now it's gone,' she was saying. 'I wake up in the mornings and then I remember, and it's like hearing him say it all over again. I lie there in bed and I don't want to get up. Because I'm thinking, what's the point? Three months ago I had everything ahead of me, and now I'm stuck living with my parents, no boyfriend, a career path I'm not even sure I want to be on any more. Perhaps I should jack the training contract in and come and work at the nursery with you. At least it would be something different.'

'And earn beggar all, like me. Great plan, yeah.'

'At least you've got Oggy!'

She raised her eyes to mine and pierced me with a tragic expression. I couldn't bring myself to make any other response than a nod.

'And you're glad you went back to him, aren't you, Frey? Basically, I mean, even if he can be a bit of a lump. He's *there*. You love him. It's less of a mess than my life, anyway.'

Against my finger the copper ring burned.

'I have to get home,' I said. There's this thing I need to do.'

★ ★ ★

As I walked back through town I tried to imagine what my days would be like without Michael around. Or Nicky. That last was a hard picture to conjure, though: she was too fond of Chester life, lunchtime shopping, browsing the Rows, stopping off for an espresso and panini or a glass of wine and a dish of olives. Her polished nails were not cut out to drive a jeep along dusty potholed roads, her feet too tender for army-style boots.

But Michael I could see. I could see him under a corrugated roof mending cars and tractors and probably generators and radios and God knows what else. His skin would bronze and he'd grow a beard and wear a sweatband round his forehead. He'd learn the native words for 'Where's it broken?' and 'It's fixed!' and the locals would all love him. Small barefoot boys would sit and watch him strip engines and pass him spanners and wire cutters on request.

But when I tried to think what life would be like here in Shropshire while he tuned machinery on the hot side of the world, that's when my imagination failed. It was an impossible idea.

I passed the supermarket, crossed the car park and stopped off at the bridge that crosses the

291

brook. Here I'd pictured throwing Oggy's ring, hurling it in a big defiant arc to land in muddy oblivion.

I put my shopping bag down and twisted the ring off. The green mark it left below my knuckle looked sickly and gangrenous, and I wondered how long that would take to fade. The ring itself I turned slowly, studying the minute figures stamped into the metal. What I'd first thought were random animals had turned out to be signs of the zodiac, identified under Geraint's bug magnifier. I found the lion now, Leo, and revolved the year between my fingertips. Where would I be in twelve months? Where would we all be? I hardly dared predict. Melody, with her burden of grief, Liv with her physical scars, Nicky re-building her dreams from scratch. And me, would I be holding a baby in my arms, lifting him up to see the mallards as they paddled underneath us with their own milling brood? Oggy sprawled on the sofa in a haze of smoke: he would still be in the same place, the same pose, this time next week, month, year.

Sunlight winked on the surface of the stream and willow branches dipped and flittered in the breeze. A crisp packet made its way lazily down to the storm drain. Near the surface stickle-back darted and hung, darted and hung, seeking out the shadows, and my practised eye could make out water-vole runs along the banks, and burrows, patches of feeding. The times I'd stood here as a kid while Liv pointed them out and took her photographs. Worlds ago.

Without warning the ring slipped from my

grasp and dropped away. I heard it splash, saw ripples spread out and a small gust of mud billow up from the stream bed, then the water flowed on over it all, as before. Seems like some decisions just get made for you.

★   ★   ★

Even as I let myself in, I could hear music coming down the stairs. It was loud, too. Some warbling, throbbing prog rock from Geraint's collection of tatty LPs that only he ever listened to. I'd known Liv would be around because she'd had chemo the day before and she always took it easy for the following twenty-four hours. But Geraint should have been out on the Moss, supervising a herptile diversity day.

I poked my head round the door of her study. It was empty, and her computer was switched off. There was no one in the living room or kitchen. I thought about calling up, but I didn't want the contact. I just wanted to be on my own.

So I slipped up the stairs, and when I got to the top I could see Liv's bedroom door was open, music blasting out. No doubt Geraint's prehistoric Bush record player had been cranked up for the occasion. Tempting to march in and demand he turn the bloody thing off, but that would be too confrontational; I could at least cut the volume by pulling the door shut, though. I stepped across the landing and reached for the handle.

Then, out of the corner of my eye, I clocked the bathroom door was open and someone was sitting in the bath. For three long seconds I couldn't tear my gaze away, enough time for me to take in Geraint — Jesus wept — Geraint naked, his hair plastered to his scalp and his beard saturated to a spindly tail, and, tucked in against him with her back to his belly, Liv. She wore no wig, and her scalp seemed so pink in contrast with his. He had his arms around her and his hands pressed protectively against her chest, and her eyes were closed in blissful calm.

I drew in a sharp breath, but they didn't hear me over the swooning guitars. The next moment I'd got myself together and was scuttling past into my room where, even through the locked door, the music followed me.

I climbed into bed and pulled the duvet up round my ears. My mammal chart, I noticed, was peeling off the wall, the dream-catcher over my bed was furred with dust. Several of my model toadstools lay scattered underneath the dressing table. Still the image of Geraint and Liv hung in front of my vision.

This house was feeling less and less like somewhere I belonged.

From Liv's diary, 12/05

Worst Christmas since Col died. She's been over, opened her presents, but it wasn't the same. Watching clock all time because Melody was picking her up & none of us could cope with M coming up path & knocking on door. I had the old decs out, Col's star & the cedar nativity set, had a go at popcorn chains (though got involved watching fieldfares on lawn & singed some of corn). Had done a stocking too, even though she wasn't there in morning to find it by her bed. When I handed it over she just looked embarrassed.

She took some cups through to kitchen for me & said 'You're managing without your home help, then?' Took me a moment to realise she meant herself. Obviously she can't have had remotest idea how hurtful that comment was. G furious. But I know if I say anything it will make F resentful & drive her even further away. No one likes to be made to feel guilty. Have to keep the way open for her to come back.

After she'd gone, went & lay on her bed for a while. G came up & gave me warm brandy. I said, 'She'd have taken all her posters down if she'd moved out permanently.' Because there's a lot of her stuff left, waiting. G says to hang on. He's convinced she'll come home. He says, 'Of course she will. You're her mother.'

A SATURDAY

September

For a week I was too frightened to do the test. Then, in the end, there was no need.

A whole twenty-one days after I should have come on, I got my period. I'd woken up feeling fine, hopped into the shower, and that was it. No baby.

Legs trembling, I perched on the edge of the bath and watched the water swirl down the plughole. I felt as though something had struck me a hard blow on the head.

I'd been so sure I was pregnant.

So that was that. I made myself wash my hands, brush my teeth, extract a pad out of the airing cupboard, get dressed. But when I got down to the kitchen I found I was shaky and weepy, and I couldn't eat the toast Liv put in front of me. Luckily no one noticed my heart was breaking. Geraint had received an email saying a member of the public thought they'd sighted a pine marten in the woods round the Moss. Liv was arguing it was probably a polecat and Geraint was busy checking the internet for maps of UK mustelid distribution. You'd think someone had reported seeing a snow leopard, the way they carried on.

I swallowed some tea and went to the toilet

and washed my hands and came out and put my coat on and grabbed my phone and opened the door and got in the car and drove to work. At the nursery I sorted through some late deliveries from the day before and re-stocked the bird food section. I took the pressure washer and cleaned the paving outside Greenhouse One, and did a litter pick along the outside verge. I wiped the entrance sign with a wet sponge. Ray came and asked me to chase up an order for slate chippings, and after that to check on the state of the herbaceous plants and pluck off any shoots or buds that looked dodgy. From there I took myself to Polytunnel Two and did some potting-up, mainly salvia and pinks. I'd felt no physical pain at all, just a general aching heaviness and a sick clamping round my chest that came and went. Melody, I kept thinking. Oh, Melody.

When work finished, I went round to Oggy's to break the news. It being a Saturday he was crashed out on the sofa in his usual weekend pose, this time watching *You've Been Framed*. I didn't even bother asking him to mute the TV, I just told him straight out.

'Thank fuck for that,' he said. There was a wave of laughter from the television. Then he remembered himself. 'Aw, shit, sorry. Are you OK and that? Do you need an aspirin?' His contrite face made him look like a droopy hound.

'I don't need anything from you. In fact, you can have your key back,' I told him, and threw it at his head. It missed, but I had the satisfaction of seeing him duck and curse.

'Calm down, Frey. I'll get us a drink.'

'I'm not stopping.'

'OK.'

But I didn't move. I suppose I was waiting for him somehow to make it better. Eventually he heaved himself off the cushions and came to put his arms round me.

'Sorry, yeah. There's no point me lying, is there? You knew what I thought about a baby.'

I said nothing.

'And be honest, you didn't *really* want all that bother, did you? You must be able to see it's for the best. I bet there's a part of you that's relieved. Go on, look me in the eye and tell me you're not.'

I wrenched myself free. 'What would you know about the way I'm feeling?'

'I know *you*. I know what you're capable of. What kind of a lifestyle you like. You wouldn't have coped with a baby. You wouldn't, though, would you? You know nothing about them. You're not the maternal type. Anyway, you'll soon be back to normal. Once the fog's cleared.' He tapped the side of his head. 'You got hooked on an idea, that's all. It'll pass.'

At that moment I hated him more than I'd ever hated anyone. He was the voice of the person I'd been, the person destined to measure out her life in plug plants and vodka shots, and I didn't want to be anywhere near him. I wished I still had his ring so I could make some other dramatic gesture, but even the green stain had faded to nothing. I took a breath: all the

298

frustration of the last months gathered itself into a great furious lungful of air, so the next thing I knew I was yelling into his face.

'I COULD have! I could, I could! I could!'

Oggy bent backwards, cartoon-style, under the force of my shouting. Any minute now the old lady in the flat below would be calling the police about domestic violence and affray.

'Could what?'

'Have brought up a baby!'

'OK. Get a grip, love. Yeah, all right, you *could* have brought up a kid. God knows, when you see some of the scuzzers who push buggies round. But you wouldn't have *liked* it. Not day after day. It's dead-end stuff. It wouldn't have got you anywhere.'

'Oh, just what I need, careers advice from the man who models himself on the three-toed sloth — actually, no, on second thoughts a sloth's way too energetic for you. You're more like one of those Antarctic starfish who only move a centimetre a year.'

'Cheers for that.'

'So don't you dare tell me how I should be living my life.'

He shrugged despairingly. 'It's no good, Frey. You're the same as me. You don't want to be tied to anything. That's why it works, you and me. Neither of us want baggage. We're drifters. We bob along in the stream.'

Happy music blasted from the TV. I wanted to hit him and hit him.

'No, Oggy. The reason we hang about together is because I've never bothered to find anyone better. I got it into my head you were all I deserved. I've convinced myself proper boyfriends were for other people, boyfriends who were prepared to talk about the future, who took you out places and acknowledged you as a partner and didn't regard you as a filler-in — '

'Don't give me that line,' he snapped.

'Why not? It's the truth.'

'Yeah? Then it's true for you as well. You get back from me exactly what you give. What have I really been, for years, except someone you call when you're fed up? We knock about but we never *do* anything. We don't *go out*. So? Why's that matter all of a sudden? Basically, I'm a mate you shag whenever. I thought that was what you wanted.'

There was a pause while I considered this. 'Then what was all that other stuff you said?'

'What other stuff?'

'How I was really 'the one', how it had taken you ages to realise it but now was the time to stop mucking about? Didn't you mean any of that? Or was it just the Tennent's talking?'

For a moment he looked genuinely confused. 'I did mean it, yeah. *Then.*'

'But today you don't. Brilliant.'

'No, I do, sort of. Jesus, Frey, I'm not dicking about for the sake of it. I'm trying to be honest here. It's just, I dunno. The way it works is I can feel a certain way, and then a week later — a day later — I can feel different. I can't explain why. That's how it is.'

'For you, maybe.'

'For you as well.' His voice rose indignantly.

'No! I'm not like you, Oggy!'

'OK, then. So tell me how you feel right now.'

'Huh?'

'Do you still love me?'

I laughed drily. 'Not much. No.'

'Well, then.'

He had me skewered on my own argument.

'But it's only because, because you — '

'Listen, Frey.' He moved away from me and collapsed back onto the sofa, swinging his legs up to lie prone once more. 'This is all the truth you need to know: we work because we're the same. Oh yes we are. You can kick against it all you like but it won't make any difference. You and me, we travel the same kind of track — '

'Like hell we do.'

' — and whether we're apart or together, you'll still be you. Motherhood? Don't make me laugh. You've had a lucky escape, you have.'

Lucky escape. The words struck home painfully. That was the trouble with Oggy. Waste of weed-soused space he may have been, but sometimes he was right on the nail.

'Well — oh, sod you,' I said. And then I left, because there was nothing else to say.

★ ★ ★

The test was still in its packet under my bed. I drew it out and read the instructions, as I'd done a hundred times in the last week. Those days that pass when you're waiting to see if you're pregnant last forever.

Now I turned the slim little box over and over

in my hands and I thought, I could still do this test. It would still show a faint positive if there'd been any kind of baby. At least I'd have that to hold onto, the knowledge that there really had been a new life growing inside me, and it wasn't just a screwed-up menstrual cycle.

But the more sensible side of my brain told me to leave well alone. The point was, there was no baby, only a baby of the mind, of a few weeks. The faintest shadow of a baby.

Instead of taking the test, I unwrapped the stick and dipped it in the glass of Ribena by my bed. Then I bundled it and its box up in tissues, and stuffed the lot down to the bottom of my waste-paper basket under the rest of the rubbish. That was an end of it. I wouldn't be telling anyone. What was there to tell?

So I put on some music, sat down at my dressing table to re-do my make-up and hair. Almost instantly found myself back in that room where Melody had given birth; saw myself sitting outside in the hospital corridor, resentful and embarrassed. A liability, a silly, useless girl.

I sprang up off the chair and ran my gaze around my bedroom, trying to shake the images out of my head. I blinked, for once seeing the room properly as though I'd just walked into it for the first time. A child in a child's room. All this junk! God. Did I need still to display my swimming certificates, school merit badges, cycling proficiency award? What was the point in hanging onto my university folders? When I was never going back to college, and their presence on my shelf was just a reminder of another dead end? I wanted to sweep it aside, start again. Scour and fumigate the lot.

I started to rip at posters. Poor, defaced Britney could come down off the wall — it would be a mercy killing — and *Children of the Damned* because it was creased and dog-eared. Under the bed I knew there was still a box of action figures, trolls and orcs: well, those I could pass on to neighbours' kids who'd get some proper use out of them. The comedy fungi could go to a car boot.

— Again I was peering into the hospital blanket —

I kicked at a pile of *Dark Side* magazines, sending them fanning across the carpet.

— standing next to the pregnant lady in the chemist's, thinking, *That'll be me in a few months* —

'It's over!' I said out loud. 'It never properly began!'

— squatting next to a pushchair while ducks and geese squabbled over the bread I'd thrown —

I threw my Freddie Kruger gloves into the bin and pressed the heels of my palms against my eyes till I felt sick. *Pull yourself together, Frey*, I imagined Michael saying. *If Melody can be brave* —

Then I spotted, wound round my jewellery box and holding the broken lid onto the base, one of those red elastic bands that postmen use. Dimly I recalled some American therapist on TV talking about using a rubber band as a kind of aversion therapy. You could keep one on your

303

wrist, she said, to stop yourself thinking bad thoughts. Every time you felt a destructive urge, you snapped the band against your skin. The pain would be enough to divert yourself onto a happier topic. Eventually, avoiding the negative would become an unconscious mental habit.

Hell, it was any port in a storm. Without hesitation I slipped the elastic over my hand and pushed it against my cuff. Then I sat down and finished my make-up, spritzed my hair, and changed my shirt.

Freshened up, I went downstairs for a roll of bin liners, brought them back to my room and had a thorough sort-out of what I wanted to keep. I made two piles: those few things that truly mattered, and the leftovers from before. Year 7 exercise books, bent *Star Wars* trading cards, a flyer advertising a pond-dipping weekend in 1995, a bundle of notes from Oggy, they were all as useless as each other. Why had I ever hung onto this stuff?

I was ruthless, it took me less than an hour. And I only had to ping my elastic band twenty or thirty times.

★ ★ ★

The doorbell rang as the text came in. By the time I'd got to the landing and peered over the banisters, Geraint was shuffling to open the front door so I took my phone back to the bedroom to check the inbox. Would it be Oggy pleading for my forgiveness? Nicky announcing she and Michael were leaving next week for the

Maldives? Or just Vodafone spam?

But it was Christian's number that flashed up on my screen.

Hv u spkn 2 Nky? was the message.

Speak to her yourself, fuckwit, I felt like replying. Or leave her alone. Instead I texted: *Nothng 2 say. Unless u wnt her back!!!*

I knew what would happen next. Within thirty seconds my phone was buzzing like a wasp in a bottle.

'What?' I snapped.

'Please don't be angry,' said Christian, tinnily. 'You're the only person I feel I can still count on.'

'What do you expect me to do? It's finished, you've told her that, so why do you keep texting and calling and pissing about?'

I could imagine him combing unhappily through his fringe with his fingers, or plucking at his flannel trousers. At last he said, 'I suppose, what it is, it's just I can't stand the thought of her hating me. She *hates* me, Freya.'

'Is it any wonder? You've publicly humiliated her, told her she isn't good enough for your exalted family — '

'That's twisting my words.'

'Are you *denying* you dumped her?'

'No, no, it's . . . Oh, hell.'

Then I had this flash of insight, and I knew exactly what it was that was getting to him. 'Oh, I understand. You can't bear to be cast as the villain, can you?'

'I'm not a villain. I simply did what my family believed was right for both of us. What *I* believe is right. Christ, you can't blame me for that. And it doesn't mean — you know, I thought, after the dust had settled, we could maybe stay friends.'

'*You and Nicky?*'

'Well. You and me, maybe. I thought you at least liked me.'

Those massed ranks of Steuers, Joan and Derek and the aunts and uncles, the neighbours, the members of Rotary and the Inner Wheel: I could picture them standing shoulder to shoulder like a firing squad. Awful to be the focus of such fury. Especially for a man like Christian who lived off his charm. There was no worse punishment.

'It's horrible, Frey,' he whispered.

That was it. Finally I saw him for what he was: a petulant, indulged mummy's boy who'd never suffered a real day's hardship in his gilded life. Imagine being married to a jellyfish like that, I'd tell Nicky later. He'd be bailing out at the first serious illness or bereavement or baby or financial blip, anything he rated a bit testing. She deserved so much better. We all did.

'Oh, why don't you bloody well grow up!' I cried, and flung the phone across the room. It may not have been the most eloquent of sign-offs, but it did the job.

In the silence that followed — a silence where Christian was almost certainly goggling at his handset in disbelief — I heard someone calling my name. I pushed the bin bags against the wall and opened my bedroom door. Liv was standing outside.

'Come downstairs. Someone wants to see you,' she said.

* * *

They were drinking elderflower cordial in the living room, Melody perched on the arm of the sofa and Michael on the tall chair by the window. Geraint stood and swayed nervously on the hearth rug.

'Doesn't Liv look fantastic!' said Melody, before I could get a word in.

I glanced across, and yes, she was looking nice. The wig suited her, and she'd pencilled in some eyebrows and put on a slick of pale lip gloss. Nor had the compliment gone unappreciated; there were sudden roses in her cheeks, and she was smiling.

'You're not doing so bad yourself,' I said, which was also true. Melody had on a grey jumper with a white collar and cuffs, and a long black velvet skirt. The effect was intense, rather than outright funereal. She'd also had her hair feathered, giving her face a softer shape, and her lips were painted a kind of brooding filmstar red. 'I thought you weren't coming back till next week.'

'She's got a job interview,' said Michael.

I blinked at him. 'Oh my God. Where?'

'It's not exactly an interview,' said Melody. 'I'm seeing a guy who runs a gallery in Chester.'

'What, an art gallery?'

'Yeah. He wants someone to coordinate events, schmooze clients, sweet talk his artists.

PA-type thing. Secretary, kind of. I'm not too clear on the detail.'

What do you know about art? I thought. Once upon a time I'd have blurted this straight out, but now I just said, 'Oh, wow. How did you get the gig?'

She giggled, and for a second it was like having the old Melody back.

'Guess,' said Michael.

'Through my *mother*,' she said, rolling her eyes. 'Abby's got friendly with this local artist, a bloke called Sean, and she introduced us. He seemed to take a fancy to me — '

'As they do,' said Michael.

' — and I ended up doing some modelling for him. He's really good. I've brought one of his sketches to show you. So anyway, when you're stuck posing in a studio, you get talking, and I told him I needed to do something different with my life. 'Course, he wanted me to move out there permanently, said I could be his muse. And he was nice, dead nice, only he's about ninety.'

'He's seventy-two, Mel.'

'Yeah. So it wasn't really on. Even if I was back on the scene, which I'm not. But one of the galleries he ships to was thinking about getting an assistant, and when Sean found out I lived nearby he gave this bloke a ring and set up a meeting. So I'm going to pop up there and have a chat, and if we hate each other on sight there's no harm done. But Sean said I'd breeze it. He said I had the right face.'

'You'd be perfect in a gallery,' said Liv.

Yeah, I thought, she would. I could see it now.

She'd sit in the window, all smoulderingly Bohemian, and passers-by would find themselves slowing their pace, stopping, climbing the front steps without even realising what they were doing. Once inside they'd be hooked. Sean was right. The job was hers.

'It'll be a change,' she said. 'Anyway, I've something to show you. That's the reason we came round.' She stood up and now I could see, shoved in between the sofa arm and the wall, a large flat folder like the one I'd used at school to cart my GCSE art projects around. Melody grasped the edge and tugged, and out it slid leaving a dark furrow in the carpet. She prised the covers open a fraction and reached inside.

What she extracted and held out to Liv was a simple ink sketch of a mother and child. Although the drawing gave the impression of having been done quickly, with bold, energetic strokes, and though the thickness of the lines was uneven as if they'd been done with something like a quill pen, I could tell at once this was good. We were looking from above at a woman with long hair holding a newborn on her lap. You couldn't see her face, but her baby was exposed and naked, its eyes black pools, one arm flung out and the tiny fingers splayed. Somehow the artist had captured perfectly the protective curve of the mother's shoulder, her wonder, and her youth.

'It's you,' I said. 'Us.'

'That's right, hun.'

'Oh,' said Liv, her flush returning.

'He took it from a photo of Abby's.'

'Has she many?' I asked. 'Only I'd like to see them.'

'Just a couple of pages in an album. Come to Ireland with me, next visit. Meet Sean.'

'Assuming he hasn't passed on from extreme old age,' said Michael.

Liv made to hand the picture back but Melody stopped her. 'It's for you, to keep. Not the original, Sean has that. This is a copy. I've got one too.'

I said, 'Can I have it for my room?' My heritage, I was thinking. My past, my history, amazing.

'It's Liv's, really. But I brought something else for you, Frey.' Melody sat back down on the sofa arm and felt around inside her canvas satchel, underneath the angora shrug. I hoped my present wasn't going to be whisky-flavoured fudge or one of those pebbles with feet and eyes stuck on. But it turned out to be a ring box made of scuffed burgundy leather. She dropped it into my outstretched palm.

When I flipped the lid open, I let out a low whistle. The ring she'd given me was gold with a chunky square-cut red stone flanked on each side by a row of minute pearls. You could tell it was old, the surface dulled and pinkish, and the mountings grimy, but it was still a lovely piece. I couldn't believe she was giving it to me.

'That's a garnet in the middle,' she explained, 'and the metal's rose gold. It was Abby's mum's, and Abby had it on her wedding day, and it was supposed to come to me when I got married. But I'm not going to, so I thought you should have it. A family heirloom. No point waiting till I'm dead. Aren't you going to try it on?'

My hands were quivering slightly as I slipped the ring over my finger, into the space that had been so lately stained with Oggy's canal-path tat.

'How does it fit?' asked Liv.

'It's a little loose,' I said. My voice was hoarse suddenly.

'We can take it to a jewellers and get it adjusted. That's so kind of Melody, isn't it? How generous of her. You must write and say thank you to Abby, too. Let me have a closer look.'

I let her lift my hand so she could examine the stone under the light. It winked and flared as I moved, as if somewhere inside whole crystalline worlds were shifting against each other, hot coals and dark blood and sunsets and deadly nightshade berries. The depths of the stone seemed unfathomable. And it felt as though all the hopes and fears of the women who'd worn this ring had been absorbed into it, and flashed out at me: *you, it ends with you.*

'Frey?' said Michael.

I blinked and cleared my throat. 'Fine. Sorry. My throat's quite dry, actually, I need a drink. No, not the elderflower. I'm just going to get a glass of water.'

I pulled off the ring and gave it to Liv, then fled.

★   ★   ★

The kitchen was an unbelievable mess. The floor was covered in chunks of dried mud that I

311

guessed had dropped off Geraint's giant boots, and the sink was smeared with black and green slime. One washing-up bowl, half full of pond water, sat by the back door and there was another on the work surface, empty except for a measuring cylinder and an eight-inch fish net. Liv's blender had been hauled out and plugged in, then filled with what looked like spinach soup but I guessed wasn't. The base-unit door below was marked with black fingerprints.

I stepped round the filth and got myself a clean tumbler out of the cupboard; let the cold tap run, swilling away some of the slime down the plughole, filled my glass and swallowed it down in a single gulp.

Michael appeared in the doorway. 'I'll have one of those.'

Without a word I re-filled the glass and handed it to him. As he drank his head tipped back, his Adam's apple bobbing. I wondered if he'd have to cut his hair short to work in a hot country.

'Bit skanky, this.' He put the glass down next to the blender and nodded at the chaos around him.

'Geraint's doing something with sphagnum moss spores. Spreading them about.'

'I'll say he is. What did you think of Melody's ring?'

'It was — I don't know. Don't tell her, but — I mean, it is classy, way too classy for me, and it was a kind thought. I was blown away, to be honest.'

'But what?'

'Oh, ignore me. I'm not myself this evening. It's been a bloody weird day.'

'And then we turned up unannounced.'

'Get off, it's always good to see you.' I let my gaze follow a string of blanket weed that stretched across the tea-towel drawer and down the front of the pan cupboard. 'I think it's that I don't feel I'm worthy, you know? A ring like that, a precious family heirloom. I haven't done enough to earn it, and I'm not mature enough to be trusted to look after it. Never mind who I'm expected to pass it on to.'

'Ah, come on, Frey. You're not even twenty-four yet. Christ, get to my age and then you can start talking like a failure.'

'I'm not fishing for compliments. I'm just saying how I feel.'

After a moment he came over and stood next to me. 'There's no catch. Melody gave you the ring because you're her daughter, her only daughter, and she loves you. It's yours by virtue of that. There's nothing to be earned. If you're worried about losing the ring, have it tightened. If you never have kids, leave it in your will to Nicky, or to a hospice, or drive down to Lands End and cast it adrift in a bottle.' He nudged me in the ribs till I smiled.

I said, 'What would I do without you?'

'You'd survive.'

'Would I?'

In the container by the door the water shivered and a piece of weed revolved under the bulk of a climbing snail. 'Hey, Kim's got herself a new man, so that's one weight off my back.'

'Is that how you see me, then, as a weight?'

He made a mock lunge at me as if his patience had finally snapped.

At the same time there came a scuffle from the dining room, a scraping of a heavy object against wood followed by a muffled crash and a series of soft thuds, one after the other. A single apple rolled into the kitchen. Geraint had knocked the fruit bowl off the window sill again.

Michael said, 'You've got Oggy, Nicky, both your mums. You'd be so busy juggling crises you wouldn't even notice if I wasn't around.'

I shook my head. 'But you're — '

Geraint was standing on the threshold with a piece of bowl in each hand, his beard drooping.

'Have we any of that superglue left?' he said.

★   ★   ★

Although I had one earphone in, I still heard the quiet tap on my bedroom door. I switched my iPod off and checked the clock: 2.15 a.m. Evidently someone else couldn't sleep either.

'Liv, is that you?' I called. She pushed the door open with her hip because she had a mug in each hand.

'I saw your light,' she said. Her kimono was loose, but she'd tied a blue scarf round her head in lieu of the wig.

'Suits you better than British Birds.' I took the cup and set it down on my bedside table.

She settled on the duvet next to me.

'These nights are a bugger, aren't they? When your mind goes racing. Geraint's snoring for

England, which isn't exactly helping. He sounds like an elephant seal.'

Looks like one, too, I thought. 'Aren't you feeling so good?'

'I'm fine. Just can't sleep. And I wanted to check you were OK. You've not been yourself this evening.'

'It was nice to see Melody looking so well,' I said, side-stepping the question. 'The job sounds perfect for her.'

'It does, doesn't it? Yes, it was good to see her. Michael too, of course. He's a lovely man. They're a decent family, really. Let's have another look at your ring.'

I passed it over and her rough fingers stroked the smooth metal sides. I could tell she was as impressed as I was. I wondered idly how much it was worth.

I said, 'Did you mind about the picture?'

Liv glanced up in surprise. 'I thought it was great. Very well done. He's a talented artist.'

'It shows me with Melody, though. Like she's sort of — staking her claim.'

Round and round she twisted the ring, studying the colours inside the garnet the way I'd done. Then she said, 'It's not about who you belong to. Maybe at first, years ago when you were very young and I was a brand new mum and not so sure of myself. I used to have these silly nightmares. But I don't think of you as hers or mine, I think of you as yourself. Gosh, look at you. All grown up.' She placed the ring back on the bed, then reached over and ran her finger down my cheek and under my chin.

'And I'd treasure any picture of you as a baby,' she went on, 'because that was the happiest period of my life, when you came along. The three years before we got you were dreadful, actually. Dreadful.'

I'd seen plenty of photos of Liv and Colin before they adopted me. When I got to twelve or thirteen, I'd become obsessed with them, poring over old albums repeatedly, unsticking every picture to see if there were any messages written on the back, taking copies to make screensavers, wallpaper for my phone, my own mini-album. There were pictures from college, wedding ones, holiday snaps and a couple of what looked like parties or work dos: Liv, in her twenties then, long red hair and full, plump cheeks, and Colin resplendent in patterned sweaters and a side parting. They seemed carefree and young. I'd never thought about them having tough years. I suppose the story I'd told myself was that one day they decided they'd like a baby, so they just trotted along to the adoption agency and got one. That simple. 'Is it hard, adopting? The process, I mean. Does it take a long time?'

She grimaced. 'You have *no* idea, Frey. God, the hoops they have you jumping through, endless. Constantly worried you're going to fail at every one. You see, whatever feelings I've had towards Melody over the years, underneath everything I'll always be so grateful to her. Because of what she rescued us from. As soon as we married we were trying and trying for a baby, and getting nowhere. People would ask when we were going to start a family — it's one of those questions complete strangers feel they can come out with — and we had to pretend we didn't want one.'

'Why didn't you tell them the truth?'

'It was easier. If you reveal you're infertile then that's the green light for a lot of intrusive and sometimes quite unkind personal questions. Pitying looks, whispers. And friends, family were all busy producing, and we'd get cards through the post with photos of newborns, and we'd have to go to christenings and I'd be given other women's babies to hold. You can't lock yourself away from it, much as you'd like to.

'Then in the end it turned out to be my fault, my dodgy tubes, and that was rotten because I felt as though I'd let Colin down. I thought he might want to walk away, to start again with a woman whose insides were in proper working order. But he was so good with me, Frey. He said, 'We're in this together.' And he kept telling me we'd be all right, he'd get me a baby somehow. I didn't think we'd ever get there, though. The paperwork and the waiting, the endless interviews. They were dark times. Very dark.'

'You never told me much about it.'

'It stopped mattering when you came along.' Her eyes were seeing something far away. 'I remember particularly, there was this one weekend when we went to Avebury — Colin booked it as a surprise, to cheer me up — and I was so sure I was pregnant. We walked all round the standing stones, and he was going on about so-called primitive societies being more sophisticated than we gave them credit for, and would someone today be able to make a polished axe head using their bare hands, and all I could think of was that I might really be having a baby. The sun was shining and there were these mallard ducklings by the car park, it was perfect. Then, on the way home, we stopped for a meal at a pub and I found out my period had started. I was inconsolable, the weekend ruined. Poor Col.'

We're in this together. What a lovely thing to say. I thought of Oggy, his disconnection, his sheer bloody uselessness, and then of the father I hardly got to know.

Liv stood up and went over to the window, drew back the curtain.

'What can you see?' I asked. From where I lay it was all reflection.

'Checking for our bat. Our little pip.'

'Is he there?'

'Can't see him. Lots of moths about so he won't be going hungry.'

Snatches of the past slid against each other and clicked into place. New patterns formed out of the darkness. There was this feel about the room, like we'd entered a charmed hour, a space where we could talk about all sorts of things we normally avoided.

'Melody's phoned you again.'

'I've chatted to her a few times lately.'

'What do you talk about?'

'Well — baby Elizabeth. Cancer. Loss. You.' She turned and smiled at me. 'Oh, you know she wants to make up my eyes with some expensive

shadow she's discovered? Give me false eyelashes, brows, the works. Can you imagine?'

'That's thoughtful.'

'I know.'

'Will you let her?'

'I can't be bothered with it. I might tell her the
chemo makes me allergic.'

She peered through the glass again.

'Do you like Melody?' I said. 'As a person,
aside from who she is.'

'I feel dreadfully sorry for what she's gone
through.'

'But do you like her?'

'I think I do, yes. Now I understand her
better.'

'You haven't always.'

Stillness, and the tiny ping of an insect against
the pane.

'Did you mind when I first got in touch with
her? I know you said you didn't, but did you,
really?'

Liv sighed. 'It wasn't for me to mind, Frey. I
always knew it would happen.'

'You were upset, though, weren't you? I didn't
get it at the time. Like, lately, when I've been
thinking back, there were all these little details I
didn't pick up on. I can see them now. I don't
know how I missed them.' I was thinking of a
trip Mel, Michael and I had taken to Alton
Towers. Getting back late, falling through our
front door, shrieking with laughter and wet from
a Coke-bottle fight, while behind me Melody
and Michael wrestled over a feathered headdress
they'd bought off one of the stalls. Liv's face

lined and stern as she stood under the harsh hall light.

'I suppose it would have been easier if *she'd* contacted *you*, then you and I would have been in it together. As it was, you were so full of your new mother, so full of new ideas. You obviously wanted to re-invent yourself. And of course Melody's so glamorous. I felt like a clapped-out old nag next to her.' She gave an awkward laugh.

'Why didn't you say anything?'

'Because ever since you came to me, whatever else has been happening, my number one instinct's been to protect you. You can't blame me. I'm a mum: it's what we do.'

'I'm grown up now.'

'My head knows that. The rest of me — it's hard to let go sometimes.'

'Which is why you won't talk to me about your cancer any more.'

She blinked, and her lips formed words I couldn't hear. Then she said: 'The trouble with mothers is we want to keep you safe against all the odds. Like King Canute battling the tide. We can't help trying, even though we're doomed to failure.'

Liv left the window and sat by me again. I could smell her aloe vera face cream, and it was comforting. When I was in the infants, she used to rub me with sunscreen that had the same scent. Her palms were always sandpapery with working outdoors. When she bent to massage my legs, her long hair would shake in a wavy curtain.

'I wish,' she said, 'I wish in retrospect you'd had a bit of proper adoption counselling. Social

Services wanted you to. They were good with me. They got me to keep a diary, just a personal one, for myself. It was very helpful, actually.'

'Did you?' I was amazed she'd never mentioned it.

'Only for a few months. Till things settled down.'

'Have you still got it? Can I read it?'

'No,' she said. I didn't know which question she was answering.

I put out my arms and buried my face against her as if I was still a little girl. When I let her go her scarf had slipped to one side. Her face was pink as she pulled the material back into place.

She said, 'I think it's been hard for you, juggling two mothers.'

'I belong to an adaptable generation. Plus it's one of those situations that probably seems much more hectic from the outside than it is.'

'I hope that's true. I've fretted for years about the effect it's had on your confidence. Because you're not very confident, are you? And I don't know why. Have I tried to protect you too much? Is it my fault? Is it Melody's?'

'It's no one's. I'm fine. Look at me, happy happy happy. Really, I am. Anyway, according to Mrs Steuer I've been 'terribly brave'. I think she's been dying for me to have a meltdown and run away or go on drugs. She talks about 'your family trouble', as though we're all marked with some terrible curse. You know she still refers to divorced households as 'broken homes'.'

'I expect she calls Melody a Fallen Woman.'

'I wouldn't be surprised. Once she told me I'd

'survived a hellish upbringing very well'.'

Liv gave a weak smile. 'Funny, I've often looked at Nicky and thought the same thing about her.'

Both of us began to snigger meanly. Joan Steuer with her forest of Swarovski, her massed ranks of Doulton figurines. Derek bringing out the after-dinner port in a silver-labelled decanter.

'God, Mum, imagine being brought up in that house. Petrified of knocking over a little table or nudging some crinoline lady off a shelf. Being made to leave your Doc Martens by the door.'

'Would she even have let you own anything as subversive as Doc Martens?'

'No way. She'd have put me into care the day I refused to wear heels. Or had me sectioned.'

'See, you could have had a worse mum.'

'Well, I could.'

Now, across the sympathetic hush that fell between us, began a weird snuffling and shuffling from the other side of the door. The landing light flicked on and off several times, followed by a thud at skirting level and a cry.

We looked at each other.

A feeble scrabble and then the door burst open: Geraint was wearing a knackered grey T-shirt with a Led Zeppelin motif, and a towel wrapped round his waist. His glasses were missing, making the top half of his face look lopsided and unfinished.

He stood and blinked at us resentfully. 'I didn't know where everyone was.'

'What the *hell* are you wearing?' I asked him.

He cast his eyes down, forlorn. 'It was all I

322

could find. Liv took my dressing gown for a badger cub, for lining its box. I never got it back.'

'Oh, God, I'd forgotten about that.' She tried to look contrite, but I could see she was struggling not to smile. 'It's probably still at Woodlands Mammal Shelter. Sorry. I'll pick it up next week, I promise. It might need a wash.'

'Aw, Geraint, that's tragic, though. Would you deprive a baby badger of its only comfort?'

'Frey! I'll go over on Tuesday, first thing.'

'But it's probably too late, isn't it?' I went on. 'They'll have made nests and bedding out of it. The staff might have cut it up for bandages. I mean, think how many poorly weasels you could splint out of a dressing gown that size. About a million, probably. And even if it's still in one piece, it'll be covered in filth. You know what frightened animals do. I'd definitely be checking the pockets before you put it in the machine, 'cause you don't want a drumful of undigested pellets. Little mouse bones poking you in the stomach afterwards.'

'I could try some fabric conditioner — '

'That lingering smell of rescue centre. Whiff of Polecat. Hint of Mink.'

'You know they don't take in mink.'

'Pong of Otter.'

'*Frey!*'

Geraint stood and peered at us for a few more seconds, then without a word he turned and walked away, closing the door behind him with an offended click. I let out a great snort of mirth. Liv flapped her hand at me to stop, but I was too far gone. Soon we were both helpless on the bed.

'He — ' She was trying to say something but she couldn't get the words out. 'He — '

'Smells of badger?'

Her scarf slipped off and there she was in her baldness, with tears running down her face. The naked skin didn't matter. 'Don't make me — He's a decent man — '

'Who smells of badger.'

My belly hurt but I couldn't stop. I don't know how long we lay together, laughing into the night.

Case Notes on: Melody Jacqueline Brewster

Meeting Location: 42, Love Lane, Nantwich

Present: Miss Melody Brewster, Mrs Abby Brewster, Mrs Diane Kozyra

Date: 10.45 a.m., 29/4/87

Some concerns raised by this visit. I found Melody very upset. Mrs Brewster said her daughter was struggling with her school-work, had not been sleeping well and had been experiencing some shortness of breath. Her GP is investigating asthma, though he'd said the breathlessness could also be panic attacks.

Eventually Melody asked if she could speak to me alone and Mrs Brewster agreed to leave us together for a short time. Then Melody told me she was worried about her baby. I asked whether she was changing her mind about the adoption, but she was adamant that she was not. However she did express the following specific anxieties: What if Fay cried in the night and the new parents didn't hear her? What if she became ill and they didn't notice till it was too late? What if the man secretly wanted a son and hadn't told his wife?

I asked Melody if she'd talked to her mother

about these fears and she said no, she didn't want to. I stressed again how carefully the adoptive parents are vetted, trained and monitored, and how much they will be looking forward to giving baby Fay a loving home. Melody said that she only wanted the best for her baby, but since she and Fay had been parted she felt as though she had 'a big black hole inside her'.

Promised she could have an additional counselling session next week.

Follow-up: contact Maureen Harper about possibly delaying the assessment by the reporting officer for a week or so.

Next visit: 08/5/87   Signed: Diane Kozyra

A SATURDAY

October

The brilliant news was that Liv had, that morning, found some hair. She still had five more chemo sessions to go, but they'd changed the drug after the first four and they did say she might get some re-growth before her final dose. She'd invited me into her bedroom to see. You had to look quite closely; nevertheless it was definitely there, tiny short baby wisps.

'I'm still wearing my wig for the autumn fair, though,' she said. 'Talking of which, chop-chop because we've a lot to do and not a lot of time to do it in.'

I knew we had to be at the fair, setting up, for nine. The display boards were ready and in the back of the Volvo, but the trickier part was that she also needed a selection of pond life for the Shropshire Mosses table. Most especially she needed newts, common and great crested, so she could do the whole legally protected species bit. It's a message she's always trying to drum home among the public. Theoretically you can go to prison for interfering with a newt.

So while she fiddled with the wig, I took the bag of wildlife kit plus two nets and a selection of plastic pots down to the pondside and started fishing. Before Liv came out to join me I'd already bagged a beetle, some unidentified larvae, several snails and about a hundred shrimp-things. 'The water boatmen keep hopping out,' I complained.

When I glanced up she was wearing not her wig, but one of Geraint's green canvas fishing hats. It made her look like one of those eco-protesters you see on TV, the type who live up trees and weave flowers round the prongs of mechanical diggers.

'OK, good start. Let's nab that dragonfly nymph and give it a pot of its own, though. Otherwise it'll eat everything else.'

I watched her decant the vicious squirming grub into solitary confinement, then picked up my net and swept it again through the weed. This time I brought up a dozen more shrimps and a lone tadpole.

'My God, look at that,' I said, shaking it in with the snails. 'It should have been a frog by now, but it hasn't even got back legs.'

She leaned over to check out my freak. 'No, it's fine. Tadpoles do occasionally over-winter in that state and develop next spring. Assuming they survive.'

'Why do they do that?'

'It varies. Not enough food to go round, colder than average weather. Pollution, in some cases.'

'Or just general crapness.'

'Yes, probably that too.'

Below the shadow of my net, pond skaters slid carelessly about, barely even troubling the surface, and for some reason I heard again Joan Steuer's voice: *I don't believe it's all been as easy as you make out.* Well, perhaps it hadn't. Perhaps I'd been a pond skater in a previous life, or a backward tadpole.

I swished again and got a leech.

'Ah-ha!' Liv pulled her net in, grinning. 'Gotcha.' That would be a newt. 'Which species is it?'

'Only a common one, and only a juvenile. But that's one down, one to go.'

She turned it out into a fresh container where it shivered and turned and then hung still. It wasn't even the length of my pinkie finger, stripy brown with delicate splayed feet. I felt sorry for the morning it was about to have. 'You'd think they'd be hibernating now.'

'Yes, it's amazing, I didn't think we'd be so lucky. I suppose it's down to this funny weather we've had, long cool summer and now this incredibly warm autumn. Everything's been delayed.' She slid her net down through the weed again, stealthily.

Here we were in sleeveless shirts, enjoying the sun on our arms. The water felt chilly, but otherwise the garden gave no hint of a winter that must only be weeks away. I saw Geraint come up to the kitchen window, his hand raised to shade his brow against the bright day. Meanwhile Liv swirled the pond into clouds, sent duckweed scattering out across the surface like blasted constellations.

'No luck?' I said.

'Nope. They probably remember me fishing them out last year so they're staying hidden. They'll be sunk down at the bottom, pretending to be dead leaves.'

'I can't really help, can I?'

She shook her head and dipped the net once more. Even in the field of environmental studies, only certain professionals are allowed to handle GCNs. You have to go on training days with titles like 'Working Towards Your Great Crested Newt Licence', and even then there are loads of rules you have to follow: care in handling and maximum containment time etc. I remembered from last year a Natural England newsletter headline announcing some firm up in Yorkshire had been fined eleven thousand for trashing a newt-filled pond. Legally, newts rule. And yet there's this smudge of a fly lives on the Moss, plain transparent wings and a Latin name I couldn't pronounce even if I could remember it, and it's so rare it's listed in Red Data Book One. In other words, if it were any rarer, it would be extinct. But no one seems bothered about saving it because it's dull and midge-shaped. Looks count for so much in this world, when you come down to it.

I said, 'I've been thinking about Melody.'

'How her new job's going? I was wondering that, too. Didn't Michael tell you last week she'd sold her first painting?'

'Yeah. It wasn't that, though. I meant, I was thinking about the baby. Elizabeth.' I made myself say the name, and at the same moment the sun went behind a cloud and the light was grey.

Liv pushed the brim of her hat off her forehead. 'I worry about Melody, too. One of those losses you never fully get over. Her due date was this month, wasn't it?'

'Yeah. Next Friday. But I had this idea for something I could do to help.'

'That's kind of you. What did you have in mind?'

'Just, we had this leaflet from one of our suppliers at the nursery about memorial topiary. It's for children, for cemeteries, and they do all animal shapes, dolphins and teddies, leaping deer, rabbits. The pictures were cool. I thought I could buy her one.'

She put her head on one side, considering. 'But there's no grave to mark, is there?'

'It could live in the backyard. They come in pots with a plaque, although she might want to choose the words for that herself. If the baby — Elizabeth — had a tree in the garden, then it would be kind of like she was still part of the family.' I could hear myself, hear how stupid I sounded.

'You know, that's a very good thought,' said Liv. 'Are they expensive, these animal trees?'

'You can get a rabbit for about two hundred and fifty. Swans are about three hundred. They're proper quality Italian plants they use, *Ilex crenata*, not just these moss-packed chicken wire jobs you can pick up anywhere. As long as Melody looked after it, it would last forever.'

'Well, how about this. It's a lot of money for you to come up with, so I'd be happy to help out. It could be from both of us. If you wanted.'

'I've got savings. I'd rather pay for it myself.'

Liv dipped her net again. 'You go ahead, then. I'm sure she'll be extremely touched.'

I felt a glow in my chest: a project gone right, a job well done.

There was a flurry of water and Liv swung her net round so it almost struck my shoulder. A line of drops silvered the pond's surface as she brought the pole in. Under the black slime, something wriggled and twisted.

She laid the head of the net down on the bank and brought some water to swill the newt clean. What emerged was nearly as dark as the mud that surrounded it: a snaky head with yellow-rimmed eyes, a ridged back, a skin texture rough and primeval. It was much longer, fatter and angrier than the common newt we'd caught earlier, and lashed its tail from side to side. When Liv coaxed it into the pot, I saw the poisonous flash of its bright-orange belly.

'Bingo!' she said admiringly. 'What a beauty.'

'Do we need anything else?'

'A ramshorn would be nice. Oh, we've none of the larger beetles, have we? Let me have another go.'

The sun came back out and, on the far side of next door's garden, a squirrel ran up and down a branch with a purposeful motion. I like grey squirrels, for all they're a pest species. In Liv's bag I knew there was a pair of binoculars, so I hauled them out and brought him into focus. It's the stop-start action of squirrels I love to watch, and the way they use their tails to steer through the air when they make an extra-big leap. This one looked to have something on its mind. It kept pausing as though it was going through some kind of mental checklist; then, satisfied, romping forward in a lazy run. I watched it spring from a high branch to a low — almost miss — swing by its front paws, tail rotating — then scramble up to pose perfectly still, the spit of one of those concrete statues we sell at the garden centre. You could tell it was in its element, up there among the twigs. And that's the cool thing about nature, how every animal's so skilled at doing what it does, there's never any dithering or confusion. Squirrels climb and jump and scrounge off the feeder and make nests and mate and try to avoid being eaten, and that's their life and they seem pretty happy on it. And good luck to you, I thought, as it dashed off again, vertically up the main trunk. I tried to track it but it must have done a sneaky U-turn or nipped into a hole because all of a sudden it wasn't there any more.

I kept the binoculars to my eyes and scanned about for something else to watch. There were jackdaws on the chimney top, a woodpigeon on the apex of the roof. Sparrows fought in the gutter. I lowered the bins till I was looking into our kitchen, at Geraint, at his wide, beardy face, the thick glasses, the unruly hair. What *was* he doing just standing staring at us like that? And then I caught the gleam of moisture under his eyes. I tweaked the focus slightly till I had him. Geraint, frozen, his gaze fixed on Liv, tears running freely down his cheeks.

I lowered the bins at once.

'Here's a great diving beetle,' she said behind me. 'He can have a pot of his own. Shove that lidded one a bit nearer, will you, so I can get at it? Actually, if you could be filling another with vegetation, that would be useful.'

I let my hand fall into the water, feeling for a rope of Canadian pondweed. It came up in a great dripping arc and I snapped a length of stalk off and coiled it round my fingers to stuff into the pot with the snails. Next, with my bare hands I plucked a ramshorn snail off the side of the bridge and added it to the collection, and I also scooped out some of the dead sycamore leaves that had clumped together round the reeds. Repeatedly I found myself glancing up at Geraint, who remained where he was, mournful kitchen sentry.

I'm sure he knew I was watching him, but he never once moved till Liv began to gather up her equipment.

★   ★   ★

It always amazes me how many hippies live in our small town. You don't see more than two or three out and about normally — the woman with the patchwork skirt who runs the herbalists, the couple with matching leather waistcoats who I think are based out at Steel Heath — but put on a certain type of event and hey presto, they materialise. Anything to do with folk music brings them out, or wholefoods, any spiritual/alternative/psychic jamboree or environmental bash and there they are.

Standing in the market hall while Liv put the finishing touches to our stand, I was struck, for instance, by how many men here had adopted the Geraint look. Some of them may have been older, some younger, taller, hairier or thinner (and none of them was wearing a grey-green fluffy jumper that looked as though it had grown from penicillin), but the general outline was the same. If Geraint wandered off at any point in the morning, we'd have hell on trying to pick him out of the crowd. It would be like a live-action *Where's Wally*.

The stall on our right was manned by a white witch selling healing crystals laid out on a black velvet cloth; on our left a fairly ordinary couple handed out Fungus Foray leaflets, and next to them was a stained-glass artist. Across the other side of the building a jaunty band played acoustic guitars and a bodhran. Liv had placed the pots of pond life down on white card so it was easier for passers-by to see the contents, and she'd provided a magnifying glass on a string, for close study.

My job was to make sure no one dabbled their fingers in the water or tried to poke the livestock. I also had to identify any newt-blessed landowners that we didn't already have on our records. Then Liv would swing into action, taking down contact details and grid references, and speaking flatteringly about 'guardianship' and 'stewards of the future'. She was good at this. I'd seen her enthuse some really resistant people.

Behind us, hidden by display boards, was a food stall; occasionally I'd hear a woman's voice saying things like, 'No, no artificial colourings,' and 'We only use local honey.' I'd glimpsed her when we were setting up, a busty girl in a kurta with hair as vivid as mine, except hers was in long plaits. If I sniffed, I could smell cinnamon, orange, vanilla, and the scent was cheering and warm. 'And are they free-range eggs?' a man asked. The hall was filling up.

I was helping a small boy use the magnifier to spot daphnia when another voice cut in: female, more strident, posh, sneering.

'I mean, it's all a big con, isn't it?'

Liv's head swung round, but the speaker was at our backs. Neither of us could see anything over the boards.

'A total bloody con,' said the voice again, and I found myself picturing a smart elderly woman with a snappish mouth and a tweedy suit.

'I'm not sure what you mean,' said the stall holder, in her soft Midlands burr.

'This organic nonsense. It's just a way of screwing more money out of the consumer, isn't it?'

The boy laid down the magnifying glass and moved on. I exchanged glances with Liv.

'Would you like a Soil Association leaflet?' said the stall holder. 'You can read more about what the organic movement's trying to achieve — '

'No I wouldn't. These poor saps might be taken in by your rhetoric, but we both know that the whole organic movement's nothing more than an attempt to discredit ordinary farmers and screw cash out of the government and get customers to pay extra.'

Geraint whispered something to Liv. I wanted to peer round the edge of the display and see this old boot for myself, but I thought that might make the situation worse.

'It's about respect for the land,' began the stall holder.

'Oh, please. Don't start that tree-hugging nonsense. I've worked the land all my life, no one knows it better than I do. This is just — See, look at this: 'chemical-free'. It's rubbish. Define chemical!'

The girl said nothing.

'Everything's *chemical*,' the boot went on. 'Water's a chemical. We're made up of chemicals. So how can you claim your — products — are chemical-free?'

'It's in the Soil Association literature. We mean anything synthesised in a lab. Produced artificially. Man-made. Not naturally occurring.'

'Your flapjacks are man-made. Or did you dig them up this morning and shake the earth off them?' I could imagine her turning round to share the joke. 'These health claims you make for organic foods, they're completely without foundation, aren't they? Outrageous lies. All the pesticides we use on our farm have been thoroughly tested for safety.'

'Like DDT was,' muttered Liv.

'People *want* perfect food. Don't you understand? They don't like blemishes and worm holes and blight on their nice shiny apples. And they *don't* want to pay for all the crops lost to disease. Why should they?'

'We feel consumers ought to have a choice,' said the stall holder feebly. I could see her in my mind's eye, her head bowed, plaits drooping.

Most of us had come with friends or colleagues, but she was manning the decks on her own.

'And what about the labelling abuse that goes on? Didn't they find that a lot of organic food *isn't*? I mean, who regulates these things, actually?'

I became aware of Geraint putting down his clipboard and standing, angling himself round, attempting to insinuate his bulk between the gap in the tables at the edge of the display. Liv put her hand on his arm but he took no notice. A brief effort and he was out into the aisle and round the corner, out of sight. Then we heard him clear his throat.

'It's to do with *environmental impact*,' he said.

'Oh, here we go again,' said the Boot.

But Geraint wasn't daunted. This was his specialist subject, his area of expertise and passion. Great useless lollop he was in so many ways, but lectures like this are what he relishes. Wind him up and off he goes, Welshly.

'Do you know,' he said, 'how many types of butterfly are under *serious threat*? How many beetles and damselflies and bees? Nearly *two thousand* species we're on the brink of losing forever, invertebrates that we'll never get back, that we depend on for pollination and to keep our natural ecology in place. A *third* of all bees and wasps! Do you know how close we came in the Seventies to losing our otters and our birds of prey to organochlorines? Lindane and endosulfan were being used in this country *right up* until a couple of years ago. Your pesticides and insecticides and fungicides and herbicides,

338

what do you think happens to them after they've been laid down? Where do you think they go when it rains? You get poison into the system and it hangs around, gets into our water, into the food chain, affects all kinds of animals and plants it was never intended for. *Twenty-five years* it can take for dieldrin to break down, and you'd still be left with a residue. We're still finding DDT and endrin in fish livers.'

The woman tried to speak, but he rumbled on over her, preacher-style.

'Let me tell you, lady, about the harvest mouse. Those little creatures are so sensitive to chemicals, we lost a whole tankful of them when someone used fly killer in a closed office *two doors down the corridor*. Then there's the animal welfare issue. Organic food *guarantees* your pig or your chicken or your sheep's been raised free from cruelty. Never mind free from hormones and routine antibiotics. Organic farms use fewer fossil fuels, too. They take less from the land all round. In fact, here's a challenge. Next summer, on a hot day, you walk round a farm where they don't use pesticides and *you count up* the number of butterflies you see. Then go walk across a field that's been sprayed. You'll *see* the difference.'

'As if I'd have — '

'And while we're here, it's been *scientifically proven* that organic milk is higher in Omega 3.'

'My, aren't you the expert,' said the Boot nastily.

We waited for more, but it never came.

After about thirty seconds, Geraint appeared

round the side of the stand clutching a flapjack and looking grimly pleased with himself.

'Well done,' said Liv.

I thought about adding my congratulations too, but decided they might sound fake, or worse, sarcastic. Besides, when I looked across, he was back on his GPS machine, head down, absorbed.

Instead I checked my aquarium. All the water creatures were busy exploring their world of plastic, shrimps circuiting in an endless quiver, nymphs shooting random trajectories, snails and leeches creeping, creeping. The dragonfly larva patrolled, searching for something to attack.

'Eew, is it a lizard? Is it alive?' a girl of about ten was asking me. She banged on the side of the tank, sending the newts into a panic.

'Don't do that!' I snapped, and she shrank back in surprise. I guess I must have sounded fiercer than I meant. Still, she needed to know. Sometimes I despair of humans.

'I think,' observed Liv, after the girl had moved on to healing crystals, 'we might be due a break. Geraint's got an appointment with a dormouse man in ten minutes, so do you want to go first?'

I took myself off to the tea counter, then for a wander round the hall. I bought myself a pair of purple fingerless gloves and, on an impulse, a Celtic bracelet for Liv. I chatted to the couple who run our local hedgehog rescue. As well as artists and wildlife folk, there were reps from the eco-coal place in Wrexham, Windtrap Turbines, Compost Awareness and Love Food Hate Waste.

By the time I was ready to go back, I had an armful of leaflets plus a special potato sack that prevents your spuds from sprouting prematurely.

I thought I'd go via the orange-plait-woman's stall, see how she was doing. Trade was brisk, I was pleased to see; flapjacks were flying off the plates. She'd stuck felt bees on wire so they floated above her jars of honey and jam, and her business card had a cartoon bee logo. *The Honey Bar*, I read. There was a row of customers in front of me so I couldn't get close enough to speak, but I gave the thumbs up, and she saw me and smiled.

Then, from the other side of the display boards, I detected Melody's voice — no huge surprise as she'd said she would drop by with my birthday present — and I was just going to walk round the corner and say hi when I heard Liv say the word 'cancer'. There was something about her tone that made me think I shouldn't interrupt. So I hung about in the aisle, and pretended to study a selection of air purifiers. 'Because I thought I'd never get to the end of it,' she was saying. 'Back in May, when I started chemo, it felt like I was standing at the bottom of a great high mountain. The first session was the worst. You don't know what to expect. Actually, it's all ghastly. Trailing backwards and forwards to hospital. And the chemo suite's as cheerful as they can make it, the nurses are lovely, but it's still a bit grim, how can it not be? Even though all you're doing is sitting around, it's exhausting. Absolutely wipes you out.'

'So seven down and five to go?' said Melody.

'You're over the hump, then. The end's in sight.'

'It's a wonderful thought. And yet — I know I should be grateful, get to spring and everything signed off.'

'You're not?'

Liv lowered her voice so I had to strain to hear. 'When I think about the chemo finishing, I'm actually petrified.'

My heart cramped with panic. I heard Melody ask: 'Is it because you don't think they've totally zapped the bad stuff?'

There was a long, dreadful pause. Then, before she could reply, some idiot passer-by butted in to ask why they had to cut some of the trees down on the Moss. Liv was forced to explain about encroachment and the need to balance habitats, and he wittered on about the old oak he used to play in as a kid. 'Forests are the lungs of the planet,' he kept saying. *Bugger off*, I vibed at him. *Hope a tree falls on your head sometime.*

At last he moved on, and after a few moments I heard her go, 'Yes, the chemo's vile, but when it's finished, where does that leave me? It's the idea that I'll be on my own. While you're having chemo, you're being treated and there's a structure to the weeks and you've something positive to battle against. It's horrible but it's also reassuring, if that makes any sense.'

'They'll keep a close eye on you after, though,' said Melody.

'Oh, they will. I'll have regular scans. The slightest concern, I can go back and see the consultant. I'll actually be safer than someone

342

who's never been ill. They've stressed that. I know I'm being silly.'

'No you're not. Jesus, I'd be bricking it, anyone would. For what it's worth, I think you've been incredibly cool about everything. Cancer — well, it's shit.'

'But once you overcome that initial shock you find yourself just getting on with things. You can't carry on being stunned forever. And also, I think you surprise yourself, what you can cope with when it comes down to it. Cancer's one of those things no one else can go through for you. People can wave encouragement from the sidelines, but really, you're on your own.'

'Like losing a baby.'

'Yes. It has been a bloody awful year, hasn't it?'

Another silence followed, the kind that suggests there's really nothing more to say on a particular topic, or that words won't do it justice, or that perhaps two women have, for a second or two, touched a level of understanding they've never reached before. I'd have put down my air purifier and walked round the corner at this point, except Liv suddenly went, 'Freya's been good.'

I froze.

'She's so helpful round the house,' she went on. 'Does nearly all the cleaning, a lot of the cooking; she's run me to hospital, even held the bowl while I was sick. She's been like a nurse. I never have to worry about whether the washing'll get done, or if we'll run out of milk or bread. She just gets on and sorts it. I don't know how I'd have managed without her. Geraint's a love but he never thinks about details like that.'

'You're telling me!' I said aloud. The man on the purifier stall looked up.

'Yeah,' said Melody. 'She was a support to me at the funeral. I really appreciated it. Michael did, too. 'Cause it can't have been easy, but it meant a lot. Thing is, Freya might not be one of these high-flyers but she is grounded, and in a shitty world that counts for a lot. You've, you know, done a decent job with her.'

'Well. It's not all been plain sailing,' said Liv.

'You've done a sight better than I could. Two babies I've had, and I couldn't keep either. I'm obviously not meant to be a mother.'

'But you are a mother.'

'Maybe a semi-detached kind of one.'

'Isn't that what all mums become in the end? If we've done the job right. I sometimes wonder with Frey, I think you might be better at treating her . . . I've found it hard — '

Something clattered to the floor; Melody made noises of concern.

Liv: 'No, no, I'm not upset. Not at all. There's a hanky in my bag.'

The blood was thudding in my ears.

'Do you need any help?' said the purifier man.

I turned away from him and put my hands to my temples. Over the roar of my emotions I heard someone new asking about reports of a great grey shrike on the heath. My face desperately needed a splash of cold water and I'd have taken myself there and then to the toilets, if I hadn't heard another voice I recognised slicing across all other conversations.

'Oh, so *you're* one of these newt fanatics?'

It was the woman who'd held forth on organic farming earlier, the woman Geraint had swept in and so neatly demolished, like a tractor running over a sapling. Only as far as I knew, Geraint wasn't on the scene right now, he was off bothering dormice.

There was no time to hang about. I left the purifiers and scooted round the corner. Standing in front of our stall was a lumpy matron of about fifty encased in an ankle-length Barbour and Dublin riding boots. Her hair was frizzy and her complexion rough, but that accent was cut glass.

'Do you know what I've been told to do with my OWN land?' she demanded, bristling. Liv just stared at her. 'I've had to put up plastic bloody fences. Right across the side of the top field, along both sides of the driveway, in case someone should drive over one of these bloody newts and squash them. Supposedly rare — hah! How can they be 'threatened' when there are dozens living in our cellar? I'll tell you, it's European jobsworths inventing directives for the hell of it. Picking on farmers, because farmers don't count, even though we stock your larders for you. I can't build my extension because I'm not allowed to drain my pond, and never mind the barn is bloody well sinking into the mire. Oh no, that doesn't matter. People don't matter, do they? Not to you lot. Thousands, it's going to cost me. Bloody Green lobby, poking about where you're not wanted. Wading up and down with your long nets. Whose land is it? Eh? Eh?'

The tirade had been completely focused on Liv up to this point, but now the Boot took a moment to check audience reaction. Her eyes lighted on Melody, who was standing at the corner of the stall and who this morning was kitted out in cream jeans and a waisted black jacket that could easily have been mistaken for riding gear. I think she thought she'd found a friend.

'You see, animal rights activists like *her*,' said the Boot, pointing at Liv but now addressing herself directly to Melody, 'believe the world revolves around them and their petty issues. They march onto your property, get in everyone's way, stick their nose in and the next thing it's letters through the post demanding you spend your own hard-earned cash on 'habitat improvement'.' A little bit of spit flew out of her mouth and landed on the desk. 'Apparently your own house can fall about your ears, but as long as the damn newts are protected, that's all right, that's fine.'

Melody signalled at me with her eyes to stay back. A dangerous smile was breaking across her face; I saw it but the Boot didn't.

'So let me get this straight. You're being victimised by a bunch of newts?' Melody said, shifting till she was between Liv and the other woman.

'It's the principle, isn't it? You feel invaded. Tied up in red tape. This country's run by officious left-wing idiots.'

'Oh dear. How very upsetting for you. You know what you want to do?'

'What?'

'Fuck off.'

The reaction was instant. The Boot's eyebrows shot up under her messy fringe. 'I *beg* your pardon?'

'You heard. Stop with your whingeing and piss off out of here. Go on, get. I don't know why you'd come to an event like this. Oh, wait a mo, yeah I do: to drop on people you don't agree with and bully them. Well you've done that now, so you can get lost. Scat. Shoo.'

Nose to nose they made an odd pair. Melody was slightly taller, but the Boot was twice as wide with arms like a weight-lifter. 'Do you *know* who I am?' she said, putting her solid shoulders back and tilting her square chin.

'They've been calling you Trout-features round here. That'll do me,' said Melody.

I definitely heard a snigger from behind the boards. The Boot took a step backwards.

'My mistake. I can see you're one of them. Nothing but a yob.'

'No, you're the yob. Cruising a bloody folk festival for fights. Jesus. I tell you what, if the biggest problem in your life right now is having to deal with a brace of newts then you're fucking lucky. You want something to complain about? When you've had the sort of year I've had, that this lady behind me's had, then you can complain. Bloody newt-proof fencing, that's the worst you can come up with? Get a fucking grip.'

There was a ripple of laughter, then an awkward scattering of applause, started, I think, by the honey girl who'd crept round to watch. I

347

clapped, and I nodded at Liv to clap too, but by now she was sitting very still with her mouth a tight pale line. Melody didn't see because her back was to the stall.

'You are a very rude young lady,' said the Boot. 'And not worth another second of my time or attention.'

We all watched as she swung round furiously and barged off down the centre of the aisle as fast as the crowds would allow. I wondered whether later she'd try phoning the police, and if so, what Melody might be charged with. Impersonating a horse-woman, maybe.

'That did it,' she said, brushing her palms together with satisfaction. 'Excellent entertainment. What a bitch, though.'

'We do usually get a tricky customer or two. Last year it was a bloke who wanted us to round up and shoot all the adders on the Moss.'

Someone touched my arm. It was the honey girl. 'Sorry, I didn't know if you'd noticed. I'm not sure your friend's very well.'

When I turned again to the stall, I had a shock. Liv's head was tipped back, her hand to her throat, and she was gasping like a fish.

I had five seconds of paralysing panic. 'Oh my God.'

'Shit. Look, stay calm. I'll get the St John's Ambulance,' said Melody.

'Let me do that.'

'No. It's important you stay with your mum.'

'But I can — '

Why was I even arguing?

'Whatever. Just go,' I said. 'Please.'

* * *

'You must have been terrified,' said Nicky, putting down her WKD and leaning across the pub table towards me. The orange lights of the fruit machine played a sequence down one side of her worried face.

'So the St John's man came and he had her breathing into a paper bag, which seemed a bit low-tech to me but apparently it regulates the levels of carbon dioxide or something, and after a few minutes she came right round again. He's pretty positive she was only having a panic attack, but she's got to go see the GP on Monday, just to make sure.'

'She's OK, then, basically?'

'We think so. She has been under massive stress this year, so it would be amazing if she didn't have some kind of reaction. It has to come out somewhere.'

Nicky frowned. 'Yeah, because she normally deals with awkward customers no problem. I remember that ex-wrestler from up your road trying to cut his hedge down in the nesting season, and she didn't half have a go at him. And I've seen her tackle hoodies for dropping litter. It's like her passion for nature overrides any sense of fear.'

'She said afterwards she was frightened for the newts, in case this woman took it out on them. So I told her to call the Wildlife Crime officer and get him to pay the old boot a visit. Remind her of the penalties for breaking Schedule Five.'

'Who'd have thought amphibians could be so

contentious. What did Geraint say? He didn't go after this woman with a cattle prod, did he?'

'That I'd have paid good money to see. Nah, by the time he got back, Liv had come round completely. Melody had scrounged a quiche off another stall and they were sitting eating it together, sharing a flask of tea. Bezzie mates.' I gave an ironic smile.

'Blimey. That won't last, will it?'

'Although it's funny, they really did look like a couple of ordinary friends, just sitting there.' Melody cutting up quiche with a Top Shop loyalty card, Liv passing the thermos lid of tea to Mel and drinking her own from a jam jar. 'Ordinary as those two could ever manage.'

'Perhaps they will be. Perhaps they're already there.'

'That would take some getting used to.'

'You always said they were too different.'

'I thought they were. Funny, but right at this very second I feel completely detached from both my mothers. It's like I've taken a step back somehow, and they've closed ranks.'

Nicky frowned. 'I wish I could detach myself from mine.'

The pub was filling up now. Girls with round young faces and excessive make-up, boys fighting spots and stubble rash swaggered about the bar, same as we used to when we were in Year 13. The sixth form seemed an age ago. *Can you remember*, I wanted to say to Nicky, *when everything was one big laugh?* A crowd of us weaving down the back lanes after closing time, provokingly loud. Drawing cocks in the dirt on parked cars, jumping gates and hedges, upending garden gnomes. Nothing terrible, although if I met us now I'd think, *Bunch of dickheads*. At the table next to us a group of girls were balling up shredded beer mats and flicking pellets at some lads by the door.

'Hey, want to know a secret?' said Nicky.

'If you must.'

She picked up her bottle and eyed the contents shyly. 'I've put my name down to train as a Samaritan.'

'Bloody hell. I wasn't expecting that. Wow. Well done.'

'I wanted to do something positive. A new start. This particular month was always going to be hell, but I'm sick of dwelling on my own problems. Which aren't even that bad when you look at what some people have to cope with.'

'You're not going abroad, then?'

'Nope. I decided I'd miss home too much. Well, the city centre. The shops specifically. And actually, I do love my job. Corporate law's way more interesting than you'd think, I get on well with the other trainees. But I did want to do something to, to *help*.'

'Your mum'll be relieved.'

Nicky pulled a face. 'It makes no odds what she thinks either way. I'm fed up of trying to please her, Frey; whatever I do, it's not enough. So from now on, the choices I make are going to be for me, based on what I want to do, full stop. Do you know, I feel as though I've had some giant kick up the backside from Fate, like, 'Get on with the rest of your life, girl. It's all out there for the taking.' So I will. Because what else is there to do? And I've been thinking, I might not even tell Mum about the Samaritans, otherwise she'll immediately broadcast it amongst her friends. It'll be 'My daughter the saint'. And from day one she'll be trying to winkle callers' stories out of me. Basically, she'll make it about herself and it won't be mine any more.'

'You'll have to come up with a cover story for when you do your night shifts.'

'I've thought of that. I'll tell her I've gone on the game.' She took a long gulp of her WKD, and replaced the bottle on the table top with a defiant clunk.

'God, Nicks. You can't do that.'

'Why not?'

'Because then she'll be making up phone-box cards for you, and getting your dad to circulate them round the Rotary.'

The pellet-flicking next to us was gathering momentum. One of the girls pulled up her top and flashed her bra at the lads near the door, prompting a ragged cheer. A glass smashed on the floor.

Nicky said, 'Can I ask you something?'

I bloody hate that line. It always heralds something at the very least uncomfortable, often disastrous. It's the sound of a tin opener puncturing the lid of a can of worms. 'Sure,' I said. 'Yeah. Fire away.'

'Would you mind if I took Michael out for a meal sometime? Or would that be too weird?'

She'd got the tone casual enough — I guessed she'd practised beforehand to get the intonation light and non-threatening — but it was her eyes that were the giveaway. She couldn't meet my gaze; her pupils were flicking around the bar, down to her drink, over my shoulder. The fire-exit sign seemed particularly fascinating.

'Oh,' I said. 'No. Help yourself.' *Help yourself?*

'I wouldn't mean anything funny by it. God, I'm not looking for anything like that, not so soon after — '

'No, obviously.' *You can't have him. He's mine.*

'But I think he gets a bit lonely, and it would be nice — '

'Michael?'

'Hmm, not lonely. Restless, maybe. As though he's missing something. Is he going abroad still?'

'Don't know. He's not really said.'

'That's good, then. For you, I mean, because he's like your mentor or something, isn't he? And I wanted to say thank you to him for the way he dealt with Corinne.'

It had been a hero's mission, apparently. After they'd collected his car parts, Michael had driven, as promised, across to Christian's house to pick up Nicky's belongings. Corinne was on the lookout for them, and he'd barely stuck the handbrake on before she was out and tapping at the window, requesting that he park round the side of the house where presumably he'd be less visible. The van stayed where it was, despite Nicky's agitation. 'Maybe the side door's wider than the front for carrying things out.'

'What are you thinking of taking?' he'd said.

353

'A grand piano?' Besides, the front entrance was a Georgian double-door affair you could have driven a jeep through.

Nicky had wanted to stay in the van, so it was Michael who went into the house to collect the sad pile of clothes and books, make-up and jewellery. Christian himself was nowhere to be seen. 'He's in Montreal,' Corinne offered, without prompting, though she didn't say why and Michael didn't ask.

Then there was some trouble with a pot of face cream. 'Oh dear, that's mine,' Corinne said, plucking it out of the holdall. 'I can't imagine how it got in there.'

Michael, unwilling to concede even the slightest ground, went back and asked Nicky. 'Oh, it is mine,' she said. 'But it doesn't matter, leave it.'

He thought the box had looked expensive, wanted to know how much it cost.

'A hundred and twenty pounds. Really, though, I'd rather leave it.'

In the end, despite her pleading, she'd gone with him and put Corinne straight. Corinne marched off upstairs and came down two minutes later, a little breathless. 'My pot's still in the en-suite cupboard, so I apologise,' she announced.

'Though it wasn't like an apology at all,' Nicky told me. 'She was crosser than if she'd caught me thieving.'

They'd been escorted to the van door, where Corinne decided without warning to make a valedictory speech. 'We do all feel so terrible about the whole business — '

'*Stop right there,*' Michael barked.

He'd helped Nicky into the cab, climbed into the driver's side, and spun a wheelful of gravel into Corinne's face.

'It would have been funny if it hadn't been so awful,' was Nicky's verdict on the excursion. 'But he really made me see I'd had a lucky escape.' I could completely understand why she wanted to say thank you to him. That was reasonable, wasn't it?

I was wondering whether to say anything more about taking him out, a warning about the type of food he disliked, or whether that might sound a touch possessive, when a familiar figure swung out of the pool room, handing over his cue as he went.

'Oh, fuck,' I said.

'What?' Nicky looked concerned. 'Oh.'

'I really don't want to talk to him.'

'What was it he did to you, Frey? Can't you tell me?'

I shook my head. 'I don't even want to think about it. I wish to God he'd just disappear.'

Oggy hailed a few people by the bar, high-fived a scruffy kid in a PVC jacket, and finally fetched up at our table. 'Howdy,' he said.

Since I'd last seen him he'd had his hair styled so it was even shorter at the sides and long on the top; when he leaned forward it swung down over his eyes raffishly. He stood, then shoved his hand into the front pocket of his jeans and wiggled his fingers.

'What is it now?' I asked wearily.

'Someone wants to say hello.' He grasped whatever it was he'd been after, drew it out and set it on the table. It was small and brown and knobbly, like an owl pellet balanced on end. 'I picked it up at the weekend. Early birthday present, if you like.'

When I squinted, I could make out little peaks all over the pellet's surface, as though someone had snipped into the clay or resin or whatever it was with a pair of nail scissors. Nicky reached across and poked it with her index finger. A snout came into view.

'I think it's meant to be a hedgehog,' she said.

'It's Hogden,' said Oggy.

I couldn't bring myself to reply.

'I've not seen him lately,' he went on. 'He'll be going into thingy, hibernation, won't he? Unless he's nipped across the road to visit his flat mate.' He tossed his fringe aside and grinned.

'I'm not speaking to you,' I said.

''Course you are.' He picked up the hedgehog and wiggled it, revealing the 75p price sticker on its base. 'Now, come on, cheer up. Hoggy wants to know what you girls are having to drink.'

Very slowly I lowered my head until my brow was resting on the table top. I felt utterly defeated. Would he *never* go away? Then again, why should he, when I always took him back? He thought we were a match because, despite it all, *I* thought we were. Every time we tried elsewhere and failed, here was where we ended up, each other's consolation prize. We'd carry on this way until one of us lost our wits or died.

Nicky went, 'Actually, can I have a word?'

'You can have any word you like, gorgeous.'

There was the clunk of a chair as Oggy pushed it out of the way, and then I heard her say, in her brisk, pleasant solicitor voice:

'Can we clear something up, Simon? *You're not wanted.* Freya doesn't want you here. You need to *go away, now.* Go right away, the further the better, we don't care where as long as it's out of our sight. Because if you bother us again this evening I'm going to take that crappy hedgehog and ram it up your arse, spikes first.'

My eyes flew open with shock. What I saw was Oggy's smile just in the process of sliding off his face, Nicky settling back with the air of a mission accomplished. She'd obviously had him leaning over her to receive the message — maybe she'd beckoned him down, held his collar, even — but now he straightened up. For a second his expression was pure confusion. Then his gaze met mine, and he scooped up the hedgehog and laughed.

'P M fucking T, or what?'

Nicky swigged her drink without concern.

'I think you forgot your evening primrose oil, love.'

'Oggy,' I began.

He simply waved his palm, a sort of *You're welcome to her* gesture, turned and sauntered out through the back door. I was left gaping at my best friend.

'Nicky Steuer!'

'Sorry, Frey. Was I very rude?'

'Erm, yeah.'

'I've just had it with tossers. I wanted this

evening to be a tosser-free zone. And you looked so unhappy.' She shrugged. 'Sometimes you have to make a stand.'

'You *never* use language like that.'

'No, I don't, do I?' She gripped her bottle by the neck as though she meant to throttle it. 'Maybe I'll start.'

The girls at the next table were still flicking their hair and gesturing to the boys by the door. PVC-jacket was leaning against the bar, flipping coins onto a beer mat. The woman serving slammed the drawer to the till unnecessarily hard. There was no one in this bar tonight I recognised, unless you counted lately released Tyler Dawes sitting by the hearth and waving his cigarette lighter under his own outstretched palm. Where were the others I used to hang around with? At home holding grown-up dinner parties, putting kids to bed, rolling around on the sofa locked in the naked arms of a new lover. I remembered Denny and Marie, the shock of her pregnancy. They'd have had their baby by now. Meanwhile I was turning twenty-four with no material change to my existence except for a couple more work scars on my hands and a mashed-up heart.

'Don't think I don't appreciate what you did. But I need a minute,' I said to Nicky, and left the table. I didn't dare look back.

I pushed past a couple kissing in the porch and came out into the beer garden. Oggy was loitering alone by the second row of picnic tables. I could tell he'd been waiting for me, which was simultaneously infuriating and comforting.

'Someone's got a strop on.'

'She was trying — '

'It's not my fault her boyfriend ran off. Can't say I blame him, sarky cow.'

'She thought you were going to start mucking about.'

'Of course I was mucking about. It's what I do. I muck about, therefore I am.'

'She thought you were going to muck *me* about.'

He sighed patiently, a man wronged and wounded. 'Freya.'

'She's right, you know, it can't carry on. I know I've said it before, but I'm really not going out with you again. You hurt me. We never get anywhere.'

'Where do you want to get?'

If there'd been an ashtray handy I'd have hurled it at his face, frisbee-style. 'What she said. Please, bugger off.'

The back door banged and a crowd of teens came out. They milled around, swearing and shouting, before gathering under the smoking shelter. Fumbling, lighter flares, smoke, laughter. Oggy said, 'I've got a boat.'

'You what?'

'I'm buying a house boat. Gonna moor it at Whixall, rent a garage off the farmer. It's neat. Thirty grand.'

'You've got thirty grand?'

'My mum's helping, and I'm getting a bank loan. It's gonna be smart. Red, it is. Flat-screen

TV, double bed, fridge.'

'That's all your needs catered for, then.'

He came forward cautiously. 'Frey.'

'Leave me alone.'

'Know what a boat means? A boat means freedom. You can go up and down the canals, wherever you want. You don't get bogged down with clutter. The cabin's small enough to heat toasty warm in the winter, and the summer you can spend on deck in the sunshine. There's shops and pubs all the way along, countryside's on your doorstep. Like a holiday the whole year round, fantastic.'

'Bully for you.'

'For us. If you want.'

My mouth went dry. At the edge of my vision I could see the youths jostling and play-fighting, high on nothing, full of energy they barely knew how to handle. I remembered feeling that way, long ago.

'Are you asking me to move in with you?'

'Yeah.'

I had been on a narrowboat a couple of times with Liv, just a few miles up the Llangollen canal and back again. I knew where to pick up supplies, how to navigate a lock, empty a Thetford loo. Knew the claims he was making were right, essentially.

'Why, Oggy?'

'Because I want you to.'

'Why?'

'Don't be so bloody awkward about it, woman. A simple yes or no'll do.'

In my mind I was trying to see it from Oggy's

point of view. What was he really after? 'You want me to go halves on the cost of the boat.'

'No.' He pulled an outraged face.

'You want something.'

'Look.' He sat himself on the edge of the picnic table and spread his hands to show he'd nothing to hide. 'If you wanted to put a few quid into the down payment, you could do, I'm not saying it wouldn't help. But I'd pay you back. You know I would. I don't mess about where money's concerned. We'd do it all proper — with receipts, if you like, so much a month, on a given day.'

'And there I was with this stupid idea that you wanted me for my own sake.'

'I do!'

Walk away now, my more sober half was telling me. *It's cold out here and Nicky's waiting and you're making a fool of yourself even listening.*

'Please, Frey. At least think it over. It's killing me, us being apart. And I've never asked anyone to live with me before. It's major, that. There's no one else I'd consider, either. If you say no, it's not like there's a back-up.'

'Glad to hear it,' I said drily, though inside I recognised the truth of what he was saying, and I couldn't help but be flattered. It was a big deal, for both of us.

'You don't have to have any cash, it was only an option. Day-to-day we'd split the bills, but that's only fair, yeah? You could share the garage I'm renting, cut across to the A49 each morning from Steel Heath. Or we could look at getting a mooring round Grindley Brook, maybe. I've

361

worked it out. It's sound on all fronts. Think about it.'

So I let myself. I thought of winter nights with the curtains drawn and the stove going, of sunny days on the towpath, passers-by waving, pots of flowers on the roof. I thought of the pleasure I'd get from telling people *I live on a boat with my boyfriend*, how Bohemian I'd look, how cool. Side-stepping the whole 'you need to get a foot on the property ladder' business, shedding at a stroke the embarrassment of admitting I still lived at home with my mum. Walking away from Geraint and his giant underpants.

'Where would I store my books and clothes? Where would I dye my hair?'

'At Liv's. You can always pop back when you need to. But you'd be living on the boat.'

I could see it. Melody of course would be thrilled with the whole idea, cooing over the painted roses and wee curtains and fold-away furniture; I could tell Michael at last I was making some sort of progression, watch his reaction. Geraint would be cheering. Liv would just go, *As long as you're happy. Are you happy?* The move would mean she'd have her space but I wouldn't be too far away if she needed help or support.

Then I pictured Nicky pursing her mouth in disapproval, making the same hard Cupid's bow with her lips that her mother favoured, though she'd be horrified to realise it. *Oh, he's not taken you in again? For God's sake, I could write the script. You could write it. I can't believe you've gone back to him. What the hell's the matter with you?*

And I might say, *At least it's a step towards this 'independence' everyone's been nagging me about.*

And she'd say, *You reckon? He wants a cook and a housemaid, is all.*

And I'd say, *It's not as if he's asking for rent off me. I don't mind housework, and anyway, there's not a lot to maintain on a boat that size. Easier than looking after Liv, actually.*

And she'd say, *He — always — hurts — you. You — know — how — it's — going — to — end.*

I'd have no reply to that.

He sat before me, his big feet on the bench, waiting.

'But you're still you,' I said hopelessly. 'Which means you'd still drop me the minute someone else happened to catch your eye.'

Now he brought his fist forward and opened it, offering up the cruddy hedgehog once more as though its simple eloquence was enough to wipe out the failures of the past.

I darted forward, plucked up the ornament and flung it in a high and reckless arc across the yard.

There was an explosion of surprised abuse from the boys in the corner as it landed near their feet, then a scuffle as they picked it out of the gloom. (''S a fucking hedgehog. They've thrown a fucking hedgehog at us.')

'Freya, I'm not that bad,' Oggy wailed.

'But I can do *better*,' I said, and began to walk away.

'Who fucking threw that? Was it you?' one lad

asked as I swept past him.

'No. He did.' I jerked my thumb over to the table where Oggy still perched.

'Oi, you!' another one called across. 'What d'you think you're fucking playing at? You got a point to make? You want to make a fucking point, do you?'

I opened the door into the warm, left them to it.

Back in the saloon, Tyler Dawes had stood up and was wiggling his hips at a girl sitting opposite. She glanced his way, then began picking the varnish off her nails. One of his mates laughed loudly.

Nicky said, 'Finished?'

'Yep.'

'All right?'

'Never better.'

She pushed my drink across the table towards me. 'I've an idea. Let's get completely smashed tonight, totally off our faces. We haven't done that for ages.'

I thought of an evening at Michael's, just after I'd left college, where Melody had got so pickled on homebrew cider she'd decided to cut her own hair, great hanks of it sliced off onto the carpet. Afterwards she wanted to start on ours too, but we wouldn't let her and then she'd passed out anyway. And I remembered a party at John Jones's house where Nicky made a cocktail out of everything she could find in the drinks cabinet, then started on the contents of the fridge. The finished cocktail had looked impressive with its yoghurt topping, except she couldn't get anyone to drink it and after twenty minutes a sediment formed at the bottom. Later that same evening, Oggy had fallen down the stairs and fractured his wrist, and none of us believed him. Happy times.

'OK. Hey, do you remember when we crashed Neil Froggat's twenty-first birthday party at Cinnamon, and Sasha Morris had us alternating vodka shots with alcoholic milkshakes? On the way home you fell in a bin.'

'Not in it, against it. And it was right on the footpath.'

'Leaped out at you as you walked past.'

'That's right. Same as the night you came round and headbutted my mother's wind chimes. Look, can I say something, Frey, without you getting rattled?'

'Why not.' I already felt as though I'd been at the booze for hours.

'It's just, I'm *bored witless* with the whole Simon Ogden cycle. I think, if you go back with him again, I'll have to have you put away. Sign you up for ECT. Because I'm not sure I can keep going through this. Sometimes you really do have to tell people to fuck off.'

I pictured Oggy in the beer garden being mauled by teens. It was a warming thought. 'Yeah, I get that now.'

'Good. Sorry. I'm a terrible friend, aren't I?'

'The worst. Come on, keep drinking. We've a lot to get through.'

From Liv's diary 12/05

It's been the very hardest part of being a mother, knowing when to step in & help & when to step away, leave her alone. I know you have to let go in the end. That's what mothers do. I know the theory. But the actual doing it, that's something else.

Because it seems to me that as F's grown older, life's got so much riskier. Shouldn't be that way, surely. Thought she was in most danger as toddler, with sharp scissors & bleach & germs & falling down stairs etc. The difference is, though, I could be there for her then, stand between her & rest of the world. Why does nature give us these fierce feelings & then expect us to quash them? Biologically pointless! A trap we spring ourselves. Some nights I'm swallowed up with fear.

I think I might be able to let her go if I thought she knew where she was headed.

TWO HOURS LATER

I didn't know what I was going to say when I reached Michael's, I just knew I had to get to him.

It's possible I'd been building up a resistance to alcohol because by closing time I hadn't felt too wobbly. As soon as Nicky was out of sight, I'd phoned for a cab. I knew Michael kept late hours, but it was a risky strategy nonetheless. The whole journey there I kept wondering whether I should text ahead, check it was OK just to appear on his doorstep out of the darkness. But what if he'd said no, actually it wasn't convenient? *Go home, Freya. Go to bed. I haven't the energy to deal with you right now.* I couldn't have stood that.

We turned onto the estate. A cluster of youths standing under a street lamp watched the car as it passed; further down, a man leaned in conversationally at a front window, his feet in a flower bed. *What do you want from me anyway?* I imagined Michael asking. His expression if I told him. If I said, Please don't get together with Nicky. She's going to ask you and I want you to say no. She's brewing a crush on you but it wouldn't work. It's too soon after Christian. And even if it wasn't, you're not right for each other. You're not the same kind of people. Promise me you'll refuse her.

Why would I want to do that, Freya?

Because, because.

When the cab pulled up, I saw with relief Michael's downstairs lights were on. I paid my fare, scuttled up the path and rang the bell. For maybe two minutes, no one came. Then the door swung open and there he was, shirtless and barefoot, his hair damp and springy. A wet towel was draped across the newel post.

'Sorry, interrupting, I'll go, it's fine,' I said.

'Don't be daft.' He stepped aside for me. 'Get yourself inside. I could do with the company.'

The house had looked bright from the street, but in the lounge only the wall lights were on and the TV, muted. REM played in the background.

I hung up my jacket and went to slip my boots off. 'No, best keep your feet covered,' he said. 'I need to get something on myself.' He went back out into the hall and returned a moment later wearing a pair of unlaced trainers and a zip-front hoody. 'There might still be broken glass.'

'Broken glass?'

'You just missed Kim.'

He turned and walked towards the kitchen, so I followed.

It's not a big space — council planners in the Thirties didn't see kitchens as a prestige area — but it would be a whole lot roomier without Michael's automobilia. I don't know anyone else who keeps the engineless frame of a Honda CBR125 propped against the back cupboard, or a carburettor on his draining board, or a range of spark plugs balanced on his window sill. The bread board's never used for bread, but it has seen plenty of engine oil over the years.

Normally half the floor's covered in boxes of metal and tubing.

Not this evening, though, because the back door was pulled open against the wall and I could see by the bulb over the lintel all his vehicle parts piled up on the lawn. Under my feet the lino was still glossy in patches where it had been swabbed, and there was a gouge out of the supporting wall, as if someone had bashed it with the claw-end of a hammer.

'This evening's special: Brick through the Window.' He closed the back door, and where the glass top half should have been was a gaping square. 'I struck out all the jagged edges and wrapped them up in newspaper. Took longer than you'd think. I can't believe I got away without a cut.'

'Shit.'

'It was a bit, yeah. While you're here I could do with you helping me pin a board over that.'

'And it was definitely Kim?'

He exhaled wearily.

'What did you do with the brick?'

'Chucked it over the bottom fence.'

This was outrageous. 'But you could have kept it as evidence. The police could have taken fingerprints.'

Michael opened the fridge and pulled out a carton of orange juice. 'Nah. I can't do that to her. She's got enough problems, a criminal record would finish her off.'

'She needs *help*. You're not being kind if you keep letting her get away with her freaky behaviour.'

He poured two glasses of juice and handed me one. 'It's only attention-seeking. She's not a real threat.'

'Not much. If you'd been in the kitchen — '

'I wasn't, though. She'd have known the room was empty because there were no lights on. I understand how her mind works. She could have thrown it through the front, but she didn't. She wouldn't physically hurt me.'

Not so far, I thought. 'You always make excuses for her. You should hear yourself.'

'They're not excuses. Some fires need fighting, and others go out by themselves. I genuinely think it's best for everyone if I don't inflict any more damage on her.'

'Although it's fine for her to damage you.'

'So easy to solve someone else's life for them, isn't it?'

Oh, bog off, Michael, I told him silently. *If you want to be pissy, be pissy with Kim. I'm not the one lobbing missiles about like a lunatic.* I could have spoken those words aloud, thrown the jibe right back at him. I could have acted hurt. Or I could have challenged him again, confronted him with the possible consequences if he let things ride. But all that would only have made him angrier, and I knew he wasn't really angry with me, he was angry with himself. Funny how a filter of alcohol sometimes gives you clearer vision.

I said, 'So are we nailing a board up over that window or are you going to let me freeze to death here?'

Any request to do with tools takes him out of

himself. Immediately he was opening drawers, lining up hammers and screwdrivers, shaking boxes of nails, frowning at the size codes. He found a torch, took it out with him to the garage and came back with an A-frame shop sign promoting cut-price MOTs. I sipped orange juice and water while he laid the sign on the floor and commenced dismantling it, undoing the back panel from the struts. When it came off I slid the spare wood away and leaned it against the cooker to give us space. Meanwhile he measured the window with his arms and came back to the panel, checking the size against the opening it was meant to cover. 'Too narrow,' he muttered, but carried on anyway.

I gazed out of the still-intact window over the sink, watching car headlights travel along the top road. A neighbour's dog was barking; someone revved an engine. I wondered where Kim had taken herself to recover. As I stared, the hedge behind his wheelie bin seemed to shudder, as if a body had passed close behind it. *Do you think she might have hung around?* I wanted to ask. But he looked so absorbed with his mouth full of panel pins I didn't like to trouble him.

He carried the board to the door and I held it in place while he knocked in half a dozen nails. He'd been right, the opening was very slightly too big for the material we had, and left a five-centimetre gap down the left side.

I assumed he'd use more wood to fill it — a leg off the A frame would have done the job if he could have freed it and cut it shorter — but instead he pulled some towels out of a drawer and stuffed them into the space.

'Will it be secure enough?' I asked.

'It'll stop the wind and rain. Be fine till Monday.'

'You might get burglars.'

Michael raised his eyebrows. 'What do I own that's worth nicking?'

'Fair point,' I said. 'Did you know it's my birthday?'

'I did.'

He put his tools away, wiped his hands and then we went back through to the lounge. It was half past midnight.

'Here,' he said, sliding a plastic bag across the carpet at me.

'Aw, no, you've not bought me something again, have you? You have to stop this, Michael. Either we do presents, or we don't.'

'They're only off the market. Impulse buy. I was going to drop them off at the nursery, only — are you working today?'

'Nope.'

'Me neither. The night is ours, then.'

He settled himself onto the sofa while I attacked his present.

'Although it does look as if you wrapped it wearing boxing gloves.'

'At least it is wrapped.'

'In Christmas paper.'

'I'll take it back if you don't shut up.'

The outer layer ripped and something grey and fluffy burst through the gap. Surely to God he hadn't bought me a teddy bear.

'What is it? Oh, slippers.'

They were those giant comedy animal feet you can get: wolf, I think these were meant to be on account they had vinyl claws sprouting from the toes.

'They called to me. They said 'Freya'.'

'Did they really? Fancy.'

'You like them?'

'A girl can't have enough fake paws, I always say.'

I wriggled my feet down into the fur, feeling ridiculous.

'They're a bit of fun,' said Michael. 'I've a card for you somewhere.'

I pointed to the side of the sofa. 'Pass us that bag, will you? It's got Nicky's present in it. Might as well open that while I'm here.'

In contrast, this parcel was done up in white and pink stripes with a white rosette on the top. Typical Nicky. Inside was a bracelet of tiny silver skulls and bells that I'd seen in a shop window in town a good six months ago and commented on. She must have gone back afterwards, bought it and put it away for me. That's how organised she is. That's the kind of thing she'd do for Michael, if they ever got together.

The accompanying card was large and bulky. I drew it out gingerly to discover a black and white publicity shot of Cliff Richard from about the 1960s. He had his hair slicked into a glossy quiff and wore a shirt so bright it was dazzling.

'Interesting choice,' I said, holding it up for Michael to see. As I did so, a zig-zag strip of card fell out onto the carpet. I bent to pick it up; read aloud: ' "WWF Wrestling Mania: Ultimate Smack-down".'

'Hmm. I didn't have you down as a wrestling fan, Freya.'

'I'm not. Mind you, I say that: I've never been.' I studied the tickets. Then I opened the card.

At once music blasted out from between the covers. '*The young ones —* ' Cliff sang out. The sound was tinny and blurred, like Geraint's old-fashioned transistor radio. I snapped the card shut and the song stopped. 'Blimey. Wasn't expecting that.'

'Open it up again.'

So I did, and it played the whole of the first verse, Cliff warbling cheerily about how we were the young ones and how we mustn't be afraid to live and love while we still had some sort of flame burning inside us because, to be brutal, we wouldn't be young for very long.

'Well there's a cheery thought,' said Michael after Cliff had finished.

'Tell me about it. Do you know what Melody bought me? Anti-ageing neck cream.'

'Neck cream?'

'Made me feel about ninety. She says necks are the classic neglected area and it's never too early to start protecting the skin there. Sometimes she soaks a scarf in almond oil and wears it round the house for an hour.'

He shook his head in disbelief. 'She is mad, isn't she?'

'Yup. Aren't you glad you don't share any of her genes?'

'Daily.'

I let the card play again while I read Nicky's message: *Thought you might like to try something different! I checked the date with Liv and next April's OK, you're not going anywhere.* ☺ X X X

Not going anywhere. Slippers. Neck cream. It was hard to avoid reading a message into my birthday gifts. Only Liv had got it spot on with a Flip video camera, and only because I'd picked it off the internet for her. But she hates buying electrical goods on principle, so I did appreciate the gesture.

I said, 'Do you think twenty-four's old?'

'Sod off, Freya.'

'No, I mean in terms of society, what people — '

But he held up his hand to shush me. 'Wait,' he whispered.

I strained my ears; at first heard only the doleful voice of Michael Stipe singing out his pain in the background, then over the top of that a scratching, clunking noise coming from the hall.

'What is it?' I mouthed, though I knew, really.

'She's posting something through the letter-box, I think.'

Dog poo? Live snakes? Petrol-soaked rags? The lounge door was ajar, so I attempted to tiptoe round and see what hideousness had made it onto the mat. The slippers made it hard to manage any other step than a shuffle, however, and I had to walk with my legs slightly astride to avoid one paw catching the other. For

375

all the tension of the moment — or possibly because of it — Michael began to laugh.

'Having a spot of bother with your footwear?'

I shot him a look. 'I'm sure there's a technique. I just have to practise.'

'Told you I was crap at presents. Next year I'll send you money.'

From where I was now I could see the hall and what had landed in it. 'She's posted you a book, I think. Unless it's a book-shaped bomb.'

'Leave it.'

'I want to see.'

I knelt on the threshold and reached across to where the paper-back lay. *Angels Inside Us* was the title. The flap on the letterbox stayed perfectly still, even though I was expecting it to fly up at any second and Kim's eyes blaze through. Nevertheless, I still had the feeling she was on the other side, crouched down maybe, ready to attack. I'd seen too many zombie hands punching through door panels.

I slithered backwards to the safety of the lounge, losing a slipper in the process.

'Here.' I held the book up for Michael to see.

'What the hell's that meant to be?'

'A romantic novel, going by the cover. No, I beg your pardon, it's a self-help guide. How to tap into your better self.'

He sighed. 'And has she marked passages out for me with a highlighter or those little sticky tabs?'

'Who cares?' I shoved it under the sofa out of sight. 'What it must be to be loved.'

'That's not love, Freya.'

'No, I know. Hey, what did you mean when you said next year you'd be 'sending' me money? Sending it from where?'

Michael laid his head back as if in exasperation. 'Don't read so much into everything.'

'I'm not. It's common sense. If you were planning to stick around, you'd talk about 'giving' me money. You really think you're off, and soon.'

The silence that followed brought a faint scratching at the front door again. We both ignored it.

He said, 'Ever since I gave you that book last year, it's been on my mind. Then I was browsing the internet and this blog came up, Project GOLE. It's an education centre in the Middle East, on the West Bank.'

'You don't still want to go out there, do you? For what? To get yourself shot? Blown up? Jesus, Michael. Talk sense.'

'It's not that bad. Project GOLE's in a town near the centre, well away from the border areas. There are other internationals out there. And what they're achieving at this place, it's fantastic. In the news you only get to hear about the violence, and yet in-between the skirmishes are all these millions of ordinary people trying to run businesses and services and keep the economy ticking over. But they've a big issue with transport because it's incredibly hard to get hold of new vehicles.'

'So you're going to fix their cars for them?'

'I'm going to teach vehicle maintenance and a bit of English.'

'Bloody hell. When?'

'End of November, ideally.'

'Before Christmas?'

'I have to go sometime, Frey.'

No you don't, I wanted to shout. *You don't have to go anywhere! Stay, be with me; Nicky, even.*

I couldn't keep the bitterness out of my voice. 'So were you planning to actually say goodbye, or just take off into the blue?'

He moved off the sofa and sat down on the floor very close to me. His bicep squashed against mine. If I'd titled my head it would have been against his shoulder.

He said, 'I would never have gone without telling you — what kind of a mate do you think I am? But there were some important details I wanted to iron out before I said anything. It's not even certain now. There's a questionnaire I have to fill in and I need formal confirmation from the centre director. It's possible they might not want me, they might not think I'm suitable. I'd have liked for it to be completely settled before I talked to you about it.'

Big of you, I thought. 'Well, that's nice. I'm going to be pretty busy myself next year, actually. I might buy myself a house boat in the spring.' Oggy and me both on the Llangollen canal, my prow approaching his prow, flicking Vs at each other as we chugged past.

'A narrowboat?'

'Yeah. Or I might even go back to college. If you think I should.'

I waited, but he knew I was bluffing and I

378

don't suppose he had the energy to pursue it. From the hall came the clunk of the letterbox again, and Kim's voice, muffled, whining. 'Mikey, Mikey.'

I said, 'Seems to me you're just running away.'

'Well, I'm not.'

Rattle, rattle, went the letterbox.

He said, 'It's only running away if you can't deal with what you're leaving behind.'

'And you can deal with this?'

'I can, yes. I'm not worried about Kim. She'll burn herself out, especially if I'm not around.'

'So you *are* leaving because of her.'

I felt him twitch with irritation. 'I'm going because I want to, Frey. Kim is not a factor. I'd be going regardless.'

'If that's true, open the door now and tell her to fuck off. Open the door with your phone in your hand and say you're calling the police so they can slap a restraining order on her.'

He let out a short laugh. 'I couldn't hurt her like that.'

'I could. Watch me.'

I struggled up again, stumbling over the loose wolf slipper in the process. 'Hoy, Kim,' I shouted. 'Let's talk. Let's sort this out once and for all.' I made a grab for the giant hairy paw and shoved it back on my foot, then stomped messily into the hall. I was aware of Michael protesting at my back, but I ignored him, wrenching at the handle and flinging the door wide. 'Kim!' I called. 'Where've you gone? We can sit down and have a lovely chat.'

The path was empty, the gate swinging. She

was nowhere in sight.

'Aw, come on, love. No need to try and climb through the letterbox. Here we are. Don't be shy.'

I padded across the front lawn and scanned the wide streets in both directions. A moment later I caught some movement by the entrance to the sheltered housing complex.

'On the other hand,' I yelled, 'I could just dial nine-nine-nine, report a case of repeated harassment. What do you say? Your choice. I know you can hear me.'

Opposite us a porch light came on. The shape in the shadows vanished.

'Kim?'

I turned and walked straight into Michael.

'Bloody hell, Freya. How drunk are you?'

I took his arm, feeling giddy and pleased with myself. 'She had it coming. No, she did. Honestly. Even *you* need someone to look out for you occasionally. Anyway, you've nothing to lose now you're leaving the country. Can I use your bathroom?'

He ushered me back into the house and waved his hand in a dazed way at the stairs. I couldn't tell whether he was genuinely cross with me or not. Surely he could see he'd given enough over the years; that however he might convince himself he'd failed Kim during the marriage, since then he'd more than paid his due. Obviously he'd be wracked with guilt right now, but when that cleared he'd see I'd done him a favour. And I'd meant what I'd said. I would report her. If she hassled him one more time, I'd be straight onto the cops, giving a statement about how I spent an evening cowering in Michael's house on a carpet of broken glass while Kim raged outside.

As I was washing my hands I rashly glanced up into the bathroom mirror and saw the state I was in. It's one of the many pitfalls of alcohol that the foxier you feel, the higher your chances of looking like a clown in crisis. My make-up was blurred, my hair mussed on one side but not the other, my pendant twisted and the neckline of my vest askew. I began to repair the damage as best I could, wiping away melted eyeliner and pushing my fingers through my fringe to re-shape it. As I fiddled, I tried to remember when I'd ever seen Nicky in anything like a similar mess, but all I could think of was the afternoon she met me in the rain to tell me about the First Big Row with Christian. Even then she'd managed to look all gorgeous and fragile, her slim arms gleaming and her lashes spiked.

Why did you come here? I imagined Michael challenging me.

Because it could be one of the last evenings where we're just us, I might say. *Because I thought something important was going to happen tonight.* Except it had: he was leaving. *Because I wanted to tell you, before Nicky gets in, that I —*

But I couldn't even admit the words in my head, let alone out loud. Let alone to him, and face the consequences. Way too dangerous.

Plus it was pointless now.

I slipped off the troublesome paws, straightened my top, and headed downstairs.

'Your birthday card. It was under a magazine.' He'd made two coffees and now he was stretched out on the sofa, zapping through his iPod with the remote. On the low table next to the mugs was a daffodil-yellow envelope with my name scrawled on the front.

I said, 'I still can't believe you're going away. Sometimes I wish someone would hand me an air ticket and fly me off somewhere. You know, present me with a fait accompli.'

He looked at me. No one's going to do that, his expression said. I slit the envelope open and drew out the card, and it was just a card: a red squirrel with googly eyes Photoshopped under the caption, *Know why I like ya so much?* I opened it up. *Cuz you're nuts!* 'Love, Michael', he'd written at the bottom. Love, but no ticket to anywhere.

'What about your terror of planes?'

'Yeah. It's a shit idea, I don't know what I'm talking about. As usual. What are you going to do with this place when you're away?'

'The house? Contact an agency, rent it out. Make sure there isn't a gaping hole in the window first, obviously.'

'Do you have to declare stalkers?' I went and sat on the floor with my back against the sofa, about level with his knees.

'I'll make sure she knows I'm not around. End of problem.'

Soft broken chords coming over the speaker, sad as anything. *Everybody hurts.*

'Michael, are you really angry that I had a go at her? Because if you are, best tell me, then we can get the bollocking over and move on. It's my birthday.'

He didn't answer, but when I turned round to check, his eyes were closed. 'I don't know, Frey. I give up. Maybe you're right. You find yourself drawn into these situations gradually and then your sense of perspective goes all to cock. I get that you were trying to help — drunkenly — and I suppose I appreciate that. So no, no bollocking this evening.'

'Good. I just don't like to see anyone bullied — '

The words choked in my throat. With no kind of warning, Kim had appeared in the doorway to the kitchen. Her hair hung lank across the shoulders of her parka, and her eyes were sunken and bleary. She looked like one of the undead. I had this flashback to when I first met her, how perky she'd looked in her snakeskin boots, how animatedly she'd talked about the store where she'd worked. Buzzing, she'd been, full of infectious energy. It had been easy to see why Michael wanted her. But we found out later the flip side of that energy was sudden slumps into depression that lasted for months. It was as if she had no control over her emotions. And that was before the miscarriage.

She brought her arm up from her side and I almost shouted out in fear. Wrapped thickly around her right hand was one of the tea towels we'd used to stuff the broken window, and sticking out from that makeshift glove was a shard of glass as long as a carving knife.

'Michael,' I said. But there was no need to warn him. He'd seen.

'Hey, Kim,' he said calmly. 'How you doing?'

At that she advanced towards the sofa, the piece of glass still half raised.

I suppose I panicked. I grabbed the cup of coffee nearest me and slung the contents at her with all the force I could manage. The hot liquid spattered in a wide dramatic splurge across the carpet, only a few drops landing on her legs and feet. She halted and looked down, then up at me.

'For God's sake, Freya,' Michael began.

The next instant she'd made a lunge like a fencer, one knee bent. I pushed myself backwards out of the way and Michael jumped up and stood facing her. 'Kim, stop, now!'

That made her retreat slightly. I thought that behind her hair she was smiling.

'Put it down.' He stretched out his hand. 'There's no need for any of this. It's OK.'

'I hate you,' she said.

'I know. I'm sorry.'

'Well, I'm calling the police,' I said. Though even as I spoke I realised my phone was in my jacket pocket, in the hall, and I'd no idea where Michael's mobile was.

He waved me silent. 'What is it, Kim? Do you want to talk?'

She laughed. 'Talk talk talk.'

'We can talk if you want to. Although it's very late. Your boy-friend'll be worried. How about we give him a ring and let him know where you are?'

384

'There is no boyfriend, stupid.'

Of course there wasn't. Another line of fantasy she'd spun him. I watched her turn the glass shard this way and that, like someone testing a key in a lock. I wasn't afraid now, I was angry. I thought, *If she hurts a hair of Michael's head, I will kill her.*

'Come on, give me that,' he said, moving towards her slowly so that she backed into the wall by the window. 'You don't want to cut yourself.'

'Don't I?'

'Nah. Dirty old bit of glass. Chuck it away. Come on, now.'

He'd almost reached her when she jerked her arm upwards and slashed down, catching the curtain and ripping the material to the hem. My heart leaped sickeningly. 'Michael!' I called out.

'It's fine,' he said, without looking round. I guessed he didn't want to take his eyes off her.

Kim let her arms drop to her sides. 'Hah. Fine, is it?'

'I meant — '

'You know, it's funny, people say they don't mean to hurt you, but they do anyway. Might as well be honest about it. I *want* to hurt you, Michael. I do. Some days it's all that gets me out of bed in the morning.'

I cast a glance at the door. However carefully I inched towards it she was bound to notice, and then what would happen?

'You don't,' said Michael. 'Not really.'

'Watch me.'

She slid away from him along the wall till she

arrived at the corner. Here she took a moment to check her weapon, pulling the tea towel tighter round her fingers and possibly admiring her reflection in the surface of the glass. I noticed her hands were perfectly steady. Then she took a great stride across the room to the sofa where we'd so lately been sitting, and in a series of short stabs tore four or five ugly lines down the top edge.

Michael said, 'Please.'

At that she spun to face him. 'Please, is it? Good one. Do you know how many times I said 'please' to you? How much notice you took? 'Please'. Oh, how hilarious that you should be saying it to me now.'

'I've said a million times how sorry I am. What else can I do?'

A flicker of something crossed her face, and again that small smile. With difficulty, because she was still gripping the glass with her right hand, she managed to nudge the sleeve up from the left wrist so the skin was bare. Then she took the shard and drew it diagonally across her forearm in one smooth movement. 'There,' she said, as if she'd clinched an argument.

'Fuck,' said Michael. 'Frey, phone for an ambulance.'

'Don't touch the phone,' said Kim.

I'd taken one step but now froze, not knowing what to do. In front of me was spread the evidence of my birthday's first hours: two coffee mugs, torn wrapping paper, an empty plastic bag, Nicky's bracelet and wrestling tickets, one visible corner of *Angels Inside Us*, the mad squirrel card and Cliff.

Cliff. He was just about in reach.

'Let me get you a bandage, at least,' said Michael. 'I don't think it's too deep.'

'I can go deeper,' she said.

If I stretched out my foot and flipped the cover of the singing birthday card with my toe . . .

'*The young ones!*' Cliff sang out once more. Kim jumped in alarm, looking round for what she probably thought was a mobile going off. In those few seconds Michael was able to dart forward and make a karate-type chop at her inside elbow which at last made her drop her weapon. He shoved it away across the carpet with his trainer. The tea towel fell to the floor.

'No, don't, Frey,' he cried as I ran to pick up the vicious shard, but I wasn't thinking. I prised it from the carpet, carried it out into the kitchen and whizzed it through the open back door. There was a springy rustle as it hit the hedge and rebounded onto the lawn somewhere.

By the time I got back in, Cliff had finished. Kim was crouched down with Michael bending over her. 'You bitch,' she said when she saw me. She sounded outraged.

'Don't speak to Freya like that, I won't have it. Frey, go phone for an ambulance. No, get me TCP first. Under the sink. And a piece of paper towel.'

'How serious is it?' I asked, peering at her arm. The coat sleeve was still pushed up and the wound clearly visible. It was shocking to see but blood wasn't pouring down her arm, only some smears near the top and a few beads welling up near the wrist. She must only have applied the cutting edge pretty lightly. Maximum effect for minimum pain. Soon she'd start crying, I guessed.

I turned to go, but as I did so I heard her whisper, 'Just promise me one thing, Mikey.'

'If I can,' he said.

'Keep your distance.'

'Huh?'

'From *her*.'

My jaw clenched with indignation.

'Do you know, I've had enough of this,' he snapped. When I looked round he'd straightened up, while she'd sunk even further to the floor and was gazing at him with round, pathetic eyes. 'Come on, get yourself together and stop talking bollocks.'

'*Promise* me, though.'

'Fuck off, Kim. No one tells me who I can and can't see. Frey, TCP.'

I started again towards the kitchen but she called after me. 'Hey, Freya.'

'What?'

She left a deliberate, annoying pause as if I was supposed to be reading her mind or something. Then she said, 'You think you're so smart, so on track. But he'll hurt you too. You see. He'll break you the way he broke me. Break you up into little pieces.'

'God but you're a mad cow,' I said, and left them to it.

All I'd done was open the sink cupboard and take out two bottles of Castrol GTX when I heard the front door slam. I was back in the lounge like a shot.

Michael was standing by the sofa with his hands on his head, staring towards the hall. 'She's gone,' he said. His surprise was genuine.

'Obviously. Like she's going to hang about for the police.'

'I told you to call an ambulance.'

'And they'll inform the police. She's been waving the equivalent of a knife around for the last twenty minutes, in case you hadn't noticed. She needs charging.'

'She needs medical help.'

'That I'm not disputing. Look, there's no point phoning for an ambulance now — where would we direct them? We don't know where she is. If you call the cops, though, they can track her down. Then they'll get a medic on the case. For what it's worth, that cut was only a scratch. It's not as though she's out there bleeding to death. It's her head that's the real mess.'

This ordinary room, scene of so much strife.

'I can't believe she hates me that much.'

'It's not you she hates, it's herself. And you can't do anything about that. Stop thinking you can.'

He looked at me wonderingly. I went to get my mobile.

★ ★ ★

After the police had left, we huddled together on the sofa drinking Amaretto.

'It ought to be brandy for shock, but this was

all I had in. This and a bottle of Bishop's Finger.' Michael laid his neck against the slashed headrest. White filling was poking out of the cushion by his ear.

'I thought the police would be ages coming out. When Derek's garage was broken into, they didn't turn up till next day.'

'Certain words trigger an automatic response. 'Wounding', in this case. Do you think they'll find her?'

'Duh, yeah. She's not some criminal mastermind who's going to melt into the night. She'll be wandering around a few streets away, or she'll have taken herself home. The cops'll nab her and then she'll be safe. We all will.'

'Are you OK, Freya?'

'Uh huh. You?'

He frowned. 'I can't believe I got it so wrong. I can't believe I put you in danger.'

'You didn't: she did.'

'Yeah, but you tried to warn me. Jesus. If she'd hurt you — '

His face was very close to mine.

'What?'

'I can't even think about it. Come here. Happy fucking birthday.' He held open his arms for me and I sank against him gratefully.

'I keep seeing her, slicing her arm open.'

Against the wall, the scene re-played itself.

'Tell me again what project GOLE's going to be like,' I said.

'I won't know till I get there.'

'You must have some idea. You researched it, you didn't just pluck a name out of the air. Use your imagination.' All I could picture was Disney's *Aladdin*.

Michael took a breath. 'God. OK, then, this is what I see . . . There are hills on both sides of the city, and light-coloured buildings climbing up the slopes, modern high-rise flats and little old square houses and mosques. It's hot and bright. Some of the walls are damaged or just crumbling with age and although the main streets are busy, the cars and buses look knackered, like they're about to fall apart. The project compound's a tall building with a flat roof and an archway through, olive trees at the corner of the street, shutters on the windows. Inside the classrooms everything's a bit worn, a bit basic, but tidy. The accommodation block's the same.'

'Wow. That's impressive.'

'Off the website, to be honest. No imagination required.'

'Ah. And will you like it?'

'Dunno. I'm prepared to give it a bloody good go. The bottom line is, I love fixing broken cars, I get such a kick out of it. To sort a blowing exhaust or clean a carb or fit a new clutch, it's sweet. But what if you were able to fix a van for someone who was absolutely desperate to get his fruit to the market before it spoiled, and his whole family were relying on what he earned that day, and there'd been power cuts all week and he'd been woken every night by gunfire? That would be worth doing, wouldn't it? The hours I spent mending that van would really count. I want to go to bed each day feeling I've done something that matters. Maybe I'm being self-indulgent. Maybe I'm going travelling to prevent a midlife crisis or make myself more interesting or pick up a nice tan. But to the people I'll be helping, my motive's irrelevant. And no, I can't explain exactly why I want to go there of all places. Just, I read about the project and something fired up in me. I can see myself there.'

There was such hope and energy in his voice. I'd never heard him speak like that before, not in all the years I'd known him. I could feel the excitement flowing out of him like an electric current.

'Am I making sense?' he asked.

I said, 'Nicky fancies you.'

A beat, and then he cracked out laughing. I suppose it was a release.

'*Nicky?*'

'I thought you should know. She wants to ask you out.'

'Oh dear. She's going to be disappointed, then. Nicky Steuer! You're joking, right?'

'Nope.'

'God, I didn't see that one coming.'

'But you like her.'

'I do, yeah. That's all, though. Bloody hell. Seriously, can you imagine her here? She'd be spreading sheets of newspaper over the furniture before she sat down. See these hands.' He held out fingers grimed around the cuticles with engine oil. 'Now picture those going anywhere near her nice clean office suits. How would that work? She's a cracking girl, I'll grant you, but she's not for me.'

'Oh,' I said.

'Is she serious?'

'I'm not sure. You might be a rebound job.'

'Makes sense. You'd better have a word, head her off at the pass. Tell her I'm off any day. That should fix it. Christ, though. I wish I could learn to read women. My life would be a whole lot simpler for it.'

My heart was beating really hard now. I thought, *What would happen now if I reached up and took your face between my palms, and kissed you?* Such a little action, in the scheme of things; the gesture of a moment. If it turned out to be wrong, then it was over and done with. Michael could keep a secret. He'd be kind. Be brave, Freya. A picture rose in my mind, unbidden, of Christian: that golden promise, yet in the end just a feeble boy still at his mother's beck and call. Nicky, meanwhile, getting on with it, making a new life for herself, making good out of bad. Then I thought of Liv dealing every day with cancer and the fear of cancer. Melody quietly grieving for Elizabeth. Geraint terrified of hospitals, more terrified of being alone. No doubt about it, life was grim and you had to be strong. How hard must it be to admit to another woman that she's brought your child up well, for instance? Or to let your adopted daughter go stay with her shiny new birth mum? Or, going further back, to give up your baby because you realise you can't cope? The world was full of small but extraordinary acts of courage, all connecting up like a great network of goodness. Two middle-aged mothers coming together to defend a newt, and each other: miraculous.

'Wait,' I blurted out. 'I said no before, but I was wrong.'

'About what?'

'I want to come with you. If there's a place for me, I want to go to Project GOLE and help.' I needed to get the words out quickly before I lost my nerve. 'I know you asked me and I said no, because I was thinking of Liv and Melody and flying and just the general scariness of, you know, everything, and it felt like too big a jump. But everything worthwhile's a jump, isn't it? I'm twenty-four, it's not the end of my story. Would I be any use out there? Do you think they'd want me?'

He stared at me, then shook his head.

'But I know about plants and pesticides, that's always useful wherever you go in the world. And I can read up on Middle Eastern horticulture. Or if they didn't want help growing stuff I could teach a bit of English. Or do canteen work, laundry. Anything domestic. I'm dead practical.'

'Frey, you'd hate it.'

'Not if you were there.'

Michael sighed and drew his hand over his jaw. 'No, honestly. I see what you're doing. You don't want me to go, do you?'

'You know I don't.'

'So you're having a flap about being left. But it's all right, I'll be back in a year. No big deal.'

'I *want* to come.'

'Oh, little Freya.' He ruffled my hair in a way that made me want to swear. 'This isn't one of your zombie films where the hero has to scramble for the last helicopter. You've got nothing to escape from. You have a perfectly OK life here.'

''Perfectly OK' isn't — '

'And the place I'm going to is, well, so different. You'd be homesick straight away. It'd be risky, too. Not out and out dangerous, probably, but challenging and hard work. Uncomfortable, sometimes. You'd have to be careful what you wore, and where you went at certain times of the day. You wouldn't have the freedom you're used to. You might not like the food — Oh, shit, you're bleeding.'

'Huh? Where?'

I followed his gaze down to my fingers and saw an orange-brown stain across three of the pads.

'You must have cut yourself when you picked the glass up.'

'I never felt it.'

'You don't when it's very sharp.' Gently he pressed on the tip of my index finger and a cut like a mouth opened, blood filling the gap. 'Ouch. Let me get you some plasters.'

'Wait.' I grasped his sleeve with my good hand and held on. 'Listen to me. Explain how is this compound place is going to be riskier than what happened in your lounge tonight. Hey? Because if I can outwit a lunatic wielding a deadly bit of window — '

His expression was so patient I wanted to slap him. 'I *know*, Frey, you were great. Really brave. And I'm really flattered you'll miss me that much.'

'Oh, for fuck's sake. You really are the most annoying man I've ever met. If I want to apply to Project GOLE, you can't stop me. I can use a search engine, I can fill in a form. I'm young, I'm sane. Why does everyone think I need protecting from everything? Why can't I at least try? God, you must think I'm rubbish.'

At last he looked serious. 'Freya, you're one of the least rubbish people I know.'

'Then why are you being so totally obstructive about it?'

'Because, because it's not the right fit for you.'

'The 'right fit'?'

'Don't get me wrong, it's brilliant that you want to go — '

'You patronising bastard! Has tonight taught you nothing?'

That did seem to check him slightly. 'You've no passport.'

'I'll apply for one.'

'Look, I'm not explaining it properly. What it is, some people are risk takers and some aren't. I *know* you're better off here with your mums and Nicky and the nursery, the things around you that you like. It's where you belong. Don't you trust my judgement?'

'Actually, no. Not any more. You're not some ruddy guru — '

'I never said I was.'

'It's not like every time you open your mouth, some great truth spills out. You get stuff wrong as well. You don't always know best.'

'I never claimed otherwise. I'm sorry if that's what you thought.'

His eyes were a boy's eyes, full of bewilderment.

'I'll email every day, I promise, Frey. Nothing'll change. Nothing.'

'You reckon? It had bloody better do.'

Without thinking, without stopping to spook myself or work myself into a state of failure, I just turned and kissed him. For a fraction of a second there was hesitation, an instant where I panicked, got ready to apologise and retreat. *God, God, sorry. I'm so drunk I don't know what I'm doing. I was just resting my face. It's my brain in meltdown after such a weird day. Forget it, forget this whole evening. I never said those things, I never touched you. I was never here.*

Then, in a rush of relief, I realised he was pressing his face against mine, surely and deliberately, kissing me back. Heat crept through me, dizzying. After a while, his fingers came up possessively to my cheeks; in turn I stroked his hair and his stubbly jaw and felt the muscles work under the skin as he moved with me. Only once he broke away to ask, 'Are you sure?'

'Yes,' I said.

Then he lay down, drawing me with him, to settle into his contours. The rightness of it made me want to cry.

What have we been doing all this while, Michael?

Nothing. Waiting for you.

Thought it would be my fault.

He tasted of almonds and coffee, he smelt of Swarfega. I said, 'You can fast-track a passport, anyway.'

'Shush.'

'Don't tell anyone yet. It's a big deal, let's give it a chance before we go public.'

'Whatever you want, Freya. Whatever you want.'

He pulled me hard against him and I wrapped my arms around his lovely warm, solid body. I felt my brain go quiet, for the first time in ages. And there we lay, holding onto each other against all danger, while outside the darkness whirled with madwomen and topiary rabbits, mutant cells and grubby, discarded wedding invitations.

When I step inside I can't for several seconds make out Michael, or any of the detail of the workshop at all. It's always that way when you come out of the bright sunlight here. Every room seems like a cave till your eyes adjust.

'Frey,' he cries when he sees me, and there's such enthusiasm in his voice I go tingly for a moment. But I soon realise it's not for me, it's for the big lump of metal he's hefting forward for me to admire. 'See what I've been doing.'

He lays it with careful effort on the concrete floor. This is a piece of cast aluminium the size of a large shoe box, marked down the sides with sets of parallel grooves and various round holes that look as if they connect up to pipes.

I take a guess. 'It's a cylinder head.'

'Excellent! We'll make a mechanic of you yet.'

'What was up with it?'

'I've been grinding it out, making the exhaust port and inlet tract bigger.'

'Why?'

'To give more power. This little beastie sits on top of the engine and feeds in petrol and air. You've got your pistons going up and down underneath, and these valves are what control the air and petrol going in and the exhaust coming out. The more efficient your head is, the more horsepower you're going to get.'

Now my eyes are used to the ordinary light I

can see his ramps and shelving, his workbench and tools, a crowd of big plastic containers, his manuals, his piles of rags. Half a year he's had to set up his oily kingdom, and I can tell he's got it exactly how he wants it. This garage could be anywhere in the world.

'What vehicle does it belong to?'

'Minibus.'

That makes sense. There are minibuses all over Nablus; also loads of Eighties cars, Opel Cadets and Novas, Fiat 127s. About half of them look to be on their last legs.

I toe the cylinder head respectfully. 'Have you got your Young Mechanics this afternoon?'

'Yup.'

'Can you knock off for lunch, though? I've got some news.'

'Is it past twelve? Yeah, OK. So long as you don't make me drink any of that sage tea again.'

He's keen on the coffee. I think it tastes like liquorice dissolved in water with some mud added for thickening. But I've only been here two and a half months, so perhaps it's an acquired taste.

While he hauls the cylinder head back onto the bench and packs away his tools, I check through my tote bag for the printout of Liv's latest email. He wipes his hands, nods at the bag. 'You still insist on having it inside-out, then?'

'It's meant to be reversible.' A patent lie. The bag lining's snagged, wonky and unfinished, threads trail at every corner. This was Melody's Christmas gift to me: a square cloth tote with wide straps and a Union Jack emblazoned on the front. 'I made it myself,' she told me. 'What I thought was, bags are always useful when you're travelling, and you won't lose sight of this one or mix it up with anyone else's. It's unique.'

'It's your jacket.' I'd recognised it at once.

'Yeah. It didn't look right on me any more. I thought I could put it to better use. I was going to make you a matching purse with the sleeve but I ran out of energy.' Working in the gallery's made her very arts-and-crafty; it wasn't a bad attempt at sewing for someone who's only ever tacked up a hem. I was sorry for the jacket, though. It meant that version of Melody had gone for good. 'Do you like it?' she'd asked shyly.

Without hesitation I'd said yes, it was brilliant, but in truth I worried about the wisdom of carrying my national flag into a conflict zone. I thought at the least it might cause confusion. Then again, there was no way I was leaving the bag behind. It's my little piece of home. Which is why I cart a bundle of ratty cloth round the streets of Nablus with me.

Michael dumps his rags in the bin and peels off his overalls.

'What have you been up to this morning?'

'Copy-editing again, for Natia.'

'For her Refugee Voices project?'

'That's the one.'

We step out into the blinding sunshine and begin to pick our way along the pavements, navigating round potholes and piles of rubble and plastic oil drums. The façades of the buildings we pass are shabby and covered in flyers and graffiti. Some are seriously damaged.

Top storeys are open to the sky, walls lean dangerously. In a house I visited this morning with Natia, sawdust and ants kept dribbling out of the window frames.

'Some boys in the street tried to lift up my skirt with a stick,' I tell him as we turn the corner.

'What did you do?'

'Natia shouted something and they all slunk off. Apparently she accused them of 'bringing shame on their country'. Works every time, she reckons. Better than any ASBO.'

Michael pulls an approving face. 'I might try that when we get back to the UK.'

The café's thick with fag smoke. Local men turn and stare, even though this is a place westerners from the project generally hang out. It's more than curiosity; Michael's talked about this sense he has sometimes of being 'owned', people he's never spoken to knowing who he is, and I'm beginning to get what he means. He likes it, says it makes him proud. I don't know what I think yet. We settle in a quiet corner and I dredge up my tatty bag once more.

'So here we go,' I say, fishing out the email to show him. 'The latest project, a joint venture. Mel and Liv Mid-Life Crises Inc.'

Liv's pasted in a photo of them both standing in the backyard at Love Lane, Elizabeth's topiary rabbit between them. In direct comparison like that, the two women look as if they've been moulded out of completely different materials. Melody's small, slender, dark and neat, in black trousers, white blouse, black waistcoat; Liv's

Amazonian, wilder, her jeans baggy and her footwear mannish. I think her hair — short, still, but her own — might be a shade greyer than when I left, or perhaps it's just the light. Makes me wonder who took the photo now we aren't around.

'Go on,' said Michael.

'OK. Everything's ticking over, basically — Melody's blooming at the gallery, Liv's had the all-clear from her last check-up so things are looking great there, plus they've found a new rare beetle on the reserve. So pretty positive, on the whole. Only now Melody's come up with this list of things they're supposed to 'do before they die'. She got the idea after they went to see the wrestling together.'

'God, the wrestling. I'd forgotten about that. Not what we were expecting, was it?'

'You're telling me. Never in a million years would I have guessed they'd enjoy watching massive men in leotards roll about.'

'But they did.'

'Liv actually called it a 'hoot'. Unless she was being ironic. Anyway, what happened was, a week or so afterwards, Melody read an article in one of her glossy mags about a nursery teacher who'd had some terrible life-threatening illness. Even though she was cured, this woman, she found she couldn't move on. She got all bogged down in the aftermath. So her best friend started a To Do list for her and there was some mad bollocks task every day, stuff like giving a flower to a random stranger, having a tattoo, or whatever. And it got her up and running again. It

403

helped her recover mentally.'

The waiter comes and takes our order. Two policemen walk past the window, coloured scarves wrapped round their automatic rifles.

'Is this two individual lists Mel's dreamed up, or one list covering both of them?'

'Two separate ones. Melody's done Liv's, and Liv's done Melody's.'

'Jesus.'

'I know what you're thinking, but listen to this: this is what Liv says her tasks are for the rest of this year.' I hold up the email and read aloud. ''Take some kind of dance lessons, go to the Notting Hill Carnival, write a fan letter, eat sushi' — only she's told Melody it mustn't be from blue fin tuna — 'and book a cruise.''

Michael winces. 'Oh, see there, her first mistake. She'll never get Liv on a cruise. Ever. Too much consumption, not enough wildlife.'

'That's where you're wrong. Liv says, after a load of research, she's 'managed to find a special nature cruise where you sail round the coast of Vladivostok in an old Russian container ship. You sleep on iron bunks and you have to do some of the cooking yourself, but the bird species you see are amazing.''

'Bet they're inundated.'

'Hmm. She's not actually booked it yet. Prising Geraint off his armchair'll be a feat in itself. Unless she goes alone. She might do that.'

'What's she come up with for Mel? Actually, don't tell me. It'll be badger-watching, installing a compost toilet — '

'Nope, you're wrong again. Nothing like that.

404

According to this she wants her to 'learn to throw a pot, train for the Sport Relief Mile, take a cookery course, tour the Houses of Parliament and attend any BBC recording of her choice.''

He looks impressed. 'No shit? I wouldn't mind having a crack at a couple of those myself.'

'I know. You thought Melody's list would be all facials and makeovers, didn't you? And Liv's all environmental.'

'Yup.'

'To be fair, so did I.'

He takes the printout from me and studies it for a long time. 'Funny girls. Ah well, if it keeps them out of mischief. Your rabbit tree looks good.'

'It does, yeah. Melody wanted to release a helium balloon on the anniversary, but Liv explained to her about them choking turtles so she bought some butterfly garden lights instead.'

'Is it strange, your mothers palling up the way they have?'

'I don't think about it.' I daren't.

Michael was right: I miss Shropshire like hell. Especially now, in May. I miss the landscape, the greenness, cold rain, the silly flock of chaffinches that used to come to our feeder every day. ''Don't forget to tell me about the wildlife,' Liv said in her very first email. But this is a busy, noisy town. All I've noticed so far are doves, storks and blackbirds, oh, and Michael says he once saw an owl. Probably a lot more lives in the desert scrubland outside the city and in the mountains.

I miss seeing the fox who visits the nursery,

and the cheeky jackdaws. I miss Ray, grumbling because he's put his coffee down somewhere and lost it. I miss tending to the plants, little seedlings pushing up, the smell of herbs and damp commercial loam.

I'm still not used to the weekend here being Thursday and Friday, and to the TV in our flat only showing two channels (both Arabic). I hate the way all surfaces are dusty, and that it's too hot to sleep. I miss the quiet, especially at night. Everyone's inside by nine and there's a lull then, but often you wake in the small hours and there are armoured vehicles trundling down the road below. Sometimes you hear shouting, sometimes gunfire.

There are days I'd kill for a buttered Welsh cake, or a pork and apple sausage, or a paper full of fish and chips. The sight of a packet of Kellogg's Bran Flakes — which, strangely, you can get here no problem — gives me a serious pang of loneliness.

Nicky I miss twenty times a day, whenever something bizarre or upsetting or fab or funny happens and I want to turn round and share it with her. She's now training in employment law, which apparently is 'even more interesting than corporate'; also she's moved out of her mum and dad's and is sharing a house in Chester with two other girls she met at the Young Solicitors' Group. It's 'ace!', she says, 'a mega-laugh!!'. I think there may be boyfriends orbiting, but nothing serious. She's too busy having a ball. Last week she emailed a photo of herself and her flatmates at some street festival, posing under the

Eastgate Clock. Nicky looks particularly gor-geous at the moment because she's had her hair layered and changed her parting and it really really suits her. She's like a new, upgraded model of herself.

My hair, in contrast, is flat and brown because I was sensible and dyed it back to its natural colour before I left England. Michael says the time for whacky hues is past, and insists it looks better anyway. Maybe it does, I wouldn't know. There are hardly any mirrors on the compound. I still find it astonishing he wasn't interested in dating Nicky, though. 'She's just too *clean*,' he always says when I ask him.

I'd like to tell Nicky, I mean to her face, about how we have to pretend we're married so we can stay in the compound together. The daily lying's a giggle, as is trying to keep track of who actually knows the truth. Should I confide in Natia, I've been wondering lately. She's young, she's western — Polish — but strict Catholic, so probably best if I keep my mouth shut. I don't want to put her on the spot. The trouble is, you can never predict who'd be cool about it and who might throw a fit.

I so miss having a girlfriend to confide in.

I daren't let myself miss my mothers.

'I get homesick too,' says Michael, taking his cup from the waiter and handing me mine. It turns out he can read my mind, this fake husband. Or is it his guilt talking? Now I'm out here he claims he tricked me into travelling through reverse psychology, that setting himself in opposition was the only way he could get me

407

to commit. Personally I think that's pants. In the end I came to Nablus because I wanted to come to Nablus. But I know he's terrified I won't hack it, that I'll have some kind of breakdown or accident, and it'll be his fault.

His expression right now's so earnest that I want to lean across the table and kiss him, not that you'd ever do that in public here. A great bubble of love swells up inside me till it seems to fill the entire room. Surely everyone else in the café can feel it? The two young men in checked shirts by the window, the old guy in the headdress, the pipe smokers in the corner, the waiter? The whole space is huge with emotion.

'You're hiding something. Something's on your mind. Look at you, jiggling your leg under the table. You're all twitchy. It's more than Liv and Melody's caper, isn't it? Come on, give.'

I'm more excited than I've ever been, but also more down because of what I've got to tell him. 'I'll just say, shall I?'

'Bloody hell, Frey.'

'I'm leaving Nablus.'

'You're going home?'

'No.'

His eyes are all confusion. 'Where, then?'

'OK. Right. There's this village outside Nablus, the one I went to last week. The one where the houses have domes on the top. Where that man was chasing a goat and he slipped on some dung. And Natia had a nosebleed while we were waiting to go through the checkpoint.'

Michael nods.

'And what it is, the woman Natia interviewed

was telling us about the group of internationals, mostly church types, who stay in one of the village houses and keep an eye on things. I think they get involved here and there with bits of farm work too. Olive-picking and stuff. So they're just a helpful presence. And it's coming time for them to change over. Plus there's a big Christian conference coming up that some of them want to attend, and they need a couple of replacement volunteers.'

'You?'

'Me and Natia.'

'Why?'

'Because she asked me. Because it's a really beautiful spot, and the locals are really appreciative.'

I wish I could tell him how it made me feel, standing in the bowl of the green-brown valley and watching the shepherds and the small sheep track their way across the dry slopes. The light was so strong it picked out every detail, every thorn and rock edge and leaf fold. There was this surreal sense of ages past, of Biblical times preserved and meeting the present. The clouds were moving over the land with a kind of sad majesty and I found myself filled up with an amazing sense of peace, which I know is mad considering how troubled this place is. Natia thought I'd had a religious experience. I told her it was sunstroke.

Michael sighs deeply. 'I see.'

'Do you?'

'Uh huh. What you're asking for is some space. You need a break. From me. Shit, I've been so happy in myself I haven't given enough thought to you.'

'No, I — '

''Cause it's all been too much, getting together after so long, and not telling the family yet, and the pressures of living in a foreign country and this secret marriage business. I mean, I've found it intense at times. It would freak anyone out. Only there's no need to leave Nablus, that's crazy. You can move to a different accommodation block. I'll have a word with Samah and he'll sort something. And you don't have to come round to the garage every day. I've so many classes to teach, I won't be bored. I can give you room to breathe, Freya.'

'No.' I shove my sage tea away in frustration. 'It's not about you. This is for me. It's like, I came out here and you'd already put everything in place for me and that was great, really kind, really helped me settle in. Only now I've got used to the routine, I want to try something for myself. Something more hands-on. The copy-editing's OK and we can still work on Natia's project while we're away, but I want to try other stuff, too. There might be something horticultural I could have a bash at in this village. If not, I know how to use a hammer and a screwdriver, I can cook, I can look after children. I want to learn some Arabic. I want my experience to be more — I don't know how to explain it. Immersed. No, that sounds stupid. Bloody hell. The place just feels as though I should be there for a bit. It's calling. I need to go.'

'You've found your sweet spot, is that what you're trying to say?'

'Yeah. My mix is right. I'm tuned. I should have started with an engine metaphor, then you'd have understood me straight off.'

He's still looking stunned. I knew he would be. Ever since I arrived, he's been like a gracious prince showing me round his domain.

'Three months, that's all. I'll only be the other side of a military checkpoint. Nothing but a soldier up a watchtower and a few metres of razor wire to stop you visiting.'

I know what he's thinking. *Aren't I enough for you? What's wrong with this?* And I almost smile because I so clearly remember sitting in his van on Christmas night eighteen months ago, overlooking the black lake, asking the same questions. How much it hurt when he talked about moving on. He'll remember that conversation too, at some point. He will catch up.

'If you have to go.'

'I think I do.'

He pushes his saucer till it's touching mine; as publicly intimate as we dare get around here. 'Strange, I always thought I had you sussed. But I don't know you at all, do I?'

'How could you? I don't know myself.'

The steam from our drinks rises and mingles, and through the window I see two men in robes wheeling a white melamine chest of drawers on a small cart between them, a boy trotting behind carrying a stool.

★ ★ ★

411

My last night in England, Melody was a wreck. Was drunk before I even got to Love Lane; became maudlin almost immediately. 'You're going to hate the Middle East,' she slurred. 'Think of the insects, and the plumbing. Plus, how are you ever going to survive without alcohol? No way, hun. You'll be on a plane home before Liv's had time to launder your duvet.'

I thanked her for the vote of confidence, at which point she collapsed into self-pity mode.

'You *and* Michael, though. Both of you gone, why both of you?' she kept saying, as if it was some great puzzle she couldn't fathom. Perhaps she guessed.

I stuck *Empire of the Flesh-Eaters* in the DVD player, and she got out the old photos Liv had sent her over the years I was growing up. Then she spread them out over the carpet in order so I could see myself, round-faced toddler through to uncertain teen. Ages she spent kneeling, picking each one up and studying it, laying it back down and squaring them all up.

'You'll be too busy at your art gallery to even notice we're gone,' I told her. But I don't think she heard me.

'I was a mess before I met you, Frey.'

'No, you weren't.'

'I was. I had a great big hole in my heart. You didn't see. How would you know? You're my best achievement.' She squatted there stroking the last picture, while behind her head a truckload of determined zombies attempted to ram raid an army base. Later on I helped her into bed. It felt like the last of the old times.

Liv was much more restrained. Whatever terrors she was feeling as I piled up my case and backpacks in the hall, she presented the usual calm front. She did hold me very tightly, and made me promise to email once a week. All the while Geraint swayed behind her, in his usual agony of awkwardness. 'You keep yourself safe, now, girl,' he'd muttered. 'Don't be doing anything daft. I'll look after your mum for you.' 'Make sure you do,' I said. And I actually found myself hugging him, can you believe it?

I'd like, now Michael's taken himself back to the garage, to take a peaceful, thoughtful stroll, but on a street in central Nablus there's no chance. Taxi horns blare, a minibus is blasting out Celine Dion through the open passenger windows, and ten yards in front of me a young man is shouting at another across the street, yelling at the top of his voice. I know if I don't keep moving, if I give even the suspicion of loitering, someone will try and talk to me. If I hang around in a shop, the owner will be over straight away. So I keep walking towards the compound, passing under hanging racks of T-shirts, under banners and wooden signs and awnings and makeshift scaffolding, past endless posters of dead men, and shelves of flat loaves and vegetables and sweets. Ahead of me is the hillside with its white multi-storeys and domed prayer tower.

I wonder what my mothers are doing right now.

It strikes me that if they were suddenly here, this second, I'd want to say thank you for

413

everything they've taught me: out of my scrambled upbringing, all those small but vital skills that make up the person I am. Liv gave me shelter, Melody gave me space. Liv raised me under the banner of my own conscience, Melody showed me how to relax and have pure, brilliant fun. I'm a product of both their worlds. It's not everyone who knows how to ID vole poo, or the best reggae track to crank you up for a night on the town ('Wear You to the Ball' by the Paragons). Never mind all the things they've taught me that I don't even know I've learned yet. I walk through this strange land wearing, as I'll wear forever, the invisible cloak of their mothering.

Of course since I've been here I've learned a whole lot of other stuff — the correct way to speak to a man holding a gun, the value of half an onion if you run into tear gas, that if you hang your washing outside you should hide your knickers between other items of clothing. That I'm not nearly as useless as I thought I was.

And that I love Michael, and he was worth every bit of the massive risk I took in telling him so. Being with him makes me happier than I've ever been, unbelievably happy, and complete. I feel stable and brave and grown up. But I've also learned from my mums that whatever alliances you make in life, ultimately you're on your own. Tonight, when I take him to bed, I'll try and explain again why I need to go away.

Afterwards we might lie awake for hours, talking or not talking, listening for the sound of heavy vehicles passing below.

And when at last sleep comes, I know I'll dream not of him or of life in the compound or the refugee camps. I'll dream of one or other of my mothers, as I have done every night since I've been here.

We do hope that you have enjoyed reading
this large print book.

Did you know that all of our titles
are available for purchase?

We publish a wide range of high quality
large print books including:
Romances, Mysteries, Classics
General Fiction
Non Fiction and Westerns

Special interest titles available in
large print are:
The Little Oxford Dictionary
Music Book
Song Book
Hymn Book
Service Book

Also available from us courtesy of
Oxford University Press:
Young Readers' Dictionary
(large print edition)
Young Readers' Thesaurus
(large print edition)

For further information or a free
brochure, please contact us at:
Ulverscroft Large Print Books Ltd.,
The Green, Bradgate Road, Anstey,
Leicester, LE7 7FU, England.
Tel: (00 44) 0116 236 4325
Fax: (00 44) 0116 234 0205

MOTHERS AND DAUGHTERS

Kate Long

Carol married young — to philandering Phil, and became a mother young — to highly-strung Jaz. But Carol put up with Phil's infidelities, suffering in silence to keep the family together. Not so Jaz. The moment she discovers her husband Ian's errant ways — a quick fumble with a woman he barely knew — she throws him out of the house. She changes the locks, refuses his calls and bans him from seeing their toddler son Matty. Carol cannot bear seeing history repeating itself. When Jaz finds out that her mother has enlisted the support of Ian's father, David, to try to reunite the couple, she is furious. There is only one way Jaz knows to get back at Carol, to hurt her most: through Carol's beloved, doted-upon grandson, Matty . . .

THE SWEETNESS OF FORGETTING

Kristin Harmel

The North Star Bakery has been in Hope's family for generations, the secret recipes passed down from mother to daughter. But Hope's life is a delicate balancing act, in danger of crumbling entirely: she's thirty-six, recently divorced, with rebellious daughter Annie and elderly grandmother Rose to care for — and a business in trouble. Then Rose reveals a shocking truth about her past and Hope, at her grandmother's request, travels to Paris armed only with a mysterious list of names. What she uncovers there could be the key to saving the bakery and the fulfilment of a star-crossed romance, seventy years in the making.

THE CRANE WIFE

Patrick Ness

One night, George Duncan — a decent man, a good man — is woken by a noise in his garden. Impossibly, a great white crane has tumbled to earth, an arrow shot through its wing. Unexpectedly moved, George helps the bird, and from the moment he watches it fly off his life is transformed. The next day, an enigmatic but kind woman walks into George's shop. Suddenly an extraordinary new world opens up for George — but no love ever comes without risk ... Wise, romantic, magical and funny, *The Crane Wife* is a hymn to the creative imagination and a celebration of the disruptive and redemptive power of love.

THE TRUTH

Michael Palin

Keith Mabbut is at a crossroads in his life. When he is offered the opportunity of a lifetime — to write the biography of the elusive Hamish Melville, a highly influential activist and humanitarian — he seizes the chance to write something meaningful. His search to find out the real story behind the legend takes Mabbut to the lush landscapes and environmental hotspots of India. The more he discovers about Melville, the more he admires him — and the more he connects with an idealist who wanted to make a difference. But is his quarry really who he claims to be? As Keith discovers, the truth can be whatever we make it . . .

BLACK ROSES

Jane Thynne

Berlin, 1933. Clara Vine is determined to be an actress. A chance meeting at a party in London leads her to Berlin, to the famous Ufa studios and, unwittingly, into an uneasy circle of Nazi wives, among them Magda Goebbels. Then Clara meets Leo Quinn who, in his undercover role for British intelligence, sees in her the perfect recruit to spy on her new acquaintances, using her acting skills to win their confidence. But when Magda reveals to Clara a dramatic secret and entrusts her with an extraordinary mission, Clara feels threatened, compromised and utterly torn between duty and love.

THE LAST TELEGRAM

Liz Trenow

As the Nazis storm Europe, Lily Verner
becomes an apprentice at her family's silk
weaving factory. When they begin to weave
parachute silk, there is no margin for error;
one tiny fault could result in certain death for
Allied soldiers. The war also brings Stefan, a
German Jewish refugee, to Lily. Working on
the looms, their love begins to grow — but
there are suspicions that someone is tamper-
ing with the silk . . . Can their love survive
the hardships of war? And will the Verners'
silk stand the ultimate test?